THE HIGHLANDER AND HIS IRISH LASS

"I'd like to take care of you, Kathleen, if you let me."

She snuggled back under his arm, as if dodging the question. "I never thought of myself as someone who needed to be taken care of."

"We all need help now and again, sweetheart."

"Even you?"

"Definitely me."

While she pondered his admission, Grant did his best to be patient. Yet all he wanted to do was kiss her breathless.

"I believe I would like you taking care of me, now and again," she finally whispered.

When he bent down to kiss her, she pressed a finger against his mouth. "But only when truly necessary."

Grant smothered a grin as he took her hand and pressed a kiss to her palm. He felt her tremble. It was slight, but telling, so he cupped her chin, finally giving in to the craving he'd been fighting for days—or weeks, if he were honest.

Taking that first, precious kiss . . .

Books by Vanessa Kelly

MASTERING THE MARQUESS
SEX AND THE SINGLE EARL
MY FAVORITE COUNTESS
HIS MISTLETOE BRIDE

The Renegade Royals

SECRETS FOR SEDUCING A ROYAL BODYGUARD
CONFESSIONS OF A ROYAL BRIDEGROOM
HOW TO PLAN A WEDDING FOR A ROYAL SPY
HOW TO MARRY A ROYAL HIGHLANDER

The Improper Princesses

MY FAIR PRINCESS
THREE WEEKS WITH A PRINCESS
THE HIGHLANDER'S PRINCESS BRIDE

Clan Kendrick

THE HIGHLANDER WHO PROTECTED ME
THE HIGHLANDER'S CHRISTMAS BRIDE
THE HIGHLANDER'S ENGLISH BRIDE
THE HIGHLANDER'S IRISH BRIDE

Anthologies

AN INVITATION TO SIN
(with Jo Beverley, Sally MacKenzie and Kaitlin O'Riley)

Published by Kensington Publishing Corp.

THE
Highlander's
Irish Bride

Clan Kendrick

VANESSA KELLY

ZEBRA BOOKS
KENSINGTON PUBLISHING CORP.

www.kensingtonbooks.com

ZEBRA BOOKS are published by

Kensington Publishing Corp.
119 West 40th Street
New York, NY 10018

All Kensington titles, imprints, and distributed lines are available at special quantity discounts for bulk purchases for sales promotion, premiums, fund-raising, educational, or institutional use.

Special book excerpts or customized printings can also be created to fit specific needs. For details, write or phone the office of the Kensington Sales Manager: Attn.: Sales Department. Kensington Publishing Corp., 119 West 40th Street, New York, NY 10018. Phone: 1-800-221-2647.

Zebra and the Z logo Reg. U.S. Pat. & TM Off.
First Printing: August 2021

ISBN-13: 978-1-4201-4707-0
ISBN-10: 1-4201-4707-2

ISBN-13: 978-1-4201-4708-7 (eBook)
ISBN-10: 1-4201-4708-0 (eBook)

10 9 8 7 6 5 4 3 2 1

Printed in the United States of America

To Abby A-P, a bright, brave lass, as well as an excellent
writer who will storm the world with her talent.
And to her mom, Dawn P, also a bright, brave lass.
Your dedication against all odds defined love and courage.

And to Maria C. It's been a true pleasure
getting to know your loving heart!

ACKNOWLEDGEMENTS

To my agent and to my editor, who always try to make the writing life easier for me—thank you! And to all the talented folks at Kensington, who bring my books into the world, also many thanks!

To my husband, my beta reader, resident grammarian, and biggest supporter. I am so blessed to have you in my life.

To my family, the outlaws, the in-laws, and everyone else. You're a big, beautiful, and complicated bunch, and I love you all.

And to a gracious God, who makes all things possible.

Chapter One

Mayfair, London
September 1823

"At least Denny and I didn't wear *real* togas," Kathleen Calvert said, as if that inane observation could forestall her impending doom.

"I think togas would have been terribly jolly," Jeannie enthused.

"But not very practical," Cara countered, as if they were having a perfectly normal conversation. "I've never understood how the Romans kept them on in the first place."

It was sweet of Kathleen's stepsisters to try to defend her from the storm of retribution headed her way. That storm went by the name of Helen, Lady Gorey. Kathleen's stepmother was the bane of her existence.

Helen stared down her daughters before turning her icy glare on Kathleen. No one did icy better than Baroness Gorey. She never yelled or ranted, or disturbed one perfect hair on her perfect head. She simply buried one with cold contempt. This time, she would surely bury Kathleen as far out of sight as she could, and for as long as she could.

"Your persistent attempts to make light of your scandalous

behavior are most distressing, Kathleen, especially for your poor father," Helen said.

"Indeed, my dear child," Papa began. "I do wish—"

"And one cannot begin to imagine the gossip," Helen ruthlessly interrupted. "I doubt we will be able to leave the house for months."

While that was a ridiculous assertion, it was true they were all but hiding out in the small back parlor. The inviting space was decorated with plump, chintz-covered armchairs, and a rather tatty velvet sofa piled high with cushions. Books, flowers, and needlework projects covered the tabletops. An easel with a half-completed landscape, along with a basket of sketching supplies, contributed to the cheerful atmosphere. Because the room's cozy disorder offended Helen's elegant soul, she rarely stepped foot inside, making it the sisters' private domain.

This morning, though, was one of those rare occasions. The family was huddled around a mahogany tea table, as if preparing for an invasion by hostile forces, a fairly accurate description of Kathleen's view of the *ton*.

Jeannie, sitting next to Kathleen on the sofa, snorted at her mother's dramatic assessment. "It's not as if Kath was dashing about with some loose screw, Mamma. It was just silly Denny Barlow. His family practically lived next door to us in Ireland, and Denny is Kath's best chum. Their race was just a bit of a rig."

When Helen leveled her Medusa-like gaze on the sixteen-year-old, it was a miracle poor Jeannie didn't turn to stone and splinter in a million pieces.

"I forbid you to use such dreadful cant, Jeanette. If you cannot behave with decorum, you will be sent to your room. Indefinitely."

"But Mamma," Jeannie protested. "It's just that—"

Kathleen jumped in. "It's just that I made a capital blunder this morning, and it doesn't matter that I made it with Denny. It's *what* I did that matters, not *whom* I did it with."

"But you were just kicking up a lark," Jeannie said. "You didn't mean anything by it."

Kathleen forced herself to say the words, for her sister's sake. "It was still very wrong of me."

Papa, sitting in an armchair near the fireplace, cast his wife a cautious but assessing glance. When he sighed, Kathleen's heart sank. Her father rarely took Helen on, and today would run true to form.

"While I am pleased to hear you take responsibility," he said, "it does not solve the problem, Kathleen. We must defer to your stepmother, since she has a better understanding of how this incident will be regarded by our friends and society at large."

Cara, perched on a padded stool near her mother, grimaced. "Not well, I imagine."

At nineteen, Cara already possessed a graceful maturity. Tall and willowy, with her mother's blue eyes and wheat-blond hair, Cara had a gentle nature which, combined with her looks, had already won her several eligible suitors.

"That, my dear child, is an understatement," Helen replied. "Really, to be racketing around at dawn on Hampstead Heath no less, with that ninny, Dennis Barlow. Your stepsister's behavior is hardly to be comprehended."

She laid her usual emphasis on that all-important qualifier, *step*, to emphasize the point that Kathleen was the wild Irish outsider and no true Gorey, as far as Helen was concerned.

Kathleen couldn't help jabbing back. "Actually, *Mother*, it was more than racketing about. It was neck and neck, cracking the whip, just like the charioteers of ancient Rome. I'm sure we broke all *sorts* of speed records."

In reality, it had been nothing more than a dash on a country road—corking good fun and a welcome escape from boredom. Thinking of it as a chariot race had simply been a silly jest between two old friends. But it might as well have been bread and circuses for the uproar it was already causing.

Jeannie flashed her an impish grin. "Did you stand up like charioteers, too?"

Kathleen was tempted to embellish but caught her father's expression. "No, dear, we quite sensibly sat. After all, we didn't wish to tip the carriages or injure the horses."

She couldn't blame poor Denny, who'd initially tried to wheedle her out of it. He'd never been able to refuse her challenges, going back when they were children in Ireland. Unlike Helen, Kathleen's mother had never kicked up a fuss over their antics. Mamma had simply urged them not to hurt themselves before sending them back out to play in the woods and fields of Greystone Court, the Gorey family seat.

"I am fully aware of your actions," Helen said, "since I received an unfortunately precise description from Mrs. Carling—who received an equally precise description from her son."

Kathleen's downfall had been the obnoxious Philip Carling and his equally obnoxious friend, Archibald Fenton. Those pair of idiots had been returning from a late night carouse somewhere out past the Heath. His mouth agape, Philip had pulled up his horse and taken a long look at Kathleen as she'd brought her phaeton to a halt. Then he'd promptly set heels to his unfortunate mare and galloped off, Archie drunkenly lurching along in his wake.

Cad that he was, Carling had immediately tattled to his

mother. Mrs. Carling, one of the worst gossips in the *ton*, had promptly shot off a deliciously horrified note to her dear friend Lady Gorey. Kathleen had barely managed to sneak back into the house before the hounds of hell were unleashed.

Stupid Philip and his stupid big mouth.

And stupid her, obviously.

"Philip Carling is no gentleman for carrying tales," Papa said, surprising Kathleen. "A grown man gossiping to his silly mother. Ridiculous."

Helen pressed a hand to the lace-trimmed bodice of her fashionable morning gown. "Olivia Carling is one of my *dearest* friends, my love. I share your opinion of Philip, naturally, but his deficiencies are hardly his mother's fault. Philip's father is far too indulgent of him. You, on the other hand, would never allow Richard to act in so disgraceful a fashion."

Richard, Kathleen's older brother and heir to the Gorey title, was spared this meeting by virtue of the fact that he was currently in Wiltshire, enjoying the hospitality of the Marquess of Bevington.

Lucky him.

"Well, tut-tut, my dear," Papa said.

"And Olivia was simply warning me," Helen plaintively added. "This sort of incident always gets out, you know—"

"Thanks to her," Kathleen interjected.

The fire from Helen's gaze almost singed Kathleen's side curls. But then her stepmother quickly regrouped and adopted an attitude both wounded and stoic, as if she were the one about to be socially martyred, not Kathleen.

"If you feel Olivia has overstepped, dear sir, I will convey that message. It will be vastly uncomfortable, but far be it from me to go against your wishes."

Alarm flashed in Papa's eyes. "I say, I don't know a thing about managing society scandals. I leave that entirely in your hands, my love."

As usual, Kathleen's father had quickly capitulated to his wife.

No point in fretting about it.

"Well then, Papa, what must I do to atone for my crime?" she asked.

He tut-tutted again. "No need for dramatics, my dear. After all, it's not as if our friends don't realize you're a bit . . ."

"Eccentric?" Kathleen wryly finished.

"Let's say dashing," he kindly replied.

Helen huffed an exasperated breath. "Kathleen's conduct has gone beyond both dashing *or* eccentric. The impact of her behavior, particularly on Richard, could be disastrous."

Papa frowned. "I do not follow, my dear."

"We all have great hopes that Richard and Lord Bevington's daughter will make a match of it," Helen explained. "That is the reason for his trip, as you will recall."

"There's not much doubt of that," said Kathleen. "Richard and Melinda have been making sheep's eyes at each other for weeks. Denny said there's even a bet at White's about the impending betrothal."

Helen looked like she'd swallowed a peach pit. "How distressing. May I remind you all that Lord Bevington has yet to give his approval to the match? He has extremely high standards, and the marchioness even more so. It is entirely possible that his lordship would refuse Richard's offer if any scandal involving our family should surface."

"Surely not," Papa protested. "Richard and Melinda are extremely well-suited."

"Melinda is not the sort to gainsay her parents." Helen

cast an ironic glance at Kathleen. "She is a good, obedient girl, and would never consent to marry a man without her father's approval."

Kathleen rolled her eyes. "That sounds rather chicken-hearted of her."

"Mamma's right," Cara said. "Melinda does *everything* her parents tell her to do."

Kathleen's stomach plummeted right through the floorboards to the root cellar. "Truly?"

"I went to school with her. She's *very* biddable."

"And given Melinda's excellent character *and* the size of her dowry," Helen said, "I consider us fortunate that Lord Bevington is even willing to consider Richard's suit."

Kathleen bristled. "Hang on, now. Richard's splendid. Melinda's the lucky one, if you ask me."

"No one asked you," her father tartly put in.

He was clearly rattled by the reminder of the importance of the impending match. The Goreys weren't pikers by any means, but Melinda's family was exceedingly rich and influential. For Richard, who had political aspirations, the marriage would be a genuine coup.

"Sorry, Papa," she muttered.

"Cara and Jeanette would also be affected," Helen added. "If one daughter can behave so outrageously . . ."

"But I'm not even out till next spring," Jeannie piped in.

"That won't matter," Helen impatiently said. "By this evening, the scandal will be all over town. I shouldn't be surprised if we start receiving callers at—"

The sound of the doorknocker echoed from the front of the house, interrupting her.

"Blast it," muttered Papa.

"Please do not suggest I marry Denny," Kathleen said, feeling desperate. "For one thing, he'd never agree."

"At this point, I doubt any decent man would marry you," Helen replied.

"Mamma!" Jeannie exclaimed, jumping to her feet. "That's an awful thing to say. If I were a man, I'd marry Kathleen right now."

Kathleen gently pulled her sister back down. "It's all right, love. We all know I'm not a patch on you and Cara. You're both much prettier *and* nicer."

"You are not without charms, Kathleen, if only you wouldn't dress so oddly," Helen said, momentarily diverted. "Take your carriage dress, for instance. Who in her right mind wears a white outfit to dash about in a dusty phaeton? Although I'll grant it's an attractive color on you."

Kathleen blinked. Was that actually a compliment?

"We must be thankful, certainly, that you didn't inherit the ghastly red hair so common in the Irish," her stepmother added, instantly ruining the moment. "And if you would only bleach your freckles with lemon water, your complexion would be much improved."

Kathleen's mother, a true beauty, had been blessed with bright copper hair and emerald-green eyes. Kathleen had not been so favored. She had ordinary brown hair and a changeable gray eye color that simply refused to settle on a specific shade. And while Mamma had possessed a charming dash of freckles, Kathleen looked like she'd been splattered with cinnamon from a cosmic fountain.

"Kath's freckles are fun," Jeannie loyally said.

Kathleen gave her sister a brief hug. "Funny, more like it. And there aren't enough lemons in England to banish my freckles."

"Since hardly anyone will be seeing you for some months, it won't matter," Helen said.

Kathleen sighed. "Rustication then, is it?"

"Yes, the country. For as long as necessary."

Kathleen froze for a moment before her brain kicked into gallop. Could it really be that simple?

"I suppose it makes sense to send me home to Ireland," she casually said. "Then I'll be completely out of sight. No one will think of me for a minute."

If she could only get back to Greystone, any amount of humiliation would be worth it.

Helen all but sneered. "Without a proper chaperone? Absolutely not."

"My former governess, Mrs. Clyde, could stay with me. That would be perfectly respectable."

"No. She was incapable of controlling you then, and I have no faith in her ability to do so now," Helen said.

One of the first actions Helen took after marrying Papa was to give the boot to Rebecca Foster, Kathleen's beloved governess. Fortunately, Rebecca had soon met and wed Mr. Clyde, a well-regarded barrister from Dublin, and she and Kathleen had remained close. She was certain Rebecca would willingly chaperone her for a spell.

She prepared to dig in her heels, because *this* was worth fighting for. "Perhaps I could stay in Dublin for a—"

A muffled yelp sounded from the hall. The parlor door flew open and in strode a tall young woman, dressed in the first kick of fashion. Their butler fluttered in her wake, wringing his hands.

Gillian Penley, Duchess of Leverton, came to a halt in the middle of the room and cast an amused gaze over the stunned Goreys. Then she winked at Kathleen.

"And how is the Gorey family on this fine day? It's a perfect one for managing a scandal, don't you think?"

Chapter Two

Kathleen's stepmother recovered first, if bristling like a hedgehog could be called a recovery. "Jensen, what is the meaning of this? We are not *at home* this morning."

Their poor butler looked ready to cast up his crumpets. "My . . . my lady, I tried to explain to Her Grace, but—"

"Her Grace wouldn't listen," the duchess cheerfully interrupted. "And there's no point in pretending you don't need my help."

"Your kindness is duly noted," Helen frostily replied. "But the situation is a private matter, and entirely in hand."

Gillian thoughtfully tapped her chin. "My husband does not share your assessment. The duke is *dreadfully* concerned about our dear Kathleen, which is why he asked me to rush over to lend a hand. And here I am, ready and willing to help."

Given the Duke of Leverton's well-known aversion to scandal, Kathleen strongly suspected that lending a hand had been Gillian's idea. Still, His Grace was a powerful man, and Kathleen could only be grateful for his support.

Papa scrambled to his feet. "Your Grace, do forgive us.

We're simply surprised to see you under the, uh, present circumstances. And so promptly, too."

Helen, recalled to her manners, rose to dip a shallow curtsy. "Indeed. We were not expecting callers so early in the day."

"Drat," Kathleen muttered. "The gossips are already making their rounds."

Gillian waggled a hand. "Barely, but there's no time to waste. We must come up with a plan."

Five years Kathleen's senior, Gillian was the illegitimate daughter of one of the royal dukes. She was raised on a remote estate in Sicily, and when she finally returned home to England, she'd struggled under the restrictions of London society. The distinguished tutelage of Charles Penley, Duke of Leverton, however, had allowed Gillian to adapt to the trickier elements of her new life. Even more importantly, Leverton had fallen madly in love with his erstwhile pupil. Gillian, now a wife and the mother of two adorable children, had become one of the most formidable and unconventional women in the *ton*.

Kathleen adored the duchess, now a fast and loyal friend.

Helen glanced at her daughters, who were staring at Gillian with dumbfounded expressions. "Girls, please stand and greet Her Grace."

Cara rose and dipped into an elegant curtsy. "Forgive me, ma'am. It's a pleasure to see you, as always."

"Probably not this morning, Cara, but it's sweet of you to say so."

"Your Grace," Jeannie said shyly, managing an awkward curtsy.

Gillian's answering smile was kind. "Ah, Jeanette, you've certainly grown since I last saw you, and you're as beautiful as your sisters. You must have legions of suitors already."

"I'm not out yet. Besides, I don't see many boys. And they can be . . ." Jeannie frowned.

"Confusing?" Gillian ventured. "They certainly can be."

"I prefer horses, to tell you the truth," Jeannie confessed.

"Personally, I find horses are more trainable than the average male," Gillian replied. "And more intelligent, in some cases."

Jeannie giggled. So did Cara, although she did her best to suppress it once she caught sight of her mother's expression.

"My goodness," Papa said weakly.

"Girls, you are excused," Helen ordered.

"But—" Jeannie started to protest.

"Come along," Cara whispered before dragging her reluctant sister from the room.

"That will be all," Helen said to their still-paralyzed butler. "Try, if you can, to see that we are *not* disturbed again."

"What, no tea?" Gillian drolly asked.

Kathleen could practically hear her stepmother grinding her teeth, while Jensen's eyes rounded with panic.

"Um, ah . . ." stuttered the butler.

"Never mind," Gillian said. "Away with you, Jensen, before your mistress has a fit."

"Really, Your Grace," Helen huffily said as their butler made a hasty exit.

"Yes, I'm completely outrageous." Gillian gracefully sat next to Kathleen. "But I really am here to help."

"How did you find out about this mess?" Kathleen asked.

"Charles was out for an early ride in Hyde Park, where he encountered Mr. Carling. The man was happy to rattle on about his son's news."

"I would truly like to murder that family," Kathleen groused.

"Agreed, but we'll manage with something less drastic." Gillian's smile was wry. "Scandals are my forte, you know."

"Yes, *everyone* knows that," Helen snapped.

Though Papa looked ready to expire from embarrassment, the duchess simply lifted a brow and studied Kathleen's stepmother with polite disdain. The normally unflappable Helen flushed pink under that silent scrutiny.

"I do have a great deal of experience, as does my husband," Gillian finally said, "and he wishes to help. We're very fond of Kathleen."

"Your assistance would be most welcome," said Papa, flashing Helen a warning glance. "I'm sure my wife agrees."

Helen fussed with her skirts as she resumed her seat. "I beg your pardon if I conveyed a different impression, Your Grace."

Gillian climbed off her high horse. "I'm sure you both wish me straight to perdition." She shifted her gaze to Kathleen. "Not the best timing on your part, dearest. You could scupper your brother's engagement."

"Yes, I . . . I'm afraid I neglected to think about that," Kathleen said. Truthfully, she'd not really thought about anything but having a jolly little lark.

Gillian patted her arm. "A tip for the future, dearest. Avoid scandals that bring others down with you. That way, if the whole thing blows up in your face, no one else gets hurt."

"Did that work for you?" Kathleen asked.

"Not according to my husband. Fortunately, my scandalous days are over." She tilted her head. "I believe it's time for yours to be over, too."

"We can *all* agree on that," Helen said.

Kathleen suspected she had a few scandals left in her future but tried to look contrite.

"Your Grace, how did your husband respond to Mr. Carling's accusations?" Papa asked.

"He told Carling to keep such rank speculations about Kathleen to himself. As Charles pointed out, his son and his dreary little friend can hardly be considered reliable witnesses, given that they were exceedingly drunk. Charles will also find a way to quietly relay that message to Lord Bevington. My husband will manage that piece of the puzzle, never fear."

"Then I won't have to leave town, after all?" Kathleen cautiously asked.

Not that she'd mind escaping London, but she'd probably end up with one of Helen's dreadful relatives. They all seemed to live in damp manor houses in Yorkshire, with bad chimneys and worse plumbing.

"Oh, you'll certainly have to leave," Gillian said. "Can't have the perpetrator hanging about as a reminder of the original crime."

"No one will suspect a thing, I promise," Kathleen replied. "I will fade into the woodwork like the biggest wallflower you've ever seen."

"On the contrary, people will absolutely suspect a thing. Besides, you're impossible *not* to notice." Gillian flashed a smile. "It's one of the reasons I like you."

"I'm glad someone does," Kathleen muttered.

"Chin up, old girl." Gillian turned to Helen. "I'm assuming you have somewhere specific in mind?"

"I do. She should spend the winter in Scotland, with her cousin Sabrina."

Kathleen practically fell out of her chair. The Scottish

Highlands, in winter? That was worse than Yorkshire. Even with Sabrina there.

Gillian nodded. "Excellent."

Kathleen gasped. "It's not excellent, it's *horrifying*. I'd rather go to Newgate than to the Highlands for the entire blasted winter. It's the bloody back of beyond."

"Kathleen, such language!" Papa exclaimed. "Besides, you love your cousin Sabrina."

"Yes, but—"

"Since Sabrina had a baby only a few months ago," Helen interjected, "she'll be delighted to have Kathleen's company. How she bears the isolation of Lochnagar Manor is beyond comprehension. But it is, thankfully, well suited to our needs."

The middle of nowhere, with *babies*.

Babies terrified Kathleen. She was always afraid she'd do something horrible, like drop them on their soft little heads.

"Absolutely not," she said. "I'm not going there."

Helen ignored her. "Because Sabrina's character is beyond reproach, she can help Kathleen recover what little reputation she'll have left after this incident. And a long stay is certainly preferable, given the extent of the damage."

When she was ten, Kathleen had once coaxed her brother into a pretend boxing match. It had been great fun until Richard accidentally punched her in the stomach. She'd collapsed to the ground, wheezing, and felt the very same sensation now. The fact that neither Gillian nor Papa refuted Helen's harsh assessment of her reputation made the impact that much worse.

"I understand I must go somewhere," she blurted out. "But Sabrina has enough to manage without me hanging about like a noxious smell."

Sabrina's letters clearly illustrated that she was happy but also had her hands full with the duties of wife, mother, and mistress of a busy estate.

Gillian darted a sideways glance at Kathleen before smiling at her parents. "Lord and Lady Gorey, I'd like to speak with Kathleen alone now."

Helen went from bristly to imperious. "The decision has been made, Your Grace, so I see nothing left to say."

"Really? Because I have several things I still wish to say," Gillian said just as imperiously.

"Of course, Your Grace," Papa hastily said, jumping up and all but hauling his wife to her feet. "Just ring the bell when you wish us to return."

He ushered Helen—who objected the whole way—out of the room.

Kathleen wilted against the sofa cushions. Her head throbbing, she was in dire need of coffee.

Or brandy. But she'd have to hide the glass, or Helen would have a fit.

"How *do* you put up with her?" asked Gillian. "I'd stab her after a day."

If even half the stories about Gillian were true, that was not an idle threat.

"You certainly put Helen in her place, so fortunately no stabbing necessary."

"My husband has taught me that words, or even looks, are often a more effective weapon than, well, weapons. Not that I don't carry a knife at all times. You'd be surprised how often a good blade is just the thing."

Kathleen burst into laughter, largely from nerves. It felt good after her ghastly morning.

"That's better," said Gillian, quirking a smile. "Now, shall we get down to hard facts? Because I think we must."

Kathleen's spurt of amusement faded. "It's truly bad, isn't it?"

"Yes, thanks to bacon-brained Philip Carling and his dreadful mamma. Even Charles won't be able to keep that nasty old tabby down for long."

Kathleen propped her aching head in her palm. "I don't really even know why I did it. It was so stupid."

"You were bored, I expect. I understand perfectly."

"You're probably the only one."

"So, did you win?"

"Of course. Denny was in a complete snit about it."

Gillian laughed. "At least there's that. But we do need to get you out of town."

"Fine, but not Scotland. While I love Sabrina, spending the entire winter in some frigid corner of the Highlands . . ." She shuddered just thinking about it.

If only she could get back to Ireland, with its lovely soft air, misty green fields, and the quiet beauty of Greystone Court.

"But Sabrina's a pip," Gillian said, "and her husband is anything but boring. He's a Kendrick, after all."

"I'm sure I'd be in the way. They're still practically newly-weds. I'd be a . . . a . . ."

"Spare wheel?"

Most of Kathleen's cousins and friends were now married and settled into their lives as young society matrons. Oh, she'd had suitors, but nothing had ever stuck. Not that she had a burning desire to wed. She'd take Ireland over a husband any day.

"I have a suggestion that might make the prospect more palatable, and still please your parents," Gillian added.

Kathleen tilted a skeptical eyebrow.

Her friend smiled. "You're still going to Scotland, but you're going with me."

Now *that* was a surprise. "Um, why?"

"As you know, Victoria Kendrick, Countess of Arnprior, is Sabrina's sister-in-law and my cousin. Vicky is the only one in my family of royal by-blows that I have yet to meet in person. I very much wish to remedy that."

Kathleen hesitated. "Would the duke and your children also be going on this trip?"

Gillian wrinkled her nose. "Charles has convinced me that it would be a ridiculously complicated venture with two small children. But I'd been thinking about a trip to Glasgow for some time. It's a happy coincidence that your gruesome stepmother came up with much the same plan as Charles and I did."

"But the duke cannot wish you to be gone for such a spell. And what about your children?"

"Charles is an excellent father, and we'll all survive a short separation just fine. Stop trying to come up with excuses, Kath."

Kathleen sighed. "Glasgow sounds fine, but once you return home, it's off to the bloody Highlands for me."

"Your stepmother will probably have forgotten all about you by then, and I'm sure Vicky will be delighted for you to stay in Glasgow for as long as you wish."

"I hope so." It sounded terribly uncertain, but Kathleen supposed she didn't have a better option. And spending time with Gillian was better than what Helen might otherwise decree by a league.

Her friend rose. "Then it's settled. I'll make all the arrangements. You simply need to pack and be ready to depart first thing in the morning."

Kathleen stood, dredging up a smile. "Thank you. Truly."

Gillian gave her a sympathetic hug. "We'll have great fun, you'll see."

"As long as I stay out of trouble."

If anything went wrong, Kathleen was fairly sure she'd spend the rest of her life in a corner of Scotland barely on the map.

"Once you're out of town, the gossip will die down and people will soon forget what happened. With a little luck, you might even be home by Christmas."

Luck.

Kathleen had the feeling her luck had run out—permanently.

Chapter Three

Kathleen nudged aside the breakfast plate of boiled eggs and smoked ham. The Leverton traveling coach was luxurious and well sprung, but it was best not to tempt fate. Except when she was handling the reins or on the back of a horse, travel made her as queasy as a vicar with a hangover.

It didn't help that after only a few days on the road, she already missed her stepsisters. Jeannie had been particularly inconsolable about the separation, convinced that her mother would turn even more rigid and censorious without Kathleen to catch fire for her. Sadly, the girl was probably right. Helen would be alert to any sign of inappropriate behavior and no doubt react with swift and merciless judgment.

Gillian sailed into the inn's private dining parlor, garbed in an elegant, hunter-green traveling dress. "Good morning, dearest. I hope you slept well."

"Very well, thank you."

Gillian eyed her. "Don't tell fibs, Kath. I can tell you didn't get much sleep. Again."

"Is it the bags under my eyes? They're almost as big as my portmanteau."

"You look lovely, as always. Just a little pale."

"Ah, my freckles gave me away."

The paler Kathleen got the more her freckles stood out. It was one of the things she most hated about them—that, and the fact that they all but glowed when she blushed. After Helen, freckles were the bane of her existence.

"I love your freckles," Gillian replied. "You look sprinkled with cocoa. I'm sure the men find it absolutely enchanting."

Kathleen snorted. "My brother once said it looked like the maid shook her duster out over my head."

"Dear me, I must be sure to accidentally trip Richard the next time I see him."

"In his defense, he was only twelve at the time."

"I'll still have to punish him." Gillian smiled at the serving girl, who'd come in with a fresh pot of tea. "Thank you. Please take away Miss Calvert's dish and bring her plain toast. Perhaps a pot of jam, too."

The girl bobbed a curtsy. "Will there be anything else?"

"I'll have scones and clotted cream. And coffee."

Kathleen sighed with relief. The odor of smoked ham was curdling her insides.

"I'm sorry to be such a pain, Gillian."

"Nonsense. Traveling does tend to make one's stomach twitchy."

"Says the woman who ate a hearty beef dinner last night."

"I've always been disgustingly healthy. One time our household came down with a dreadful case of the grippe, and Charles was positively green around the gills, poor lamb. But I never turned a hair."

"That was lucky."

"Hardly. Aside from the cook and a groom, our butler

was the only other person who didn't fall ill, so he and I had to take care of most everyone. I took on the muckiest tasks because I was terrified he would give his notice."

Kathleen laughed. "That does sound awful."

"At least I discovered that I'm a capable nurse." Gillian narrowed her gaze. "Which leads me to believe it's more than a twitchy stomach for you. You're fretting."

Kathleen busied herself by pouring another cup of tea. "You're right that I didn't get much sleep. My room looked out over the stable yard."

"Ah, yes. The larger inns can be annoyingly busy. And the service is dreadfully slow, isn't it? If the girl doesn't come soon with my coffee, I'll have to storm the kitchen."

"Not with daggers drawn, I hope."

"I never threaten the people who prepare the food." Gillian paused. "Goodness, what is all the thumping out in the hall?"

When another loud thump was followed by a protesting yelp, they exchanged startled glances.

Kathleen stood. "I'll go—"

The door flew open and one of the Leverton grooms marched in, his hand firmly clamped on the shoulder of a stable boy trying to wriggle from his grasp.

Except it wasn't a stable boy.

"Sorry to interrupt, Your Grace," the groom said. "But here's a bit of a problem."

"So I see." Gillian glanced at Kathleen. "Dearest, I believe that is—"

"My sister," Kathleen whispered.

"Let go, you poltroon," Jeannie hissed, struggling to escape.

Kathleen pressed a hand to her roiling stomach. "Oh, my God."

"It's all right, Simmons," Gillian said. "You can release Miss Calvert."

Simmons still maintained his grip, albeit at arm's length. "She gave me a right good kick in the knee when I helped her out of the boot. Almost took me down."

"You didn't help me out," Jeannie snapped. "You *pulled* me out."

"Only because you wouldn't *come* out," the groom protested.

Kathleen rushed over. "Jeannie, you should never kick anyone."

"That will be all, Simmons," Gillian said. "Tell the coachman we'll be delayed. Oh, and find that blasted serving girl and tell her to bring another pot of tea along with my coffee."

The groom released Jeannie and backed away, as if she were a wolf about to spring. "Yes, Your Grace."

After Simmons limped out, Kathleen grasped her sister's shoulders. "Are you all right? Are you hurt in any way?"

Jeannie rolled her eyes. "Don't fuss, Kath. I'm fine."

"My groom, however, is apparently not fine," commented Gillian.

"He shouldn't have pulled me out of the boot like that," Jeannie said. "I tried to tell him who I was, but he wouldn't listen."

"How dreadfully rude of him. I must instruct my grooms forthwith to ignore all stowaways in the boot of my carriages. I assume that's where you've been since we left London."

Kathleen goggled at her sister. "You were in the boot for over two days? That's insane!"

Jeannie winced. "No need to shriek. I'm *fine*. Just a bit hungry."

As if on cue, the door opened and the serving girl hurried in with a fully laden tray.

"Coffee at last." Gillian nodded at the girl. "And please bring some ham and eggs for the young l—"

"Boy," Kathleen cut in.

The serving girl looked flummoxed. "You wants me to serve the likes of him? In here with you?"

Jeannie, who had shoved her thick, wheat-blond hair under a droopy knit cap, was garbed in dust-covered breeches and a smock that was topped with a leather jerkin two sizes too big. Kathleen couldn't imagine where her sister had found such an appalling outfit.

"Yes," Kathleen replied. "He's . . . he's our coachman's son and is under the weather. He needs a good breakfast to, er, perk him up."

With a dismissive shrug, the serving girl thumped down the tray and departed.

"Very quick thinking on your part, Kathleen," Gillian said.

"What difference does it makes if people guess I'm a girl?" Jeannie dropped into a chair and poured a cup of tea. "No one knows who I am."

"They know who I am, and they certainly know the Duchess of Leverton," Kathleen replied, still trying to recover from her shock. "The entire point of my exile is to avoid a scandal, not start a fresh one."

After taking a large gulp of tea, Jeannie began removing her knit cap.

Kathleen flapped a hand. "Please leave it on. You have to maintain that gruesome disguise until we leave."

"Why? It's not as if anyone cares about me." Jeannie's tone was now surly. "I'm not you or Cara."

Gillian patted her arm. "Kathleen certainly cares about you, dear. She doesn't want you damaged by cruel gossip."

Jeannie pulled a face. "It's not fair. Kathleen kicked up the stink, but Mamma was acting like I was just as bad. She threatened to lock me in my room. What choice did I have but to run away?"

Guilt stabbed at Kathleen. Still, now was not the time to fret about unintended consequences or fruitlessly dither. Unfortunately, devising a plan to get Jeannie safely home, without causing gossip, currently felt beyond the skills of her frazzled brain.

"Think," she whispered to herself, pressing a fist to her forehead.

"Kath," Jeannie said. "Are you all right?"

"Not really." Kathleen sank into her chair. "You, however, seem remarkably sanguine for someone who just spent two days in a carriage boot. How ever did you manage it?"

"Oh, it was—"

Kathleen put up a warning hand as the maid came in with a tray. The girl set it down, darting curious glances at Jeannie while she unloaded plates of eggs, scones, and ham.

"That will be all," Gillian sternly said.

The maid curtsied but cast a suspicious look over her shoulder before she closed the door behind her.

"I'm assuming your servants will not gossip with the inn staff?" Kathleen asked.

Gillian shook her head. "They know I'd stab them if they did."

Jeannie giggled. "Would you really?"

"Let's hope not," Kathleen said as she began stacking food on her sister's plate. "Now, please tell us how you managed this mad scheme."

"It was dead easy," Jeannie replied around a mouthful of eggs she'd immediately shoved into her mouth.

"Don't choke yourself, dear," Gillian said. "There's no rush."

Kathleen grimaced. "I'm afraid there is. We have to get her back to London as soon as possible."

Jeannie's fork paused in midair. "I'm *not* going back."

"Did you at least leave a note for our parents?"

"Not that I was going with you, silly. They would have come after me."

"Won't they, anyway?" Gillian asked. "I'm surprised we've not had a rider catch up with us already, since we're traveling with two heavy carriages."

Jeannie sawed at a chunk of ham. "That's why you never saw me. I hid in the boot of the second carriage. You weren't taking any luggage from that one, and it was just Your Grace's maid traveling in that coach. I was very quiet and careful, so neither she nor the grooms ever suspected a thing."

"Clever girl," Gillian said, shaking her head.

"That doesn't explain why Papa hasn't apparently sent anyone after us," Kathleen noted. "Or how you snuck out in the first place."

"I took some clothes from the stables, then I told the upstairs maid I wasn't feeling well and was staying in bed all day. Then I got dressed and snuck out to wait for the carriages. I had to crouch down in one of the window wells until they pulled up in front of our house. Fortunately, it was raining, so everyone was rushing to load the luggage and not looking around. As soon as the second carriage was ready, I dashed out and climbed into the boot." She grimaced. "It was a tight squeeze. I'm *so* glad to be out of there."

"I can imagine," Gillian said. "But full marks for pulling it off."

Kathleen cut her friend an exasperated glance. "Really?"

Gillian shrugged. "Sorry, but it's exactly the sort of thing I would have done—or you would have, for that matter."

"It's true, Kath," her sister earnestly said. "Whenever things get sticky, I try to think what you would do."

Kathleen resisted the urge to curse. "But *why* didn't anyone come after us?"

"I left a note saying I was going home to Ireland." Jeannie reached for a scone. "Mamma knows I like Ireland, too, so I thought it made sense to send them in that direction."

"But . . ." Kathleen sighed. "That's rather brilliant, I admit."

Her sister grinned. "I thought so."

"But Papa and Helen must be frantic with worry," Kathleen said, regrouping. "This was not well done of you."

Her sister's chin tilted up at a mutinous angle. "They were being awful to both of us. They deserve a good scare."

Because Jeannie was tall and blooming into a beauty, it was easy to sometimes forget she was so young and naïve. Kathleen had been given a long leash while growing up, allowed to roam the countryside with her brother or Denny, riding horses, climbing trees, and dashing through the local villages. They'd indulged in more than a few risky adventures that had taught Kathleen how to take care of herself. Jeannie's childhood, however, had been sheltered and strictly supervised. That she'd managed to pull off such a daring escape was terrifying.

"Awful or not, they love you," Kathleen countered. "And if anything had happened to you . . ."

It could have gone wrong in ways too horrible to contemplate.

"The only hard part was sneaking out when the carriage stopped so I could use the necessary and find something to eat."

"Are you sure no one saw you?" Kathleen asked.

"No one that matters. I brought money along so I could nip in and buy a pie or pasty whenever the carriage stopped at an inn." Jeannie shrugged. "Everyone just thought I was a boy."

Gillian nodded. "People generally only see what they expect to see. Jeannie's costume is quite effective and deflected from her, ah, other attributes."

She meant Jeannie's already blossoming figure.

"And now we can be together, Kath," Jeannie said. "You won't have to go to those dreary Highlands by yourself. Won't that be splendid?"

Kathleen steeled herself against her sister's pleading gaze. "We'll have to hire a carriage. Gillian, perhaps your maid could escort Jeannie back to London?"

"Of course, if that's what you truly wish to do."

"It's not what I wish to do," Jeannie protested. "And you can't make me."

Kathleen tried another tack. "Sweetheart, do you really want to spend the entire winter in a musty old manor house? It's bound to be dreadful. We'd probably hate each other by the end of it."

"It's only three months. I heard you talking to Papa."

"You mean you were eavesdropping."

"Papa said that if you stayed out of trouble for that long, then you could return to London."

Kathleen had wangled an even bigger promise out of her father, of which Jeannie was unaware. After an embarrassingly frank discussion about her utter ineptitude on the marriage mart, they'd reached an agreement. If she willingly spent three months at Lochnagar, scandal-free, Papa would let her return to Ireland for a trial run at pursuing a quiet life at Greystone.

But he'd emphasized the *staying out of trouble* part, or their gentleman's agreement would be off.

"Jeannie, how do you think Helen would react if I were to whisk you off to Scotland?"

"All Mamma cares about are Cara and Richard, and getting them leg-shackled. I'm just in the way."

Sadly, there was more than a nugget of truth in that assessment.

"But there's your coming out in the spring to plan for. You don't want to miss that," Kathleen said with an encouraging smile.

"I don't care," Jeannie flatly said. "And I swear I'll run away again if you make me go back. I know how to do it now."

Kathleen's heart lurched. "That would be a terribly foolish—not to mention dangerous—thing to do."

"I think you don't want me along because you're afraid I'll make trouble for you."

When Jeannie suddenly looked down at her lap, her defiance crumpling as she blinked back tears, Kathleen wanted to cry, too.

You've made an epic mess of everything, Kath, old girl.

"No . . . nobody wants me," her sister gulped. "And I don't know what to do."

Kathleen slid out of her chair and went down on her knees, pulling Jeannie into a tight embrace. "Darling, I love you *so* much, and I would happily keep you with me if I could."

Gillian leaned forward. "Might I make a suggestion?"

Kathleen glanced over with relief. "Please."

"Allow me to send an express post to my husband, explaining the situation. I'm sure he can speak with your parents and smooth things over."

"B-but I still don't want to go home," Jeannie quavered. "Please don't make me, Kath."

"Kathleen, I suggest Jeanette come to Glasgow with us," Gillian said. "It would be the best way to avoid scandal, for one thing, since Charles and your parents can put it about that she joined us at the last minute. Then she can return to London with me at the end of my visit."

Jeannie turned a teary, pleading gaze on Kathleen. "Please say yes, Kath. *Please*. At least let me stay for a visit."

Kathleen wavered, unsure whether Gillian's solution made sense. Jeannie was a handful at the best of times. "Well . . ."

"You'll have both me *and* Lady Arnprior to look after Jeannie," Gillian said, clearly reading her mind. "Vicky used to be a governess, and knows all about entertaining, er, active young ladies."

Jeannie bounced in her chair. "I'll be good as gold, I promise."

Kathleen mentally rolled her eyes. "The duke would truly be willing to explain all this to our parents?"

Gillian twinkled at them. "I won't give him a choice."

Kathleen recognized the desperate eagerness in her sister's expression. It was a need to be loved and accepted, to know she was truly wanted. She'd felt the same more times than she could count.

How in God's name could she say no?

She nodded. "Thank you, Gillian. That would be splendid of you and the duke."

"Huzzah!" Jeannie jumped out of her chair and began dancing around the room.

Kathleen pointed at her sister. "But you must *promise* to listen to me. No more running off or doing silly things."

Jeannie twirled to a halt and clasped her hands in a prayerful attitude. "I will be a perfect angel, Kath. I promise. Now that we're together, what could go wrong?"

Chapter Four

Glasgow
September 1823

Bored.

Grant Kendrick knew the feeling would pass. He was too busy to indulge in foolish bouts of dissatisfaction.

And yet . . .

He leaned back in his desk chair and cast a jaundiced eye at the ledger before him, where the figures marched across the page like soldiers in battlefield formation. Business was its own sort of battle, fought with brains, instinct, and numbers.

Always numbers, unrelenting and precise.

Grant was certainly precise, from the neatly arranged bookshelves in his office, to his daily attire of plain tailcoat in dark blue or green, with gray vest, pale breeches, and top boots. Why wear anything different? He spent most of each day in the warehouse or down at the port when a ship was off-loading, so there was no point in dressing flash.

He closed the ledger and stood, stretching his arms to work out the kinks, almost touching the massive beams overhead. Then he picked up the rest of the leather-bound volumes stacked on his desk and carried them to the oak bookcases that lined the opposite wall. He barely had to look to put them back, since every ledger, every file, and every scrap of paper was perfectly organized, so that the right information would be at his fingertips whenever he needed it.

He was good at organizing and, since coming to work for his older brothers three years ago, Grant had discovered that he was good at making money. Everyone in the family had a talent, and raking in the blunt had turned out to be his. Helping to grow Kendrick Shipping and Trade for his family—for the future of his nieces and nephews—was a grand thing. Grant had built a useful and worthy life, and there wasn't a damn thing worth complaining about.

Except you're bored out your damn skull.

"You're an idiot," he muttered as he shoved the ledgers back into place.

It hadn't always been this way. He and his twin, Graeme, had spent years raising hell. But Graeme was married now. He'd moved on from his freewheeling days, and was now settled into an eminently respectable life on a small Highland estate. In Graeme's case the respectability was rather hilarious, since he'd always been the truly wild one in the family, practically immune to any correction.

Grant, though? For him, the wildness had never come naturally, and the life he now led suited him as nothing else ever had. Everything was exactly as it should be. After years of heartache and trial, the Kendricks were finally at peace.

Except for how you actually feel.

He scowled to himself as he pointlessly rearranged a few ledgers.

"What's amiss, laddie?" barked a voice from the doorway. "Numbers not adding up?"

Grant turned to see his grandfather leaning against the doorframe. Angus looked particularly disreputable today in an ancient kilt, scuffed boots, and the tatty Highland bonnet he'd worn ever since King George had admired it on his visit to Scotland last year. The attire, along with his bushy white eyebrows and correspondingly wild hair, made Angus look like a Highland ancient run amuck from the glens.

Yet, his grandfather was an extraordinarily canny man. Though not bookish, no one pulled anything over on Angus. Every Kendrick brother had tried at various times over the years but all had failed.

"Mayhap ye should let me look at yon ledgers," the old fellow added in a hopeful voice.

Grant swallowed a sigh. Angus was a marvel, except when it came to numbers. When he'd served as estate steward at Castle Kinglas, the seat of Clan Kendrick, Grandda had made a massive financial mess of things. Nick, Grant's oldest brother and head of the clan, had finally been forced to banish their grandfather from the estate office unless he was there with him.

Still, even that drastic measure had failed to convince Angus that he was anything less than a financial genius.

"The ledgers are fine, Grandda." Grant crossed back to his desk to snuff out the lamp. "I'm just packing up for the day."

His grandfather sidled in and reached for one of the leather-bound volumes. "Remember ye got yer head for numbers from me, lad."

Grant plucked the ledger from his hand. "Perhaps another time."

Angus scowled and straightened his sagging bonnet.

"Ye always say that, and somehow that *other time* never arrives."

"Grandda, why are you here? And does Vicky know you're wandering about town dressed like the ghost of Rob Roy?"

Grant's sister-in-law usually managed to keep Angus on the right side of respectable. This time, though, he'd clearly slipped the net.

"I dinna need any lassie tellin' me how to dress," Angus indignantly replied.

"Apparently you do, though. I'm sorry, Grandda, but that bonnet is wretched."

"Yer brother *the laird*," Angus said with unnecessary emphasis, "sent me forthwith to fetch ye. And I'll nae have ye insultin' my bonnet. King Georgie himself wished that he had one just like it, ye recall."

"Yes, you remind us of that repeatedly." Grant gently propelled his grandfather into the hall. "And we all wish you'd given it to the king as a going away present. The blasted thing smells like a peat bog."

Angus glowered as they walked along the upstairs corridor. "This bonnet was worn by one of yer ancestors when he fought at the side of the Bruce himself. I'll nae have ye disrespecting our history."

Grant cast a quick glance into the various offices as they made their way to the stairs. The warehouse manager and three senior clerks were already gone, probably a good hour ago.

"Grandda, that's *your* bonnet, and it's not that old. It's only pathetic because the moths got at it when you shoved it into a trunk and forgot about it."

"It's the point I'm makin' that matters, lad. It's all numbers and work for ye. It's nae good for ye, all this toilin' away by candlelight."

Grant snorted at the sudden change in topic. "What I ken is that your bonnet and my work are completely unrelated subjects."

Grumbling, Angus preceded him down the stairs to the front office, where junior clerks, now gone for the day, tallied the inventories of timber, furs, and other goods arriving from Canada.

While the headquarters of Kendrick Shipping and Trade was in Halifax, Canada, Grant's older brother, Logan, had established a large office in Glasgow and a smaller branch in Edinburgh. They hoped to expand to London within the next six months, after Logan and his family returned to Scotland. Logan, Donella, and their children had spent the better part of two years in Halifax, but would soon be moving back to Glasgow.

The night porter was a sharp young fellow from the small village near Kinglas. He rose from his seat by the fire when he saw Grant.

"All settled in for the night, Sam?" Grant asked.

"Aye, sir. And thank ye for loanin' me yer copy of *Ivanhoe*. It's a corkin' good story."

Grant nodded. "That it is."

Angus snorted. "Och, a fat lot of nonsense written by a Lowland nincompoop. Now, dinna ye be neglectin' yer duties, lad, reading that historical twaddle."

When Sam's eyes widened with alarm, Grant nudged his grandfather toward the door. "Sam knows his responsibilities perfectly well, Grandda. No need to lecture him about reading a harmless novel."

"I'll lock up behind ye, sir," the young man gratefully said.

"Ye needn't shove me," Angus protested as he stepped

down onto the cobblestone street. "Ye'll be breakin' my puir old bones."

"I did not shove you. Besides, you're as sturdy as a billy goat."

Angus tottered, doing his best to look frail. "And how would ye ken that? What with yer bein' at work all day and half the night, a slave to yer ledgers. I could be lyin' dead in my bed for a week and ye'd never notice."

Grant cupped a hand around his grandfather's elbow and steered him down the street. "I might not, but our housekeeper surely would."

"Not the point, laddie boy."

"Then what is?"

"All this fussin' about Royal leavin' the business, it's got ye in a stew."

Grant repressed a grimace at the home hit. He *was* worried about his older brother's impending departure. Royal was Logan's right-hand man and knew Kendrick Shipping and Trade from the bottom up.

"I'm not—"

"And yer oldest brother—that would be *the laird*—agrees with me," Angus triumphantly added. "Yer frettin' aboot all the things ye'll be havin' to do once Royal leaves."

Royal's wife, Ainsley, had recently inherited a tidy estate up near Cairndow. Since Royal had always favored the country over the city, and since Ainsley would love nothing more than managing an estate, they'd decided it was time to quit Glasgow and move north. The family was happy for them, though it meant responsibility for the Scottish end of the business would fall entirely on Grant until Logan returned.

Grant felt more than up to the task. Yet it *would* require

a great deal of hard work—something his family seemed unable to comprehend.

"Is that why Nick sent you to fetch me? He thinks I'm working too hard?"

Angus pulled out his battered claymore pipe. "Nae, that's not the reason he sent me."

Grant waited patiently while his grandfather got a light from a street vendor with a brazier. Then he took Angus by the elbow and hurried him across Queen Street.

"If ye were in such an all-fired hurry, we could have fetched a hackney," Angus protested.

Grant threw him a disbelieving look. "You're the one dragging me out of the office, presumably because I'm late for something. But if you want me to flag a coach, I'm happy to do so."

"Och, ye need the fresh air after bein' cooped up all day. Yer practically growin' moldy."

Lately, Grant did find himself longing for good mountain air, and a visit to Kinglas, the family's ancestral home on the shores of Loch Long, was overdue. Caught between water, sky, and snowcapped peaks, Kinglas was the most beautiful place in the world to him.

Gloriously beautiful, but haunted by memories, many of them desperately unhappy. Those memories were ones he'd rather avoid right now.

"What's amiss, son? Yer lookin' a bit squirrely now," his grandfather quietly said.

"Nothing's wrong, Grandda."

Angus blew out a cloud of smoke. "I know everything about ye, so dinna be pretendin' with me."

"All right, I'm squirrely because I still don't know why we're rushing home."

"Have ye forgotten the guests arrivin' today? Yer brother wanted us all on hand when the duchess made her appearance."

Grant sighed. "Oh, hell."

He'd completely forgotten about the Duchess of Leverton. Vicky had never met her royal cousin and was as nervous as a cat in a thunderstorm. And whenever Vicky got fashed, Nick got fashed. That meant *everyone* got fashed, if they knew what was good for them.

"Vicky wants us all to make a good impression. Yer brother is nae happy yer late."

They turned into a quiet side street. "I'm sorry I wasn't there, though my absence could not possibly have made a worse impression than your outfit. You look like you've been rolling about in a patch of thistle."

"Nae, I was dressed right and proper for the grand arrival. I changed when Nick sent me out to fetch ye home. Ye ken I canna stand wearing fancy dudes for long."

"Well, you can't sit down to dinner looking like that." A nearby church tower began to toll out the hour. "I'll have to change, too. It's already seven o'clock."

He'd also have to perform the appropriate amount of groveling for his late showing. The duchess's visit would no doubt prove to be massively inconvenient, since Nick would expect Grant to do his bit by squiring Vicky and her cousin around Glasgow, since most of the brothers were out of town.

"I don't have time for this," he muttered as he hurried his grandfather along.

"Dinna fret. Vicky pushed dinner back an hour."

Grant shot him a glare. "And you couldn't think to tell me that?"

"Just keepin' ye on yer toes, laddie boy."

"You are a pain in the arse sometimes, Grandda."

Angus snickered. "Somebody has to keep life interestin' around here."

"In future, when such is required I will alert you immediately," Grant said as they entered the small square that fronted Kendrick House. "In any case, Vicky didn't need to push dinner back on my account."

"Happens it was necessary. The ladies made quite a ruckus when they arrived. They needed to get settled."

"Ladies? I thought the duchess was making a solitary visit."

"Vicky gave us the details at breakfast a few days ago, which ye clearly dinna recall."

Grant had a dim recollection of the discussion. He'd been studying an agricultural journal at the time, so the details had escaped him.

"A companion of some sort, wasn't it?"

Angus shook his head. "Yer hopeless."

They cut through the square, whose trim lawns and tidy paths were a favorite daytime haunt of the nursemaids and their charges from the surrounding mansions. Now it was quiet, softly lit by the glow of street lanterns and lamps in nearby windows.

Grant suddenly had a bad feeling. "Grandda, whom did the duchess bring with her?"

"Well, she's a bonny young lass, *verra* bonny. And she'll be that happy to meet ye, I ken."

Grant came to a halt, looking up at the darkening sky. "Really? This again?" Most of the Kendricks, and especially Angus, were annoyingly inveterate matchmakers. "I bloody well don't have time for you or anyone else playing Cupid, Grandda."

"I'd never play Cupid. He was a bloody *Sassenach*."

Grant stalked off, leaving his grandfather to scamper after him. "You're failing to grasp the main point," he said when Angus caught up. "And Cupid was Greek, by the way."

Angus ignored that. "Speaking of *Sassenachs*, this lassie's a rich one. And she's Sabrina's cousin, too."

"Splendid, but I'm not on the lookout for a wife, even Sabrina's cousin."

"Have I mentioned that she's bonny? Rich and bonny?"

Grant stopped at the foot of the marble steps of Kendrick House and gave his grandfather a stern look. "First of all, you don't give a damn about money. And secondly, I'm too busy to deal with such nonsense. Logan is depending on me, remember?"

"Fah," Angus scoffed.

Grant forced himself to remain calm. Most Kendricks tended to yell when frustrated, but Grant always made a point of doing the opposite. "Now, Angus—"

The old man started up the steps. "Och, fine. Ye can sit in a corner and be yer usual gloomy self. Not that the bonny lass will have time for the likes of ye, anyway. She'll be too busy keepin' her wee sister in line. That one's waitin' to pop off like a bottle rocket, I reckon."

"Good God, just how many people did the duchess bring with her?"

"Including the maid and the grooms?"

"You're incredibly irritating." Grant rapped on the door, ignoring his grandfather's chuckle.

Will, the under-butler, answered. "Good evening, Mr. Grant. I hope you had a productive day."

"I did, until a lunatic Highlander forced his way into my office."

Will didn't bat an eyelash. "The family and guests are

beginning to gather in the drawing room, sir, but you and Mr. MacDonald have time to change."

"Thank you. I'll just be . . ."

The words died on his tongue as he caught sight of a young woman floating down the staircase. He blinked, and then blinked again.

Grant was used to living with beautiful women. His sisters-in-law were all stunners, the sort that stopped men dead in their tracks.

This girl, though? She was just a wee dab of a thing. If lost in thought, a man might pass her on the street and never notice. But with a closer look, there was something . . . something fey about her, as if she'd just stepped out of a fairy ring in a deep Highland glen.

That impression grew stronger as she reached the bottom of the stairs, her skirts seeming to drift on a mountain breeze. The gown was eccentric and charming, a confection of pink silk and white lace that skimmed over her figure. An extraordinary number of gold spangled ribbons encircled her slender waist and cascaded down the front of the gown, some gently flaring as she came toward them. As she passed under the huge chandelier of the center hall, she seemed to shimmer, as if a thousand tiny stars were embedded in the fabric of her gown.

You're daft, man.

Girls didn't shimmer or float, or any other stupid image his brain kicked out.

She *was* very bonny, just as his grandfather had said. With wide-set, pewter-gray eyes, narrow cheekbones, and a sharp little chin, her face looked more elfin than human.

Except for her mouth, which was definitely human and very lush, with a Cupid's bow curve and a full lower lip. Set against her ethereal features, it made for an intriguing contrast.

Grant liked intriguing. He decided he liked pink gowns and spangled ribbons, too.

The young woman drifted to a halt a few feet away, her mouth tilted in a crooked half smile, as if unsure of her reception.

"You're starin', laddie," Angus whispered.

Of course, what his grandfather considered a whisper could be heard half a block away.

Stop acting like a dolt.

He dredged up a smile. "I take it this is one of our guests. Perhaps you could introduce me, Grandda."

"That would be preferable to us staring at each other like boobies," the young lady responded.

The vinegary reply was offset by her light voice and an appealing trace of a brogue—not Scottish, but Irish. That was also intriguing.

After a fraught pause, Grant nudged his grandfather. "Angus?"

"Och, I'm forgettin' my manners. Happens all the time, ye ken."

When the girl smiled—a real smile, this time—Grant almost forgot his own name.

"Lady Arnprior warned me that you didn't have any manners," she said to Angus. "So I shouldn't mind if you say something outrageous."

Good God.

Angus gave her a wink. "I'll be havin' a wee chat with her ladyship, defamin' me like that."

The girl laughed. "Oh, drat. Now I've got us both in trouble, haven't I?"

"Nothin' we can't get out of together, lass. Just follow my lead."

She dipped him a saucy little curtsy. "I will be sure to do so, Mr. MacDonald."

"A-hem," Grant said.

Angus gave a fake start. "I almost forgot about ye. Miss Kathleen Calvert, allow me to introduce my grandson Grant Kendrick."

Grant bowed. "Miss Calvert, it's a pleasure to meet you. Welcome to Kendrick House."

"Thank you, sir." She tilted her head back, studying him with a thoughtful frown. "I thought Lord Arnprior was tall, but you're almost a giant. It's all the clean living, I suppose, not to mention the log tossing. I've been told that Scots are fond of log tossing. By your size, I would say you do quite a lot of it."

Grant's mind blanked for a moment. "Er, is that a question?"

Miss Calvert studied him for a moment before letting out a sigh, as if disappointed. "I suppose we should go in. The others are waiting."

When she calmly walked off toward the drawing room, Grant turned to his grandfather. "What just happened?"

"Ye got rolled up, son, that's what happened. Ye'll have to do better than that."

"Do better at having bizarre conversations? That's your forte, not mine."

Angus snorted. "At least my conversations don't bore young lassies to death."

With that annoying and probably truthful bon mot, his grandfather beetled over to the stairs, heading up to the family apartments.

Grant blew out a frustrated breath, then looked at Will. "Is it just me, or is my entire family insane?"

"Dinner in thirty minutes, sir," the young man politely responded.

Shaking his head, Grant stalked up the stairs.

Chapter Five

It's because he's so tall.

Kathleen mentally cursed, annoyed with her inane response to Grant Kendrick. But even in a family of tall, impressive-looking men, he'd stood out.

She paused outside the drawing room door, taking a deep breath. Men never rattled her. Never. And she'd always thought that rather a shame, since she imagined it might be fun for an attractive man to ruffle her feathers.

But then she'd seen him standing in the hall and had promptly lost her ability to form a sensible thought.

That wasn't much fun at all.

In addition to his height and impressively broad shoulders, Mr. Kendrick was handsome, with rather austere features and a manner that had little in common with the languid dandies or bored Corinthians of the *ton*. In fact, he was slightly intimidating. Not that he'd done anything impolite, except stare at her with those extraordinary eyes. His gaze had tracked her all the way down the stairs. That had made her feel self-conscious and awkward, as if she'd said or done something tremendously silly.

Unfortunately, as soon as she'd opened her mouth that

was exactly what she did. His russet eyebrows had shot up in surprise, and an incredulous expression had filled his jade-colored gaze. Until today, Kathleen had never seen eyes of such a startling color. Combined with his dark red hair, burnished like an autumn leaf, Grant Kendrick seemed on first glance the epitome of a dashing Highlander warrior, stepped right from the pages of a poem by Sir Walter Scott.

On both second and third glance, however, Mr. Kendrick struck her as a man who took the business of life very seriously. That was probably why his gaze had transformed so quickly from surprised to disapproving. It was not an uncommon reaction. Men often found her disconcerting, if not downright strange.

Kathleen almost jumped out of her shoes when a quiet voice spoke up behind her.

"Miss Calvert, may I get the door for you?"

She smiled weakly at Henderson, the Kendricks' very correct butler. "Yes, I was rather woolgathering, but I shouldn't keep the others waiting."

"There's no rush, ma'am. Dinner will not be served until the entire family has assembled."

The older man's kind smile was probably why she blurted out yet another admission. "I think I was rather rude to Mr. Kendrick. Mr. Grant Kendrick, I mean. Just now, when I met him. Back in the hall."

Good God. What was wrong with her?

Henderson didn't turn a hair. "I think you'll find that the Kendricks value forthright speech, Miss Calvert. And Mr. Grant is the kindest of men, I assure you. He would never take offense."

Kathleen wasn't quite sure about that, but she appreciated the butler's attempt to settle her nerves.

"Are you ready to join the others now, ma'am?" he patiently asked a few moments later.

Kathleen gave him a nod, deciding to ignore the residual effects of Grant Kendrick. It made not one whit of difference what he thought of her, even if he *was* terribly handsome.

"Ah, there you are," Gillian said as Henderson ushered Kathleen into the spacious and elegant drawing room. "And looking very dashing, I might add. That color is simply splendid on you."

Lady Arnprior, seated next to her cousin on a green velvet chaise, gave her a warm smile. "Indeed. You look absolutely charming."

Overdressed, more like it. For some demented reason, Kathleen had chosen a gown suited to a grand London ball at the height of the Season. By contrast, both Gillian and the countess were dressed in simple, elegant gowns perfect for a family dinner. No wonder Mr. Kendrick had stared at her.

"You should see me when I really put in the effort," she joked.

Lord Arnprior came over to escort her to the group. "As my wife noted, you indeed look charming. We are fortunate to have so many lovely ladies in our midst."

"You look top drawer, Kath, as always," Jeannie said, beaming up at her.

Her sister was plopped down in front of the grand chimneypiece—marble, in the Adam style if Kathleen wasn't mistaken—to play with the family dogs. The two Skye terriers, messy mopheads, were snuggled close to Jeannie, one of them drooling on the hem of her gown. Helen would have fainted dead away at the sight, but since no one else seemed perturbed by such casual behavior, Kathleen refrained from comment.

In fact, Kade, the youngest of the Kendricks, who'd respectfully stood when Kathleen entered the room, settled back down on the floor next to Jeannie. Although a tall, dignified young man in his early twenties, Kade seemed comfortable sitting cross-legged on the carpet, playing with dogs.

The Kendricks were a warm and welcoming clan—with one exception, whom she refused to think further about at the moment.

Kathleen smiled at Jeannie, steadfastly ignoring the paw print on her sister's white cambric skirts. They'd managed to pick up a few dresses for the girl while on the road, but the need for a shopping expedition was urgent. As informally charming as the Kendrick family appeared, Kathleen was determined that she and her sister make a good impression. Their arrival had already kicked up a bit of a fuss. Causing trouble could result in unpleasant consequences for both of them.

Lord Arnprior, a distinguished man in his early forties, escorted her to the chaise where his wife and Gillian sat.

With her usual unaffected grace, Gillian hopped to her feet. "Kathleen, sit and have a nice chat with Vicky. You've barely had a moment to exchange more than a few words, what with all the bustling about. Such a commotion we caused."

"That's because you two brought so much luggage," Jeannie cheekily said, as if there'd been nothing awkward about her unexpected arrival.

"Piles and piles of it," Gillian agreed, sliding over the moment. "We are rather like the Viking hordes."

"Except no longboats." Kathleen heaved a dramatic sigh.

"And I am sorry to say I misplaced my axe somewhere on the road."

"I could lend you one of my knives," Gillian replied. "I always pack extra."

Lady Arnprior laughed. "In that case, I must be sure to warn the maids, so as to avoid any unfortunate accidents."

The countess obviously thought her cousin was joking, but Kathleen would bet a bob that Gillian did pack extra knives amongst her stockings and stays.

"Gillian has been telling me how much you've been looking forward to this visit to Glasgow," Lady Arnprior said as Kathleen sat down next to her.

"Indeed," said Gillian with a mischievous twinkle. "A very *long* visit."

As usual, the duchess was as subtle as a sledgehammer.

"Although I'm sure Sabrina is eager to see you, you're welcome to stay as long as you like," said Lady Arnprior. "Glasgow isn't London, but it can be quite charming this time of year."

Kade rolled his eyes. "Charming might be a bit much. Still, there are some interesting places to visit, both in town and the surrounding countryside."

"I do hope you'll be able to show us," Jeannie enthused. "All the best spots, if you please."

Kade flashed her a very engaging grin. "It would be my honor, Miss Jeanette."

"Please call me Jeannie," her sister responded, gazing at the young man with rapt attention. "Everyone does."

Although quite a bit younger than his brother, Kade bore a great resemblance to Lord Arnprior. With a vague sense of alarm, Kathleen realized that his dark good looks were just the sort to make a powerful impression on a sensitive girl like Jeannie.

Lady Arnprior darted a glance at Kathleen before nodding at her brother-in-law. "Kade, would you fetch Miss Calvert a sherry?"

"I'll get it," Lord Arnprior said, crossing to the chinoiserie-style sideboard that held a collection of crystal decanters and goblets.

"May I have a sherry, too?" Jeannie asked.

"No," Kathleen firmly said.

When her sister scowled, Kade touched her hand. "Do you want me to tell you where I think we should visit first?"

Jeannie was instantly diverted. "Yes, please." Her big, cornflower-blue eyes shone with what could only be described as burgeoning hero worship.

Gillian, observing from a chair next to the chaise, tapped her chin. "That could turn into a bit of a problem," she quietly said, as Jeannie and Kade chatted away.

Kathleen sighed. "Drat."

Lady Arnprior patted her hand. "Kade is the most decent young man in Scotland. He would never engage in inappropriate behavior."

"He's not the one I'm worried about," Kathleen replied.

Gillian crinkled her nose. "Chaperoning is a thankless task, I must say."

"You and I are not exactly well-suited to it," Kathleen dryly replied.

"I, however, am exceedingly well-suited," said Lady Arnprior. "All will be well, I promise."

Kathleen cast her a grateful smile. "Thank you. We're such a dreadful imposition. You're to be spending your time with Gillian, not keeping an eye on two ramshackle Calverts."

"Vicky and I will have plenty of time to talk," Gillian

said. "After dinner, I intend to drag her back to my room, where I expect we'll be gabbing most of the night."

"I can't think Lord Arnprior will approve," Kathleen replied. "He seems very much—"

A masculine throat clearing interrupted her. "Your drink, Miss Calvert?"

She looked up and managed to give the earl a weak smile. "Oh, yes. Thank you, sir."

Her stepmother was right. She truly did not know how to behave in polite company.

"And if you think I'm going to let you keep my wife up half the night," Arnprior said, giving Gillian a mocking glance, "you will be much surprised. That is my job."

Kathleen almost choked on her sherry.

The duchess waved a negligent hand. "I outrank you, Nicholas. You'll just have to go without."

"This is a most improper conversation," Lady Arnprior said in a stern tone. "Nicholas, you will embarrass poor Miss Calvert."

Lord Arnprior smiled at Kathleen. "You must forgive us. Despite my wife's best efforts, I am apparently still an untutored Highlander."

"Frankly, the entire lot of you is hopeless," her ladyship replied. "Except for Kade, of course. He's perfect."

Her brother-in-law had caught the tail end of the conversation and now grinned. "Vicky, you have to say that because you were my music teacher."

"True, but you're still perfect, my dear."

"You seem *quite* perfect to me, Mr. Kendrick," Jeannie said, staring at Kade with an unfortunately ardent gaze.

Kade looked momentarily nonplussed by her enthusiasm. Then he gave her a cheerful nod, clearly oblivious to the pitfall looming before him. "Please call me Kade.

If you keep calling me Mr. Kendrick, I'll think you're referring to one of my big brothers."

"I could never mistake you for one of your brothers," Jeannie replied.

"Uh-oh," Gillian muttered.

"Speaking of your brothers," Lady Arnprior pointedly said, "perhaps you could go look for them. They seem to have disappeared."

When Kade obligingly hoisted himself to his feet, Kathleen ignored her sister's frown and flashed the countess a grateful smile. "Your grandfather and Mr. Kendrick had just returned when I came downstairs."

"Thank goodness. Some nights, we practically have to drag Grant home from the office. I take it Angus introduced you?"

At the memory of that embarrassing encounter, Kathleen's face grew hot. "Yes, although it was quite a short introduction. We—"

"Found one of them, anyway," Kade said as he walked back into the room.

Following on his heels was Royal Kendrick, whom they'd met on their arrival. His wife and children had departed a few days ago to travel to their estate up north, and from what Lady Arnprior had explained Royal would soon be departing as well.

"Good evening, ladies. Your Grace," Royal said as he bowed over Gillian's hand. "I trust you've settled in."

From the first, Royal had struck Kathleen as a man possessed of a kind and steady temperament, inclined to let the other members of his family take center stage. Not that he could ever be anything less than noticeable, with his slight limp and dramatic good looks that put one in mind of a poet. Unlike Grant's, his hair was more auburn than red, but they shared the same vibrant green gaze.

The Kendricks were certainly a handsome lot, although none that she'd met were as intensely masculine as Grant.

Don't be a ninny. You barely had two minutes with the man.

"None of that *Your Grace* nonsense, if you please," Gillian said. "You Kendricks certainly don't stand on ceremony, and neither do I."

"Hmm," Kathleen said. "I think I've heard that about you." She snapped her fingers. "Oh, right, from your husband."

Gillian snorted. "Cheeky lass."

"I've heard that before, too."

Royal laughed. "I take it you've recovered from the rigors of your trip, Miss Calvert?"

"Yes, thanks to Lady Arnprior and her excellent housekeeper."

"My excellent housekeeper will be pitching a fit if we don't get in to dinner," the countess said. "Where is Grant? And please don't tell me he snuck back to work again."

"Does he do that often?" Kathleen couldn't help asking.

"Grant hates dinner parties," Kade said. "He says they're a waste of time."

Gillian laughed. "That's rather insulting, given that we're the dinner party tonight."

"It's also completely untrue," said the topic of discussion as he walked into the room. "I only hate boring dinner parties. And from what Graeme has told me, the Duchess of Leverton is definitely not boring. In fact, he said she is *the* most interesting woman in London."

For a few moments, all Kathleen could do was stare. She'd thought Grant Kendrick handsome before, dressed as an ordinary businessman. Now, garbed in stark black and white evening kit, he looked spectacular.

Gillian scoffed. "He only says that because he destroyed a very expensive Chinese screen at one of my parties. He's still trying to make it up to me."

"I remember that night," Kathleen said. "He'd caught someone trying to cheat an elderly lady at cards, as I recall."

"Yes. Graeme was quite . . ."

"'Fashed' is the word you're searching for," Grant said in a wry tone.

"Exactly. My screen also became quite fashed, since your twin tossed the cheater right into it," Gillian replied.

"That's our Graeme," Royal said.

"I thought it one of the most entertaining parties in quite some time, actually," Kathleen said.

Gillian laughed. "My poor husband did not entirely agree."

"Sabrina's calmed the lad down," Royal said. "Wives tend to do that sort of thing."

"Depends on the wife," Gillian quipped.

"Which is why you won't be bored tonight," Kathleen said to Grant. "Gillian won't allow it."

Something sparked to life in Grant's expression as his gaze flickered over her. Something that looked like . . . interest.

"I suspect you wouldn't allow it either, Miss Calvert."

He had a lovely voice. Deep and warm, with a slightly rough edge that almost made her shiver.

Almost, because shivering over a man's voice would be ridiculous.

"It's more of a challenge than one would expect," she replied. "Most people are awfully dreary, you know."

When Grant's expression turned blank, she winced.

"Present company excepted, of course," she hastily added.

"Of course," he said.

"Shall we go in to dinner?" the countess brightly suggested.

"I'd hold up on that for a wee bit, lassie."

Angus had slipped into the room, wearing a sheepish expression.

The countess narrowed her gaze. "Grandda, what have you done now?"

"Not me," the old man said in a defensive tone. "It was Nancy. She got ahold of a wee little dish in the pantry. Nothin' to speak of, ye ken."

Lord Arnprior shook his head. "Can you not keep that little hellion under control?"

"She's nae hellion," Angus protested. "Just high-spirited."

"Grandda, Nancy is a disaster on four legs," Grant said.

"Who's Nancy?" Jeannie asked.

"Another one of Grandda's terriers," Kade explained. "She's only a year old, so her manners aren't very good yet."

"I think we can all agree that none of your grandfather's dogs have very good manners," Lady Arnprior tartly added.

The butler stepped in, a pained expression on his dignified features. "I beg your pardon, my lady, but dinner will be delayed. There has been an *incident* in the pantry."

"Yes, so we just heard." The countess sighed. "How bad is it, then?"

"The kitchen maid and the junior footman attempted to retrieve tonight's joint of beef from Nancy, giving chase."

"I take it they were not successful," Grant dryly said.

"The footman *quite* foolishly tripped over Nancy when she swerved during the chase. He then compounded the error by knocking over the table with the soup tureen *and* the fish course."

"How very clumsy of him," Gillian said, trying not to grin.

"Words fail me, Your Grace," said Henderson, looking cut to the soul.

By now, Royal, Kade, and Jeannie were all laughing, and Kathleen was doing her best not to aggravate the situation by joining them.

Grant simply crossed his arms and shook his head at his grandfather.

"It's nae my fault, ye ken," Angus said, protesting the silent reprimand.

The countess glared at him. "It's *entirely* your fault. I take it Cook is in hysterics?" she asked Henderson.

"Smelling salts have been applied, but to little effect."

At that, even Lord Arnprior couldn't hold back laughter.

His wife pointed a finger. "This is no laughing matter, Nicholas."

"Of course not, my love," he said in a choked voice.

"Grant is the only man in this house with any sense," she said with disgust. "And the only one who will get any dinner, if I have my way. Come along, Henderson. We must do our best to restore order."

She paused at the door to scowl at Angus. "And you and I will be having a discussion about this particular incident, and about your *very bad dogs* in general."

Angus bristled. "Now, see here, lassie—"

"I wouldn't, Grandda," Arnprior warned.

With an indignant huff, the countess sailed out of the room, followed by her faithful retainer.

"A lot of botheration over nothin' if ye ask me," Angus

said with commendable nonchalance. "Now, how about a wee dram to hold us over?"

"You're ridiculous." Grant clamped a hand on his grandfather's shoulder and steered him to one of the needlepointed armchairs by the fireplace.

"There's nae need to manhandle me," Angus protested. "It's just a wee bit of fuss."

"I think they're very nice dogs," Jeannie said, crouching down to give the other two terriers a pet. "I wish I had one."

Angus beamed at her. "One of my girlies up at Kinglas will be whelpin' a litter soon. Ye shall have yer pick, Miss Jeannie."

Hell and damnation.

"That's very kind, sir," Kathleen hastily put, "but we're not in the position to have a pet just now."

If Jeannie returned to London with a scruffy terrier in tow, Helen would be apoplectic.

Her sister glared at her. "You always had a dog when you were growing up."

"Every bairn should have a dog, ye ken," Angus unhelpfully added.

Grant, who'd fetched his grandfather a whisky, shoved the glass into his hand. "I'm sure Miss Calvert has her reasons, Grandda. We should respect them."

The old man subsided with a mutter.

Jeannie, unfortunately, did not. "I think you're being very unfair, Kath. And mean."

Kathleen tried not to wince. "Dearest, perhaps we could talk about this later."

"Och, nae need to be embarrassed, lass," Angus said. "We Kendricks yell it out all the time."

"Not a helpful observation, Grandda," Arnprior sternly said.

"Fah," the old fellow trenchantly replied.

"Fah," Jeannie echoed, lifting a defiant chin.

Grant cast a swift look at Kathleen before hunkering down next to Jeannie. He reached out and ruffled the head of one of the dogs, earning a slobbering lick.

"The pups won't be whelped for another few weeks," he said to the girl. "And they won't be able to leave their mother for several more weeks after that. In the meantime, I think my grandfather would be happy to lend you little Daisy here. She's a very sweet dog, as you can see, and she can be your special companion while you're staying with us."

Jeannie shyly returned his smile. "That . . . that would be splendid, as long as your grandfather doesn't mind."

"Daisy would be happy for the attention," Angus said.

"Can she sleep in my bedroom?"

Grant glanced over his shoulder at Kathleen and lifted a questioning eyebrow.

"Please say yes, Kath," Jeannie pleaded, blinking a few times.

Kathleen's heart throbbed with a small, sad ache. Despite her pampered upbringing, Jeannie's life had not been easy under Helen's thumb. All the things Kathleen had enjoyed as a child—riding horses through the countryside, climbing trees, larking about in the gardens—were freedoms her sister had never tasted. Sitting there on the floor, hugging one of the dogs in her lap, Jeannie looked more like a lonesome child than a blossoming girl on the cusp of womanhood.

And in a flash, it occurred to Kathleen that she'd not fought hard enough for her stepsister, not *nearly* hard enough.

"Of course, love," she said. "And if you want to take home a dog, we can talk about that later, too." She smiled. "Although I think we can guess how Mamma would react to that."

Jeannie's pretty features lit up with joy. "Oh . . . oh, that's wonderful, Kath. Thank you." She stared earnestly up at Grant. "And thank *you*. I promise I'll take very good care of Daisy."

"I have no doubt of that," Grant said as he rose.

For such a big man, he moved with true masculine grace, his long, muscled legs flexing as he stood.

"You're staring, pet," Gillian murmured.

Kathleen felt her skin flame as she tried to ignore her friend's warning.

"Thank you, sir," she said to Grant.

His gaze lingered for few moments on her face, probably taking note of her freckles. They always glowed like beacons when she blushed, much to her lasting frustration.

"It was nothing," he said before moving away to speak to Lord Arnprior.

"I think he likes you," Gillian said in an unfortunately loud stage whisper.

"Don't be an idiot," Kathleen hissed.

Gillian grinned, but refrained from further comment when Henderson returned to the room.

"Dinner," he said, "is *finally* served."

Chapter Six

Kathleen fiddled with her empty teacup as the ladies waited for the gentlemen to rejoin them in the drawing room, only half listening to the conversation.

Initially, she'd been pleased to be seated next to Grant at dinner. His kindness toward Jeannie had been touching, and had even made her feel a bit wobbly around the knees. Beneath that stoic exterior lurked a man of both perception and heart.

As a dinner partner, however, Grant Kendrick had been a decided failure.

Naturally, he'd been polite, tilting his head with a thoughtful frown whenever she'd asked him a series of what she thought were interesting questions. Unfortunately, all his replies had been succinct to the point of terse. By the time they'd reached the meat course—the fricassee of veal that had replaced the late, lamented joint of beef—Kathleen gave up trying to draw him out. If Gillian hadn't taken pity on her to talk across the table, it would have been a silent march through the cheese and dessert course.

When Lady Arnprior had finally risen from the table, Kathleen had breathed a sigh of relief. Grant had cut her a sharp glance before his expression again turned politely bland as he pulled back her chair. He'd then resumed his seat without a backward glance as she left the room.

Why she should let that bother her was a mystery, since the man was obviously a dead bore. Then again, perhaps he found *her* boring, or simply a pest with her lighthearted questions about the city and his family. She now realized that sort of thing could very well irritate a man of such serious temperament.

Perhaps a few cogent commentaries on Plato's Republic *would have done the trick.*

When Gillian tapped her on the arm, she almost dropped her teacup. Her friend nimbly snatched it away and put it on the table in front of the chaise.

Kathleen crinkled her nose. "Sorry, what were you saying?"

"Victoria was asking if you'd like another cup of tea." Gillian's mouth curved into a sneaky grin. "But you were obviously thinking of something else. Or *someone* else?"

"Whatever it was, it's not worth remembering," she firmly replied. "Thank you, but no, Lady Arnprior. After that wonderful dinner, I don't think I have room for anything else."

"Please call me Victoria, or Vicky," said her ladyship. "After tonight's disaster, it's safe to say you've been initiated into the family."

"Your staff made a splendid recovery, though."

"Thanks to Henderson, really. He all but cooked the rest of the dinner himself."

Jeannie, again on the floor with the dogs, flashed a grin. "I thought it was quite lovely and the most fun I've had in years."

"You have to admit it was hilarious," Gillian said. "Surely

the look of stoically pained outrage on Henderson's face was worth the upset, Vicky."

"You didn't have to deal with my cook," her cousin wryly replied.

"Still, Jeannie's right," Kathleen said. "It was a lovely dinner."

Mostly.

"I'm glad you both enjoyed it," Victoria said. "It's kind of you to overlook our little foibles."

"By that I suppose you mean Angus," Gillian commented. "I already adore him. Next to him, I look positively ordinary."

Kathleen raised her eyebrows. "Ordinary? Is that even possible?"

Gillian laughed. "You are definitely what Angus would call a cheeky lass. And speaking of possibilities, what were you and Grant discussing during dinner? Anything interesting?"

Kathleen refused to respond to that obvious lure, instead frowning at her sister. "Sweetheart, Daisy has caught her paw in your lace trim. She might rip it."

Jeannie rolled her eyes but carefully removed the dog's snagged paw.

"If there's any damage, my dresser will repair it," Victoria said. "She's had plenty of experience with just that sort of thing."

"How many dogs do you have?" Jeannie asked as she hoisted a drooling Daisy higher onto her lap.

"Three here and seven at Castle Kinglas. Angus would cart all of them about with us if we let him. I fear both Henderson *and* my housekeeper would quit if they had to manage the whole lot."

Gillian reached down and ruffled Daisy's fur. "They're

sweet, but I prefer a good mastiff. Now *that* is a dog you can count on to cover your back in a fight."

Jeannie perked up. "Have you been in lots of fights, Your Grace?"

"Well, let's see—"

Kathleen discreetly elbowed Gillian.

"These dogs are the descendants of the original terriers of Angus's daughter," Victoria smoothly interjected. "There have been many generations at Kinglas since then, with every dog equally silly. But Angus is devoted to them."

Jeannie dropped a kiss on Daisy's head. "He's so lucky to have them."

Again, Kathleen felt that cramp in her heart, as if she'd failed her sister all these years and not even known it.

The men chose that moment to join them, dispersing about the room. Lord Arnprior went to the sideboard to pour drinks.

"May I fetch something stronger for the ladies?" he asked.

"I'll have some of that excellent whisky I keep hearing about," Gillian said.

"And you, Miss Calvert?"

"It's Kathleen, please, since your wife has kindly informed me that I am now one of the family. And sherry is fine."

"Of course yer family, ye and yer sister both." Angus retrieved a battered pipe from his pocket and winked at Jeannie. "Especially if yon lassie on the floor will fetch me a spill for my pipe."

Jeannie giggled and started to carefully remove the dogs from her lap.

"You stay right there, Jeannie." Kade quickly fetched a spill from a brass container by the fireplace.

Jeannie gazed up at him with all the wonder of a young girl in the grip of her first crush. "Thank you."

"Uh-oh," Gillian muttered.

"If you don't stop saying that, I will bash you," Kathleen whispered back.

"Kade," said Grant, who'd taken a seat across from them. "Perhaps you could set up the card table for a round of whist. I heard the duchess remark that she'd like to play a hand."

"Right-o," said the young man.

Jeannie pulled a face at losing the object of her adoration, while Kathleen turned to direct a grateful smile at Grant. Unfortunately, he'd already stood and was going over to join Royal.

"How did things go at the office today, Grant?" Royal asked.

That prompted the men to launch into an animated discussion of problems with shipping supplies to the new whisky distillery at Lochnagar Manor. Grant came alive, his gestures growing more dramatic and his brogue more pronounced. His green gaze glittered with quick intelligence as he responded to questions and comments.

His sudden passion rendered him even *more* attractive, even if it was only in the service of growing the family fortune. No wonder she'd bored him at dinner. She should have asked him about the latest accounting methods if she'd wished to attract his attention.

Victoria shook her head with humorous exasperation. "The lads are always like that when they start on business. Not Kade, though. His great interest is music."

"He's a very talented pianist, isn't he?" Jeannie inquired. "I hope I get to hear him play."

"Since he practices at least five hours a day, you will certainly get the chance."

"He's not the only talented musician in the family, I understand," Kathleen said.

Victoria waved a hand. "I'm an amateur. Kade is genuinely brilliant."

"Yes, but you were his music teacher," Gillian said.

"He quickly outshone me. In fact, he's been asked by the king to play a series of concerts in London. Then he wishes to go to Italy for further study. Both Rome and Venice. Then, who knows?"

Jeannie clasped her hands reverently to her chest. "That means he'll be coming to London. I do hope I'll be able to see him then."

"I certainly envy him a trip to Italy," Kathleen put in. "I've always wanted to visit Rome."

Victoria pulled a slight grimace. "Such a nomadic life is not what we wish for him, but his talent is undeniable. It would be cruel to try to keep him from doing what he loves."

Kathleen could certainly understand that. "It's wonderful that you don't stand in his way. It's . . . it's very hard to be denied the chance to do what you love."

"And what do you love doing, Miss Calvert?" asked a deep voice from the side.

Kathleen almost toppled from her seat. She'd not even noticed Grant rejoin them.

Gillian hopped up from the chaise. "Grant, sit next to Kathleen. I wish to ask his lordship a question."

Argh.

That her friend was playing matchmaker was now thoroughly confirmed. The fact that she and Grant were clearly unmatchable should be obvious to anyone.

When he started to sit, Kathleen held up a hand. "Best not."

He blinked. "Why not?"

"Your hair will clash with my dress."

When he stared at her with mild incredulity, Kathleen wanted to bite her tongue. The dratted man was truly scrambling her brain.

Suddenly he unleashed a smile that had her staring at him like a ninny. He had an absolutely riveting smile.

"As long as we're not seen together in public, I believe we should be fine," he said, taking a seat.

"Not being seen together shouldn't be a problem, I would think."

Good God.

She'd done it again. Even Jeannie was looking appalled by her inane remarks.

Grant simply continued to study her, as if she were some minor but annoying problem to be resolved.

"What I meant," she said, "is that you're obviously very busy. We would just be gadding about town, which would of course be a waste of your time. Your very busy time," she added after a fraught pause.

"It's true that I am especially busy right now," he politely replied.

Kathleen decided she didn't like his bland voice, where his brogue faded away. His brogue wasn't boring.

"Well, then, we'll be sure not to pester you," she brightly responded.

"Och, that's nonsense," Angus piped up. "Grant will be happy to escort ye about town. It's nae proper or safe for ladies to be wanderin' aboot by themselves. Ye'll nae be wantin' to wander into the fleshpots, ye ken."

"Grandda, there really aren't many fleshpots in Glasgow," Kade said.

"Even if there were, I need neither a chaperone nor protection," Gillian interjected.

"Yes, but the citizens of Glasgow might need protection from you," Kathleen teased. "You're positively dangerous under the right circumstances."

Victoria chuckled. "I'm sure those stories are quite blown out of proportion."

"Not according to my twin," Grant said.

Gillian aimed a finger at him. "That's enough out of you, laddie boy."

"Angus is correct, however," Victoria said. "You should have an escort when I can't go about with you."

"I'm sure Grandda would be happy to do it," Grant said.

His grandfather waved his pipe, scattering ashes on his lap. "Aye, delighted, but I fancy the ladies would much rather have a braw lad like yerself."

"I wouldn't wish to clash with Miss Calvert's dress," Grant said. "Besides, Kade is much better company than I am."

"That's a low bar, since you lock yourself away in that dreary office all the time," Kade said.

"Says the lad who spends hours on his music."

Victoria held up a hand. "You both work too hard. It's quite ridiculous."

"Agreed," said Royal. "An outing with the ladies would do you both a world of good. Perhaps even two outings. Yes, I know," he continued when Grant frowned at him. "Fresh air, and during daylight hours. How shocking a concept."

"Ye may recall I'm a wee bit busy right now, thanks to ye," Grant tartly replied.

The lovely brogue was back, and stronger than ever.

No doubt it had surfaced because he was annoyed at the prospect of spending time with her.

Lord Arnprior shook his head. "I find it appalling that any Kendrick male would hesitate to leap at the chance to escort such lovely ladies."

"Quite right, Nicholas," Gillian said. "You'd think we were a trio of madwomen escaped from Bedlam."

"To be fair," Kathleen said, "that's not quite an inaccurate description for the three of us."

Thankfully, almost everyone laughed, as she'd intended. Even Mr. Stodgy and Stoic Grant Kendrick cracked a smile.

"Perhaps Grandda and I could take you for a drive around Glasgow tomorrow," said Kade. "We could point out the highlights and then go for pastries at Monroe's."

"What's Monroe's?" Jeannie asked.

Kade smiled. "Only the best cake shop in Scotland."

"From what I hear about Scottish cuisine, that's not saying much," Gillian teased.

Angus pointed his pipe at Gillian. "I'll nae have ye disparaging our pastries, ye saucy *Sassenach,* even if ye are a duchess."

Gillian heaved a dramatic sigh. "Is it to be pistols at dawn, then?"

"We could take the ladies up to Mugdock one day," Grant unexpectedly said.

Kathleen mentally blinked at that, and because he was now staring directly at her. "Mugdock? That sounds . . ."

"Disgusting," Gillian put in.

Kathleen rolled her eyes. "I was about to say *nice.*"

Actually, she hadn't been sure how to respond, since the sudden intensity in Grant's eyes had again momentarily flustered her.

Angus nodded his approval. "The ladies will love Mugdock."

Jeannie looked doubtful. "What is it?"

"The ancestral home of Clan Graham," Kade explained. "And one of the oldest castles in the district."

Jeannie brightened. "That sounds lovely, and very romantic."

"I'd say interesting rather than romantic," Grant said. "But it's got tremendous history and excellent views of the countryside."

"Just about any place can be romantic with the right sort of company," Gillian said. Then she turned to Kathleen with a sly smile. "Don't you agree, pet?"

It was all Kathleen could do to keep her jaw from sagging open at her friend's astounding lack of subtlety.

"No," she bluntly replied.

When Grant's expressive eyebrows ticked up, she repressed a grimace.

You are an absolute ninny.

Her sister came to her rescue, apparently unintentionally.

"Is the castle haunted?" Jeannie asked.

Kade waggled a hand. "Maybe."

"No," Grant said at the same time.

Jeannie wrinkled her nose in disappointment.

"But the views truly are spectacular," Grant added, by way of consolation.

When Jeannie snorted, Kathleen almost felt sorry for the poor man.

"It does have a bloodthirsty weapons collection," Kade said. "Positively gruesome."

Gillian winked at Jeannie. "Now, that sounds promising, doesn't it?"

Jeannie beamed, her good humor restored.

"It sounds fascinating," Kathleen said. "I'd love to visit."

She smiled at Grant, who gave her just a brusque nod in return. Honestly, men could be *so* very confusing.

"Mugdock is a splendid place to visit," Arnprior said. "I'm sure Grant and Kade will enjoy showing it to you."

"It's a shame you won't be here long enough to visit Kinglas," Victoria said with a sigh. "Glasgow or even Edinburgh can't compare."

"Perhaps next summer, when my children are older," Gillian replied. "As it is, two weeks is all I can manage before Jeannie and I must return to London."

"I don't want to go back to London," Jeannie said. "Certainly not in a paltry two weeks."

There was a fraught pause. Kathleen crushed the impulse to bang her head against the wall. They'd only just arrived, and her sister was pushing for more.

Of course, that sort of pushing against boundaries was exactly the sort of thing Kathleen had done her entire life. Jeannie had clearly picked up her burgeoning rebellious streak from her.

"We can talk about it later, dearest," she said. "Let's just try to enjoy Glasgow, shall we?"

Jeannie's chin took on the now-familiar tilt. "All right, but I still don't want to go home. I want to go to Lochnagar with you."

Kathleen's brain froze. "Ah . . ."

"Lochnagar's a grand place," Angus filled in. "Can't blame the lassie for wantin' to visit."

"No, but perhaps we can let Miss Calvert and her sister sort that out later," Grant suggested.

The old man simply shrugged.

"There's nothing to sort out," Jeannie stubbornly insisted. "I want to stay in Scotland."

Kathleen tried to look firm. "Jeanette—"

"You're not in charge of me, Kath, so don't even try," her sister replied.

"More tea, anyone?" Victoria asked in a bright voice.

Kathleen suspected that even a good belt of whisky would fail to do the trick. It was going to be a long two weeks.

Chapter Seven

Grant hastily stepped away from Jeannie's wobbly swing. "Steady, lass."

An old broadsword was hardly a toy at the best of times. In the hands of an enthusiastic sixteen-year-old, it was a lurking disaster.

"Aye," said Angus. "We dinna want yon laddie losin' any body parts, especially not the good bits."

He capped off that bon mot with a wink to Kathleen, who turned bright pink. The pretty *Sassenach* wasn't the shy type, but Grandda's matchmaking was obvious and embarrassing.

Kathleen had captured his grandfather's fancy as a potential bride. Angus had a soft spot for girls with both brains and beauty, not to mention ones also possessing an excellent dowry. The dowry insight had been relayed by Gillian, another participant in the matchmaking quest. That Kathleen was less than enamored with Scotland and him were impediments easily brushed aside by the coconspirators.

It was a hell of an impediment for Grant, even though he was certainly not on the lookout for a bride.

"I value all my bits," he said as he sidestepped another swing and snatched up a lamp, saving it from imminent destruction.

After putting the lamp on a side table, he plucked the sword from Jeannie's hand as she prepared for a practice lunge.

"But some more than others, I reckon," Angus replied, tapping his nose as he tried to look both subtle and sly.

Grant contemplated whacking the old fellow with the flat of the blade but contented himself with a glare. Angus blatantly ignored the silent reprimand as he puffed on his pipe, safely ensconced in the ancient, elaborately carved oak chair by the fireplace, far away from the swinging.

Kathleen had been wandering around Mugdock's weaponry hall, peering at the various lethal items and moldering stag heads. Now she glanced at her sister.

"Dearest, perhaps you'd best let Mr. Kendrick keep the broadsword for now," she said. "It's heavy and hard to control."

Jeannie rolled her eyes, a remarkably consistent response to her sister's interventions. "It's not that heavy. Besides, I'm just practicing. Kade said he would teach me, and how can I learn if I can't swing it?"

Grant lifted questioning eyebrows at his brother, who was also standing well out of harm's way.

Kade gave him a sheepish smile. Jeannie was running rings around the poor fellow, and Kathleen was clearly not happy about it. But the girl's infatuation had evolved with a speed that had caught them all off guard—especially Kade.

Too kind to crush the girl's sensitive spirit, Kade was struggling a bit to keep her at a friendly but appropriate distance.

Still, Grant reckoned it was all fairly harmless. Jeannie

was too young to know what she truly wanted, other than Kade's attention. As long as he and Kathleen kept an eye on the lass, all should be well.

Unfortunately, Grant found himself wanting to spend most of *his* time keeping an eye on Kathleen—a very close eye. Not that he'd had much chance, given the whirlwind of female shopping that had taken place over the last several days.

Little Jeannie had arrived in Scotland without much of a wardrobe. There was a mystery there that seemed to generate a fair bit of tension between the sisters. Vicky no doubt had a better understanding of the situation, which meant Nick would, too, but Grant had steadfastly resisted making attempts to discover the truth. The less time he spent thinking about Kathleen Calvert and her troubles, the better.

It was a challenge, though, because he found the lass fascinating, charming, and quirky, and a whole host of other adjectives he could conjure up. It was impossible not to notice her, since she talked quite a lot in her sweet voice, with its hint of an Irish lilt, and laughed even more. Kendrick House, almost always a lively place, was even livelier now thanks to Kathleen.

She also had an eccentric habit of leaving her belongings strewn about the house, thus constantly reminding one of her presence. More than once, Grant had found a gauzy scarf draped haphazardly over a chair, or jeweled hairpins or dainty hankies dropped on the floor. For some deranged reason, he found the habit endearing.

Aye, she was a handful, Kathleen Calvert. Along with her rambunctious sister and the madcap Duchess of Leverton, they'd turned Kendrick House into a bit of a circus. Which was why Grant had made a point of staying at the office as much as possible, hoping that everyone had forgotten his impulsive suggestion for an outing to Mugdock Castle.

It hadn't worked. At breakfast yesterday, Nick had acerbically pointed out to him that everyone else was doing his social duties by the ladies, and now it was *his bloody turn*. Grant had responded that he was much too busy to be larking about, but big brother had simply ordered him to *get it done*, before retreating behind his morning gazette.

"You used to like larking about," he muttered to himself as he placed the broadsword back on its pegs.

"Did you say something, Mr. Kendrick?" Kathleen asked.

He turned. "No, Miss Calvert. Nothing at all."

Grant felt his artificially polite smile suddenly turn into something genuine. It was a hell of a thing, but Kathleen Calvert just made a fellow want to smile.

When he'd caught sight of her coming down the stairs this morning, he'd had to smother a grin. Because it was another pink outfit—this time, a brightly colored walking dress, trimmed with elaborate red braid on the sleeves that also marched down the front of her bodice. That, naturally, drew his attention to her breasts, curves lovely enough to satisfy even the most exacting of tastes.

It wasn't much of a surprise to discover that Kathleen exactly fit his particular tastes.

Forgetting for the moment that he had piles of work at the office, he'd gladly handed her into the barouche, where Kade, Jeannie, and Angus were already waiting. Grant could barely remember the last time he'd been out of the city, and found the country drive to Mugdock surprisingly enjoyable.

So had Kathleen, who'd perked up as soon as they left the outskirts of Glasgow, growing ever more appreciative as the countryside rolled by. The steady climb to Mugdock took them through colorful meadows of bracken and heather, and a sun-dappled forest of oak and birch. The leaves were just beginning to turn, and flashes of red and yellow sparked out in the clear light of an early autumn day.

Her pretty features framed by a lavishly trimmed pink bonnet, Kathleen had tilted back her head to catch the sun. Her skin was cream, and her freckles a splash of cinnamon across her nose and cheeks. She'd breathed out a happy little sigh, then her lush lips had curled up in a lovely smile as the sunlight danced over her features. To Grant, she appeared as if lit from within, and that inner glow turned her from pretty to glorious. Quite the most glorious girl he had ever seen in his life.

Unfortunately, Mugdock had so far failed to elicit a similar happy reaction. Grant couldn't entirely blame her for that. Mugdock was no fairy-tale castle. Rather, it was a grim-looking fortification of gray stone, built for battle during the days when clan fought clan and marauders roamed the countryside.

Jeannie loved it, of course, expecting phantoms to be lurking around every corner. Her favorite room thus far had been the weapons hall of the old manor house. Its collection of claymores, dirks, and broadswords was set on the wall amongst ancient heraldic banners and moth-eaten stag heads.

Kathleen, on the other hand, seemed unimpressed, and was currently inspecting the stags with a critical eye.

"They're such magnificent creatures," she said. "It's a shame to see them moldering away on a wall."

"They do look rather tatty," Grant replied.

Kathleen squinted up at an impressive twelve-point

buck mounted high over the fireplace. The poor thing had seen better days, alive and dead.

"Still, if one squints," she added, "I suppose it does convey a certain grandeur of days gone by."

"The *Sassenachs* in the family tend to call the style 'Heroic Highlander,'" Grant said. "It's not meant as a compliment."

That earned him a crooked, charming grin. "I cannot say that I disagree."

"One of the first steps Vicky took at Kinglas was to remove most of the animal heads. She said they attracted moths and were a dusting nightmare for the maids."

Angus gloomily sucked on his pipe. "A sad day. I fair wept into my dram, seein' our history come down like that."

"You had more than a dram," Grant replied. "Nor did you weep. You yelled at poor Vicky at some length, as I recall."

"And *I* recall that the lassie yelled right back," Angus retorted. "Besides, all I was doin' was teachin' family history to her."

Kade, who stood with a shoulder propped against the mantel, snorted. "Is that what we're calling that particular incident? A history lesson?"

Angus adopted a dignified look. "I was simply explainin' things, but our countess refused to listen."

"No, you refused to back down until Nick threatened to toss you into the loch," Grant said.

"Och, the laird sided with me, ye ken."

Kade shook his head. "Grandda, I distinctly remember Nick was going to throw you into Loch Long."

"Yer mistaken lad. I was there, ye ken."

"We were *all* there, unfortunately," Grant said. "You're off the mark, Grandda."

"Fah," Angus replied, curling a lip.

Kathleen chuckled. "I have to agree with the countess. I'm not fond of animal heads littering the walls, either."

"There are mounted heads in our Wiltshire manor house," Jeannie said.

The girl had given up on broadswords and was now craning up to pluck a big old yew bow from the wall.

"Only a few in Papa's library. One hardly notices them," Kathleen replied.

"Except for that Christmas when you draped them in mistletoe and stuck candles on the antlers. That was fun."

Kathleen winced. "Please don't remind me."

"It didn't turn out well?" Grant asked.

"I basically set the room on fire."

He laughed.

"These ones are much nicer than Papa's old things," Jeannie said as she pointed the bow at the twelve-point buck. "Can you imagine how difficult it must have been to shoot him?"

Kathleen crinkled her nose. "I'd rather not."

Jeannie tried to bend the bowstring, without much success. "I think it would be exciting. Like Robin Hood and his comrades in Nottingham Forest."

"It takes a great deal of skill and strength," Kade said. "And if you only wound the poor animal, you often have to spend hours chasing it down. You cannot let it suffer."

Jeannie frowned. "That part doesn't sound like fun."

"Definitely not," Grant quietly added.

Kathleen shot him a curious look. "Did that ever happen to you?"

It was a memory he particularly hated. "Yes, I was hunting a stag. It wasn't with a bow, but my shot missed the mark. Took almost a full day to track the poor fellow down."

He'd only been seventeen at the time and still mad for hunting. When he'd flubbed the shot, the poor beast had taken off into the woods around Kinglas. Nick had ordered Grant not to come home until he'd tracked the wounded animal down. Their father had drummed that rule into their heads from an early age. Always respect the animal, and never let it suffer.

But that poor stag had indeed suffered. By the time Grant and Graeme had tracked it to a secluded fen hours later, the animal had collapsed, half-dead from distress and blood loss. Graeme, bless his soul, had offered to finish the job, but Grant had done it. It was his mistake, and his duty to fix it.

The creature had barely moved, gazing up at him in exhausted, mute agony. That had been the end of Grant's days hunting bigger game. At Kinglas, he still shot the occasional partridge or grouse, but only to give it to local crofters who needed the extra food.

"Ye just had a bad bit of luck with that one, son," Angus said. "Yer a fine shot. Best in the family, after me."

Grandda was a notoriously bad shot, in fact. Truthfully, though, Angus also hated hunting. He loved animals of all sorts, and had too soft a heart to kill them.

"Do you still hunt, Mr. Kendrick?" Kathleen asked.

"Very little, in fact," Grant replied.

"Did you ever shoot a person?" Jeannie asked. "The duchess has, you know. And she said your twin shot lots of people when he was a spy."

Kathleen grimaced. "Jeanette, that is all *extremely* inappropriate."

Grant smiled at Jeannie. "I think the duchess has exaggerated Graeme's, er, prowess. And, no, I have never shot anyone."

"But ye could if ye wanted to. You'd plug the bastard right between the eyes," Angus said, as if offering Grant a consolation prize. "Just like yer twin."

"Also an inappropriate comment," Grant said, sternly eyeing his grandfather.

"Your twin does sound like a very exciting person," Kathleen said with a grin.

"And fun," Jeannie added.

Unlike Grant, seemed to be the unspoken implication.

"Graeme's settled down since his marriage," Kade said. "Now he's the local magistrate, which seems to involve paperwork more than cracking heads or shooting. He's also managing the new distillery and helping Sabrina with estate business."

Jeannie scrunched up her face. "Ugh, how boring."

"Very necessary, however," Kathleen said. "Although I'm afraid I would find that sort of work a bit of a bore, too. I'd rather spend my days outdoors, or in the stables."

"I canna blame ye for that," Angus said. "No one in his right mind would choose a moldy old office in Glasgow when he could be spending his time, say, on a grand outing to a castle with two lovely lassies."

"The Kendrick offices are neither moldy nor old," Grant felt compelled to say.

"They're dusty, too," his grandfather added for good measure.

Grant bit his tongue to stop himself from engaging in an inane discussion about the levels of dust in his office.

"Perhaps we should take the ladies up to the southwest tower," Kade tactfully suggested. "We don't want to miss the chance to take in the views before the housekeeper sends us on our way."

"Yes," said Kathleen in a bright voice. "I'm dying to see the views."

"Views are boring," Jeannie said. "I'd rather see the dungeons, or go looking for ghosts."

While Mrs. Graham, the castle's inestimable house-keeper, had assured Jeannie that no ghosts existed at Mugdock, she obviously remained unconvinced.

"No dungeons at Mugdock, I'm afraid," Grant said.

"Nor ghosts, apparently," Kathleen wryly said.

"Ugh," Jeannie repeated.

Kathleen looked at Grant, crinkling her nose in silent apology.

Despite the splendid tea the housekeeper had provided on their arrival or the allure of all the bristling weaponry, their expedition to Mugdock was not proving to be a rousing success.

"I think you'll like the tower," Kade said to Jeannie. "It's very gloomy. If we're going to find a ghoulie anywhere in Mugdock, it'll be in the tower."

"Huzzah! Then what are we waiting for?" Jeannie grabbed Kade's hand, practically dragging him from the room.

"Drat," muttered Kathleen, hurrying after them.

"Ye'd best rescue yer brother," Angus said. "And be gettin' on the stick yerself, son, or Kade will be gettin' hitched before ye. Wrong sister, wrong Kendrick, ye ken."

"You are *massively* unhelpful, Grandda," Grant retorted as he strode for the door.

His grandfather snickered, and followed leisurely after him.

Kathleen's boot caught on the uneven stone steps. As she started to slip, large hands clamped around her waist from behind, all but circling it. Grant was a big, brawny man, which evoked certain sensations she didn't care to examine, at least not when he was looming over her.

He's boring. Remember?

It didn't matter how big or how handsome he was. Grant Kendrick had the soul of a businessman, which was apparently his one true passion in life. That he was finding today's expedition a chore was becoming quite clear.

Not that she and Jeannie were covering themselves in glory. One couldn't wonder if he found them a pair of bottle-headed pests.

"Careful, Miss Calvert." His subtle brogue rumbled in her ear. "You don't want to go arse over teakettle on these stairs."

She looked over her shoulder. He stood three steps below her on the narrow staircase, so they were all but face-to-face, so close she could see into the smoky-green depths of his remarkable gaze. Her stomach took an odd little flop because those depths sparked with heat.

"Commenting on my anatomy, Mr. Kendrick?" she said. "Very shocking of you, I must say."

What was truly shocking was how effectively he rattled her. For a supposedly boring man, he had quite a knack for it.

He froze and then retreated a few steps. "I apologize for my intemperate language, Miss Calvert."

"It's fine," she said with an airy wave. "I'm not prudish about that sort of thing."

"Yes, I've noticed that," he said in a neutral tone.

Lovely.

He obviously thought she was some sort of loose fish. When it came to Grant Kendrick, Kathleen could not seem to navigate a sensible course.

She carefully climbed the ancient stairs toward the second floor. No wonder Angus was giving the tower a miss, choosing instead to have a *wee dram* and a chat with the castle's housekeeper. Although the day had started enjoyably—she wouldn't forget the appreciative smile on Grant's face when he saw her this morning—their little outing had turned into something of a slog. Much of that was due to Jeannie, although Kathleen carried her share of the blame. Since arriving in Glasgow, her sister's behavior had continued to deteriorate, and Kathleen hadn't a clue how to keep her in check.

She'd die before admitting it, but part of her was starting to look forward to Jeannie's return to London, and now even found a certain sympathy for Helen. Trying to keep Jeannie out of trouble and a moderately respectable distance from poor Kade had turned into a challenging task.

Her sister stuck her head through the hatch at the top of the staircase. "Hurry up, Kath. We'll never get up to the roof at this rate."

"Coming, dearest, but I don't wish to slip and break my noggin."

Her sister scoffed. "You would never be so clumsy as to do that," she said before disappearing from view.

"Jeannie obviously has a great admiration for you," Grant said.

Kathleen couldn't tell if he thought that a good or bad thing.

"She's always tended to put me on a pedestal. It's silly, really. I'm such a dreadful role model."

"For a young girl, you mean."

Bad thing.

"Especially for a young girl," she lightly said.

"I can understand why. I felt the same toward Graeme. Still do, actually."

She cast him a startled look over her shoulder. "Was that a compliment? I can't tell."

His lips moved in a barely-there smile. "Careful with the top step. It's very worn."

Since he was not going to answer her question, she faced forward and stepped into the room.

Her sister rushed over in a whirl of enthusiasm. "Isn't it splendid, Kath? It's so dreadfully gloomy. One can imagine all sorts of horrible things happening in a room like this."

Kathleen took a slow turn. They were on the main floor of the southwest tower, the only one of the four tower structures that was still intact and livable. Not that she could imagine anyone voluntarily living in such a place.

"It's certainly something," she said as she eyed the high timbered ceiling and the large, soot-covered fireplace.

"Damp, for one thing." Grant strolled over to peer out one of the windows.

There were only two. Both were fairly narrow and covered with iron bars, obviously for defensive purposes. That meant the room was cast into twilight, even with the sun shining outside. The iron chandelier, empty of candles, did nothing to dispel the dreary atmosphere.

One could feel the weight of history in the thick gray walls, and it didn't take much imagination to conjure a vision of fearless, tartan-clad warriors, guarding their keep with broadswords.

Oddly enough, Kathleen could imagine more than a bit of that warrior in Grant. Despite his impeccably tailored coat and breeches and his polished boots, he fit the rugged environment. Taking in his brawny shoulders, stern expression, and burnished hair, Kathleen fancied there might still be a wild Highlander lurking under the man's sober demeanor. She couldn't help wondering what it would take to tease that inner warrior to the surface.

And what might happen if she managed it.

Don't be a ninny.

She didn't give a biscuit about Grant's inner warrior, or anything else about him, for that matter.

"This room must be freezing in the winter," Kade said. "No wonder the fireplace is so large."

Kathleen rubbed her arms. "It's not exactly balmy in here now."

Jeannie made an audible noise of disdain for that piddling complaint, and then bent down to peer under the massive oak table dominating the center of the room.

"Dearest, what are you looking for?" Kathleen asked when her sister all but crawled under the table.

"There might be a secret cubbyhole inside this table, with a treasure map or some old family papers."

Grant threw Kathleen an amused glance. "Sorry, Jeannie. All you're likely to find is a few cobwebs and a spider or two."

Jeannie straightened up. "How boring."

Kathleen fancied she saw Grant wince, but the expression was fleeting.

"Graeme and I searched this tower from top to bottom when we were lads," he said. "Sadly, we never found any secret papers, treasure maps, or anything else remotely exciting."

"Not even a skull or two?" Jeannie asked in a hopeful voice.

"Not even one."

"What about in the dungeon?"

Grant shook his head. "There's no dungeon, only a moldy cellar used for storing broken furniture, I'm afraid."

"That is so b—"

"Boring," Kathleen finished for her. "Yes, dear, we know. But there's a great deal of interesting history about Mugdock. It's the traditional seat of Clan Graham, and they've owned it for centuries. That's rather fascinating, you must admit."

Jeannie studied the room, as if looking for the ghosts of long ago Grahams. "I suppose they had some rather splendid battles here."

"They did," said Grant. "Bloodthirsty ones."

Kade nodded. "Gruesome beyond belief. Heads chopped off and everything."

Jeannie brightened. "Can you tell me about those battles?"

"If you like," Kade said with a kind smile.

"You can tell Jeannie about it on the roof," Grant said as he consulted his pocket watch. "We'll have to start back soon, and we don't want to miss taking in that view."

With a flourishing bow, Kade indicated the narrow staircase up to the top floor of the tower. "Shall we, Miss Jeannie?"

She giggled and started up the steep staircase, with Kade in her wake. Grant and Kathleen followed.

The next level was a duplicate of the lower room but

devoid of any furniture. Another set of narrow stairs led up to a small trapdoor in the ceiling.

Kade glanced at his brother. "Who should go up first?"

"Why don't we all go up?" Kathleen suggested.

"There's barely enough room for two," said Grant.

"Much less a giant like you," his brother joked.

"But you're *ever* so tall yourself, Kade," Jeannie said.

Kathleen swallowed a sigh.

"I'm a scrawny beanpole compared to my brothers," Kade cheerfully replied. "Here, Jeannie, let me go up first and open the door. Then I'll help you onto the parapet."

From the expression on Jeannie's face, one would have thought Kade had just asked her to marry him.

Kathleen started for the stairs. "Dearest, I think—"

Grant reached out a long arm to snag her wrist. "Don't worry. Kade will take care of her."

"It's not Jeannie I'm worried about."

He smiled. "Kade won't let anything like that happen, either."

"My sister is *very* persistent."

"That she is." He glanced up at Kade, who had unlocked the trapdoor and thrust it open. "Kade, keep that door open, and make sure you stay close to it, all right?"

His brother glanced down, a wry expression on his youthful features. "Understood."

Grant gently squeezed Kathleen's wrist before letting go. For a brief moment, she wondered what it would be like to actually hold hands with him.

Nice.

She firmly put that image out of her mind. "Jeannie, be careful, all right? Do everything Kade tells you to."

"I'm always careful," Jeannie shot back before clambering up to disappear through the door.

Kathleen grimaced. "She's actually the opposite of careful."

Grant propped a shoulder against the wall at the bottom of the staircase. Kathleen knew he was standing in that spot to keep an eye on things up above.

"Something tells me that you weren't very careful at her age, either," he said.

"No, but I was horse mad. Boys held little interest for me."

"And now?"

Kathleen's heart jumped. "Um, now what?"

"Are you still horse mad?"

"Oh, of course."

That was a bit deflating. For a wild moment, she'd thought he was flirting with her. But it was already stupendously apparent that Grant Kendrick was not the flirting type.

"I spent a great deal of time in my father's stables at home in Ireland," she said to cover her awkward response. "We had an excellent stablemaster. I learned much from him."

He tilted his head, as if listening to the murmur of conversation drifting down through the door. "And did you spend as much time in the stables after you moved to England?"

"We only spend a few months in the summer at Papa's estate in Wiltshire, because my stepmother prefers the city. I do try to ride as much as I can in Hyde Park, and I occasionally take my phaeton out to Richmond Park." *Or racing on Hampstead Heath.* "But it's not the same as driving or riding in the country."

When a scuffling noise sounded from overheard, Kathleen started for the stairs.

"They're fine," Grant said in a gentle tone.

She dredged up a weak smile.

He settled his shoulders more comfortably against the window frame. Once more, her attention was drawn to the fact that those shoulders were indeed very broad. As was his chest, which tapered down to a lean waist and hips. For some reason, she found his legs quite fascinating. They were long and exceptionally muscled, a fact made obvious by his well-fitting breeches.

For a dreary businessman, he certainly cut an imposing athletic figure.

"Miss Calvert?"

Kathleen jerked her attention back to his face. She could only be thankful that the room was so poorly lit, because she could feel her cheeks glowing like fiery embers.

"Yes, Mr. Kendrick?"

He stared at her for a moment before answering. "I was suggesting that you not worry too much about Jeannie. She's energetic, but she's a sweet lass for all that."

She wavered for a moment. There was something dependable and trustworthy about Grant, and it seemed so silly not to tell him. Then again, she was reluctant to air her family's dirty laundry with a near stranger.

"You don't have to tell me," Grant said. "But I can tell you're worried about something. Whatever it is, have you talked to Vicky about it? She's very good with wayward lads and lassies. I speak from painful experience on this issue," he added with a wry smile.

She couldn't help but chuckle, and suddenly she did want to confide in him.

"Jeannie ran away from home to follow me to Glasgow. She stowed away in the boot of the luggage carriage for two days before she was discovered by one of Gillian's grooms."

He jerked upright. "Was she all right?"

"Just hungry and annoyed with us for dragging her out of there. It's been a challenge to keep the episode under wraps, quite honestly."

"How did she pull it off?"

Kathleen sighed. "She dressed as a stable boy."

"Good Lord." He glanced up at the open door. "I assume you told Vicky."

"Yes. She's much better at controlling Jeannie than I am. I'm afraid my sister no longer listens to me like she used to." She crinkled her nose. "She's too much like me, I'm afraid."

"Och, you're much too hard on yourself. And Vicky was a governess, don't forget."

When another scuffling noise sounded above their heads, they exchanged a glance.

"On second thought . . ." Grant started to climb the stairs.

Kade stuck his head through the trapdoor. "I'm sending Jeannie down. Stand by the bottom of the steps, will you?"

"Aye, that." Grant stood on the bottom rung, waiting for her.

Jeannie's feet and skirts appeared a moment later, as she lowered herself through the trap. Grant grasped her waist and handed her down to the floor. Kathleen couldn't help noting that her sister looked very put out.

"Did you enjoy the view?" Grant asked.

"No," Jeannie snapped.

Kathleen frowned. "Dearest, Mr. Kendrick was simply—"

"Leave off, Kath, would you?"

Jeannie turned on her boot heel and headed down to the lower level in a huff.

"Careful," Kathleen called after her.

By this time, Kade had clambered down the stairs.

Grant rested a hand on his brother's shoulder. "Everything all right, lad?"

Kade grimaced at Kathleen. "I'm so sorry. I *did* actually try to show her the view and talk about the castle's history."

"Tried to kiss you, did she?" asked Grant.

Kade flushed bright red, looking more like a guilty schoolboy than the accomplished young man he was.

"Sorry," he said again to Kathleen.

"I'm the one who should be apologizing to you, Kade." She pointed a finger at Grant. "I told you."

"And I'm sorry I didn't take it seriously. Our Jeannie was even more assertive than I imagined."

"I almost fell over the parapet when she went to kiss me," Kade admitted.

Kathleen was torn between laughter and irritation at the ridiculous situation. "Oh, dear, that's dreadful."

"Well, no real harm done, except to the poor girl's pride," Grant said. "Try not to worry, Kade."

"I hated hurting her feelings."

Grant pulled him in for a brief hug. "Aye, but the truth had to come from you, I'm afraid. She probably wouldn't have listened to anyone else. This I know from sad experience, ye ken."

"Someone gave you the boot, did she?" Kathleen asked.

"You have no idea," he dryly replied.

And, now, she was insanely curious to know what kind of woman would pitch over Grant Kendrick.

"Should I apologize to her?" Kade asked.

Kathleen shook her head. "That would just embarrass her even more."

"Go rustle up Angus and have him play chaperone," Grant said. "And have Mrs. Graham fetch Jeannie a nice, calming cup of tea. Then tell our coachman to ready the carriage to go home."

When Kade headed down the stairs, Kathleen started after him.

"Don't you want to see the view?" Grant asked.

She frowned. "But we're not chaperoned, either."

"Are *you* going to try to kiss me?"

"Of course not!" she indignantly said.

"Then I think we're fine. Besides, the carriage will take at least a half hour to organize. And the view truly is spectacular."

When she hesitated, he tilted an eyebrow. "Do you really want to face Jeannie right now?"

"Well, no." Her sister would probably rip a strip off her.

"Smart lass. I'll go first so I can help you through the trapdoor. Be careful on the steps."

"I promise not to go arse over teakettle."

He snorted and climbed up to the door, thus affording Kathleen an excellent view of his muscled legs and equally muscled, well, arse—not to be delicate about it.

She started up, pausing halfway as he squeezed through the small trapdoor. His shoulders filled the opening. For a moment, from his annoyed muttering, it seemed he might get stuck.

His finally squeezed through, hoisting himself up and out of sight. Quickly, his head appeared, and he reached down a long arm to help her through the door. He lifted her off the top step with effortless strength and carefully deposited her on the narrow parapet that ringed the top of the tower. His big hands circled her waist, holding her steady as she regained her footing.

She did feel a bit wobbly, although she suspected that

had more to do with his presence than from the dizzying height of the tower.

"I trust heights don't bother you," he said in a slightly gruff tone.

Kathleen placed both hands on the stone parapet, regaining her mental balance. "Not in the slightest. You may release me now, Mr. Kendrick. I am perfectly steady."

When he edged over to the side, leaving a few feet between them, she repressed the impulse to be disappointed.

Silly girl.

"What do you think?" he asked.

She'd been so busy trying to ignore her fluttering heartbeat that she'd not yet taken in the view. Now, she uttered a gasp of delight.

"I had no idea how lovely it would be. One doesn't really get the sense of it on the drive up."

He leaned his forearms on the parapet, letting his gaze scan the landscape stretched out before them. "I'd forgotten how spectacular it is, especially on a clear day."

The castle stood on a high hill, surrounded by sloping meadows full of purple heather and wild cranberry bogs. Beyond them ran the woods through which they had traveled, their leaves a dappled texture of various greens laced with vibrant autumn colors. Near the ring wall on one side of the castle, a small lake glittered under the late afternoon sunshine.

Mugdock might not belong in a fairy tale, but the setting certainly did.

She gazed down at the lake. "Are those swans?"

"Yes, whooper swans. The Grahams are quite proud of them. Been here for generations."

"That was the final romantic touch this vista needed, I must say."

He shaded his eyes to smile down at her. In the dazzling sunlight, his hair seemed gilded with fire.

"When Graeme intended to charm a young lady, he would bring her up here."

Kathleen couldn't resist. "And what about you? Did you employ similar methods?"

"In fact, I do believe you're my first." Then he frowned, as if registering what he'd just said. "Not that I'm trying to charm you, of course. At least not like that."

Hopeless.

"Well, I declare myself perfectly charmed," she said after a short but awkward pause. "Mugdock Castle has redeemed itself."

He raised incredulous eyebrows. "You mean you're not charmed by crumbling walls, dank privies, and dust-covered cellars, no matter how historic?"

"Is it even possible for privies to be historic?"

"It is if Robert the Bruce used it."

She had to laugh. "All right. I can appreciate the historic nature of Mugdock while still having no desire to sleep under its roof."

"Jeannie would not agree."

She smiled. "I'm quite surprised to discover that she's the romantic in the family. That was supposed to be me."

"That's a shame."

She shot him a sideways glance, but he was absently gazing out over the countryside, as if not really seeing it.

"Maybe we should show her the privies," Kathleen said.

He laughed. "All right, if Mugdock isn't your style, what is?"

She didn't have to think about it. "Greystone Manor, my family's estate in Ireland."

He turned toward her, leaning a hip against the parapet. "What's it like?"

"Not like Scotland, and certainly not like Mugdock. Not that I don't think it's beautiful up here," she hastily added. "But there's something so rugged about Scotland. It's got its own sort of beauty, but it's . . ." She trailed off, not wanting to offend him.

"Harsh? Wait till you see the Highlands."

"That's what I'm afraid of," she ruefully said.

"Och, ye'll be fine."

Kathleen wasn't so sure about that.

"So, tell me more about Greystone," he prompted.

"Well, the house itself isn't historic. It was only built in the last century. It's elegant and pretty, and very much in the classical style."

"And no dank privies."

She held up a finger. "All the most up-to-date plumbing. Helen insisted."

He gently nudged her around to the other side of the tower. "You don't strike me as a lass who spends all her time indoors, no matter how good the plumbing."

She was momentarily distracted by the new view. "That's quite amazing."

"It's not Ireland, but still rather nice."

"I never said that Scotland wasn't beautiful," she said, ignoring his grin.

He might not flirt, but Grant could clearly tease, when he put his mind to it.

"Just not as nice as Ireland," he said.

"Nothing's as nice as Ireland. But this is quite wonderful, I must say."

"Those are the Campsie Fells." He pointed to a high ridge of hills in the distance. "On a really clear day, you can catch a glimpse of the mountains around Loch Katrine." His gaze was locked on the horizon. "Sometimes I swear you can see all the way to Castle Kinglas."

She couldn't help being curious. "What's Kinglas like?"

"Grand," he thoughtfully said. "A great, grand old castle tucked between lake and sky, with mountains to keep it company."

She blinked at the poetic description—and at his handsome, austere profile. He seemed to be looking at something far, far away.

"It sounds very romantic," she softly said.

His gaze snapped into focus as he glanced down at her. "It's certainly in better shape than poor old Mugdock. Kinglas is a working estate, and it takes a great deal of management and work from Nick and Victoria and the staff to maintain it. It's a constant battle to keep the bloody place from falling apart. With these old castles, romantic generally only runs to the surface."

She frowned at the sudden change in attitude. "But you still love it."

He shrugged, his broad shoulders shifting under his coat. "Yes, but it's not really home for me anymore. And it has its bad points. It's bloody cold and snowy in the winter, for one thing. Sometimes we'd get snowed in for weeks. That, I assure you, isn't the least romantic."

It could be, with the right person.

"That is a commendably realistic view of life," she said instead.

"I am nothing if not realistic, Miss Calvert."

Turning slightly away from him, she propped her chin in her hands and drank in the view. "Well, as I said before, it's not Ireland, but I like it."

He snorted. "What makes Ireland so much better than Scotland or England?"

"Fewer *Sassenachs*."

When he laughed outright at that, for a moment the breath caught in her throat. He had a deep laugh, full of warmth and life. In response, her body came alive with a joy that somehow seemed part of everything around them, from the stones beneath their feet to the crystal-blue vault of the sky.

"That's certainly one mark in Ireland's favor." The warmth of his laugh lingered in his smile. "What else?"

A jumble of words gathered on the tip of her tongue. Words like *lush*, *green*, *soft*, and *welcoming*. Cherished images flooded her mind . . . the rushing brook that ran through the bluebell meadow, the deep, cool woods, and the thick fields of clover. But words could never really catch the feel of the place and what it meant to her.

In the end, only one word did. "It's home."

Even more importantly, it had been her mother's home. Where Mamma had lived and loved her husband and children, creating a haven of peace and beauty for everyone blessed to know her.

His gaze turned thoughtful. "And you miss it."

Kathleen had to swallow against the sudden emotion that had tightened her throat. "More than anything."

"But I understand you haven't been back since you were sent to school in Bath."

She mentally frowned. How did he know that sort of detail?

"That is correct," she cautiously answered.

"Don't you think it might have changed? Be different now from your memories?"

She flushed under the disconcerting intensity of his gaze.

"No, I don't think so. I grew up there, with my family. With my mother." And her mother's memory made all the difference.

He glanced away for a moment. "Of course, your mother. Forgive me, Miss Calvert. It makes perfect sense that you would miss her, and your old home."

There was something in his voice she couldn't quite interpret. Regret? No, that wasn't it.

"I . . . I understand that you lost both your parents at a young age," she hesitantly said.

Silence stretched between them, broken only by the snapping of the heraldic banner flying above them, and the cry of a hawk circling overhead.

"I was seven when my mother died," he said. "And I . . . we lost my father two years later."

His tone was flat. Too flat.

A quiet sorrow that had as much to do with her mother as with his terrible loss rustled in her chest.

Kathleen reached out and touched his arm. "I'm so sorry."

His gaze shifted to her hand resting on his sleeve. "You needn't be. It was a long time ago."

"But—"

Grant suddenly leaned over the parapet and looked down. "Ah, there's Angus, waving at us. The carriage must be ready."

When he turned back to her, his polite smile was firmly back in place. "Shall we go, Miss Calvert?"

The message was clear. Her sympathy—or anything else she might offer—was not wanted. As far as Kathleen was concerned, that was perfectly fine.

Chapter Eight

Will, the Kendrick's under-butler, deftly caught the perfectly thrown cricket ball.

"Wide," called Angus.

Kade whipped around to stare at his grandfather in disbelief. "Grandda, that bowl was *not* wide."

Angus shrugged. "Looked wide to me."

"It was well within Her Grace's reach, and you know it."

At the opposite end of their makeshift pitch, Gillian grinned as she casually leaned on her bat. "There's no need for titles whilst playing cricket, my boy. And if it was such a good bowl, then why didn't I strike it?"

"Because you know that Angus is throwing the match your way?" Kade retorted.

Kathleen smothered a laugh. A dreadful umpire to begin with, Angus had clearly decided to side with the ladies. He'd already made several outrageously bad calls against his grandson's team, composed of Will, a footman, and two of the Kendrick grooms, one of whom switched between teams to fill in the gaps.

It was possibly the most ridiculous match in the history of cricket, and Kathleen had spent almost as much time laughing as she'd spent fielding the ball. It could barely qualify as a real game, given the small size of their teams and how the rules were being largely ignored by almost everyone but Kade and Kathleen.

Restless after two weeks away from her family, Gillian had suggested a match as a way to *shake out the fidgets*. Jeannie had thought it a smashing idea, and Kathleen had been unable to refuse. She loved cricket and was the best fielder in the family, though she rarely got to play since Helen disapproved of girls playing cricket.

Angus had suggested using the small park in front of Kendrick House for their field and had also agreed to serve as umpire. The other team members had been dragooned from the staff, and Gillian had decreed that the teams would be the ladies against the men. Kade had protested, since he was the only member of his team who'd actually played cricket. The duchess had insouciantly ignored his objections.

Playing in the public square had given Kathleen a bit of a qualm. True, the pretty little park was generally quiet, especially in the late afternoon, but it was still surrounded by houses. So far, their visit to Glasgow had been scandal free, and she wanted to keep it that way.

"We'll ask Vicky," Gillian had suggested. "If she says no, I suppose we'll just have to go for a another walk to get some exercise."

"Ugh," Jeannie had said with a grimace. "I'm sick of walks."

Victoria, going over the monthly accounts with Henderson in her study, had absently given her approval. So after they'd unearthed the necessary equipment out of the attic, they'd marched out to the square. Gillian and Kade had measured out the pitch, and Kathleen had explained the basic rules to Will and the somewhat bemused staff.

But if not for the blatant advantage provided by Angus, the men's team would probably win. Kathleen had grown rusty, and Jeannie's powerful swing was erratic. Gillian was the only member of their team with the athletic skill to offset superior male strength.

Angus, grabbing the kitchen stool meant to serve as a wicket, pretended to be outraged by Kade's accusation. "Are ye truly accusin' yer old grandda of being a cheat? Because if ye are, yer not too old for me to paddle yer bum."

"You can borrow my bat if you like," Jeannie offered with a sly grin.

Kathleen knew her sister had yet to fully forgive Kade's appropriate but embarrassing rejection at Mugdock. Kade, fortunately, had been nothing but patient with Jeannie ever since, although he'd been careful to avoid too much contact with her.

Still, he'd readily agreed to their absurd plan this afternoon, and Kathleen was now relieved to see Jeannie behaving more comfortably with him.

"Don't encourage him," Kade wryly replied. "He might actually take you up on it."

"You did accuse him of cheating," Jeannie said.

"Because he is." Kade frowned at his grandfather. "And why are you taking the stool? That's supposed to be our wicket."

"I need to sit myself down," Angus said, perching on the stool.

"We need a wicket to play the bloody game," Kade retorted.

The old fellow began to refill his pipe with tobacco. "Ye'll manage."

Kade scoffed. "This is the silliest game of cricket in history."

"Yes, but it's good fun, don't you think?" Jeannie replied as she took practice swings with her bat.

Kade hastily stepped to the side. "You say that because you're winning."

Jeannie's laugh echoed through the small park, drawing the notice of two matrons on a stroll. They paused, eyeing the cricketers with vague disapproval. Still, when Kathleen dropped a curtsy and flashed a smile, one of the ladies gave her a friendly nod.

"Stop jabbering and throw the ball," Gillian yelled from her end of the pitch.

She'd assumed her stance, slightly crouched, waiting for Kade to bowl.

The matrons, after giving them now decidedly disapproving stares, disappeared into a mansion a few doors down from Kendrick House.

"Perhaps we should lower our voices," Kathleen suggested. "We don't want to disturb the neighbors."

"Och, nae need to worry about Mrs. Buchanan and her sister," Angus said. "Vicky always turns 'em up sweet."

Kade flexed his arm, preparing to bowl. "Mrs. Buchanan secretly likes all of us, especially Grant. We can always send him over to charm her if she kicks up a fuss."

"Why Grant?" Kathleen couldn't help asking. Of all the Kendricks, he seemed the least likely to charm anyone.

He charmed you, though, didn't he?

She steadfastly ignored that inner voice.

"That's because our Grant is an old sobersides, just like Mrs. Buchanan," Angus said. "She was married to a vicar, ye ken. Says Grant reminds her of yon late husband."

Kathleen laughed.

"Course, our lad wasn't always that way," Angus added with a broad wink. "He just needs to find the right lassie to remind him how to have fun again."

Kathleen mentally winced. After their Mugdock outing, Grant seemed to be avoiding her. That was rather a shame, since she'd caught a glimpse of a different sort of man up there on that high tower. Grant had been the opposite of boring, then. He'd displayed an intensity she'd found both attractive and disconcerting.

But by the time they'd returned to Kendrick House, he'd reverted to form—politely bland and mostly disinterested. He'd been that way for the last five days. And, yes, unfortunately, she'd been counting.

Yet, what difference did it make? She wouldn't be changing her plans for Grant or for any man. And those plans were proceeding well. Jeannie would soon be returning to London, her enthusiasm for Glasgow dimmed after her falling-out with Kade. Jeannie wasn't wild about returning home, but she'd come to accept it as inevitable.

As for Kathleen's situation, Victoria and Lord Arnprior had made it clear that she could spend as much time as she liked in Glasgow and even spend the winter holidays with them at Castle Kinglas. Although she still planned to travel to Lochnagar to visit with Sabrina, she would no longer be required to spend the entire winter in a dreary corner of the Highlands.

You'll be spending more time with Grant, too.

Again, she tried to ignore that annoying little voice. "Are you ready, Kade?"

"I've been ready for ten minutes."

"Ye'll have to wait a few more." Angus waved at a groom standing halfway between wickets in a fielding position on the right. "Young Ian, will ye run inside and fetch me a light for my pipe?"

The groom nodded and started toward the house.

Kade shook his head. "This match is *beyond* absurd."

"I canna properly umpire without a smoke," said Angus.

"Grandda, you couldn't properly umpire to save your life. Too bad Grant couldn't be here. His calls are always fair, and he actually knows the rules."

Angus, clearly unimpressed, curled a lip.

Gillian, meanwhile, flapped an emphatic hand at the departing groom. "Ho, Ian, get back in position. You can't trot off in the middle of an inning."

The poor man stopped a few yards off the pitch, looking resigned to yet another period of confusion.

Kade snorted. "She's right, Ian. You'd best get back to your position. If this insanity keeps up, we'll never finish."

"What a tragedy that would be," Kathleen drolly said.

"But I still need my turn at bat after Gillian," Jeannie protested.

"You heard the girl." Gillian thumped her bat on the ground.

Angus pointed at the duchess. "Verra well. But dinna be thinkin' that I'll be throwin' any more calls your way, lassie. Yer on yer own, now."

Gillian resumed her stance. "I assure you, sir, I need no one's help to win."

Kade retreated a few feet before taking a short run and then unwinding a fast bowl. Gillian swung hard and solidly connected, driving the ball in Ian's direction.

Jeannie and Gillian both took off, running for opposite ends of the pitch. Kathleen blew a two-fingered whistle of support as the ball sailed over the groom's head, just out of his reach and bouncing across the park.

"That's an impressive whistle ye have, lassie," Angus admiringly said.

Kade tugged on his ear. "It's certainly loud."

Gillian arrived at the wicket in a flurry of skirts and triumph, as Jeannie reached the opposite wicket, scoring the run.

"Huzzah for our side," the girl cried, waving her bat over her head.

"Told you I didn't need help," Gillian teased Angus.

"Aye, but I'll still be wantin' a puff of my pipe."

Kathleen looked at the small watch she'd pinned at her waist. "We should probably finish. It's almost time to change for dinner."

"True," Gillian said, "but we did promise Jeannie a turn at bat."

Kathleen glanced at Kade.

"Might as well," Kade said with a good-natured smile. "Thanks to Grandda, my team has been thrashed."

Gillian casually spun her bat. "We would have won anyway. Just ask my husband."

"So ye didn't need my help after all, cheeky lass," said Angus.

The duchess doffed an imaginary cap. "Your chivalry, however, is duly noted."

Kathleen rolled her eyes. "Cheating counts as chivalry?"

"There's all sorts of chivalry, lass." Angus flashed a beatific smile. "Why, take Grant. He'd lay his cloak on a puddle for *ye*, just like Bothwell did for Mary, Queen of Scots."

Gillian choked back a laugh.

"That wasn't Bothwell, and it *definitely* wasn't Queen Mary," Kade said.

"Are ye sure, lad? I could swear it was."

"And there are no puddles here," Kathleen firmly said.

Gillian made a show of frowning. "And no Grant. It's a shame we see so little of him. I wonder why that is?"

Having retrieved the ball, Ian trotted up, interrupting the embarrassing conversation. "Sorry. Yon ball went under those thick bushes."

"Are we playing or not?" Jeannie yelled from her end of the pitch.

"Yes, dear," Kathleen called back. "Get ready."

Kade went into his short run and unleashed another perfect bowl. Jeannie whipped up her bat in a hard, angled swing.

Crack.

The ball shot nearly sideways at a ferocious speed. The other groom lunged for it, but it hummed well over him and headed directly for the nearest house on the square.

"Uh-oh," Kade said.

The ball smashed through one of the sash windows on the main floor. Glass flew, with shards scattering on the pavement.

"Och, that's nae good," Angus muttered.

"That's a bit of bad luck," said Gillian.

Kade winced. "You have no idea. That's the Trim house. They're the worst twiddlepoops in the square."

Kathleen shook off her paralysis. "Jeannie and I will apologize immediately, and of course I'll pay for the damages."

By this time, her sister had rushed up, looking guilty. "I'm sorry, Kath. I didn't mean to hit in that direction."

"Of course not, pet. We'll just go and apologize, shall we?"

"Best let Kade go, instead," Angus suggested. "He knows how to handle old Trim."

As they briefly debated that point, the door to the house

flew open. A footman scurried down the steps and took off across the north side of the square. In his wake came a portly, middle-aged gentleman who looked rather rumpled, as if he'd just awakened from a nap. He also looked mightily aggrieved, pulling clouds of righteous outrage in his wake.

Jeannie retreated behind Angus.

"Och, young Trim," the old man said. "He's even worse than old Trim."

"I'll try to forestall him," Kathleen said.

As she hurried across the lawn, Kade joined her.

"I can handle him, if you'd rather," he said.

"Thank you, but it's only a broken window."

"You don't know Matthew Trim. He doesn't like women. Or children."

"He'll like me."

Men always liked her. After all, she was such a jolly good sport, as her friend Denny used to say.

"My dear sir," she said as Mr. Trim stormed up. "I sincerely apologize for breaking your window. I'll be happy to—"

He cut her off. "Young woman—I do not call you lady, because you are clearly not one—"

"Now, hang on," Kade indignantly interrupted.

"I have no wish to speak with you, either, Kendrick," the man barked. "This entire spectacle is a disgrace, if not an outright violation of the regulations governing use of the square. My father will be making the appropriate complaints."

Kathleen glanced at Kade. "Regulations?"

He shook his head. "There's nothing formal. Children play games in the square all the time."

"You are not a child," Trim snapped. "Nor are these

others, including that sorry excuse for a grandparent. His behavior, as always, is disgusting and outrageous."

"My grandfather has every right to use the park," Kade retorted. "And my brother, Lord Arnprior, will not be best pleased with your insults."

"Believe me, I will be speaking with Lord Arnprior. That ball crashed right into my father's study. It's a miracle he was not physically injured, although I cannot vouch for an injury to his nerves. I have already sent my footman to fetch our physician. *After* he fetches the constable."

Angus stomped up, followed by Will, who was obviously playing guard—or keeper.

"Fetchin' a constable?" Angus snapped. "Why the bloody hell would ye do that, ye ninny?"

"Not helping, Grandda," Kade warned.

Kathleen glanced over her shoulder. Gillian, thankfully, was still hanging back. She had her arm around Jeannie and was directing the grooms in a cleanup of the incriminating evidence.

"Again, I am so sorry, Mr. Trim," Kathleen said. "I'm sure we can clear this up without a constable. Please let me apologize directly to your poor father and try to make amends."

Trim looked outraged, as if her very existence was an insult to the good order of the city.

"And Mr. Trim was not hurt, thankfully," Kade added, while discreetly trying to wave Angus back. "So, really, no harm done but to the window."

Trim's cheeks puffed out like red balloons. "Do you take me for a fool, young man?"

When a sudden breeze wafted the man's wispy, combed-over hair straight up like a billowing curtain, Kathleen had to swallow an exceedingly inconvenient laugh.

"Best check yer head, young Trim," Angus said. "Yer about to lose what few sprouts ye have left."

Kade sighed. "Good God."

The other man froze for a moment before reaching up to smooth down his hair with offended dignity.

"Angus, perhaps you could take Jeannie and Gillian inside," Kathleen hastily said. "I'm sure Kade and I can sort this out."

"There is nothing to sort out," barked Trim. "You are all to wait right here until the constable arrives."

Kade ignored him. "Grandda, please take the ladies inside. We already have an audience."

Kathleen glanced over and mentally cursed. Mrs. Buchanan had appeared in her doorway, and people in at least two other houses were now peering out their windows.

"Nae, lad," Angus stubbornly said. "I'll stay right here with ye and Kathleen, in case ye need a hand."

Kathleen stepped in front of Angus, trying to keep him well away from Trim. "Sir, please let me speak with your father. I'm happy to explain what happened and offer restitution."

Trim jabbed a finger in Jeannie's direction. "Hooligans, all of you, especially that one over there." Then he glared at Kathleen. "And you're nothing but a hoyden. I'm amazed Lady Arnprior would put up with such nonsense."

By now, Trim's voice had reached bellowing proportions. More doors opened, as perplexed-looking footmen peered out. Mrs. Buchanan, now joined by her sister, was no doubt taking mental notes of the gruesome scene.

"Don't you dare shout at my sister," Jeannie yelled, storming up.

Gillian followed closely behind. "Sorry, Kath. She rather got away from me."

"It's fine." Kathleen grabbed Jeannie by the arm.

"There is nothing fine about any of this," Trim blustered. "And do *not* think my father won't be writing to Lady Gorey. She'll be as shocked as I am about this dreadful situation."

"Oh, hell," Gillian muttered.

Kathleen's heart seized. "You know our parents?"

"My father is related to Lady Gorey on his mother's side."

"Then Kathleen and Jeannie are your relatives," Gillian pointed out. "So perhaps you could try for a little familial charity, instead of acting like a nincompoop."

"Gillian, please don't," Kathleen warned.

Trim snorted. "You're clearly a hoyden as well."

"You'll have to do better than that if you want to insult me," Gillian said with a smile that was mostly teeth.

Kathleen chopped down a hand. "Everyone, stop. Mr. Trim, may we please go inside and talk?"

"There is nothing to talk about. My father will be writing to Lady Gorey and informing her that her daughters are ill-mannered hussies."

Jeannie suddenly shoved in front of Kathleen. "You're a mean old man."

"And *you* are a nasty guttersnipe."

Before Kathleen could react, Jeannie delivered a swift kick to Trim's right shin. He staggered but, with astonishing speed for so portly a man, grabbed Jeannie by the wrist.

Her sister tried to break free. "Let me go!"

Kathleen stepped forward and planted a hand flat on Trim's chest. "Jeannie, stop struggling. And you, sir, release my sister. *Immediately*."

"I'll be handing you both off to the constable, is what I'll be doing," he angrily replied.

Angus practically crawled over Kathleen's shoulder. "I'll kill ye myself, ye scaly bastard."

"And I'll stab you right where you live," Gillian snarled, crowding in from the other side.

Kathleen wasn't entirely sure what *that* meant but knew it should be avoided at all costs—especially since two large footmen had erupted from Trim's house. Both looked ready to start throwing punches.

"No one is stabbing anyone," Kathleen yelled over the growing commotion.

She doubted anyone could hear, since Kade was now shouting at Trim, while Angus and Will intercepted Trim's footmen and commenced a yelling match. Gillian, meanwhile, was now calmly bending over and reaching for her boot, which no doubt contained a knife.

"Gillian, no," Kathleen ordered as she tried to clamp a madly wriggling Jeannie to her side. If Jeannie kicked Trim again, all hell would break loose—if Gillian didn't stab the man first.

"Mr. Trim, if you value your safety, let go of my sister," Kathleen added.

The man froze as his gaze jerked up and over her shoulder. He suddenly let Jeannie go and scuttled back several steps.

Oddly, his footmen also retreated. Everyone suddenly stopped yelling, and silence fell over the square, broken only by the sounds of Jeannie's outraged sniffles.

"Trim, if ye touch either girl again, I will twist yer damn arm off."

The threat was uttered in a calm yet utterly terrifying tone. Trim took another step back.

"Aboot bloody time ye showed up, laddie," Angus said.

Turning around, Kathleen got quite the shock. Grant's

gaze was as terrifying as his tone. Daggers practically shot out of his eyes and drilled into Trim's balding skull.

Hastily, Kathleen dragged Jeannie out of the way.

"Don't . . . don't threaten me, Kendrick," Trim spluttered.

Grant's gaze flickered off to the side. "Please put that away. It is not required."

"Spoilsport." Gillian slipped a small, wicked-looking blade back into her boot.

"That's a dandy little shiv," Angus said in an admiring tone.

"Isn't it?" Gillian affably responded.

Trim stared at her in disbelief. "You . . . you pulled a knife on me? I will have you arrested as soon as the constable arrives."

"I don't see a knife," Grant said. "Kade, do you see a knife?"

Kade shrugged. "Honestly, I don't even know what we're talking about at this point."

Trim waved a hand at Jeannie. "This girl attacked me— that is what we're talking about. *And* my house was damaged and my poor father scared out of his wits."

Grant looked to Kathleen for clarification.

"Jeannie accidentally hit a cricket ball through Mr. Trim's window," she said.

Grant's calm deserted him. Now he looked massively annoyed. "And that's what prompted an all-out melee in the park?"

"I did apologize. And I was offering to pay for any damages when—"

"When that nasty little hoyden kicked me," Trim interrupted.

Gillian shook her head. "I am *definitely* going to stab you."

Beneath Trim's outraged bluster about constables and arrests, Kathleen heard Grant blow out a sigh.

"Your Grace, it might be best if you returned to the house," he said.

Trim paused in his tirade. "Your Grace?"

"I take it you have not been formally introduced to the Duchess of Leverton?" Grant's tone was as dry as three-day-old toast.

Gillian swept a mocking curtsy. "Charmed, I'm sure."

Trim blinked. He'd obviously forgotten there was a duchess staying at Kendrick House, albeit an unconventional one.

"Angus, please take the duchess back to the house," Grant said.

Gillian scoffed. "I'm staying right here."

"No, you're not," Grant replied.

The two locked gazes. Much to Kathleen's surprise, Gillian capitulated with a sardonic snort.

"Oh, very well," she said. "You clearly want to impress Kathleen, so I'll leave you to it."

Angus took Gillian's arm, and the two reluctantly retreated from the field of battle.

They'd barely departed before Trim started waving a frantic hand. "Now we'll see what's what," he said in a snippy tone.

Grant glanced over his shoulder, then back at Trim in disbelief. "You really called a constable over a broken window?"

"Have you forgotten that I was attacked?"

"Mr. Trim," Kathleen firmly said, "you called the constable *before* my sister kicked you. And she only kicked you because your language was offensive."

Grant's gaze returned to her. "Was it now?"

"He was being very nasty to Kathleen when she was sincerely trying apologize," Jeannie said.

Grant studied Trim with aristocratic disdain. Kathleen had never seen him do aristocratic disdain. She quite enjoyed it.

"What sort of man calls the constable on a young girl and her sister for playing a game in the park?" he asked with undisguised contempt.

Trim, who'd begun to recover his countenance, flushed red again. "We'll see what the constable has to say, sir."

The lawman trundled up, a bit out of breath.

"It's about time," Trim angrily said.

Grant smiled at the constable. "Mr. Hugo, I'm afraid you've been called out for nothing."

The genial-looking, middle-aged man heaved a sigh. "Och, Kendrick business, is it? Is yer twin lurkin' about? Ye two were a whole pile of trouble, back in the day."

Kathleen perked up. "Really? That sounds interesting."

The constable gave her a sly grin. "I could tell ye a story or three."

"This is ridiculous," huffed Trim.

"It certainly is." Grant nodded at Will, who'd been standing by, ready to lend assistance. "Will, please take Mr. Hugo to the house for a dram. Angus will be pleased to see him."

The constable brightened. "Now, that's a fine suggestion, sir. Thank ye."

"But—"

Trim's protest withered under Grant's lethal gaze as Will promptly took the constable off to the house.

Impressed by Grant's efficient handling of the situation, Kathleen smiled at him. "Now what?"

"Now we all apologize to Mr. Trim, arrange to fix his window, and go home."

"But he grabbed me," Jeannie protested.

"You kicked me," Trim snapped.

Grant went back to looking flinty. "No gentleman should lay a hand in anger on a woman, much less a girl. Do I truly need to remind you of that?"

When Trim fumed in outraged silence, Grant turned to Jeannie. "Maybe everyone got a wee bit fashed and over-reacted?"

Since Jeannie was beginning to look mutinous again, Kathleen nodded. "Yes, I think we *all* overreacted, for which I certainly apologize."

Grant crouched down to meet Jeannie's gaze. "Lass?"

She finally relented. "I'm sorry, too."

He gently tapped her cheek. "Good for you, sweet lass."

"Matthew, is everything all right?" called a querulous voice from the steps of the Trim house.

Kathleen glanced over to see an elderly man wearing a shawl and leaning on a cane as he peered at them.

"Everything's fine, Mr. Trim," Grant called. "Lady Arnprior will visit with you later today, to see how you get on after this unfortunate incident."

"Her ladyship is always welcome," the old man said. "Matthew, come back inside. All this standing about cannot be good for us."

"But, Father," young Trim protested, "this whole business—"

Old Trim waved his cane. "If Lady Arnprior is satisfied, then so am I."

"Oh, very well." Young Trim glared at Kathleen. "But I *will* be writing to Lady Gorey to inform her of this afternoon's distressing events."

He stomped off, followed by his footmen.

Kathleen rubbed her forehead. "Well, that's just splendid. Helen will be *so* pleased."

"Sorry, Kath," Jeannie said in a small voice.

She dredged up a smile. "It's not your fault, dearest. Except for the kicking, but one can hardly blame you. That man was positively dreadful."

Grant nudged them toward the house. "Perhaps we could move this inside, away from our audience."

Mrs. Buchanan and her sister were still observing from their doorstep.

"It really was just a ball through a window," Kade said. "And Kathleen did her best to apologize."

"Not much success there, I'm afraid," Grant said.

"I'm not used to being the coolheaded one in a crisis," she said. "It threw me off."

He snorted. "At least you didn't pull a knife."

"Aye, it's a mess," said Kade.

"Especially when that old twiddlepoop writes to Mamma," Jeannie morosely added.

"And Mrs. Buchanan saw the whole thing from start to finish. You know what a gossip she is." Kade brightened. "But the old gal is fond of you, Grant. You can give her a visit and butter her up. Try to contain the damage, as it were."

Coming from such an old sobersides, Grant's quietly muttered oath was remarkably colorful.

Chapter Nine

"Grant, be a good lad and fetch me another dram," Gillian said. "This has been a most annoying day."

"Partly thanks to you, pulling a knife on Trim like that," he sardonically replied as he took her glass over to the drinks trolley.

"Nonsense. I was merely *about* to pull my knife. Your heroic entrance forestalled that need."

Grant threw her a disbelieving look. "Gillian, I saw the damn thing in your hand. So did Matthew Trim."

"Oh, well," she said with an insouciant shrug. "He was a dreadful ninny, you must admit."

"Ye can hardly blame the lass," Angus said from his customary seat by the drawing-room fireplace. "Young Trim was itchin' for a fight."

Royal, who was lounging across from him, scoffed. "You didn't need to scratch that itch so thoroughly."

"I was the soul of patience, ye ken. A veritable saint."

"More like the soul of idiocy." Grant splashed whisky into Gillian's glass and then poured himself a hefty one. "I suspect you were getting ready to drub Trim with a cricket bat before I arrived."

Angus let out a disgusted snort. "Och, I didna even think of usin' the cricket bat, more's the shame."

"Losing your touch, Grandda?" Royal teased.

"No sass from you, laddie boy."

Nick, who was sitting across the room reading a letter, finally gave up trying to ignore the discussion. "I'm extremely disappointed that the men in this family were not able to protect our guests from such a ridiculous scene. Especially you, Angus. You should have immediately taken the ladies into the house. Instead, you displayed not one whit of common sense."

Grant snorted. "Nick, have you actually ever met our grandfather?"

His brother's gaze narrowed to glittering shards of blue ice. "And you, Grant. Where were you when this window breaking was going on? You were to be looking out for the ladies, as well. I specifically asked you to do so."

"I'm not a babysitter," he protested.

"You're a terrible one if you are," Gillian airily commented. "You've all but abandoned us, alas and alack."

"Exactly my point," Nick said.

"I *do* have a job," Grant retorted. "And I pulled everyone's arse out of the fire today, I might add. If not for me, this sorry lot would have been spending the night in the clink."

"Och, nae," Angus said. "I had everythin' under control."

Kade rolled his eyes. "No, you didn't, Grandda. None of us did, I'm sorry to say."

Grant smiled at his little brother. "As far as I could tell, you and Will were the only ones trying to calm things down, unlike certain other participants."

Gillian raised a hand. "Guilty as charged. Seriously

though, Grant, you did a splendid job managing a difficult situation once you arrived."

After escorting Kathleen and Jeannie home, Grant had taken up Kade's unwelcome but sensible suggestion to visit Mrs. Buchanan. Unsurprisingly, the old gal had been properly shocked by the antics in the park. Having both excellent vision and hearing, she'd seen and heard everything, including Gillian's threat to gut boneheaded Matthew Trim.

Not that a little gossip would hurt the Duchess of Leverton. But Kathleen and Jeannie *were* vulnerable. The on-dits would no doubt spread to London, because even if old Trim didn't write to Lady Gorey, somebody else would. There were twenty houses that lined their little square, and a fair number of residents had observed the ridiculous scene. One wouldn't have to exaggerate the details much at all when the Duchess of Leverton was part of the mix. The scandal sheets practically wrote themselves.

Thanks to a silly game of cricket and one errant ball, Kathleen and Jeannie were now waist-deep in pig manure. And since the scandal had happened on Kendrick watch, the chief of Clan Kendrick would naturally see it as the family's duty to sort it out.

As did Grant. He felt responsible for Kathleen, and for her scapegrace little sister. If he'd been there to keep an eye on the two lasses, as Nick had asked, none of this would have happened.

Grant *had* been avoiding Kathleen these last few days, and that had been both stupid and selfish. The truth was that Kathleen Calvert made him feel a hell of a lot of emotions he'd rather not have to face at the moment. Their time together at Mugdock had made that crystal clear. He was starting to tumble for the lass, which was massively inconvenient given the current state of his life.

Tumbling for her was also pointless, since the fair colleen was obviously determined to return home to the old sod. Grant didn't need to be a genius to figure that out.

Vicky entered the room and plunked down next to Gillian on the chaise, heaving a sigh. "This situation is my fault. I should have known that having a cricket match in the square was tempting fate. I *will* call on the Trims tomorrow. I should have gone this evening, but Matthew Trim is such a prissy bore that my nerve quite failed me."

Nick crossed the room and leaned down to drop a kiss on the top of Vicky's head. "It's not your fault, love. Apparently, we cannot expect either our family or our guests to conduct themselves like rational adults."

"You should just blame everything on me, Nicholas," Gillian cheerfully said. "No one will question that in the least."

"I'm sure we can all agree that there's more than enough blame to go around." Nick stared pointedly at Angus. "Some in larger measures than others."

"I was the soul of brevity," Angus indignantly replied.

"Grandda, that makes no sense," Royal said.

"Fah," their grandfather replied with a dismissive wave.

"Regardless of who is to blame," said Gillian, "I feel perfectly dreadful about having to rush off tomorrow. But I'm afraid it cannot be helped. My husband's letter made that point *quite* clearly."

Vicky patted her hand. "We were all sorry to hear about your mother-in-law's accident, and we hope the dowager duchess makes a speedy recovery."

At the same time as the cricket debacle, an express post

had arrived from the Duke of Leverton. The dowager duchess had been visiting her son and grandchildren during Gillian's absence. While playing with her grandson in the back garden, the old gal had tripped on a paving stone and taken a fall, breaking her wrist. The dowager, understandably, had kicked up a fuss and was now insisting that her son escort her back to the country, where she could recover away from what she called the dreadful noise and bustle of the city.

"I feel terrible for the dear old dragon," Gillian said. "Though you'd think we were living in the middle of Seven Dials instead of an enormous mansion in boring old Mayfair. But the country it must be. And since Charles will not leave the children until I'm home . . ."

"That means you must return posthaste to London." Vicky let out a wistful sigh. "I'll miss you dreadfully, though. We've had very little time together."

"I know, pet. But I'll return next summer, with Charles and children in tow. We'll camp out with you for weeks and weeks until you're thoroughly sick of us."

Grant had to smother a laugh at the look of alarm on Nick's face.

Vicky, however, beamed. "That sounds simply lovely. We'll all go up to Castle Kinglas and have a nice, long visit."

"Nicholas will be thrilled with that prospect," Gillian replied, giving him a wink.

"I'll be on pins and needles until your return," he wryly said.

She laughed. "At least I'm getting Jeannie out of your hair. That girl rather makes me look like a piker."

"Nonsense. She's lovely," Vicky stoutly said. "Jeannie

simply has a great deal of energy and doesn't quite know what to do with herself."

Kade winced. "True enough."

"Runs in the family," Grant couldn't help adding.

Vicky tilted a questioning eyebrow. "Kathleen is a delightful young woman, Grant. And you seem to get along with her quite well."

Nick, who was almost as annoying as Angus on the matchmaking front, perked up his ears. "I am happy to hear that. I hope you've been paying Kathleen the attention she deserves."

"You did seem to be having quite the discussion on the steps this afternoon," Royal said with an annoying smirk. "Anything you'd like to tell us?"

"There was nothing pleasant about that particular discussion," Grant said in a tone he hoped would end the conversation.

Gillian pointed a finger at him. "Really, dear boy, Kathleen did not need a reprimand from you on the front steps of the house. She truly did her best with that awful young Trim."

Nick scowled. "You reprimanded Kathleen?"

Grant rolled his eyes. "Of course not. I simply suggested that she needed to exert a bit more control over Jeannie."

"Och, ye all but bit the poor lass's head off," Angus scoffed.

"Grandda, you weren't even there," Grant said.

"I was watchin' out the window, ye ken."

"Of course you were," he dryly replied.

Vicky leveled her best governess scowl. "Grant, I am *quite* surprised to hear this about you. I do not approve."

"And I thought you were the nice Kendrick," Gillian drolly said to him.

Kade raised his hand. "That would be me."

"I am not best pleased about this, Grant," Nick said in a stern tone.

"Hang on, everybody," he protested. "I was perfectly polite. If anything, she was rude to me."

Angus clucked his tongue. "And ye wonder why yer still unmarried, what with yer moods and all."

Argh. And his family still wondered why he spent all his time at the office.

Royal, smothering a laugh, decided to take pity on him. "Is Jeannie reconciled to her early return to London?" he asked Gillian.

"I thought she was, yet now she's resistant again. We tried to discuss it with her after dinner, but . . ." Gillian wriggled a hand. "I'm ashamed to admit I beat a hasty retreat and left poor Kathleen to deal with the rebellion."

"Of course the wee lassie wishes to stay with us," Angus said. "We're a damn sight nicer than her own mother."

Gillian nodded. "Sadly true. Lady Gorey will probably lock the poor child away on some remote country estate."

Vicky grimaced in sympathy. "That's dreadful. Perhaps—"

Kathleen hurried through the door. "Please don't get up, gentlemen. It's dreadfully rude of me to be late for tea, but Jeannie was quite upset."

Nick led her to an empty armchair. "No apologies are necessary. May I fetch you a sherry, perhaps, or even a whisky?"

She flopped down with an endearing lack of formality.

Grant had to admit that such naturally graceful charm was one of the many things he loved about her.

Loved.

His brain stuttered over the word until he regrouped and told himself to stop thinking like a feckless moron.

Kathleen gave Nick a grateful smile. "A brandy, please. In fact, perhaps you might bring me the entire decanter."

"Something wrong, Grant?" Angus asked in an innocent tone. "Yer looking a wee bit fashed."

"The only thing I'm fashed about is my empty glass," he said, starting to rise.

Nick plucked the glass from his hand. "I'll fetch it. You sit and talk with Kathleen."

Kathleen looked startled. "Talk to me? About what?"

"Ah . . ." Grant started.

"About his apology," Gillian said. "Which he'll be making right now."

Good. God.

Kathleen looked perplexed for a moment. Then her brow cleared. "You mean about this afternoon? No apology is necessary. In fact, I'm the one who should be apologizing to all of you for causing trouble." She crinkled her nose at Grant. "Sadly, a great deal of trouble."

She looked so adorably rueful that he had to smile. "Och, dinna fash yourself, lass. We'll get it sorted."

"I have a suggestion, Kathleen," Vicky said. "Why don't you and Jeannie simply continue to stay with us? I am happy to write to your stepmother and extend the offer."

"That's so kind of you, but when Helen gets wind of what happened . . ." Kathleen gratefully accepted the brandy glass from Nick and took a healthy sip.

"I can talk to the old bat . . . er, your stepmother when I get back to London," Gillian offered. "Smooth things over."

"I'm afraid there's no smoothing this over," Kathleen morosely said. "After discussing the matter with Jeannie . . . well, I've decided to take her north with me to Lochnagar. Immediately."

Her pronouncement produced a surprised silence.

"Are you sure that's the best solution?" Grant cautiously asked. "Jeannie is . . . a wee bit of a handful."

Kathleen bristled. "Are you implying that I can't control my own sister?"

"Well . . ."

He saw a heartbreaking mix of anxiety, defiance, and vulnerability in her lovely gray gaze. Somehow, in a room full of supportive people, she seemed very alone.

"I'm simply trying to understand," he continued in a gentle tone. "She's been running you in circles for the last two weeks."

"Running all of us, quite frankly," Gillian said with a sympathetic grimace.

Kathleen breathed out a heavy sigh. "I know, and I *am* worried about that. But Helen will just make the poor girl utterly miserable if Jeannie goes home. I can't bear the thought of it."

"I suspect you're also afraid she'll do something foolish if you send her back to London," Victoria added.

"It's more than likely," Kathleen replied.

"But wouldn't it be better if the two of you simply stayed with us?" Grant couldn't help asking. "We won't let anyone pester you."

He'd bloody well start breaking heads if anyone tried.

Kathleen gave him a smile so warmhearted and sweet that it made his heart twist.

"You're all so incredibly kind," she said. "Still, Helen will be furious if we stay in Glasgow any longer, especially after today's incident. She might even travel up here to drag Jeannie back herself."

"What about Kinglas then?" Victoria suggested.

"Since my parents made it clear I'm to go to Lochnagar at some point, I think it's best to go there. Helen is very fond of Sabrina, so she'll be more inclined to let Jeannie stay. I simply need to get my sister out of Glasgow before Mr. Trim or anyone else has a chance to write to my step-mother. She might still pitch a fit, but I'm fairly convinced she'll let Jeannie stay if we're at Lochnagar." She flashed a wry smile. "After all, it *is* rather remote."

"So, it's off to the Highlands for the lassies, eh?" Angus said. "Well, ye'll have a grand time with Sabrina and Graeme."

Kathleen dredged up a polite smile. Though clearly not thrilled with the idea, she was loyal to the bone and would not abandon her sister.

"It makes perfect sense when you explain it like that," Vicky said. "But we'll still miss you."

"Well then," Nick said. "I suppose the only question is who will escort you to Lochnagar."

Kathleen waved a hand. "I'll hire a coach. I was hoping you could lend us one of your footmen to attend us, though we're quite capable of looking after ourselves."

"Nonsense," Nick said. "You'll be going in our traveling carriage."

"That's kind of you, but—"

"And you will certainly need an escort," Vicky added. "It's not safe for young ladies to travel unattended."

"And who do you have in mind?" Gillian asked, glancing at Grant with a sly smile.

Oh, hell.

"Angus can go, if he's so inclined," Nick said.

But before Grant could let out a relieved breath, his brother looked straight at him. "And Grant, of course. I think we can all agree on that."

Kathleen cast Grant a horrified glance. He could only assume he was wearing a similar—if not identical—expression.

"I . . . I . . ." she stammered.

"Well, that's settled," Gillian cheerfully said. "Goodness, it's getting late, and there's so much packing to do."

The duchess hauled Kathleen to her feet. "Come along, pet. We'll have a nice little chat while we get organized."

Vicky also stood. "Excellent. We can leave the men to make all the necessary arrangements."

Kathleen, whom Gillian was dragging inexorably toward the door, cast Grant a panicked look over her shoulder.

"Vicky," Gillian said, looking back, "fetch that decanter of brandy, will you? Since it's our last night together, we might as well make the best of it."

Grant had spent the last ten minutes trying to explain to the men in his family exactly why he couldn't leave Glasgow right now. Sadly, he was failing.

"Kathleen and Jeannie will need a competent escort, so it might as well be you," Royal said, summing up the general opinion.

Grant wrestled his rising temper. "I remind you again that I have a business to run. Especially with you leaving at the end of the week for Cairndow to rejoin your family."

"That's not a problem. I can delay my departure for another week or two. Ainsley will perfectly understand."

Angus nodded. "Aye, she will, especially since it's for such a grand cause."

Grant rolled his eyes. "There is no grand cause."

"Och, romance is the grandest cause of all, ye ken."

"And there *is* no romance, ye daft old man."

Angus tapped the side of his nose, trying to look wise. "I've seen ye and the lassie together. There's something there, ye ken, if ye give it half a chance."

"That sounds promising," Nick said with an approving nod.

"Look what happened when our Graeme and Sabrina went north last year," Angus added. "All that canoodling led to marriage, a wee bairn, and even a knighthood for yer twin."

Grant resisted the urge to bang his head against the marble surround of the fireplace. "Grandda, this is not remotely the same situation. Besides, you've already agreed to go with the ladies. There's no need for an additional escort."

"I disagree," Nick said. "Your grandfather is not a young man anymore. If there was trouble on the road . . ."

For a moment, Angus seemed unsure whether to be insulted at the suggestion that he was getting old or to play the necessary role to bolster Nick's argument. After a brief struggle, he chose the latter.

"Yer right about that," he said in a quavering voice, raising a now trembling hand to his brow. "If we were attacked by highwaymen or stranded in the middle of nowhere—"

"Oh, for God's sake," Grant interrupted.

Angus dropped the act. "Yer stuck in a rut, son, and ye know it. Ye need to shake things up."

"Grandda's not wrong," Royal said. "You're all but chained to that desk of yours. No wonder you're bored."

"Who says I'm bored?" Grant protested.

"We all do," Angus said. "And there's nae better cure for boredom than a nice bit of—"

Grant shot up a hand. "Do *not* say it."

"A nice bit of travel, ye ken," Angus indignantly finished. "And if ye think I was goin' to say something randy, yer way off the mark."

Royal snorted. "Of course you were going to say something randy."

"I am the soul of concupiscence," Angus said in a pious tone. "Like a monk, I am."

"That is not what that word means," Royal said.

"It doesn't matter," Grant impatiently cut in. "I'm too busy right now. You'll have to find someone else—Royal, for instance." He flashed a mocking smile at his brother. "If you're able to stay an extra week or two in Glasgow, then you surely have time to escort the ladies north."

Royal shook his head. "I have a number of matters to clear up in Glasgow before I head to Cairndow. I can take care of those now without having to rush, while I'm filling in for you."

"Grant, don't you wish to visit with Graeme?" Nick gently asked. "You must surely miss him."

"I . . . yes, of course I miss him."

More than any of them could ever know. His twin's absence was like a small but ugly rip in the fabric of his life that could never be mended. But he would be damned if he showed any sign of the depth of that feeling. After a long, tough slog, Graeme had finally found happiness. Grant would throw himself off a cliff before he made his twin feel the slightest bit guilty for deserting him.

He didn't desert you, idiot.

"Then take this as a chance to visit with him," Nick said. "Besides, if you don't go, I'll have to do it. And you know how busy I am at this time of year with the harvest at Kinglas. I was planning on going up next week to deal with a few problems, so it would be a great favor to me if you agree to do this, Grant."

Grant mentally sighed. His big brother so rarely asked for help. Nick was the one who was always there for them, pulling various Kendricks out of the fire, time and again. He'd stood in as parent, teacher, and mentor after their parents had died all those years ago. If not for Nick, God only knew what would have happened to a family all but sundered by tragedy and misfortune.

It was more than loyalty owed to their brother and laird. Nick had given all of them love, shelter, and support when everything in their lives had gone so terribly wrong.

Angus reacted to Nick's words like a hound to a scent. "There's trouble at Kinglas? I can help ye with that, lad. I can even go up tomorrow and have a look at the books and a wee chat with the tenant farmers before ye arrive. Get the lay of the land, as it were."

Nick looked appalled. Grant knew his poor brother already had enough work on his plate without Angus royally mucking things up.

"No, you'd best come with me, Grandda," Grant said, now resigned to his fate. "You're much better at managing young ladies than I am."

Again, Angus looked torn for a moment before he brightened. "Well, I suppose yer right, lad. And mayhap I can give ye a few tips on courtship and such when we're alone."

"Now, that is a conversation I'd like to hear," Royal said with a chuckle.

"There will be no such discussion," Grant firmly replied. "We will escort the girls to Lochnagar, and then I'll be returning immediately to Glasgow."

Angus rolled his eyes. "Now, lad, yer passing up a chance—"

"Good man," Nick interrupted, clapping Grant on the shoulder. "I knew I could count on you."

That was exactly the problem. Everyone could always count on him, no matter how annoying or unpleasant the task. And being cooped up in a carriage for several days with a woman who obviously found him a dead bore was shaping up to be a very unpleasant task. Especially since he found that particular woman the polar opposite of boring.

Chapter Ten

When the carriage rocked around another curve in the road, Kathleen had to resist the urge to close her eyes. Her insides were already wobbling like an off-balance top. Closing her eyes could only make it worse.

After four gruesome days of travel, she was ready to stay put for a long time—no matter how dreary Lochnagar might turn out to be. It would likely take her stomach at least three months to recover from such a dreadful trip on increasingly dreadful roads.

"Not much longer now," Grant said in a kind voice.

From the opposite bench of the Kendricks' traveling coach, he studied her with concern. She couldn't help feeling sorry for the poor man. That he had been dragooned to serve as their escort was fairly clear. Even worse, he'd been all but forced to play nursemaid thanks to her fractious insides. It was mortally embarrassing, but there wasn't a thing she could do about either her stupid stomach or the wretched scandal that had forced them to slink out of Glasgow.

Angus, seated next to his grandson, peered out the window to confirm Grant's assessment.

"Maybe an hour, ye ken," he loudly whispered. "Then the lassies can have a nice, wee rest from all this jostlin' aboot."

Angus had taken to whispering on the assumption that it would help calm her unsettled state. Since his whispering voice was almost as loud as his regular one, it was rather a failure in that respect. Not that such measures made one whit of difference, but she did appreciate the effort.

Kathleen mustered up something that she hoped resembled a smile. From the expressions on the men's faces, she'd obviously failed. Their concern now seemed tinged with alarm. If she'd had the energy, she'd say she was beyond the desire to toss up her crumpets. Now she simply wished someone would shoot her.

Jeannie, who never turned a hair from travel sickness, looked up from her book and shifted on the luxuriously padded seat to peer closely at Kathleen.

"You're looking pretty green, Kath. Do you want us to stop?" She put her book aside and started to dig around in her reticule. "Or I can give you my smelling salts. I packed them in my reticule in case you got sick again."

For a moment, Kathleen did close her eyes. Nothing would send her bolting for the nearest bush faster than the odor of smelling salts.

"No, thank you," she finally said. "I'll be fine until we reach Lochnagar."

Angus scrunched up his face. "Are ye sure? Because ye look fair ready to shoot the cat."

She managed a weak chuckle. "All cats are safe, if I correctly deduce the meaning of that expression."

Grant's smile was wry. "Grandda has many interesting phrases and expressions, at least one for every occasion."

"And I've had fair cause to use 'em over the years, thanks to Grant and his brothers. Why I could tell ye some stories—"

"You have, Grandda," Grant interrupted. "Repeatedly, over the last four days."

"I like Mr. MacDonald's stories," Jeannie said. "They're fun. I've never been allowed to have fun like that."

Angus had done his best to while away the tedious hours of travel with outrageous tales about the Kendrick brothers, especially the twins. Kathleen suspected there was a fair amount of poetic exaggeration involved, at least when it came to Grant. It was well-nigh impossible to believe that the calm, perfectly proper gentleman sitting opposite her was, in fact, the young hellion his grandfather made him out to be.

That Grant was a thoughtful and decent man was beyond doubt. But Kathleen simply could not envision him tumbling from one madcap escapade to the next.

He gave Jeannie a smile. As always, Kathleen couldn't help thinking what a wonderful smile he had. Unfortunately, she rarely saw it. Grant was so carefully polite with her that she was beginning to find it annoying.

"My brother and I never asked anyone's permission, so there wasn't much *allowing* going on," he said. "Nor was it always fun, despite what my grandfather claims."

"Of course ye had fun, ye jinglebrains," Angus scoffed. "I remember one time—"

When they lurched through a particularly large pothole,

Kathleen bounced several inches off her seat. When she landed, it took her stomach a few seconds to catch up. She braced a hand on the seat and swallowed hard.

"Miss Calvert," Grant said, "we can easily stop. There's plenty of daylight left, so we'll arrive in good time, regardless."

"Thank you, but the sooner we conclude this journey, the better."

It wasn't just the usual bother of travel that was twisting up her insides. Word of their scandal was bound to have reached their parents by now, and there was no predicting their reaction. Papa could easily squash Kathleen's plan to return to Ireland, and God only knew what he and Helen would do about Jeannie.

God only knew what *she* would do about Jeannie, too. Right now, the prospect of keeping her little sister out of trouble for the next three months seemed daunting in the extreme.

Grant reached inside his greatcoat and extracted a small twist of paper. "I've got one more ginger lozenge. I thought I'd keep it in case of emergency."

She gratefully accepted the small packet. "I'm sorry to be so much trouble for everyone."

Angus waved a dismissive hand. "Och, we're just right sorry ye've had such a hard time of it."

"Thankfully, your suffering is almost at an end." Grant took out his pocket watch and flipped it open. "We should be at Lochnagar well within the hour."

His suffering was almost at an end, too. Grant was clearly itching to return to Glasgow, and Kathleen had little doubt he'd be back on the road within a few days. She couldn't blame him. If she were Grant Kendrick, she would have run screaming for the hills by the end of their first day of travel.

The trip had started off badly for her, thanks to a massive headache induced by a late night of packing and, well, drinking. Gillian had insisted that they celebrate their last evening together by polishing off the brandy. Their packing session had turned into quite a lot of fun, thanks to Gillian, and had been an excellent way to bring their time in Glasgow to a close.

But when morning came too soon, Kathleen awoke to the realization that she'd made an epic mistake. When she'd gingerly climbed into the traveling coach an hour later, Grant had taken one look at her and let out a small sigh.

At the stop for their midday meal—which she'd not been able to eat—Grant had disappeared. When he finally returned, he had stomach powders from an apothecary and ginger lozenges from a sweet shop.

For the rest of the trip, he'd gone to every effort to make her comfortable. He'd ordered warm bricks for her feet, installed her in the quietest room at every inn, and rustled up meals that were simple and bland. Even more importantly, he'd kept a close eye on Jeannie. In doing so, he'd relieved Kathleen of her greatest worry.

While Grant Kendrick might not be the most exciting man she'd ever met, he was certainly the nicest. Given even the slightest encouragement, a girl could easily fall in love with him.

Fall in love with Grant?

It was such a startling thought that she couldn't help frowning. Yes, she liked him, quite a lot as it turned out. But the idea of falling in—

"Miss Calvert, are you all right?"

Grant's deep voice jolted her out of her thoughts.

"Oh, ah, yes," she stammered.

"Kath, are you getting a fever?" Jeannie asked. "Your face is like fire."

"I'm perfectly—"

Crack.

Grant whipped back the shade on the carriage window, craning sideways to see out. Kathleen also leaned forward, straining to see around his broad shoulders.

"Did somebody fire a pistol?" she asked in disbelief.

"Pistol?" Jeannie squeaked.

"Sounds like." Angus had peered out the other window before glancing at Grant. "A hunter, ye think?"

They heard a shout from the coachman before the carriage gave a hard jolt as it picked up speed. Kathleen fell forward, practically into Grant's lap. He easily caught her, lifting her straight up and back onto her seat.

"Hold on tight, lass."

Angus sighed. "And me without my pistol, for once."

Grant shoved down the window glass. He stuck out his head, took a quick look around, and then pulled back in. His grim expression sent Kathleen's heart hammering against her ribs.

Reaching inside his greatcoat, Grant pulled out a pocket blade and slipped it into his boot.

"You have your knife?" he asked his grandfather.

Angus patted his chest. "Right here."

This was obviously *very* bad.

The carriage slowed, then jerked to a halt, rocking on its frame. Kathleen grabbed onto her sister, trying to keep them both from sliding off the seat.

"I take it by your actions that we're about to be held up," she asked in as steady a voice as she could manage.

"Looks like," Grant tersely replied.

Her head swam. Everything, including the light streaming into the carriage from the late afternoon sun, seemed unreal.

"But it's broad daylight. Who does that?"

He flicked her a veiled look. "We're about to find out."

When Kathleen's stomach all but crawled up her throat, she sternly ordered it down. She would *not* toss up her crumpets during a robbery. With her luck, she'd probably do it on one of the robbers and be promptly shot.

"Yer popper's packed in the boot, I take it," Angus said.

"Like yours." Grant sounded enormously frustrated.

The old fellow looked disgusted. "Och, we're growin' soft. Well, knives it'll have to be."

"Do *not* take yours out unless I tell you to. There are at least four of them, and they've obviously neutralized our coachman and Robby. We would only be endangering the ladies." Grant had gone back to looking out the window but now glanced over his shoulder at his grandfather. "We only fight if absolutely necessary. Understood?"

The old man nodded. "All right, lad. We'll play it yer way."

"Good."

Grant looked at Kathleen and Jeannie. Although his gaze had gone as hard as marble, he remained calm. More than anything, *annoyed* described his expression, as if one of the horses had thrown a shoe, causing a slight delay.

"I know you're scared," he said. "But if you'll both keep quiet and do exactly what I say, everything will be fine."

"You promise?" Jeannie asked in a quavering voice.

He flashed a brief smile. "I promise. Nothing bad will happen to you or Kathleen."

"Out of the carriage, now," shouted a muffled voice.

As Grant reached for the door handle, he glanced at Kathleen. "I mean it. Keep quiet, all right?"

His repeated warning was slightly irritating, especially since she didn't feel the tiniest inclination to say anything to a highwayman. Her only plan was to keep her sister safe.

Grant cautiously opened the door. He muttered a quiet curse before stepping out and clicking the carriage door shut behind him.

"Stay right there, mate," someone barked.

"I've no plans to run off, since you're holding a pistol on me," Grant replied. "Now, who is in charge of this misadventure? The sooner we can conclude our business, the better."

Kathleen blinked. Grant was a quiet man, even self-effacing. And certainly no one would ever call him a snob. Right now, though, he sounded both imperious and righteously offended.

Even though Jeannie was huddled against her, Kathleen shifted closer to the window. If she leaned forward enough, she could see him.

Grant looked as haughty and irritated as he'd sounded. He also seemed entirely in control by his demeanor. It was quite remarkable, since a man with scarf wrapped around his face held a pistol just six inches from Grant's nose.

"That's our lad," Angus said as he too looked out. "He'll soon have this sorted."

Kathleen practically plastered her ear to the glass. "They're arguing."

"Nae, they're negotiating, lass." He patted her knee. "It's all just part of the game, ye ken."

It didn't seem like a game, since the argument seemed to be growing more heated. And from the tone of Grant's voice, it was clear he was frustrated.

"What's going to happen to us?" Jeannie whispered.

The poor girl was as pale as a slipper moon, and her pupils had dilated with fear.

"Nothing, dearest," Kathleen said in a soothing voice. "Mr. Kendrick will protect us."

Angus patted Jeannie's knee. "Och, they'll just take a bit of blunt and be on their way."

Kathleen jerked back when Grant opened the carriage door. His gaze had narrowed to fiery green slits, and his features were tight with anger.

"I'm afraid you'll have to get out." His calm voice was at odds with his furious expression.

Angus made a disgusted noise. "Bloody idiots, I ken?"

"Ye ken correctly," Grant replied.

A large figure loomed behind him and jabbed a pistol into the back of Grant's skull.

"Get 'em out now," growled the man, "or I'll blow your bloody brains all over the inside of this fancy carriage."

Kathleen gasped. Grant, however, simply looked massively annoyed.

"If you will cease jabbing that blasted weapon at my head," he replied, "I will be able to step back so the others can alight."

"Bloody pounce," the man snarled as he stepped back. "I oughta blow yer brains out."

Grant moved aside to let Angus climb out. Then he reached in to help Kathleen and Jeannie down.

Jeannie, however, huddled against Kathleen, refusing to move.

"Dearest, we have no choice," Kathleen whispered.

Jeannie buried her face in Kathleen's shoulder. "No."

"Jeanette, look at me," Grant said.

She reluctantly lifted her head.

"I told you I won't let anyone hurt you or Kathleen," he said in a patient voice. "If you just do what I say, we will all be fine."

"Get a bloody move on it," yelled the bandit. "Or I *will* blow someone's brains out."

Jeannie flinched.

"Och, man," Angus barked back. "She's just a child. Yer scarin' the wits out of her."

"Not true." Grant took Jeannie's hand. "She's a brave lass, is our girl."

"Certainly braver than I am," said Kathleen. "She's always been that way."

Grant gave a gentle tug, and Jeannie moved onto the step. After he lifted her down, he turned back to help Kathleen step out. She lined up with her sister and Angus by the side of the carriage. Grant stood in front of them in a protective stance, braced as if ready for a fight.

A fight for which he and Angus were greatly outnumbered, she gloomily observed. Danvers, their coachman, along with Robby the groom, were sitting on the verge, hands behind their heads and held at gunpoint by a man on a horse. Another man had dismounted and was holding the reins of two horses while keeping a pistol pointed at Kathleen, Jeannie, and Angus.

A third man stood several feet away, his weapon leveled on Grant. All wore scarves and hats tugged low. Identical greatcoats made them almost indistinguishable. The one holding the pistol on Grant was particularly tall and powerful looking, but they were all big men.

Kathleen cast a quick glance around. They were on a deserted stretch of road, surrounded only by windswept meadows, with a stand of woods in the distance. Not a farmhouse or cottage was in sight, and she suspected there wasn't one on the opposite side of the road, either. Even though she knew they weren't far from the hamlet attached to Lochnagar Manor, the area seemed lamentably perfect for a highway robbery.

The villain aiming at Grant—presumably the head bandit—leaned forward to stare at Kathleen. Although the brim of his hat shadowed his eyes, she could feel his gaze crawl over her. She forced herself to stare back, refusing to be rattled.

Grant stepped slightly to the side, coming between her and the man.

"I wouldn't," he said in a cold voice.

The thug snorted. "Ye couldna stop me if ye wanted to, ye big oaf. I'm the one with the gun."

Grant crossed his arms over his chest. Kathleen could see the flex of his shoulders even through the fabric of his coat.

"And I'm the one whose brother is the local magistrate. That would be Sir Graeme Kendrick, brother of the Laird of Arnprior. Harm me or one of mine, and you'll rain hell and Clan Kendrick down on your damned heads."

That dire threat took the fellow slightly aback. The other two bandits exchanged a glance, obviously disconcerted.

"Och, that ain't good," said the one on the horse.

"I thought ye looked familiar," opined the one watching the coachman and groom. "I heard about Kendrick havin' a twin. Yer him, I reckon."

"You reckon correctly. So you'd best be having a care if you want to keep your necks from getting stretched."

"Shut yer bleedin' mouth," snarled the leader.

A thump came from the back of the carriage. Kathleen craned back to see yet another bandit heave a trunk onto the road. When it hit the dirt, the latch gave way, spilling out some of the contents.

"Those are my things!" Jeannie yelped, jerking forward.

Kathleen pulled her back. "It doesn't matter. We can replace everything."

"That's using yer brains." The leader studied her again. "I can think of something else I'd like to use, too. Ye've got a pretty arse, from what I can tell. I'm thinking—"

"Think about it again, and I'll rip out yer damn tongue and shove it down yer feckin' throat," Grant snarled.

Kathleen blinked. Grant's voice had deepened to a terrifying, guttural brogue. She couldn't see his face, but his shoulders had bunched up, as if he were about to spring at their captor and carry out his gruesome threat. He radiated a dangerous, masculine ire that she found immensely reassuring.

The bandit leader obviously found it intimidating, since he took a quick step back.

"Ye'd best listen," Angus said in a sanguine tone. "Kendricks always keep their word, especially when it comes to killin'."

The leader turned his pistol on Angus. "We'll see who's doin' the killin'. I'd shoot ye as soon as look at ye, old fool."

Grant chopped down an impatient hand. "No one with a brain should kill anyone today. Now, why don't you lot prove you have a few brains amongst you and get on with this business."

"Oy, Heckie," said the bandit who'd been rummaging through the boot. "What do you want me to do with this 'ere stuff?"

His leader rounded on him. "Don't use my name, ye

bloody moron. Just go through the rest of them trunks and be quick about it."

"No need to get tetchy," the man protested. "I'm workin' as fast as I can."

Kathleen mentally frowned. While the other three men were obviously Scottish, this one was not. He was English, with what she thought was a—

"Oh, no," Jeannie moaned as the bandit dumped the entire contents of her trunk onto the road.

Kathleen gave her sister a hug as the villain quickly sifted through the pile, strewing items willy-nilly.

When the Englishman got up and pulled Kathleen's trunk from the boot, Heckie waved his gun at Grant.

"Now empty yer pockets, and collect them lasses' purses while yer at it."

Grant extracted his money clip from his coat—a very fat money clip—and threw it at the varlet's feet.

"You too, old man," barked Heckie.

Angus turned his pockets inside out. "I dinna have a shilling to my name. I'm a puir man, ye ken."

"Ye'll be a dead man in a minute. I'll be happy to plug ye right between the eyes."

"You're horrible." Jeannie's voice quavered.

"Ye have no idea, girl. But I'll be happy to show ye if I don't get yer damn purses right now," Heckie said, leering at her.

When Kathleen felt Jeannie shudder, anger surged through her body, pushing aside fear. "Lay a hand on her, and I'll beat you to a bloody pulp," she snarled.

"I'll fetch their purses now," Grant said. "Then you bastards can be on your way."

"Too right," said the man still fiddling with the lock

on Kathleen's trunk. "Don't want some bleedin' villager stumbling along."

The leader waved his pistol again at Grant. "Don't be tryin' anything funny, or I'll shoot that barmy old bastard and take the pretty girl for myself."

Grant turned on his heel so quickly that his greatcoat flared out like a cloak. Although his features were stone-like, his eyes glittered like icy green shards. Fury pulsed off him in waves—a cold, hard force that was utterly terrifying.

The sober-minded businessman had turned into a fierce Highland warrior.

His gaze flickered over her, and some of the fury retreated.

"All right?" he murmured to her.

She nodded.

"Good lass."

He reached into the carriage to retrieve their reticules, then tossed the small bags at the leader's feet. The man swiped them up and shoved them in the pocket of his greatcoat.

"Get that bloody thing open," he barked at the bandit still struggling with Kathleen's trunk. "Shoot the lock off if ye have to."

Kathleen sighed. "There's a key in the green velvet reticule."

"Why didn't ye say so, ye silly bitch."

She resisted the impulse to reply with an unhelpful comment.

The leader found the key and tossed it to his companion, who swiftly opened her trunk and dumped out the contents. Kathleen winced as her new satin evening gown—an unfortunate shade of cream under the circumstances—landed right on top of what looked like horse dung.

It doesn't matter.

None of her clothes mattered, as long as they didn't find—

"Oy, looks like we gots a false bottom 'ere," the bandit triumphantly said.

Kathleen had to force down her horror as he pried away the inner lining with his knife. He extracted a rolled silk pouch, tied with a braided cord.

"Oh, no," Jeannie whispered.

Crouching down, the man opened the pouch, unrolling it on the dirt road. Finely cut stones glittered in the rays of the late afternoon sun. Two diamond-set bracelets, a number of gold chains, and a truly splendid set of pearls Kathleen had received for her sixteenth birthday. Of much less value but infinitely more precious was a small garnet ring, its pretty stone set on a plain gold band. It was the first piece of jewelry Kathleen ever owned, given to her by her mother. The thought of losing it . . .

Heckie nodded, clearly pleased. "Aye, then, let's be off."

"But Kath, that's your mother's ring," Jeannie protested.

"It's fine, dear," Kathleen managed. "It's just a ring."

"But you love it so!"

"Take everything else and leave the ring," Grant said in a hard voice. "It's just a trinket."

The man barked out a laugh. "And why would I do that?"

"To prove yer not a complete piece of shite?" Angus said.

"I've had enough of you, old man," Heckie sneered, turning his pistol on the old fellow.

"All right," Grant snapped. "You've got what you want. Just get on your blasted horses and be on your way."

"I'll be on my way, but what's to stop me from shooting that old coot before I go?"

Grant stepped directly in front of Heckie. "The certainty that wherever you go, I'll find you and kill you."

It was hardly the worst threat made during this gruesome

episode. But Grant's tone was so chilling and the truth of his words so evident that only a fool wouldn't take it seriously.

"Someone's comin'," barked the man on the horse. "I can hear a rider."

Grant leaned in closer to the leader. "Best be on yer way. *Heckie*."

Kathleen could see the man glare at Grant from under the brim of his hat. "We're not done, Kendrick. I promise ye that."

"I'll look forward to our next meeting," Grant replied.

Heckie retreated to his horse. Once they'd all mounted up, they were off, jumping a short hedge and thundering across a meadow toward the woods.

Grant swiftly turned and came to Kathleen and Jeannie. "It's all right now. It's over."

"It's fine," Kathleen managed. "We're fine."

"That was awful," Jeannie said in a tearful voice. "I thought we were going to die."

Grant pulled her in for a quick hug. "They just wanted our money, Jeannie. The rest was bluster."

"But they took Kath's jewels, too."

He grimaced at Kathleen. "I am truly sorry, lass."

"It's fine," she repeated. "As long as we're safe."

It wasn't fine. It was awful, and she wanted to cry over the loss of her mother's ring. Still, they were alive and whole.

"I'm grateful they were scared off," she added. "Is there really a rider coming?"

Angus, who'd gone to talk to the coachman and Robby, gazed up the road. "Aye, there is." Then he snorted. "It's the bloody village vicar, ye ken. Come to our rescue."

Chapter Eleven

"Found it!" The vicar triumphantly held up Jeannie's shoe.

While Angus helped the girls reorganize their trunks, Grant and the vicar retrieved various bits of clothing and personal items scattered about the roadside and ditch. Robby and the coachmen, now armed, kept a careful watch on the surrounding countryside.

Given the unsettled situation, Grant had been tempted to leave the trunks and their contents, returning for them once the sisters were safely stowed at Lochnagar. Kathleen, however, had pointed out that the bandits had taken everything of value, and she refused to leave her undergarments strewn about the roadside for everyone to see. Grant had declined to point out that the road into Dunlaggan was hardly a bustling thoroughfare, which was why they'd been robbed in the first place.

After a few tartly exchanged words, he'd reluctantly given in. But he would not rest easy until the lasses were behind the sturdy walls of his brother's manor house.

"Thank goodness you arrived when you did, Mr. Brown," Jeannie enthused to the vicar, clasping the other shoe to her chest. "We probably would have been *killed* if you'd not come along to rescue us."

Grant swallowed a snort. Though he had an athletic build, Brown was an exceedingly peaceable and rather absent-minded fellow. It was impossible to imagine him affecting any sort of rescue, much less taking on a gang of highwaymen.

Nevertheless, the sound of Brown's horse had spurred the gang to quit the scene. That was a good thing, since Heckie's interest in Kathleen had crossed the invisible line in Grant's head. He'd been seconds away from gutting the man despite the likelihood that he'd have been shot as a result.

Grant had been damned careless with the safety of those in his charge, and for that he wouldn't forgive himself. Still, who could have foreseen highwaymen operating this close to Lochnagar? It didn't make any sense. Not on Graeme's watch, practically under his magistrate-brother's nose.

"You're very kind, Miss Jeanette," Brown said as he climbed out of the ditch. "But it was lucky the poltroons didn't know it was I who was the rider. Vicars aren't very intimidating, you know, except from the safety of our pulpits."

When he handed Jeannie her shoe, the girl gazed up at him with a dazzled smile. "Oh, no. You definitely saved us. Didn't he, Kath?"

"Every little bit helps," replied Kathleen as she carefully tugged a thistle that was enmeshed in a delicate lace scarf. When the lace ripped, she sighed and pitched the scarf into the trunk.

"Sorry, lass," Grant said with a sympathetic grimace.

He finished dusting off her books with his handkerchief before placing them back in her trunk.

Those books had surprised him. Expensively bound, they contained detailed illustrations of gardening plans and beautiful drawings of various types of fauna. She'd clearly been distressed to see them so casually tossed aside—and a little embarrassed when Grant had retrieved them from under the carriage. Muttering something about her *hobby*, she'd then hurried off to rescue a blushing Mr. Brown, who'd discovered her stays behind a bush.

Grant had not taken her for the gardening type. Then again, his *Sassenach* beauty was full of surprises, she was.

His brain mentally stumbled over the notion of thinking of Kathleen as *his*, before refocusing on her.

"What's that, Miss Calvert?" he asked.

"I said that it's not your fault," she carefully enunciated, as if he were both slow-witted and hard of hearing. "At least they missed your bags, which is a small blessing."

Grant's plain carpetbag, along with his grandfather's, had been shoved in the back of the boot, behind everything else. In any case, except for his silver-chased pistol, which might as well have been a decoration for all the good it had done them, anything of his could easily be replaced.

"I'd much rather they'd taken mine than yours," he said.

She shrugged, doing her best to put on a brave face. "They're just things, you know. The important thing is that we're all safe."

"Aye, that."

He hated that she'd been robbed of her jewelry, especially the little garnet ring. By her reaction, it obviously held great sentimental value.

She frowned as she rolled up her now mucky evening gown. "I must say that I had no idea the roads in the Highlands were so dangerous. I wouldn't have brought Jeannie along if I'd realized."

"I'm just as surprised as you are," Grant dryly replied.

Fiddling with the broken lock on Kathleen's trunk, Angus nodded. "There haven't been highwaymen in these parts for years. Now, London is a different story, ye ken, with its fleshpots. Full of rum coves and all sorts of diddlers and cheats."

"Dear me," said Brown, looking scandalized by such reckless use of cant.

Almost as scandalized as when he'd found Kathleen's stays. With two fingertips, he'd carried them at arm's length, his face as red as a strawberry. Kathleen had quickly stuffed the offending object into her trunk, but not before Grant glimpsed pink satin ribbons and a lot of pink lace. He'd had a sudden, wildly inappropriate desire to see more of her underthings, specifically while she was wearing them.

"Kath and I have never been robbed in London, though," Jeannie dubiously said. "Not that we ever stray very far from Mayfair, much less go to the fleshpots."

"Goodness, one certainly hopes not," exclaimed Brown.

Angus tapped his nose. "Well, Vicar, I could tell ye some stories—"

"Grandda, you have never even been to London," Grant interrupted as he closed Kathleen's trunk and hoisted it into the boot. "Much less to any fleshpots."

"Now, see here, laddie—"

"May I remind you and everyone else that we have just been robbed by armed bandits," Grant said with asperity. "We need to go. *Now*."

Kathleen briskly nodded. "Quite right. Thank you for giving us the time to gather up our things."

She plucked the shoes from her sister's hands and bent

over to place them in Jeannie's trunk, shoving down the rumpled contents so the lid could be closed.

"I'm sure we're fine, especially with Mr. Brown here to protect us," Jeannie said as she regarded the vicar with a worshipful gaze.

Kathleen glanced up at her sister with some alarm. Then, muttering something under her breath, she went back to her struggle with the overstuffed trunk.

Brown failed to notice his new admirer's youthful enthusiasm, since he was currently transfixed by something else—namely, Kathleen's shapely arse. Grant had to repress an overwhelming impulse to toss the right, bloody reverend into the ditch.

Angus dug an elbow into his side. "Looks like ye might have a little competition."

"Don't be an idiot," Grant replied.

He stalked past Brown and hunkered down next to Kathleen, who was now struggling with the lock. "Here, lass, let me do that."

She breathed out such a sad sigh that it almost broke his heart. "My fingers don't seem to want to work."

"You've had a bad shock, but we'll get you to Lochnagar and you can have a nice rest."

"I'd rather a nice brandy, to tell you the truth."

Since she was still pale, her freckles standing out like a fey dusting of spice, Grant agreed that a stiff drink was in order.

He clicked the lock shut and stood up holding the trunk.

"Careful, sir," Kathleen said. "It's quite heavy."

"Here, let me help you," Brown said.

"No need." Grant brushed past him.

Well, *shoved* past him might be a more accurate

description. And, yes, his grandfather's chuckle made it clear he was acting like a jealous boob.

After he stowed the trunk, he moved around to the front of the carriage. "All set, Robby?"

The groom, who was standing guard with Grant's pistol, nodded. "All set, sir."

"I'll take the pistol, then. I'm going to ride up top with Danvers. You'll ride inside with my grandfather and the ladies."

Kathleen frowned. "Surely that's not necessary. I cannot imagine those bastards—"

"Goodness," Brown said with a cough.

"Er, those dreadful men will return," she finished.

Grant bit back a smile. "It's just a precaution."

Then he glanced at Brown, who was staring at Kathleen. The blasted idiot couldn't seem to keep his eyes off her.

"Don't let us keep you, Vicar," he said.

Kathleen's delicate eyebrows shot up, probably because he'd sounded as hostile as he felt.

Brown, oblivious to his tone, beamed at Kathleen. "I wouldn't dream of abandoning the ladies in their hour of need. I will happily escort the carriage to Lochnagar."

Jeannie clasped her hands together. "Would you, sir? I would feel *so* much safer if you came with us."

"Of course, Miss Jeanette."

"Please call me Jeannie."

"Oh, God," Kathleen muttered.

Obviously recovered from the Kade debacle, it appeared Jeannie had found a new object for her impulsively romantic attentions.

"Thank you, but your services aren't required, Vicar," Grant said. "Besides, you don't even carry a pistol."

Brown reached into his pocket and gingerly extracted a small pistol.

"Got a little popper, do ye?" Angus said.

"How dashing," Jeannie exclaimed.

Actually, Brown was the opposite of dashing. Nor, as far as Grant knew, had the vicar ever needed to carry a weapon in these parts. True, there'd been a spot of trouble with local smugglers at one point, but Graeme had taken care of that. Lochnagar and the neighboring village were now as peaceful and safe as the local kirk.

"Why the hell are you carrying a pistol?" Grant asked. "Do you even know how to use it?"

The vicar all but bristled with clerical dignity. "Of course. And may I inform you that Sir Graeme himself suggested I carry it."

Angus grimaced. "Och, that's nae good."

"That, Mr. MacDonald, is an understatement," Brown morosely replied.

"Have another cup of tea," Sabrina suggested. "It's just the thing to settle your stomach."

Kathleen smiled at her cousin. "My stomach is fine, surprisingly. Highwaymen would seem to be an outstanding cure for twitchy insides."

As soon as the villain had shoved his pistol against Grant's head, Kathleen no longer thought about her digestive ills. Though upset about the theft of her jewels, she was supremely grateful that their party had escaped unharmed. Later, perhaps, she'd have a good cry over Mamma's ring. For now, she would be happy they'd finally arrived at Lochnagar, safe and sound.

"Try one of these cheddar and chive scones," Jeannie said. "They're excellent."

Her sister, although still rattled, had mostly recovered from their ordeal—due in no small part to the arrival of the attractive Mr. Brown. Kathleen had the distinct feeling his timely appearance might turn out to be a mixed blessing where Jeannie was concerned.

"Yes, I'd best have one before you eat them all, pet," Kathleen joked.

Jeannie shrugged as she plucked up another scone. "I can't help it. I'm starving."

"I admire your fortitude, especially after such a dreadful experience," Sabrina wryly said.

Kathleen smiled at her cousin. "We're very relieved to be off the road. And you've made us feel so welcome that it's like coming home after a long journey."

Sabrina, seated next to Kathleen on the stylish Hepplewhite settee, reached for the silver teapot and refilled Kathleen's cup.

"That is exactly how I want you to feel. Whatever you need, Graeme and I will do our best to provide it." She smiled at Kathleen. "I know this wasn't your first choice for social exile, but I do hope you will be comfortable here."

Kathleen wrinkled her nose. "Sorry, I don't mean to be ungrateful."

Her cousin's sapphire-blue gaze twinkled with good humor. "We all know where you'd like to be, if given a choice."

"Ireland," Jeannie said around a mouthful of scone.

"Well . . . true." Kathleen cast an admiring glance around the drawing room. "But Lochnagar is splendid. You've done a bang-up job with the place, Sabrina."

On their arrival a few hours ago, she'd discovered that Lochnagar was more than just a necessary port in a storm. A tower house in the classic Scottish style, it was sturdily built from lovely weathered stone. It stood on top of a gradual rise and commanded a splendid view over rolling glens and meadows, with craggy peaks looming in the distance. The old manor, with its tall, matching towers flanking the center hall, perfectly fit the rugged landscape.

While neither the house itself nor the surrounding countryside was anything like the lush and gentle environment of Kathleen's childhood, Lochnagar held a stark beauty, nonetheless.

Still, it was mind-boggling to see her sophisticated cousin, always so comfortable in her luxurious Mayfair existence, in such a setting. As soon as Sabrina had rushed out of the house to greet them, Kathleen could tell that she was deliriously happy with her new life. Always a lovely and cheerful person, she now radiated joy and vitality. Sabrina was a wizard at organization, and had found her perfect life managing everything and everyone in her orbit, including her adoring husband.

And although they had yet to meet Sabrina's baby son, since he was napping, it was clear motherhood agreed with her, as well. It was clear that *everything* agreed with her.

Kathleen was thrilled for her but couldn't suppress a mild tinge of envy. Not over the husband and baby, of course. She had *no* desire for anything of that sort. But Kathleen longed for the day when she too would be where she most wished to be, finally in charge of her life and settling down in the place she loved most in the world.

"It's taken quite a bit of work to get the place up to scratch," Sabrina said as she offered Kathleen a scone from the generous tea service. "And we still have much to do in the oldest parts of the house." She rolled her eyes. "Don't even ask me about the water closets."

Kathleen laughed. "I won't. This room is beautiful, though."

The main drawing room, which faced the front lawn and looked out over fields toward the road, was an elegant yet comfortable mix of antique and current styles. A pair of fashionable striped silk wing chairs flanked the fireplace on the opposite side of the room, along with a scattering of padded benches and another Hepplewhite settee.

The men were gathered on that side. The twins, along with Mr. Brown, were drinking whisky and discussing today's events, keeping their voices low so as not to upset Jeannie.

"This room was utterly grim when we first arrived," Sabrina drolly replied. "The curtains were in tatters, mice had got at the carpet, and the chimney gave off the most blood-curdling moans."

Jeannie suddenly looked worried. "You don't have ghosts, do you?"

"It was just from an old bird's nest stuck in the chimney," Sabrina replied. "There are no ghosts at Lochnagar. Graeme wouldn't allow it. He says ghosts are bad-tempered morons who don't have the brains to get themselves off to where they belong. He absolutely refuses to have one on the premises."

"That's a refreshing viewpoint," Kathleen said.

Jeannie whooshed out a relieved sigh. "Good. It's fun to think about ghosts, but I don't think I'd like to stay if you actually had one."

Sabrina held up a hand, as if taking an oath. "Word of a Kendrick. No ghosts, ghoulies, or anything else of a supernatural constitution."

"Just obnoxious bandits, I'm afraid," said Graeme, reaching down to swipe up a macaroon from a stacked plate of pastries.

Kathleen hadn't even noticed him cross the room.

"Darling, you really shouldn't creep up on us," Sabrina gently scolded. "You're worse than any ghost."

"But I'm better looking than any ghost." He popped the macaroon into his mouth.

Grant strolled over to join them, Reverend Brown trailing in his wake.

"Since ghosts are generally dressed in grave clothes and often missing an eyeball or various appendages," Grant commented, "that's no high bar even for you."

"Och, dinna forget that I'm the good-looking one here, laddie," his twin retorted.

Jeannie frowned. "But you both look exactly alike."

In one sense, that was true. Their physical resemblance was startling, and already Kathleen had noticed they shared certain mannerisms. But they were also quite different. Graeme was clearly the more restless of the two, and seemed disinclined to sit in one place for too long. In contrast, Grant's personality conveyed a quiet steadiness and an almost unimpeachable sense of calm.

Except when he was threatening to rip out a man's tongue and shove it back down his throat. He'd rather lost his calm in that particular moment.

Graeme winked at Jeannie. "No, I'm definitely the good-looking one. Ask anyone."

Kathleen pretended to study them. "Now that you mention it, I believe you *are* the better-looking twin."

Grant lifted a sardonic eyebrow. "But I'm the smart one. Ask anyone."

Jeannie, who tended to take things literally, shook her head. "I still think you look exactly alike." She cast a dubious look at Grant. "Are you really smarter than Sir Graeme?"

"Absolutely," Grant said. "Just ask Sabrina. She'll vouch for me."

Despite the unpleasant events of the afternoon, Kathleen had never seen Grant so relaxed. Clearly, he was happy to be with his twin again, even under less than propitious circumstances.

Graeme smiled at his wife. "I don't need brains anymore. I've got Sabrina to do all my thinking for me."

"That shouldn't be very taxing," Grant teased.

"And it means I win all the arguments," Sabrina added.

"Not all the time, love." Graeme's smile suddenly went sly. "In fact, just last night—"

Grant elbowed him. "I think it's time for more tea."

"Ouch," Graeme said. "That actually hurt."

"And there's more where that came from, if you don't behave yourself." Grant slightly jerked his head in Jeannie's direction.

"You've all had a difficult day," Graeme protested. "I'm just trying to lighten the mood."

"Don't strain yourself," his brother dryly replied.

Graeme's extremely mild innuendo had naturally sailed right over Jeannie's head. Mr. Brown, however, was blushing again, which Kathleen supposed was the appropriate reaction from a vicar. The poor man had almost fainted dead away when he'd stumbled upon her undergarments in the bushes.

"Miss Jeannie, I do hope you're feeling much more the thing," Brown said, as if eager to change the topic.

"Such a dreadful introduction to Lochnagar for you and your sister."

When he directed a warm smile at Kathleen, a tiny frisson of warning filtered into her brain. She thought she'd caught a few admiring glances since their chance encounter, but one generally didn't expect to win a gentleman's admiration in the aftermath of a holdup—especially with one's unmentionables strewn about the countryside.

"I'm ever so much better," Jeannie earnestly said. "It was frightening, but then you came along and scared those awful men away. It was so *terribly* brave of you."

The vicar looked momentarily disconcerted by Jeannie's girlish enthusiasm. And knowing her sister, Kathleen was *massively* disconcerted by the adoring look in her big, blue eyes as she gazed up at the vicar.

As if this day hadn't been bad enough, it now seemed clear that Jeannie had found another inappropriate object for her affections.

"It truly was an accident that I stumbled upon you when I did," Brown modestly replied. "Nothing brave about it at all."

"That's certainly true," Grant commented.

His response sounded almost hostile.

Apparently, Kathleen wasn't the only person who read it as such. The vicar was peering at Grant with some puzzlement, while Graeme was making a poor show of hiding a smirk.

"We must all be grateful that no one was injured," Sabrina smoothly interjected. "One's health is what truly matters. Belongings can always be replaced."

"Except for Kath's jewelry," Jeannie said. "Some of it was her mother's."

"Yes, and I'll be dealing with that," Graeme said, turning

serious. "We'll get to the bottom of this, Kathleen. I promise we'll find your jewels."

That seemed a rather dicey promise to make, even if Graeme was a former inquiry agent.

"Thank you," she said. "But I don't want to put you to any trouble—or put you in danger. Not over silly pieces of jewelry."

"It's not silly," Jeannie said with dogged loyalty. "Your mamma gave you that ring."

"Yes, but the fact that *you're* safe is what truly matters to me," Kathleen replied.

"That you are *all* safe," Brown said, soulfully pressing a hand to his chest. "Miss Calvert, your safety counts more than any piece of jewelry, no matter how precious."

Grant's eyes narrowed to irritated slits as he studied the vicar.

"Thank you," Kathleen hastily said, hoping Brown didn't notice Grant's rather mystifying disapproval.

"If there's anything I can do to help," Brown added, "you need simply ask. You and your sister both, of course."

Jeannie clasped her hands. "*Thank* you, sir."

Kathleen tried to ignore the fact that the twins were now regarding the vicar with identically sardonic expressions.

Then Grant looked over at her. "Never fear, Kathleen. Graeme will find your jewels."

She blinked, startled by the use of her given name as well as by the quiet confidence in his voice.

"Ah, yes," she said, blushing like a complete idiot.

Kathleen knew herself to be the opposite of shy, but there was something about Grant Kendrick that made her go warm and cozy inside, as if he'd just snuggled her up in a deliciously warm blanket.

Idiot. You'd have better luck with the vicar.

Sadly, she didn't want the vicar's attention.

"I'd make more progress with this problem if you weren't so ready to hare off back to Glasgow," Graeme said to his twin.

"Please don't run off, dear," Sabrina added. "You know we'd love for you to stay."

Grant's gaze remained on Kathleen for a moment before he gave Sabrina a polite smile. "I'd like nothing better, but I can't leave Royal in a lurch."

"Och," Graeme said. "Royal can manage."

"Sir Graeme, please feel free to call on me if you need any assistance," Brown earnestly said. "I am more than happy to do what I can to assist you in addressing these nefarious incidents."

Grant, again quite pointedly, rolled his eyes.

Jeannie put down her teacup. "What nefarious incidents are you talking about? Have there been other robberies?"

"Nothing at all to worry about, my dear." Sabrina transferred another scone to the girl's plate. "Kathleen, I cannot tell you how happy I am that you're here. My gardens are a dreadful mess. Our gardener, a lovely fellow but *quite* elderly, desperately needs some expert help."

That was a clear dodge, of course, intended to distract Jeannie.

"I'm simply an amateur," Kathleen replied, "though I'm certainly happy to help."

"How interesting," Grant said, picking up the discussion. "Do you actually design gardens?"

"Kath knows everything about gardens," Jeannie said. "She even planted one of the kitchen gardens at Greystone Court, in Ireland."

"Goodness, Miss Calvert," the vicar said in an admiring tone. "You are clearly a woman of many talents."

That unfortunate compliment arrested Jeannie's attention, and her gaze flickered suspiciously between Kathleen and Brown.

"I only did some of the work, dearest," she hastily said. "I simply helped our head gardener. It's really a hobby more than anything else."

It was more than that, of course. But she rarely had the opportunity to exercise one of her few true skills, because Helen wouldn't let her anywhere near the ornamental gardens.

Sabrina gave her an encouraging smile. "The preliminary designs you sent along are excellent."

Kathleen wriggled her fingers. "I'm a bit rusty. I do hope your gardener won't mind me mucking about and experimenting a bit."

"Since our gardener spends most of his time dozing in the potting shed," Graeme said, "you'll be just fine."

"I also enjoy gardening," Brown said. "Please call on me, if needed. And if you and your sister wish to leave Lochnagar at any time, perhaps to visit Dunlaggan, I would be happy to escort you—especially after today's distressing events."

"Which will *not* be repeated," Graeme firmly said.

Brown gave him a gracious nod. "I have every confidence you will see the villains brought to justice, Sir Graeme. Given how busy you are, I am simply expressing my willingness to serve as escort for Miss Calvert and her sister. You cannot wish the ladies to go about alone."

"That's why we have footmen," Graeme replied. "To escort the ladies."

"And your parish work must keep you busy," Grant added in a bland voice. "All those elderly widows must take up a fair bit of your time, not to mention the preparation for your sermons. They're rather long, as I recall from my last visit."

Graeme choked out a laugh that he quickly smothered when Sabrina scowled at him.

"Blasted macaroons," he said. "Coconut always gets caught in my throat."

"My widows are no problem, Mr. Kendrick," Brown said in a dignified tone. "And I am *quite* efficient when it comes to writing my sermons. I will have plenty of time to help Miss Calvert. With anything."

Hell and damnation.

On top of everything else, why did she need the blasted vicar complicating her life?

Behind Mr. Brown's back, the twins looked at each other and rolled their eyes at exactly the same moment.

"Goodness, look at the time," Sabrina said, making a show of peering at the gilded bronze clock on the mantel. "Gus should be awake by now."

Graeme snorted. "If not, Angus will have seen to it."

Almost as soon as they'd stepped foot out of the carriage, Angus had insisted on going to the nursery to see his new great-grandson and namesake. Sabrina had tried to persuade him to wait until the infant was awake, but the old fellow was not to be denied.

"You know Grandda and babies," Grant said with a wry smile. "An entire *Sassenach* brigade couldn't keep him away from the latest Kendrick bairn."

"The poor nursemaids will probably smother Angus with a pillow before the week is out," Graeme commented.

The vicar, predictably, looked shocked.

"I can't wait for you to meet our darling boy," Sabrina said to Kathleen. "Even though he's mine, I think he's the most adorable baby ever born."

"He's a fine boy, Lady Kendrick," Brown said.

"Even if he did scream all the way through his christening," Sabrina joked. "I hope he'll be better behaved for our guests."

Kathleen mentally sighed. Crying babies—it wanted only this to make life perfectly annoying.

An awkward silence descended on the group.

"Well, I suppose I should be going," Brown finally said with reluctance.

"I suppose you should," Grant replied.

Kathleen almost gaped at him.

Sabrina, as usual, smoothly covered the awkward moment.

"My dear David, thank you so much for your help." She rose to give the vicar her hand. "We're ever so grateful."

"Can't Mr. Brown stay for dinner?" Jeannie asked in a plaintive voice. "He's had a trying day too, you know."

"Er," Sabrina said in hesitation, as Brown looked at her hopefully.

They were interrupted by the fortuitous appearance of Angus, carrying a small bundle wrapped in a gaily colored tartan plaid. Sadly, the bundle was emitting considerable and decidedly unhappy noises.

"The laddie's awake," Angus said. "And he's a wee bit chippy."

"Oh, dear." Sabrina hurried over. "He's been colicky, poor love."

She took the bundle from Angus, murmuring soothing coos as she expertly rocked him in her arms. Unfortunately, the wailing only grew louder.

Jeannie scrunched up her nose. "Do all colicky babies cry like that?"

"I'm afraid so," Graeme said, raising his voice over the racket.

The vicar looked appropriately sympathetic. "Poor little tyke."

"It's the wind," Angus said. "It'll pass."

Graeme winked at his grandfather. "Literally, one hopes."

"Takes after his da," Angus commented. "Graeme was always a windy one. All but blew the puir nursemaids out of the room."

He punctuated that bon mot by providing a verbal approximation of such windiness.

"I really *must* be going, Lady Kendrick," the vicar quickly said as he turned three shades of red.

Sabrina gave him a pained smile. "Graeme, please show David out."

"Not necessary." Brown was now backing toward the door. "Miss Calvert, I hope to see you—"

The baby suddenly emitted a sound that remarkably echoed his great-grandfather's verbal effort.

Brown turned and fled.

"Goodbye," Kathleen called after him. "Thank . . . oh, well, I suppose I'll have to thank him later."

"Grandda, that was quite rude," Sabrina sternly said.

"It was a bit much, even for you," Graeme added.

Angus shrugged. "Did the trick, though. Yon parson couldn't wait to escape."

"Finally," Grant said.

Sabrina jiggled the crying baby. "David is a very nice man, if a bit earnest."

"And that *nice man* has a schoolboy crush on my wife," Graeme said. "Which is more than a little annoying."

"Nonsense, dear. And David is an excellent vicar."

"Excellent at unexpectedly calling at dinnertime," her husband replied.

"He's just a little lonely."

"He can be lonely with someone else for a change." He flashed a sly smile at Kathleen. "Like—"

Jeannie jumped to her feet, her cheeks flushed. "I think he's splendid, and I intend to tell him just that. In fact, I'm going to ask him for a drive around Lochnagar. Maybe I could send him a note tomorrow."

"That was very nice of him to offer, dear," Kathleen said. "But perhaps we could settle in a bit before imposing ourselves on Mr. Brown. He is, after all, a busy man."

Jeannie whipped around to glare at her. "He already said he had time. Why are you being so mean about him?"

Kathleen held up her hands. "I'm not being mean, but we just met the man. Not to mention we just got robbed, and I'm sure—"

"I don't care about any of that," Jeannie exclaimed. "And I don't care what anyone says. I think Mr. Brown is wonderful."

"Yes, dearest, but—"

Jeannie stalked from the room.

"Our Miss Jeannie is obviously a feisty lass," Graeme wryly said.

Kathleen sighed. "Sorry. She's not usually this . . ."

"Fashed?" he supplied.

"I suppose that's as good a word as any. Again, I apologize for her behavior. How dreadful that we've both been foisted on you."

"Nonsense," Sabrina said. "We're thrilled that you're here."

"Jeannie's a grand little lass," Grant said to Kathleen.

"She had a proper fright today, so she's unsettled. She'll get over it soon."

"I hope she gets over the vicar soon," Kathleen gloomily replied.

"Well, at least she's over our Kade," Angus said.

Graeme lifted an eyebrow. "Do I even want to know?"

"Definitely not," Kathleen said.

Sabrina smiled. "We'll get Jeannie sorted. Right now, it's time to meet Master Angus Musgrave Kendrick, better known as Gus."

Kathleen mustered a smile. "I would be delighted, of course."

"Would you like to hold him?" Sabrina asked, bringing him over.

"Oh, best not," Kathleen hastily said. "He's still crying."

"He'll do that anyway," Graeme said. "You should probably get used to it."

"Still, ah—"

When Sabrina plopped the baby in Kathleen's arms, she had no choice but to take him.

Her cousin arranged Kathleen's left arm. "Just shift a bit to support his little head."

She carefully made the adjustment. "I'm not very good with babies, Sabrina."

"You're doing fine. Just rock him."

She awkwardly rocked the baby, clutching him tightly. No matter how windy or loud he got, she would *not* drop him.

"Huh," said Angus after several moments. "Would ye look at that?"

Kathleen glanced at him. "Look at what?"

"He's stopped cryin', ye ken."

Kathleen looked at the bundle in her arms, truly focusing for the first time. A red-haired baby with flushed, damp cheeks and a soft green gaze stared up at her, apparently transfixed. And although he gave a few quiet hiccups, he had definitely stopped crying. In fact, he seemed to be smiling at her.

"You're a natural," Sabrina said, beaming.

"Thank God," Graeme said. "You can help out the nursemaids. I swear they're ready to give their notice."

"But I'm terrible with babies, and children, too," Kathleen protested as she rocked Gus. "Just look at Jeannie. I can't do anything to make her behave."

Grant strolled up to her, a warm smile lighting his eyes— eyes that were the same color as the baby's fascinated gaze. That warm smile rather muddled her insides.

Or perhaps it was just her astonishment that she had not dropped Gus, and that he appeared content in her arms.

"Well, lass," Grant said, his deep voice infused with his lovely Highland brogue, "it seems that yer, in fact, the very opposite of terrible."

Chapter Twelve

Grant held up his glass as Graeme joined him at the hearth. His twin's small study was well appointed with sturdy furniture and a splendid view out the bay windows to the peaks in the distance.

"I thought Brown would never take himself off, but leave it to Angus to do the trick," Graeme said as he poured Grant a dram.

"If there's one thing Grandda excels at it's offending the best sorts of people."

Graeme settled into the matching leather club chair on the other side of the hearth, propping a booted foot against a cast-iron firedog. "You weren't on your best party manners with Brown, either, I noticed. What set you off, old man?"

Grant leisurely studied the pale liquid in his glass, then took a swallow before he replied. "This is excellent. Almost as good as the stuff we used to distill at Kinglas."

Graeme snorted. "It's a damn sight better than our old home brew. Although I will say that our youthful escapades have been surprisingly helpful in setting up the new distillery."

"Is that what we're calling it now? Youthful escapades?"

After they'd been booted out of university, Grant and Graeme had returned home and set up an illegal still in a remote glen on Kinglas lands. Angus had come up with the idea to keep them busy and out of trouble. It also put extra blunt in their pockets, since they were able to sell three or four small casks a month to local publicans who were willing to keep secret their source.

Poor Nick had known nothing about the mad scheme until customs agents had come knocking on the castle door. Their big brother had been forced to pay a large fine to keep them out of trouble. It had resulted in a tremendous row, exacerbated when Angus had insisted it was the God-given right of any Scotsman to make his own whisky, *Sassenach* laws be damned. Vicky, Kade's governess at the time, had finally convinced Nick not to toss them all out on their sorry arses.

From that moment on, Vicky had made it her mission to see that *all* the Kendrick men trod the straight and narrow before they drove her future husband completely out of his mind. Given what hardheads they all were, especially Angus, she'd been remarkably successful.

Graeme flashed a crooked grin. "Sometimes a spot of crime does actually pay."

"And you call yourself a magistrate."

"Rather ironic, you must admit."

"'Insane' is the word I'd be inclined to use. But on a serious note, oh great Sir Graeme, why the hell are highway-men roaming about your district? And why did you need to drag me away from the others to discuss it?"

"Drag you away from Kathleen, I believe you mean," his brother said with an annoying smirk.

"That is not what I meant, and stop trying to bait me. It won't work."

"No? Then why are you scowling at me?"

"Because you're a tosser?"

His brother laughed. "All right, but you *were* fashed with Brown. Admit it."

"I admit to nothing except for concern that the ladies apparently can't step foot outside the house without protection."

Graeme shook his head. "I'm thinking Jeannie is the biggest worry. That girl seems like an accident waiting to happen. And I cannot tell you how thrilled I am to be the one now tasked with keeping her out of trouble for the next three months."

"Sorry, old man, but it wasn't my idea," Grant replied with a sympathetic grimace.

Graeme frowned at the small peat fire simmering in the grate. "I know. It's just that I'm up to my ears with a new baby, a new distillery, and a very *not* new estate to get back in order. Poor Sabrina is also run off her feet, although she puts a good face on it."

"From what I can tell, you've done a bang-up job on the estate. It's looking miles better than it was the last time I was here." Grant held up his glass. "And you're clearly having success with this, too."

"Who knew that a motley band of former smugglers could produce such an excellent product?"

That was yet another amusing irony of his twin's life. Lochnagar Distilleries had grown out of a local smuggling ring Graeme had broken up last year. The smugglers had even kidnapped him at one point. That's when Graeme had met Magnus Barr. Magnus had never been comfortable with a life of crime and had leapt at Graeme's offer to open a legal operation, made possible by recent changes to the law. As it so happened, the former smuggler was already crafting some of the finest whisky in the Highlands.

With Nick helping to secure the appropriate licenses, Lochnagar Distilleries was well on its way to becoming a grand success.

"Apparently *you* knew," Grant said. "But now it appears that someone is throwing a spanner into the works."

"Unfortunately true."

"You obviously don't want to talk about it in front of the ladies or Angus."

Truthfully, Grant had not put up much of a fight when his brother suggested they repair to his study on the pretense of discussing distillery business. He'd made a complete fool of himself over Kathleen by snapping at the vicar, for one thing. It was becoming embarrassingly obvious that his Irish lass was turning him into an addlepated moron.

"And here I thought I was being so subtle," Graeme joked.

"The great spy is losing his touch, I'm afraid. Must be all the wedded bliss."

"Och, Sabrina keeps me on my toes, ye ken." Then he winked at Grant. "And keeps me up—"

Grant held up a hand. "Don't. Bad enough I have to put up with all the happy Kendrick couples making sheep's eyes back in Glasgow. Revolting, it is."

"Perhaps you need a bit of happy coupling yourself, eh lad? It's the cure for what ails, ye ken."

"I am happy to report that I am in fine health. Now, shall we get on to discussing *your* problem, before I am forced to bash you in the noggin?"

"Message received. But the thing is . . ." Graeme grimaced. "I do actually need your help, brother. The situation around here is not good."

Grant sighed. "More than just a bit of bad luck that we ran into highwaymen, I take it?"

"Why do you think I told Brown to carry a pistol?"

"That was probably a mistake. He hasn't a clue how to use the damn thing."

"Then he'd better learn."

Grant's twin was the most capable and fearless person he knew, and the one least likely to raise the alarm. "Stop talking in riddles, lad. What's going on?"

"What's going on is . . . well, I suppose a crime spree is the best way to describe it."

"In sleepy, little Dunlaggan?"

The local village was more of a hamlet, and peaceful. Besides Lochnagar, there were only a few other estates in the vicinity, and most were parceled out to tenant farmers or crofters. The quiet district, tucked away in a corner of the Highlands, was not a place where one expected crime sprees.

"And not related to the smuggling gang you broke up last year?" Grant added.

"Not at all. Jackie Barr, the gang leader, is sitting in prison in Edinburgh. The other members of the Barr family were happy to escape that life and are now gainfully employed as crofters or workers at the distillery. A few of them have even been victimized lately."

"What sort of crimes are we talking about?"

"Until recently, it was a combination of petty thefts and vandalism. Clothing stolen from a drying line or a small item or two from local shops, and a few windows broken overnight at the distillery." He twirled a hand. "You know."

"Not much different from some of the things we got up to when we were lads," Grant said.

"That's what I thought at first—just a few cheeky lads out for a lark. I figured I'd track them down and put a proper scare into them, but no such luck."

"What else is happening?"

"In the last three weeks, the crimes have become more serious. Two of the local crofters had livestock stolen. And two houses in the village were broken into last week. Money was taken, along with some rather good pieces of silver."

"Definitely not cheeky lads, then."

Graeme shook his head. "Neither of us would have had a clue how to get rid of stolen cattle, back in the day."

"Are there any towns around here big enough to merit a pawnbroker who traffics in stolen goods?"

"Only one, and I paid a visit there last week. But nothing."

"Nothing, as in no contact, or nothing as in not willing to speak to a local magistrate?"

Graeme scoffed. "The proprietor was unimpressed with my credentials and had no problem informing me of such."

"How shocking. He must have been deranged."

"Or thinking that he was innocent," Graeme dryly replied. "The terms cakedoodle, nincompoop, and totty-headed noddy were applied to me rather liberally."

Grant had to laugh. "Are you sure you weren't talking to Angus?"

"He was worse than Angus. And I might be a cake-doodle, but I'm a cakedoodle who also happens to be a magistrate. Anyway, I'm convinced the man was telling the truth. He was also certain that none of the local nibblers were involved in this, either."

Grant propped his foot against the other firedog. "Why

Dunlaggan? It's hardly rich pickings for your average thief."

"Aye. It makes no bloody sense."

"How are the locals taking it?"

"They were annoyed by the pilfering, but now they're genuinely worked up. Understandably so."

"Which means Sabrina is worked up."

Graeme sighed. "She actually lost her temper with me the other day. Called me *Sir Graeme* and told me to do my blasted job or else she'd do it for me."

"That must have been a terrible blow to the great spy's pride."

Graeme reached over and punched him in the arm. "I'm not a spy anymore, ye silly prat."

"Still, no fun having the wife of one's bosom ringing a peal over one's head."

"The poor girl doesn't get much sleep these days, what with the wee laddie being so tetchy. I've hired two bloody nursemaids, but Sabrina still insists on sitting up with Gus half the bloody night."

"I'm thinking it's not the nursemaids who sit up with the bairn the rest of the night. Am I right?"

Graeme scowled at him. "Look, they have to take care of Gus during the day. Besides, when I try to put him down, he cries. Can't let him cry now, can I?"

Grant repressed a smile. "So, Sabrina is sitting up one half of the night, and you're sitting up the other half. Which means neither of you is—"

His brother jabbed him again. "I thought I was the one with the mind in the gutter."

"As I was going to say, neither of you is obviously getting enough sleep."

"We've had our hands full, to tell you the truth. Between

trying to restore the manor and the home farms, helping our tenants and the villagers, and getting the distillery up and running . . ."

"You're run off your feet, and the last thing you need is a gang of bloody bastards running amuck."

Graeme all but growled. "And what happened today takes it to a new level. It's not just a few petty thieves taking advantage of a peaceful village. It's a well-organized dangerous gang."

"I got that impression when a gun was shoved against my skull," Grant wryly said.

His twin grimaced. "I'm so sorry, lad."

"Not your fault. So, what's the plan?"

"I have to find a way to get on top of it. Someone's bound to get hurt, sooner or later. If nothing else, a villager is going to get twitchy one night and accidentally shoot a neighbor just on his way home from the pub."

"You'd best retrieve that pistol from Vicar Brown, then. He's likely to shoot himself accidentally."

His twin snorted. "Yer not likin' our good vicar. Again, why?"

"Mind your business, laddie boy. Again, what is the plan, and how do I come into it?"

"I know you're planning on heading back to Glasgow almost immediately, but I really could use your help, Grant. I need someone to bring fresh eyes to this problem and also do some poking around. Try to get wind of something. Of *anything*, at this point."

Grant was silent for a few seconds.

"I know it's a lot to ask," Graeme apologetically added.

"Don't be a moron. Of course I'll stay. I was just thinking through what needs to be done in Glasgow. Royal will have to stay on in the office for a few more weeks. Still, he was already willing to do that, so it shouldn't be a problem."

"You know I wouldn't ask if I didn't truly need your help. I know how much I'm imposing on you."

This time, Grant leaned over and jabbed his brother. "Stop. I'm always here for you, Graeme. Always."

Just as his twin had always been there for him, no matter the trouble. Of course, Graeme was usually the instigator of the trouble, but that hardly mattered. His brother's love and loyalty had always been boundless. Whatever was asked was given, without question or hesitation.

"It's incredibly lucky I am, to have you as my brother," Graeme quietly said. "I'd never have made it without you."

A surge of emotion tightened Grant's throat. Angus had been right all along. He'd not been paying enough attention to his family these last months, especially to his twin. He'd been a selfish prat, narrowing his life down to the demands of his work and numbers in a ledger.

Graeme tilted his head. "All right?"

"Aye, that." Of course Graeme would know exactly what he was thinking. "You do know this means you're stuck with Angus, too. He loves *spy business*, ye ken."

"I know, but I'm hoping he'll be so taken up with Gus that he'll be too busy to interfere."

"Told yourself that, did you?"

As if on cue, the door flew open and Angus stomped in.

"Well, is it sorted?" He wagged a finger at Grant. "We'll not be leavin' yer twin in the lurch, ye ken. I willna be havin' it."

Grant shot his brother an incredulous look. "Did you really discuss this with Angus before you spoke with me?"

Graeme rolled his eyes. "Of course not."

Angus dragged a padded bench over to join them. "Och,

I raised ye both. I know what ye both are thinkin' before ye do."

That was sadly true.

"Yes, Grandda, I'm staying," Grant said.

The old fellow rubbed his hands with anticipation. "So, what's the plan, lads? I'm guessin' we'll be wantin' to look for the gang's bolthole. Start squeezin' the villagers for information. There's got to be someone around here who knows somethin'."

"There is no plan," Graeme tartly replied. "Especially not one that involves you barking at the locals like a mad dog. They're already rattled enough."

"I'll be as gentle as a lamb, and subtle as a snake. They'll never even know I'm squeezin' them."

"You're as subtle as a rampaging bull," Grant said. "And you're not to go poking about the countryside looking for trouble, either."

Their grandfather scoffed. "I never *look* for trouble."

"And yet you always manage to find it."

"But ye need my help, so ye'll have time to be courtin' the fair colleen. Ye have to up yer game, or else that poncy vicar will be cuttin' ye out."

Grant sighed. "It never stops, does it?"

Graeme adopted a mock-thoughtful expression. "Brown is just the sort of pretty fellow the ladies swoon over. Half the girls in the village are mad about him, not that our good vicar ever notices."

Angus pulled out his pipe and tobacco pouch. "He noticed a certain lass today."

"He did seem quite taken with Kathleen." Graeme pointed at Grant. "As Grandda said, you'd best look lively, or our clerical friend will cut you off at the pass."

Grant scowled at his brother. "You're just as ridiculous as Angus."

"I seem to remember a certain brother—my twin, in fact—who did his best to push me directly into the path of a certain Lady Sabrina."

"You needed Sabrina. I don't need anyone."

Graeme and Angus exchanged a look.

"Besides," Grant felt compelled to add, "I'm not here to run after pretty girls—"

"So you *do* think she's pretty," Graeme cut in.

"Of course I think she's pretty. What difference does that make?"

"Ye dinna want to be courtin' a girl ye don't have a fancy for," Angus patiently explained. "Much less marry her."

"This conversation is completely deranged," Grant said. "And I'm not marrying anyone."

Angus heaved a sigh. "I dinna ken why yer so dead-set against marriage. Look at how much good it's done for yon laddie."

"True enough, Grandda," Graeme said. "I even got a knighthood out of it."

"No one will be handing out knighthoods to marry Kathleen Calvert," Grant acidly replied. "Although they probably should, given the trouble she gets up to."

Angus beamed at him. "That's why she needs ye, lad. To keep her out of trouble."

Grant resisted the impulse to start shouting. "Let me explain something clearly. I am staying to help my brother track down a gang of thieves. Since my time is valuable, I will do everything I can to expedite the process. Again, that means no time to court ladies."

Angus now heaved a dramatic sigh. "To my way of thinkin' there's nothin' sadder than an old bachelor, ye ken."

"I am *not* old. And this is—"

"You know Sabrina thinks very highly of Kathleen," Graeme interjected. "And from what I've seen, she's a verra bonny lass."

Grant put his glass down. "Let me make something else perfectly clear. Aside from the fact that I do not have the time for this, Kathleen Calvert has no interest in me. None." He formed his thumb and forefinger into an oval. "Zero. There is literally *no point* to this discussion."

"That's only because ye won't put yer back into it," Angus countered. "Not like the old days, when ye used to have the lassies swarmin' all around ye like flies on a side of overripe beef."

"That is a disgusting analogy, Grandda. And I was an idiot back then, remember? So pardon me if I decline to fall back into old ways in order to charm a woman who is absolutely not interested in me."

"Are you interested in her?" Graeme unexpectedly asked.

Grant's brain momentarily stumbled. "Er . . . of course not."

His brother tilted a skeptical brow at his reply.

Grant finally waved an impatient hand. "It doesn't matter. What *does* matter is that I help you with your problem and then return home where I belong."

Angus leaned forward to fetch a spill from a brass container by the fireplace. "Yer a terrible liar, laddie boy."

"He's actually a very good liar," Graeme said. "It's just that we know him and can see through it."

Grant slapped his hands on the arms of the leather club chair and started to push up. "Right. Since we're now going in circles . . ."

"It's because of yer da, I reckon," Angus said. "He's in yer head again. That's nae good for ye, son."

Grant's entire body froze. His mind froze, too. "What does my father have to do with any of this?"

"It's all that guilt ye still carry around. Grant, ye were just a wee lad back then. It was a terrible thing, but there was nothin' ye could have done to change the outcome."

Grant slowly sank back into the chair as that terrible memory filled his mind. He could still see the blood and hear the sounds of an animal in distress. For a moment, he could even smell the damned heather in the damned field.

Then he slammed the door shut on the memories, as he always had.

"I know that," he said in a calm voice. "I am perfectly fine."

"That's my line, old son," Graeme said.

Grant met his twin's gaze and saw nothing but sympathy and understanding. He also saw the shadow of a long-ago sorrow, one that should definitely be left in the past.

"I've made my peace with it, Grant. So should you," Graeme added.

This time, Grant did stand up. "By talking about it? No, thank you."

His twin shook his head. "All right. You win. No need to get fashed about it."

"I'm not the one who gets fashed—that's you and Angus."

Graeme held up his hands in mock surrender.

"And we're clear that my purpose here is to help you get this mess sorted, correct?" Grant added. "Not court young ladies or any other such nonsense."

"Absolutely clear, old man."

Grant shifted his focus to Angus, who was now making

a show of lighting his pipe. "And you, Grandda? You won't be causing trouble on that front either, correct?"

Angus puffed away, all but enveloping himself in smoke. "Of course not, lad. I'm just a frail old man, ye ken. Couldna cause nae trouble even if I wanted to."

Oh, hell.

"Have another drink?" Graeme asked.

Grant sank back into his chair. "Possibly two."

Chapter Thirteen

"Are you warm enough?" asked Sabrina as she and Kathleen stood at the bottom of the kitchen gardens. "It can get nippy this time of year, even with all this glorious sunshine."

Kathleen, mentally replanting the herb bed, nodded. "This pelisse is quite sturdy. Sabrina, I'm wondering if we might plant basil and perhaps even some lavender over by that brick wall. It's sheltered enough and seems to get quite a bit of sun."

"We're just as likely to get rain and mist, I'm afraid, and the winters can be quite dreadful. Nothing like the mild climate around London, or what you're used to in Ireland."

"The lavender might be pushing it, I suppose." Kathleen snapped her fingers. "Perhaps you could build a small succession house, one for herbs and potted orange plants. Wouldn't that be delightful?"

Sabrina adopted an apologetic smile. "It would. But I'm afraid Cook would be deeply suspicious. When I asked her to make a true English pudding for Christmas, she complained for a week. If I start importing orange trees, I might be forced to deploy smelling salts."

Kathleen scoffed. "Now you're just being silly. I can make a few preliminary sketches of a small greenhouse, if you like. It would tuck in quite nicely between those two outbuildings and the stables."

After she'd taken a proper look at the garden this morning, she'd started drawing up plans in her head. At the very least, it was a welcome distraction from yesterday's distressing events on the road. Also, Jeannie had been difficult, and it had taken a concerted effort to smooth the girl's ruffled nerves and get her comfortably settled.

And then there was Grant. Thinking about him had kept her tossing for half the night. Finally, she'd fallen into slumber, only to be awakened early by some commotion at the other end of the hall. While the fuss had died down almost immediately, images of Grant had again intruded into her muddled brain. One that particularly stood out was the image of him looking at her yesterday when she was holding the baby. His emerald gaze had glittered with a warmth that had set her nerves dancing like fireflies on a summer night.

She'd never imagined Grant Kendrick as a man who could seduce a woman with just one look, but that particular expression had convinced her otherwise.

He'd left the room shortly afterward to speak with his brother. By the time they'd all reconvened for dinner, he'd reverted to his usual polite self, almost as staid and boring as the day she'd met him.

It was all very confusing. It didn't surprise her, though, since she found men in general to be confusing.

Kathleen firmly refocused her thoughts on the garden. "In fact, if you pulled down one of the outbuildings, you could build an even bigger succession house. Then you could have fresh fruit and vegetables all year."

After studying her with an amused expression, Sabrina hooked a hand around Kathleen's arm and led her through a wrought-iron gate at the base of the garden.

"I think you should rest for a few days," her cousin said as they turned right along a neatly graveled path.

It ran along a brick wall that enclosed the kitchen gardens before gently winding away through a meadow behind the manor. The path afforded a lovely view over a rolling landscape of field and glen, broken by the occasional stand of poplar and birch trees. A herd of shaggy cattle grazed in the next field, and smoke curled up from the chimney of a crofter's cottage. In the distance, slate-gray peaks towered in the bright blue sky. It was dramatic and even a bit lonely, but it held its own sort of peace, born of rock and sky, and a horizon that stretched up to the heavens.

"You and Jeannie just arrived," Sabrina continued. "There's no need to throw yourself immediately into work."

"Gardening isn't work." Kathleen breathed in the crisp, clean scent of the Highlands. The bracing air cleared one's head and made anything seem possible, even surviving a winter in Scotland.

"It is up here, because you never know what the day's weather will bring." Sabrina flashed her a smile. "You know what they say—if you don't like the weather in Scotland, wait ten minutes and it's bound to change."

Kathleen laughed. "I'm not sure I approve of such erratic behavior."

"Are we still talking about the weather or about a certain handsome Highlander?" Sabrina asked with a mischievous twinkle.

Drat.

Sabrina had always been adept at reading other people's emotions. But Kathleen was no longer the messy little girl who worshiped her older cousin, no matter how smart and sophisticated she might be.

"The weather," she responded in a breezy voice.

"Really? Because you looked quite odd for a moment, as if you were thinking of someone."

"I was merely trying to recall if I packed any flannel wrappers. It certainly sounds like I'll need them."

Sabrina winked at her. "When one has a brawny Scotsman in one's bed, flannel is not only unnecessary but rather beside the point."

"You're supposed to be teaching me how to behave like a proper young lady, remember? I'd say you're making a rather poor job of it so far," Kathleen wryly said.

Her cousin laughed. "Forgive me, dearest. I'll stop teasing—for now."

Kathleen ignored the last bit. "We'd best step lively if we're going to catch up with the others."

"We've been dreadful dawdlers. Graeme and Grant are likely halfway to the distillery by now."

"They're not the ones I'm worried about."

Sabrina wrinkled her nose. "Yes, Jeannie has developed quite an interest in our poor vicar. And so quickly, too."

Kathleen sighed. "She's turning out to be as impulsive as I was at her age, and she's in love with the idea of being in love. Mr. Brown, alas, is quite attractive, too, which doesn't help."

"You've nothing to fear from David. He is everything a vicar should be, and more."

"Jeannie's not the one in danger, I'm afraid."

Sabrina laughed. "She did rather drag him off, didn't she? When he so clearly wished to spend time with you."

"Rats. I was so hoping that wasn't the case."

"It is definitely the case."

"That won't make life with Jeannie any easier. I'll have to do what I can to discourage him." She flapped a hand. "It's quite ridiculous, since he only met me yesterday, and under less than propitious circumstances."

Circumstances like her undergarments strewn all over the road and beyond.

"While I'm not the least surprised he finds you attractive," said Sabrina, "David's behavior is a bit out of character. He's quite shy, though he certainly seems eager to spend time with you."

"I'm a complete scandal. He should be running in the other direction."

"He doesn't know you're a scandal," Sabrina said in a consoling tone. "Just give it time."

"Thank you for that vote of confidence," Kathleen sarcastically replied. "Perhaps I can scatter more of my undergarments along the drive to the house. That might scare him off."

"Really? I imagine the sight of your frillies did quite the opposite."

"Bloody hell," Kathleen couldn't help muttering.

She'd been surprised that Brown had come calling so quickly, volunteering to take her and Jeannie for a tour in his curricle. Jeannie had responded with enthusiasm, apparently forgetting that Kathleen and carriages did not generally mix.

While she'd been casting about for a polite refusal, Grant had come to her rescue. In a blighting tone, he'd informed Brown that pleasure excursions with young ladies should be kept to a minimum as long as bandits were roaming the countryside. When Graeme had backed up his brother, the vicar had been forced to concede.

When Jeannie had started to argue the issue, Sabrina had

tactfully suggested a group stroll to Lochnagar Distillery, which was on the estate and only about a mile from the manor. The recommendation met all the necessary requirements. Brown could visit with the ladies, and the ladies would be safe on estate grounds, escorted by the gentlemen.

Picking up the pace as they rounded a curve in the path, Kathleen breathed a sigh of relief when she spotted Jeannie and the vicar a few hundred yards ahead. Her sister, clinging to Brown's arm, was chattering away like a magpie. It all looked harmless enough.

"There, nothing to worry about," said Sabrina. "And I see the terrible twins not far ahead of them, so David is properly chaperoned."

"I do apologize for foisting my handful of a little sister on you, Sabrina. Truly, I didn't know what else to do. Jeannie's really very sweet—just a little lost and lonely right now."

Kathleen's throat suddenly constricted. She knew what it meant to feel that sort of loneliness, as if no one understood you. Again, she silently vowed to be there for Jeannie, no matter what.

Sabrina gave her arm a squeeze. "Graeme and I are delighted that you've both come to stay with us. And I am *especially* delighted that little Gus has taken a shine to you. It's rather a miracle, that."

"Believe me, I am just as surprised as you are."

After dinner last night, she had gone—reluctantly, she wasn't too proud to admit—with Sabrina to the nursery. Her cousin had fed the baby and helped the nursemaid put him to bed. Gus had been fine while his mamma was feeding him, but as soon as she'd gently transferred him to his cradle, he'd kicked up an unholy fuss. He'd wriggled under his little blanket, wailing away until his cheeks turned as red as polished apples.

The nursemaid had suggested rocking him in the cradle but, sadly, that had failed to do the trick. Sabrina had finally picked up her son, but Gus had still continued to fuss. Just when Kathleen had been tempted to sneak from the room, Sabrina had turned and swiftly plunked Gus in her arms. Gulping, she'd clutched the little bundle awkwardly to her chest.

And then, as if a spigot had been closed, Gus had stopped crying. When Kathleen had cautiously eased her grip and peered down at him, he stared back, looking just as amazed as she was.

Kathleen had then spent the next half hour trying to get the little devil to sleep. Every time she tried to hand him over to his mother or put him down in the cradle, his sleepy eyes had popped wide and he'd start to wind himself up again. Resigned to her fate, she'd paced the floor with the baby, whiling the time away by chatting softly with Sabrina. Her cousin had entertained her with mind-boggling stories about her courtship with Graeme, and Kathleen had found herself confessing her frustrations with life in the *ton*. Sabrina had listened with quiet sympathy, not making judgments or offering advice.

It was a far cry from Kathleen's life in London. Yet last night in that peaceful nursery tucked under the eaves of the old manor house, she'd felt a sort of contentment she'd not had for a very long time.

"I'm not sure Angus is very happy with me, though," Kathleen added. "He seemed quite put out by my hitherto unknown ability to soothe fractious babies."

"He's always been the one with the knack for handling

difficult babies. He probably fears you've knocked him off his pedestal."

"Oh, dear. I suppose that's why he decided to stay back at the house with Gus."

"Yes, he said he intended to *get the nursery sorted.* I shouldn't be surprised if the nursemaids quit by the end of the day."

"Good God, I hope not. You'll make me spend all my time in the nursery."

"With Angus," Sabrina drolly replied.

"Gus will likely yell his poor little head off the next time he sees me, in which case I will happily cede my position to Angus."

"I certainly hope not. This is the first time my little angel has slept through the night, which means it was the first time Graeme and I slept through the night since he was born. When we awoke this morning, Graeme leapt out of bed in absolute terror, convinced something was wrong with Gus. He bolted upstairs to the nursery without even putting his breeches on. He frightened poor Abby—that's the junior nursemaid—out of her wits."

Kathleen almost choked. "Did she scream? I thought I heard a scream this morning."

"She most certainly did. Fortunately, Hannah had already taken Gus into the other room to bathe him," Sabrina said, referring to her maid. "*Un*fortunately, Abby's screech brought Grant running upstairs too, also sans breeches. He thought someone was being murdered, so there was no time to waste on clothing."

By now, Kathleen was wheezing with laughter. "Were they at least wearing their smalls?" she managed.

"Thankfully, yes."

"They must have made quite the impressive sight, though. Kendrick men are splendidly . . ."

She'd been about to say *well endowed*, but realized what an inappropriate term that was under the circumstances.

"Well built," she finished.

Sabrina waggled her eyebrows. "You have no idea."

Kathleen had to admit she'd like to catch a glimpse of Grant Kendrick wearing only his smalls.

"Hannah, however, was not impressed," added Sabrina. "She gave the lads a good scold for scaring the nursemaid and told Graeme that fellows running about in their skivvies was not how proper folk behaved. She also called them carrot-topped madmen, larking about in their unmentionables. Needless to say, the twins meekly apologized and slunk back to their rooms."

Kathleen laughed. "I must say that Lochnagar seems a rather unusual household."

"Well, I do hope to convince my spouse to keep his breeches on, at least *outside* our bedroom."

Kathleen pressed a dramatic hand to her chest. "Is this truly my cousin Sabrina? The most perfectly polite, perfectly correct woman in London?"

"It's the Kendrick influence. It tends to addle one's brain."

"As well as other parts, apparently."

Sabrina raised her eyebrows. "Now who's being the naughty one?"

"Guilty as charged. That's why I've been foisted on you, old girl."

"I, for one, am exceedingly grateful for the foisting. As much as I love my life, Lochnagar can a bit overwhelming, even with the help of our truly wonderful staff." She pretended to shudder. "I still get nightmares thinking about the state of our water closets when we first arrived. Add in smugglers, wood rot, crumbling stonework, stubborn tenants, chimneys that smoke . . ."

"And a husband and baby to care for. You've been run off your feet, haven't you?"

"I will admit that I'm grateful to have your help, especially with the gardens."

"Well, I'm as good with gardens as I am with babies, so never fear," Kathleen stoutly said.

"Your baby-tending skills are a most welcome bonus. And I'm so grateful that Grant has decided to stay, too. Graeme needs his help."

Kathleen's foot seemed to catch on a small stone. "Um, he's staying?"

"Yes. He and Angus both are. After yesterday's unfortunate events, it's clear our crime spree is officially out of hand."

"But what can Grant, er, Mr. Kendrick do to help?"

"I'm sure you've noticed how competent Grant is. And he and Graeme understand each other. Each *always* knows exactly what the other needs." Sabrina's smile was wry. "It can be disconcerting at times, especially when they finish each other's sentences. Or have an entire conversation without even talking."

"Still, they're quite different. In personality, I mean."

"Yes, Grant is a very serious man, although Graeme tells me that he wasn't always that way. They were both absolute hellions when they were younger."

"Angus told a few stories on the trip up, but they were amusing rather than outrageous." Thanks to Grant, who'd shut his grandfather down more than once. "Honestly, though, men get to have all the fun. It's *so* unfair."

Sabrina's eyes twinkled with mischief. "I'm sure Grant

would be happy to tell you about his adventures. You might learn a few new tricks."

Kathleen recollected herself. "I've given up my life of nefarious doings, remember? From now on, I walk the straight and narrow path. Besides, I'm sure Mr. Kendrick will be much too busy helping your husband. And I'll be busy helping you, so we'll hardly see each other."

Sabrina shot her a much too perceptive glance. "I know Grant is quiet, but that doesn't mean he's boring. He's the opposite, once you get past his armor. All the Kendrick men wear a bit of armor, you know. But once they drop their shields, so to speak, you'll find they're entirely worth the effort."

"Sabrina, I'm not really sure why we're having this conversation," Kathleen cautiously said. "Mr. Kendrick is not interested in me, nor I in him."

"Are you sure?"

"I'm sure he finds me a terrible nuisance."

"And I'm sure he doesn't."

Kathleen flapped a hand. "It doesn't matter, because I'm not interested in him."

Much.

"I think the two of you would get along splendidly, if you just gave him a chance."

"Are you deranged? We're complete opposites."

"So were Graeme and I. Do you think anyone in our London set could imagine me married to a wild Highlander and former spy?"

"True, but I'm not looking for—"

"Kath, hurry up!" Jeannie suddenly called out.

She breathed a sigh of relief, happy to forgo the suddenly awkward discussion. "Coming, dearest," she called to her sister.

Jeannie and Mr. Brown waited by a sturdy iron gate in what appeared to be a newly built brick wall. Beyond was a stand of pine and birch trees, through which Kathleen could catch a glimpse of a long building, presumably the distillery.

"Yes, but hurry up. You're taking forever," her sister yelled.

The vicar winced. Jeannie was standing right next to the poor man, and she had a very healthy pair of lungs.

"Shall we go rescue Mr. Brown?" Sabrina asked. "We can finish our conversation about Grant later."

Kathleen had no intention of finishing *that* particular conversation. "I will say that Mr. Brown has done his duty by Jeannie."

"Yes, he's a very kind man."

If a trifle dull, especially compared to Grant.

She mentally blinked over her sudden conviction that Grant Kendrick was, in fact, not dull in the slightest.

Mr. Brown doffed his round hat as she and Sabrina approached.

"Ladies, I do hope you enjoyed your stroll."

The man was looking straight at her with a decidedly warm glint in his eyes. Why in the name of all that was holy did he have to take a liking to her?

Kathleen mustered what she hoped was a bland smile conveying no enthusiasm whatsoever. "Yes, thank you. The countryside is very pretty, although not as pretty as Ireland's, I'm sorry to say. Then again, Ireland is home, so I'm biased in that respect."

"How can you say that?" Jeannie protested. "The scenery here is so dramatic, and the history is, too. Mr. Brown has been telling me wonderful stories about Highland history."

She gazed at the vicar with girlish enthusiasm. "I think I could live here forever."

Mr. Brown, clearly oblivious, gave Jeannie a kind smile. "I certainly hope you and your sister have a lengthy visit with us, if not forever. That is indeed a very long time."

Kathleen scrunched her nose up. "What an awful prospect for poor Sabrina and Graeme. We're both absolute terrors, Mr. Brown. Our parents hardly know what to do with us."

"You're the one who's the terror, Kath," Jeannie said. "I'm as good as gold."

She heaved a sigh. "Sad but true, pet. I'm a complete romp."

Brown looked shocked—probably by both her language and frank assessment of her character. Unfortunately, he quickly recovered.

"I refuse to believe you are anything but charming, Miss Calvert," he gallantly said. "No one in his right mind could say otherwise."

Jeannie's brows snapped together as she shot the vicar a suspicious glance.

Double drat.

"I do believe the men are waiting for us," Kathleen said.

"Indeed they are," Sabrina replied, waving to her husband.

The Kendrick twins waited by the center door of a two-story, whitewashed building. They stood in identical postures—legs braced, arms crossed over their broad chests, faces shadowed by the brims of their hats.

Kathleen would have laid bets they were also wearing identical expressions of irritation at all the dithering about. Kendrick men, even the calm ones, radiated restless energy whenever they wanted to get on with something.

"Hallo," she called, madly waving both arms. "We'll be right there."

When the twins exchanged a glance she could practically read that one, too. After all, she was behaving like something of an idiot.

Jeannie frowned. "Kath, why are you acting so strange?"

Kathleen took her sister by the arm. "Whatever can you mean? This is how I always act."

Sabrina pressed a hand to her mouth, trying not to laugh.

"Step lively now, my girl," Kathleen said, layering on an Irish brogue. "We don't want to keep the gents waiting."

She swept her sister along the path to the distillery, leaving an amused Sabrina and a perplexed Mr. Brown to follow in their wake.

Chapter Fourteen

Grant watched Kathleen haul her sister toward the distillery. Jeannie was clearly protesting, and just as clearly her big sister wasn't having it.

"What's that all about?" Graeme asked him.

"I imagine Miss Calvert is trying to discourage her little sister's enthusiasm for the vicar."

"Ah. Which would leave room for the vicar's enthusiasm for the big sister," Graeme replied.

Grant had to ignore the impulse to growl at his twin. If Kathleen wished to spend her time with boring clergymen, so be it.

"For a wee slip of a thing, she's quite masterful," added Graeme.

"I'm well aware."

"And very bonny. As our Mr. Brown has clearly noticed, unlike some other fellow around here."

Grant threw him an exasperated glance. "Did we not agree that this subject was closed for discussion?"

"I don't think I recall that discussion."

"Since it took place less than twenty-four hours ago, I can only conclude you've turned into a moron."

"Maybe, but I'm still your favorite." Graeme dug an elbow into Grant's side. "Although I suspect that will be changing any time now."

"Yes, because I'll have murdered you for being so moronic."

"Och, you'll be shocking the lassies with such blood-thirsty talk," Graeme teased.

Grant just smiled as Kathleen bustled up, Jeannie in tow. Halfway down the path, Sabrina and Brown followed at a more reasonable pace.

"Please excuse us for dawdling." Kathleen sounded a trifle breathless. "So kind of you to wait."

"We didn't dawdle," Jeannie groused. "I have a stitch in my side from running up that blasted path."

"I'm very sorry, dearest," Kathleen said, not looking sorry at all.

"You and Sabrina were the ones who were dawdling, not the vicar and me," Jeannie replied. "Mr. Brown said we had to keep up with Grant and Sir Graeme, and not linger by ourselves to look at the scenery." The girl twirled a hand. "Because of the bandits, you know. He's very concerned for our safety."

More likely, the vicar was concerned about Jeannie's reputation—and his. According to Graeme, Brown was the very soul of clerical propriety. Grant suspected, though, that yon vicar would happily cast all vestiges of propriety to the winds when it came to Kathleen.

Not that he could blame the man. She looked entirely fetching in the beribboned straw bonnet that framed her sweet, freckled features, and the pink spencer that was buttoned tightly over her breasts. It did an excellent job of showcasing her neat figure. Now a dandy little breeze was whipping her skirts tight around her legs, flattening the material against the top of her thighs, perfectly outlining the delicate notch between—

"Here we are," Sabrina gaily announced as she walked up with Brown. "I apologize for keeping you waiting. I'm still getting back into fighting trim after my confinement."

Graeme leaned down to give her a kiss on the nose. "You're in perfect fighting trim, my love, as I *well* know."

"Goodness," said the vicar.

Sabrina poked Graeme in the chest. "None of that nonsense, sir, or I'll be forced to box your ears."

Jeannie giggled. "He's too tall for you to box his ears."

"I'll climb on a chair. It wouldn't be the first time," Sabrina said, winking at the girl.

"Then we'd best get on with the tour," Graeme said, "before my wife takes it upon herself to engage in acts of physical discipline."

The mildly off-color remark sailed over Jeannie's head. Brown, however, blushed and then darted a furtive look at Kathleen.

Bastard.

And here *he* was, jealous of the bloody vicar, apparently the most mild-tempered man in Scotland. And wasn't that just ridiculous?

"Ready, everyone?" Sabrina brightly asked.

"Aye," said Kathleen, "and I'm especially hoping for a taste of your foine Lochnagar brew. It's that eager, I am, to compare it to a good Irish whisky. There's nothing like a dram or two of whisky to remind one of home, as they say in the auld sod."

Jeannie peered at her sister. "Kath, why do you keep talking like that?"

"Like what? This is how I always talk."

"No, it's not."

For some reason that Grant couldn't fathom, Kathleen had adopted a comically prominent Irish accent. It reminded him of all the times he and Graeme had broadened their brogues to annoy various members of the family, especially the *Sassenachs*.

"We cannot possibly disappoint the old sod," Sabrina said, trying not to laugh.

"Och, I'll put my foine brew up against your Irish whisky any time, lassie," Graeme said. "There'll be nae contest, ye ken."

Mr. Brown darted a glance between Kathleen and Graeme, looking confused.

"Since we're reaching the point where we won't be able to comprehend each other," Grant said, "I suggest we go in."

Graeme winked at him. "Aye, that."

"I don't understand," Jeannie said. "Is everyone joking?"

"No, lass, my brother is simply acting like the village idiot," Grant replied.

"A frequent occurrence," Sabrina cheerfully concurred.

"Aye, that," Graeme teased as he ushered his wife through the door.

Jeannie looked suspiciously at her sister, who simply opened her eyes wide as if to suggest nothing at all was amiss. The girl shrugged and latched on to Brown again, all but dragging him inside.

Kathleen huffed out a sigh before starting to follow her sister.

Grant held her back. "What's afoot?"

"Why, nothing."

"A foine brew?" he said.

She seemed to debate with herself before her lovely mouth curled up in a sheepish smile. "I'm dancing on the head of a pin, if you must know."

"And it's Vicar Brown who has placed you there?"

"You noticed?"

"Which part? The part where Jeannie's mooning over him, or the part where he's mooning over you?"

"Unlike Jeannie, *I'm* certainly not encouraging him. And I'm hoping that my ridiculous behavior will put him off."

She bristled so adorably that he couldn't help teasing her. "Aye, but the fella seems mighty taken with ye. Not that I blame him, ye ken. Yer mighty fetchin' in that wee bonnet of yers."

"Good Lord, you're worse than I am."

"Aye, that."

She started to laugh but then caught herself. "I'm going in."

When she sailed right past him, Grant followed, shaking his head. What the hell was he doing?

You're flirting with her.

Fortunately, what he saw inside the building was interesting enough to momentarily distract him from the woman who was turning his brain inside out.

When Grant had last been up for a visit, the distillery was still in the construction stage. It was now completed, with three copper stills running on the spacious ground floor, with room for at least three more double stills. Fires burned in the large brick hearths behind all the gleaming copper, and stairs at the back of the room led up to what would be the mashing floor.

A lanky young fellow was tending the hearths, carefully restocking the flames with peat. He glanced over at them with a smile but continued in his work.

Grant breathed it all in, the scent of peat and mash filling his nose. The heady scent was replete with memories of his wild youth, memories that made him feel rather wistful.

He and his twin had been a pair of jinglebrains, as Angus liked to say, and they'd had some splendid adventures together. Running an illegal still had probably been the stupidest escapade in their careers of mayhem, but it had been rather grand for all that. For the first time in their lives, they'd made something and earned money by their own hands. As foolish as it was, it had felt like a real accomplishment.

In the difficult days of their youth, when tragedy had so often brought the family teetering to the brink of destruction, he and Graeme had actually *done* something. They'd built something that worked.

Together.

From his earliest memories, Graeme had always been inseparably by his side. Because of his twin, Grant had never had a chance to be lonely, even on the darkest days. Graeme had been wild, yes, but always there, the rock on which Grant could find his footing.

And that was the root of the problem, wasn't it? His family had all moved on from those tumultuous times, settling down and building happy, purposeful lives. While he had built a useful life too, in service to family and clan, it was a rather solitary one. Even surrounded by Kendricks, as he was most days, he often felt alone.

Graeme quietly moved to his side, his gaze warm with understanding. "All right?"

He mustered a smile. "Always."

"Brings back memories, doesn't it?"

"Aye, that."

"God, we were stupid."

Grant laughed. "Incredibly stupid. But you've done a splendid job with this. Everything looks top-notch."

"Not like the old days, eh? That crazy still we cobbled together. It's a miracle we didn't blow ourselves up making the blasted stuff."

Sabrina joined them. "How satisfying that your misspent youth has transformed into something so productive. Kendricks have an interesting way of going about life, I must say."

"You mean the most difficult way," Grant said. "Taken only by hard-headed Scotsmen who can never make life easy on themselves."

"Or the rest of us," Sabrina wryly commented.

Kathleen, who'd been inspecting one of the stills, glanced up. "Are you saying you distilled illegal whisky?"

Her skeptical tone seemed to suggest that Grant couldn't possibly do something so interesting.

"As a matter of fact, we did."

"Best brew in the district," Graeme added.

"So you two were both . . ." She twirled a hand, as if words failed her.

"Criminals?" Grant finished for her.

"I was going to say smugglers. I assume you had to smuggle your ill-gotten gains to market."

"Those casks weren't going to walk themselves out of that glen, now were they?" Graeme said. "Grant excelled at developing the distribution network, which is no surprise."

"I think you mean I was simply better at outrunning the excisemen," Grant replied.

Kathleen pressed a hand to her lips.

"One mustn't be too shocked at such goings-on, Miss Calvert," Brown said. "The taxes imposed by the British on the legal trade were punishing. Although quite wrong, one cannot be surprised that some locals engaged in a spot of illegal distilling."

"I'm not shocked," said Kathleen. "As I said to Sabrina earlier, men get to have all the fun, which is *quite* unfair."

"I'll say," Jeannie piped in.

Brown looked startled by their responses, but then he mustered a gallant smile. "Yes, but what would we do without the ladies to keep us in line?"

"Become smugglers, apparently," Kathleen replied.

Grant smothered a grin. Brown would have to do better than that to keep up with his sweet lass.

Och, yer doin' it again. Kathleen was most definitely not *his*.

"Ye canna blame us," said the young man tending the hearths. "Them bloody *Sassenachs* almost bled us dry." Then he bobbed his head at Sabrina. "Beggin' yer pardon, milady. I mean, the bloody *English*."

"Never mind, Dickie," Sabrina said. "I'm used to it."

"Don't forget you're half Scottish, love," Graeme added.

"And it's that proud we are to be workin' for ye, Lady Kendrick." Dickie smiled at Grant. "And a pleasure it is to be seein' ye again, sir."

"And you as well, Dickie. You've done a splendid job, here. I'm mightily impressed."

The young man blushed. "Och, it's all Magnus, sir. I just does what he tells me to."

Dickie was cousin to Magnus Barr, Graeme's chief distiller. The cousins were part of the smuggling ring that had operated on Lochnagar lands. Graeme had put an end to it, primarily by asking Magnus and Dickie to join him in setting up a legal operation. Magnus was a genius at coaxing a fine elixir from his stills, which he lovingly tended like they were his bairns. His talent, combined with Sabrina's money and Graeme's leadership, had spurred Lochnagar Distilleries to be on its way to turning a profit by next year.

When Grant happened to glance at Kathleen, her polished-pewter gaze was fixed on him with intensity.

"What?" he asked.

"You really were a smuggler?"

He frowned. What the devil was she getting at?

"Yes."

"But you should know that I was the true mastermind of our evil doings at Kinglas," Graeme quickly said. "Grant was simply watching over me and trying to ensure that I didn't kill myself or end up in prison."

For some deranged reason, Grant was annoyed at such a lackluster description of his contribution to their youthful indiscretions.

"Angus came up with the original idea," he pointed out. "Although I was the one who developed the plan and designed the still. Graeme was simply the muscle."

"I was more than just the muscle," Graeme indignantly stated.

Grant raised an eyebrow.

"I was also the chief taster," his twin said.

"You certainly drank up more than your share of the profits."

His brother heaved a dramatic sigh. "Och, stabbed in the back by one of my nearest and dearest. It's a sad life, ye ken."

Sabrina patted her husband's arm. "It's certainly true that you have very nice muscles."

He snorted. "Thank you. And Grant is correct. He *was* the brain of the operation."

"It all sounds quite jolly," Jeannie enthused.

"I had no idea you were so dashing, Mr. Kendrick," Kathleen said, flashing Grant a cheeky smile.

In other words, she'd continued to think him a dead bore until now.

"Grant can certainly be dashing," Graeme said. "I remember one time, just before we were sent down from school—"

Since Grant knew exactly which embarrassing tale his brother was about to relate, he elbowed him in the side. "Definitely not."

"Let's have that tour then, shall we?" Sabrina tactfully interjected. "Dickie, perhaps you could do the honors."

"I'd be happy to, milady. I can take ye upstairs to show ye where we start the mashin'."

"Is Magnus about?" Graeme asked. "I'd like a word with him while you show the others around."

"He was called over to the gristmill, sir, 'bout an hour ago."

Graeme frowned. "Is there a problem?"

"I canna say, sir. He beetled out before I had a chance to speak with him. But his mam is in the office, if ye'd like to ask her. She's goin' over the inventory for the next few months, like ye asked her to."

"I'll just pop in and have a chat with her, then."

Graeme strode over to a door at the other end of the distillery. When he opened it, a small bundle of gray streaked past him and straight to Dickie.

"You have a cat," Jeannie exclaimed.

"Aye, that's Mrs. Wiggles," Dickie said, as the cat wound herself around his legs. "She's our mouser."

Jeannie crouched down, clicking her tongue. The sleek

feline scampered over and pushed her head against the girl's hand. "Can I pick her up?"

"Of course, dear," Sabrina said. "Mrs. Wiggles is quite spoiled. She loves nothing better than to be carried and fussed over."

"Huzzah." Jeannie hoisted the cat into her arms.

Mrs. Wiggles promptly settled and began purring loudly.

As Dickie ushered the others up to the second floor, Kathleen paused at the bottom of the staircase, clearly waiting for Grant.

He raised his eyebrows.

"I'd quite like to hear that story about you and Graeme," she said.

"Which one?"

She rolled her eyes. "The one you cut short."

"It's not for polite company, I'm afraid," he said.

Well, it was more a story too stupid to relate to anyone with a brain. He couldn't count the times he and his brother had acted like complete idiots back then.

Kathleen's gaze suddenly lit up with mischief. "That's exactly why I want to hear it."

He couldn't help returning her smile. Everything about her seemed to sparkle, as if she were a spangled scarf catching sunlight. Her very presence filled the room with vibrant, joyful life.

Grant couldn't resist leaning down, coming within inches of her Cupid's bow mouth.

"Och, ye'll be wantin' to hear all my secrets now, will ye?"

Her cheeks pinked up, making her freckles practically glow. Instead of retreating, she gave him that adorably saucy smile.

"You'll be thinking me a forward miss, kind sir," she said with her teasing Irish lilt. "But it's that curious I am, and no denying it."

My God. She was actually flirting back.

And wasn't that a grand surprise? Grant would be happy to satisfy her curiosity about a number of things, and his own, as well. Like how far her freckles trailed down her body, and if they reached her—

"Hurry up, Kath," Jeannie called. "Everyone's waiting."

Kathleen jerked back, knocking her elbow against the oak banister. "Ouch."

Grant reached for her. "Be careful, lass."

"I'm fine, sir. And you're correct. I should be more careful." Quickly, she turned on her heel and marched up the stairs.

He slowly followed. Kathleen Calvert was as changeable as her beautiful eyes—one minute, bright silver with humor, the next, dark gray with frustration. He didn't know where he bloody well stood with her from one moment to the next.

So let that serve as a warning to you.

By the time he reached the upper floor, Grant had himself firmly under control. Kathleen didn't even bother to look at him as she adroitly inserted herself between Jeannie and Brown. And while that clearly pleased the vicar, who beamed at her with undisguised delight, it did not please Jeannie. There was trouble brewing there. If he had a brain in his head, Grant would steer clear of the whole lot of them.

He was here for only one reason—to help Graeme bring a gang of thieving, troublesome bastards to heel. What Kathleen Calvert chose to do with her time was no concern of his.

Now properly sorted, Grant turned his attention to his surroundings and was impressed once again.

Three large mash tuns were installed in the center of the long, low-ceilinged room, with space for at least two more. The design of the room was excellent, and the quality of the equipment top drawer. With Graeme running the show, Grant had no doubt that Lochnagar would soon be one of the finest distillers in Scotland.

Dickie gestured toward the containers. "These here be called tuns. That's where we mix the grist with hot water and start fermentin' things."

"The grist is actually malt, grown from barley," Brown explained to Kathleen. "Once the barley is harvested, it's soaked in warm water for a few days, then spread out to dry in a malting house. It's then dried some more in a kiln before it's ground to flour at the mill. That is the grist Dickie is referring to."

Dickie nodded. "Aye, sir, that's correct."

His tone suggested he was a wee bit annoyed that Brown had stolen his thunder. Grant didn't blame him. He was beginning to conclude that yon vicar was a bit of an officious prat. In all fairness, he'd never thought that about the man before, but he'd never been in competition with him for a fair lady's hand.

And you're not, you ninny.

"You seem to know quite a bit about whisky, Mr. Brown," Kathleen said. "I take it you're a tippler?"

The vicar looked shocked. It was his default expression, as far as Grant could tell.

"Goodness, no," he exclaimed. "But any self-respecting Scot is familiar with the process."

"My Irish granny always used to say that a dram a day

kept the doctor away," Kathleen replied with an airy wave. "It was grand advice, I'm thinking."

Jeannie shook her head. "But your granny was a tee-totaler, Kath. She said she hated the taste of spirits, remember?"

When Kathleen let out a tiny sigh, Grant decided a spot of chivalry was in order.

"Dickie, I take it the barley is still milled off the premises."

"Aye, Mr. Grant. We use the barley from some of the local farms, and two of them have malt houses and kilns for the dryin'. They were part of our smugglin' rig, ye ken, before we turned legal."

Brown clucked his tongue. "The less said about those days, the better."

"Aye, Reverend," Dickie said in a long-suffering tone.

"But why work with other farms?" Kathleen asked. "Wouldn't it be easier to consolidate everything into one operation?"

"That's an excellent question, dearest," Sabrina said.

"I'm not just another pretty face, you know," Kathleen joked.

Brown pressed a dramatic hand to his chest. "Brains and beauty. A formidable combination, Miss Calvert."

The vicar's ponderous gallantry had Grant contemplating whether to dump him into one of the mash tuns.

"I'm pretty and smart, too," Jeannie said, looking rather sad as she cuddled Mrs. Wiggles.

"Darling, you are much prettier and smarter than I am," Kathleen cheerfully exclaimed. "By a country mile, as we all know."

Brown smiled. "Dear ladies, such comparisons are

entirely unnecessary. I have rarely seen sisters who shared such beauty, both inside and out."

Jeannie scrunched up her face. "Kath and I aren't related, Mr. Brown. We're stepsisters. So we couldn't possibly look like each other."

The irrepressible vicar looked daunted by Jeannie's artless observation.

"Did you say something, Grant?" Sabrina asked with an innocent air.

Since he'd been trying not to laugh, it took him a moment to answer. "Ah, not really."

Kathleen's mouth quirked. "Perhaps you were answering my excellent question?"

Vixen.

"Yes, that was it," he replied. "Up until recently, most people brewed their own liquor and ale as a regular part of the farming seasons. They had malting houses and kilns, and they supported each other more or less as a collective."

Brown held up an admonishing finger. "It was illegal, nonetheless."

"How dreadful of everyone," Jeannie said, who'd gone back to gazing at the man with girlish adoration.

Kathleen pointedly cleared her throat. "You were saying, Mr. Kendrick?"

"Right now, Lochnagar is still in the building stages," Grant explained. "So it relies on local farmers to provide the finished grist. But all the distillation and production will take place here, so as to ensure a consistent product."

"We're hopin' to roll some of them farms directly into the operation," Dickie said. "Bring 'em into the fold, as Sir Graeme likes to say."

Sabrina nodded. "We want to provide as much work as possible for the locals. We'll be relying on the farmers for barley, and the crofters for harvesting peat for the fires and kilns."

"And as we expand," Dickie added, "we'll be bringin' in more villagers to work."

Brown smiled at Sabrina. "It's splendid that you and Sir Graeme are providing work for Dunlaggan, even if one cannot entirely approve of the end product."

"I do believe we were promised a sample of that *end product*," Kathleen said. "This tour has been so interesting, but I swear I'm parched. I'd love to wet my whistle, Sabrina."

"Er," Brown said, clearly disconcerted by Kathleen's behavior.

One could only hope the vicar was finally realizing that the cheeky lass would be more than a handful for the likes of him.

Grant had to admit he'd like nothing better than getting a sweet handful of the cheeky lass, preferably while she was wearing one of those frilly underthings and not much else.

Sabrina hooked arms with Kathleen. "Why don't we repair to the office? Graeme has several bottles of Lochnagar's finest tucked away there, exactly for emergencies such as this."

"Hardly an emergency, Lady Kendrick," Brown said with a nervous chuckle.

"That remains to be seen," Kathleen muttered.

The ladies trooped downstairs, followed by Jeannie and Brown.

"What's amiss with Vicar Brown?" Dickie asked Grant. "He's actin' right strange."

"Maybe he's been out in the sun too long."

Dickie snorted, then followed Grant down the stairs just as Graeme was emerging from the office.

"Enjoy the tour?" Graeme asked with a smile.

"Dickie is very good at giving tours," Sabrina replied.

Grant snapped his fingers. "Tours—that's just what you need. Everyone's mad for the Highlands these days. Half of England is coming up here on holiday. Once you get fully up and running, you should give tours of the distillery. You can put up some of the whisky in specially designed bottles and sell directly to *Sassenach* tourists."

"Tourists? Really?" Sabrina asked in a doubtful tone.

"Scotland is crawling with *Sassenachs*, thanks to Walter Scott and that ridiculous spectacle with the king last year. Might as well make some blunt off it. God knows you two have certainly earned a slice of that particular pie."

His sister-in-law had played an integral role in King George's visit to Edinburgh, and she'd snagged Graeme as a result of it.

"What do you think, dearest?" she asked her husband.

Graeme flashed a smile at Grant. "Actually, I think it's bloody brilliant. I always knew there was a reason I liked you."

"I'm the smart twin, remember?" Grant said. "As well as the good-looking one."

Graeme scoffed. "That's debatable, but—"

The door was flung open and Magnus Barr stalked into the room, Angus on his heels.

Graeme frowned. "Grandda, what's wrong?"

Sabrina hastened forward. "Is Gus all right?"

"Och, the wee lad's fine. It's other trouble we've got, ye ken."

Magnus, a veritable giant of a man with the soul of a puppy, was looking mightily fashed.

"Aye, that," he said in a grim tone. "At the mill. That's why I popped over there." He grimaced at Sabrina. "Sorry to interrupt yer visit with yer guests, my lady."

"Don't apologize," said Sabrina. "Magnus, this is Miss Calvert and her sister Miss Jeannie."

Magnus respectfully doffed his hat. "It's my pleasure. I'm right sorry I weren't here to show ye around."

"Never mind that," Graeme impatiently said. "What's wrong at the mill?"

"Somebody broke into the storage room overnight. The blighters cut open the sacks of grist and dumped it all over the place. Some went out the back window. It's a right mess."

Graeme muttered a curse and threw a meaningful glance at Grant.

"I'll go right over and look about," Grant said, starting for the door.

Angus held up a hand. "That's not all the trouble. A lad ran up from Dunlaggan. Yon kirk has been vandalized too, I'm afraid."

"What?" Brown gasped.

Angus grimaced. "I'm sorry, Vicar, but it sounds like they mucked up a mess in there. Made off with the silver, too."

Chapter Fifteen

Kathleen was on her knees repacking the dirt around the morning glories and trailing vines when a familiar masculine voice nearly startled her out of her wits.

"Miss Calvert, what are you doing out here alone?"

Resisting an impulse to press a gloved hand to her thumping heart, especially since that hand was covered in dirt, she twisted around to see an irate Highlander glowering down at her. For a man who prided himself on self-discipline, Grant had been bearish these last few days. Of course, it was in everyone's best interest, as he and his equally overbearing twin had made abundantly clear.

"You shouldn't sneak up on people like that," she replied. "I didn't even hear the garden gate open."

A reasonable person would expect that Grant and his twin would thump about the place making a great deal of noise, as befitted any proper giant. But at least twice now, she and Sabrina had been discussing the Kendrick brothers when the subjects of their conversations all but popped out of the woodwork like ghosts.

Of course, that quiet quality didn't hold when having

an argument with a Kendrick male. In those circumstances, yelling tended to be the order of the day.

"That's because I stepped over the gate," Grant said, "which anyone could have done if they'd wanted to sneak up on you."

"And you apparently wished to do."

"No, it's just easier to step over it."

Although the low fence fronting the vicarage came up past Kathleen's knees, for Grant it would be nothing but a trifle of sticks, easier to step over than waste any energy pushing against the creaky old gate.

She clapped her hands to shake loose the dirt before starting to push up from the grass border that edged the pretty flowerbeds between the kirk and the vicarage. At least they *had* been pretty before the mystery bandits had taken several large whacks at them. The crime was petty and stupid, but infuriating nonetheless.

"Allow me." Grant cupped his hands under her elbows and lifted her straight up.

One second, she was kneeling on the ground. The next, she was on her feet, carefully deposited as if she weighed no more than a feather pillow. The man's casual strength was both unnerving and . . . stimulating.

"Thank you," she replied, rather breathlessly.

Grant frowned. "You've been working too long in the sun. You'll wear yourself out."

"Nonsense, it's a lovely day. And it's splendid to see the sun out in full force. You must admit that yesterday was very dreary."

"Because of the weather, or because we all spent the day arguing over highwaymen and such?" he dryly asked.

"Oh, is that what we were doing? I hadn't noticed."

Then she happened to catch sight of her low boots and let out a sigh.

"You've stepped in a bit of muck there, lass," Grant pointed out.

In fact, her boots were caked in mud. Annoying, that, since she'd not be trotting off to one of the local stores for a replacement pair in Dunlaggan. The tiny hamlet had only about eighty souls living within its small boundaries. There was one linen draper, who also served as haberdasher and shoemaker. Dunlaggan certainly had its share of rustic charm, but a location for stylish fashions it was not.

"Mr. Kendrick, would you mind serving as a wall for a moment? I'd like to clean off these boots before they're completely ruined."

"I live to serve, but don't think we're done talking about you jaunting around Dunlaggan by yourself. I thought Graeme and I both made it clear that you, Jeannie, and Sabrina were to stay put at the manor house."

She braced a hand on his rock-hard bicep and began scraping her muddy boot with a trowel. "You and Sir Graeme did indeed make that abundantly clear, not only on the day of the incidents but carrying on into yesterday. *Unfortunately* carrying on, one might add."

"Yet our suggestions failed to take, at least in your case."

"As I recall, they were rather more lectures than suggestions. Very loud lectures."

"You're thinking of Graeme. I never shout."

She carefully finished scraping her boots, and then stuck the trowel in a plant pot. Grant radiated impatience, which was rather fun. Kathleen was surprised to realize how much she enjoyed teasing him.

"Mostly never," she finally replied.

His burnished eyebrows snapped together. "And when did I yell?"

"When I agreed with Sabrina that it was foolish to uproot the entire household and run off to Glasgow over some incidents of vandalism. As distressing as those incidents were," she hastily added when emerald fire sparked in his gaze.

She'd seen that fire more than once in the last few days. Once they reached the Highlands, Grant had seemed to turn into quite a different sort of person from the staid, Glaswegian businessman she'd first met. That she found this new version of Grant increasingly attractive was a discovery she intended to keep to herself.

"The vicar seemed fair distressed about all this, ye ken," he sarcastically said, waving a hand at the garden.

She grimaced as she eyed the wreckage. Two large rhododendrons, clearly the vicar's pride and joy, had been viciously hacked to bits. The flowerbeds had been trampled, and two stone flowerpots had been overturned, one shattering into pieces.

But that was nothing compared to the damage done to the kirk itself. Although the vandalism had been fairly minimal in there—the sacristy door had been forced and the drawers and cupboards ransacked—the theft had been significant. The thieves had taken a very fine set of silver candlesticks, an enameled crucifix over three hundred years old, and a chalice inset with semiprecious gems. It was a terrible loss for such a small parish. Mr. Brown had been devastated, and the inhabitants of Dunlaggan were equally upset by the attack on their kirk.

Since the incidents, the Lochnagar ladies had been under strict orders from the Kendrick men to remain safely at home. Since yesterday had been rainy, Kathleen hadn't minded. But today had been sunny and warm, and being cooped up had given her the fidgets. And while she lacked the required skills to help track down a gang of thieves, she could do her bit by setting Mr. Brown's garden to rights.

It was her small act of defiance in the face of such unfathomable ugliness.

"Poor Mr. Brown," she said. "I did feel like I needed to help in some small way."

"Not small. You've done a splendid job repairing the damage to the garden." He cast an appraising eye over her work. "You've a true talent, lass. Brown will be thrilled."

His praise made her feel foolishly girlish—and happy. *Don't be such a ninny.*

"Even if you did have to sacrifice your boots," he wryly added.

She smiled. "They'll be my contribution to the cause."

"Hannah will sort them out. She wages constant battle against the effects of country life." He chuckled. "And my brother. Hannah's determined to get him sorted, too—much to Sabrina's amusement."

"I've never seen a lady's maid scold the master of the house before. It's refreshing."

"Hannah believes a proper scold now and again will prevent Graeme from reverting to his former ways."

"You mean Highland hellion ways? From what Sabrina tells me, that's a family trait. Except for Lord Arnprior, who is very dignified. And Kade is terribly sweet."

"Nick has his moments. Just ask Vicky."

"I shall certainly do so."

She hesitated. *Nothing ventured, nothing gained.*

"And what about you, Mr. Kendrick? Do you ever revert to your hellion ways?"

Again, heat flared in his gaze as it tracked over her. Kathleen's mouth suddenly went dry as that heat some-how transferred to her body, sending a flush dancing over her skin.

A moment later, however, she had an uncanny sense that Grant had just taken a mental step back.

"Miss Calvert, what is of concern is not my past behavior, but your present behavior. As in, wandering about on your own."

Men. They were *so* bloody confusing.

"I believe we finished that discussion," she replied.

"I'm not sure where you got that idea."

"Well, *I'm* finished with it, anyway." She retrieved a pair of clippers from the gardening basket she'd unearthed from the vicar's shed.

While she carefully trimmed a few bedraggled bits off the rhododendron, she could all but feel Grant fuming behind her.

After a minute or so of fraught silence, he finally blew out an exasperated breath. "Lass, are you just going to ignore me?"

She threw some trimmings onto a pile of debris. "It would appear so."

"Miss Calvert, you simply cannot—"

She rounded on him. "If you don't stop calling me *Miss Calvert* in that annoying tone of voice, I swear I will stab you with these clippers."

Grant simply tilted his head. "What should I call you, then?"

"You might try Kathleen. We've been practically living on top of each other for weeks. It seems silly to be so formal, especially since I refer to Graeme by his Christian name."

His expression went blank. Then a slow smile curled up the corners of his mouth.

Kathleen decidedly liked his firm-lipped, masculine mouth. It was hardly the first time she'd noted such and suspected it wouldn't be the last.

"That's true," he said. "Your bedroom is right down the hall from mine."

She'd already noted that fact, too. His room was two doors down, on the right.

"I hadn't noticed. Is it a nice room?"

He narrowed his gaze. "That is entirely beside the point, *Kathleen*. Why are you riding about Dunlaggan by yourself? It's not safe."

"Well, Grant," she drawled. "I didn't come alone. Your grandfather escorted me."

He made a show of looking around. "Apparently, Angus has added invisibility to his many talents. Either that or you stashed him in the shed, so he wouldn't annoy you."

She had to laugh. "Such drastic measures weren't necessary. Your grandfather escorted me here and then took our horses to tie up behind the pub. I'm to meet him there when I'm finished."

"He shouldn't have left you alone."

"I asked him to keep me company, but apparently gardening is not his forte."

"Och, I'll be havin' a wee chat with him," Grant said with a scowl. "With yon vicar gone to report to his bishop, ye shouldna be here alone, ye ken."

She patted his arm, inordinately pleased by his quick transformation into a growling, protective Highlander.

"I'm teasing, sir. Angus kindly volunteered to stay with

me, but Mr. Brown's housekeeper is here, as is the kitchen boy. They've been keeping a weather eye on me."

As if called, Mrs. Adair pushed open one of the vicarage's casement windows. "Good day to ye, Mr. Kendrick. Can I be gettin' ye a cup of tea, or something a little stronger?"

Grant waved. "I'm fine, thank you, Mrs. Adair. Just here to escort the lady home when she's finished up in the garden."

The housekeeper, a brisk woman in her early fifties, shook her head. "I never thought to see such goings-on in Lochnagar. It's enough to make a body afraid to go to sleep at night."

"Try not to worry. We'll get it sorted," Grant sympathetically replied. "My brother will be posting a watch in the village both day and night, and we'll not rest until we bring the poltroons to heel."

"I ken Sir Graeme will get the best of them eventually. But the villagers are that upset, I can tell ye. It's nae good all around."

"Sir Graeme will be speaking to the villagers, too," Grant assured her.

"Well, I'd best be gettin' back to my pies," the housekeeper said. "Give a shout if ye need anythin'."

"See?" Kathleen said after the window closed. "She's been hovering all morning like a mother hen with one chick."

"While that relieves me somewhat, don't forget this particular crime . . ." He paused to gesture at the garden and kirk. "It happened in broad daylight, yet no one apparently saw anything. That's alarming."

She waved her arms with frustration. "How is that even possible?"

He deftly took the clippers. "Careful, or you'll hurt someone."

"I'm extremely adept with gardening tools, sir. I only hurt someone when I mean to."

"Then you should keep a pair with you all the time. And now, time to have a wee rest, I think." He led her to a rustic stone bench under a nearby ivy-covered trellis.

Kathleen gratefully sank down, since she'd been working steadily all morning under a bright sun. She'd not realized that she needed a respite, but Grant had an eye for that sort of thing. And he seemed to be able to quickly sense what she needed, which was both disconcerting and . . . lovely.

He propped a booted foot on the other end of the bench, leaning a forearm on his thigh. Kathleen tried and failed to avoid staring at the enticing line of rock-hard muscle showcased by his close-fitting breeches and boots.

"In some ways, it was clever of them to pick late morning to do their dirty work," he said. "The villagers were either working in the shops, at Lochnagar, or at one of the tenant farms. And since the vicarage is at the far end of the village and is somewhat secluded, it made for an inviting target." He pointed beyond the house. "They must have come over those fields, from the direction of the woods."

"It is worrisome, I admit. Jeannie's anxious and upset for Mr. Brown's sake."

One of Grant's brows went up in an ironic tilt. "Which is why Graeme and I suggested you ladies should head back to Glasgow until we track the bast . . . er, the gang down."

"I suspect the bastards are just as likely to attack us on the road."

He snorted. "Och, lass."

"I know. I'm completely shocking."

"Charmingly so. However, I would think Jeannie's inappropriate fascination for the vicar would be an excellent reason for returning to Glasgow."

"Have you ever tried talking reason to a sixteen-year-old girl?"

He smiled. "No, but I clearly remember being a sixteen-year-old boy. Neither Graeme nor I had a farthing's worth of common sense between us."

"Then you will understand my dilemma. Besides, I won't leave Sabrina."

"Commendable, but—"

She held up a hand. "I will not budge on this, sir."

"Not even if it gives you a surefire excuse to escape the back of beyond? No one would blame you, Kathleen."

"I would. Sabrina needs me."

His mouth twitched up into a wry half smile. "It's a kind lass, ye are."

She couldn't help bristling. "Does that surprise you?"

He studied her for a moment, then leaned forward and gently tapped her nose. "Not one wee bit."

"Oh, um, thank—"

"Then since you will continue to be stuck with us," he briskly cut in, "what do you intend to do about Jeannie and the vicar?" He shook his head. "That sounds like the title of a very bad melodrama, doesn't it?"

She made a concerted effort to regroup. "More like a farce, I'm afraid. Mr. Brown seems entirely unaware of Jeannie's enthusiasm for him, which is surprising."

"I believe he's failed to notice because he's been distracted by something else," he replied in a carefully neutral tone. "Or, I should say, someone else."

She pointed to herself. "That would be me."

That pulled a reluctant grin from him. "I was trying to be discreet."

"Surely you've learned by now that such measures are pointless with me," she cheerfully replied.

"Has anyone ever told you that you're a rather unusual young woman?"

"Odd is the way most people would put it."

"There's nothing wrong with being odd. My entire family fits every definition of the word. If you were to look it up in Mr. Johnson's excellent dictionary, I suspect you'd find an illustration of Angus, ratty old tam included."

She laughed. "You seem to be the exception to the rule. You're very . . ."

"Normal?" he dryly finished.

She echoed him. "There's nothing wrong with being normal."

"That is very reassuring," he said. "Now, getting back to yon vicar, we agree that his penchant for *you* is the reason he's unaware of Jeannie's penchant for *him*."

"His *inappropriate* penchant for me," she said, determined to make that clear.

"There's nothing inappropriate from his point of view. It's perfectly reasonable that a man like him should wish to court such a bonny lass."

His unexpected compliment threw her off balance—yet again. The blasted man was turning her brain to mush.

Make a joke of it.

"Really, can you imagine me as a vicar's wife? I would be sure to do something dreadful, like drink up all the communion wine or insult the parishioners."

He grinned. "How shocking that would be for poor Mr.

Brown. I wonder if he realizes what a narrow escape he's made."

"Apparently not yet, which is why I continue to do my best to discourage him. Besides, poor Jeannie will have an absolute fit if she gets the idea that I'm trying to cut her out." Kathleen had to repress a very real shudder. "The consequences of that scenario would be appalling for all of us."

"Then I suggest you cease repairing the man's gardens. Doesn't that send a mixed message?"

"You'll notice that I waited until he left town this morning before I commenced the repairs."

"Mrs. Adair will certainly tell him who did it. That'll send him straight to Lochnagar on his trusty steed as a suitably sedate and clerical version of a fairy-tale prince."

She sighed. "It'll be a gothic nightmare if Jeannie twigs to it. And you're right, of course. But I couldn't bear what those awful men did to this poor garden."

To her mind, it had been another form of desecration— destroying God's beauty both inside and outside the kirk.

He leaned closer again, his gaze now glittering with intent. It made her stomach flutter like ladybugs taking flight.

"As I mentioned earlier," he murmured, "you're a very kind lass."

It was astonishing how so *normal* a man could so thoroughly scramble her wits. Something was happening here that she didn't entirely understand.

He's flirting with you.

That revelation almost knocked her sideways off the bench.

"I suppose I should have restrained myself because now he'll get the wrong idea," she said, trying to rally.

"You could try the Irish brogue again. That seemed to throw Brown off his feed."

"It certainly threw off my sister. She's unused to me talking like an Irish barmaid."

"Och, lassie, ye sounded like the fairest of colleens. As foine a maiden as ever graced the emerald sod."

She laughed. "That's very impressive. You just sounded more of an idiot than I did."

"Graeme and I spent years practicing our technique." His smile turned wry. "It used to drive poor Nick mad. How he put up with the pair of us is a complete mystery."

"I expect it's because he loves you."

"We certainly didn't deserve it," he softly replied, as if more to himself than to her. Then he grimaced and pulled out his watch. "It's getting late, don't you think? Sabrina will be wondering where we are."

Well. Obviously the flirting had come to a conclusion.

She leaned over to look at his watch. "Goodness, I'd best clean this mess up before collecting your grandfather."

"I'll help, then I'll escort you down to the pub." He gave her a hand up from the bench. "No wandering about alone, understand?"

She snapped off a salute. "Aye, aye, Mr. Kendrick."

He tapped her chin. "No cheek, lass."

When he leaned a little closer, her mind seized. *He's going to kiss you.*

Involuntarily, her lips parted on a small gasp.

He suddenly straightened up, as if someone had poked him in the backside.

"I'll just collect these cuttings, shall I?" He gestured to the pile of debris she'd stacked up.

Drat and double drat.

"Of course," she replied, mentally cursing the blush rising in her cheeks. "Take everything around to the garden shed, please." She reached for the whisk broom. "I'll sweep up the walkway."

She commenced sweeping with a great deal of vigor. It was rather silly, really. Of course she liked Grant. What sane woman wouldn't? That didn't mean anything would come of it—or *should* come of it. Despite some minor indications to the contrary, they truly had nothing in common. Besides, she had a plan for her life, and it didn't include either a husband or living in Scotland.

"I saw your designs for Lochnagar's gardens."

She turned to find him only a few feet away. "What did you think of them?"

"They're very good," he said. "You have an excellent eye for composition."

"You sound surprised."

Dappled sunlight through the trees made his hair gleam like polished copper. "I don't mean to."

She narrowed her gaze on his inscrutable features. Grant Kendrick was very good at hiding his thoughts. "You don't think women are capable of that sort of thing?"

"Don't be daft."

"Then what?" she challenged.

"Gardening seems a rather staid avocation. And you are anything but staid, Kathleen."

"I thought you liked staid."

He gave an exaggerated wince. "Touché. I'm afraid we can't all be as exciting as Mr. Brown."

She laughed. "That was actually rather mean."

"It was, wasn't it? But you *are* talented, and I *am* interested. Why gardening?"

The answer to that question was tangled up with so many memories, some of them painful.

He patiently waited. Kathleen had the feeling he could wait for a hundred years if he really wanted to know something.

"It's because of my mother," she finally said. "Our estate, Greystone Manor, has some of the prettiest gardens in Ireland. Parts of it were planted over three hundred years ago. Mamma loved to garden, and she spent a great deal of time tending to them and expanding on the original designs. Our gardens became rather famous because of her. They were her favorite place in the world."

For that reason, they would always be Kathleen's favorite place, too.

"You obviously inherited her talent," Grant said. "Both your designs and your drafting skills are excellent."

His praise made her feel a bit shy. "I'm not a patch on my mother. After she died . . . well, learning how to draft and design gave me something to do."

Truthfully, it had been much more than just *something to do*. It was a major source of comfort in the dark months after her mother's unexpected death.

She hesitated, but then shrugged. "Gardening makes me feel like she's still with me, at least a little bit. Does that sound silly?"

"Anything but," he quietly replied. "When you lose a parent at a young age, you look for them everywhere. And you try to hold on to them by loving what they loved."

Kathleen had to swallow twice before she could answer. "Yes, you lost your mother at a young age, too."

"I was seven." He had that faraway look again, as if he were gazing down a long, black tunnel that led to nowhere good.

She rested a tentative hand on his chest. "I'm so sorry, Grant."

His hand came up to cover hers, pressing it close. Through the fine wool fabric of his coat, through the solid muscle of his brawny chest, she could feel the beat of his heart, strong and true. Darkness still lurked in his gaze, though it seemed to lift as he stared down at her.

Time slowed as the breeze softly rustled through the trees. A sparrow flitted overhead, returning to its nest in the apple tree. The air, scented with heather and the faint tang of smoke from the vicarage chimney, was so lovely and crisp she could almost taste it. Everything about the moment seemed as clear as a polished windowpane, imprinted on her mind's eye so she would never forget it.

As she gazed up at Grant, a soothing peace drifted over her, settling deep in her bones. When he slowly bent his head, her fingers curled into his coat. Her lips parted, his mouth a mere whisper away. Finally, *finally*, he was going to—

"Hallo in the vicarage," called a loud voice.

They jerked apart, Kathleen stepping on the broom at her feet. Grant lashed out a hand to steady her. When she glanced up at him, she had to swallow a semi-hysterical giggle at the incredibly annoyed look on his face.

After blowing out an exasperated breath, he turned and stepped onto the walkway, partially shielding her.

"Can I help you?" he curtly asked.

"I hope so, old man," came the hearty reply.

After taking a breath to steady her nerves, Kathleen

moved around Grant and saw a tall, broad-shouldered man regarding them with a grin barely concealed by an impressive mustache. His beaver hat was tipped at a jaunty angle over curly brown hair, and his many-caped driving coat was negligently pushed back by one hand propped on his hip.

His grin broadened as he took in Kathleen. "Well, and how do *you* do, good lass?"

The casual insolence set her teeth on edge. "As the gentleman said, can we help you?"

"I'm looking for the vicar. Do you know if he's in?"

"Not at the moment," Grant replied. "Who wants to know?"

The man swept off his hat and gave an extravagant bow. "I'm his brother. Captain John Brown, at your service." He winked at Kathleen. "Especially yours, my dear lady."

Chapter Sixteen

Grant jumped the bay gelding over the low wall that separated Lochnagar lands from the road to Dunlaggan. He'd spent the morning riding through the more remote corners of the estate, where the rugged countryside of gorse-filled ravines, hidden glens, and deep caves all held potential boltholes for criminals. So far, he had found nothing. If the gang had a camp near the hamlet, they were doing a damn fine job of hiding it.

He was quite sure no locals were involved, since most were gainfully employed and intensely loyal to Clan Chattan. That was Sabrina's clan, to which most people in the area were related by blood or marriage. He couldn't imagine any of them creating such havoc in their own community.

A bit of smuggling was one thing, as recent history had shown. But holding up travelers, stealing cattle, and breaking into churches? Those were entirely different. The villains were professional thieves, and dangerous ones at that.

Why had they chosen this part of the Highlands for their mark? While Dunlaggan was both rural and remote, making it easier pickings, those pickings weren't exactly generous.

Grant wondered if the gang was always on the move, cleaning out one spot before moving on to the next. He'd already written to Nick for help. No one had more contacts throughout Scotland than his big brother, so Grant was hopeful that some piece of information might result.

Still, it was a faint hope. At the moment, he had only questions that kept him up half the night.

Thoughts of his Irish colleen were keeping him up at night, too—and in a state of sexual frustration. That day in the garden, he'd come within a whisper of finally taking her lush lips. Kathleen had been more than willing until the vicar's obnoxious brother had rudely interrupted them. Although their conversation with Captain Brown had been short, it had thoroughly embarrassed Kathleen and destroyed any chance for a romantic interlude.

Even more frustrating, the lass had gone skittish, retreating behind a courteous and even shy façade or avoiding him entirely. Since Kathleen was anything but shy, he could only assume she was having second thoughts about the *garden incident*, as he'd come to think of it.

Not that there had been any opportunities for *first* thoughts. But that she was very conscious of him was evident when they encountered each other. Her lovely Irish complexion would fire up, setting her whimsical freckles aglow. She would then either flee the room or engage in a dementedly bright conversation about nothing at all—usually with Sabrina or Jeannie, if they happened to be there.

Of course, what Grant was hoping for, aside from the opportunity to discover every freckle on her sweet body, was still a bit of a mystery to him.

Solve one mystery at a time, lad.

Keeping everyone safe by ending the crime spree was

his first order of business. Once he'd accomplished that, he could turn his mind to Kathleen and what the future might hold for them.

He trotted the bay along Dunlaggan's single street, heading for the Deer and Hound. Tracking down elusive villains was thirsty work, and the hamlet's only pub was the best place for gossip and getting a feel for how the locals were doing. Graeme and Sabrina were greatly worried about that. Sabrina's father had been an absentee landlord who cared not a farthing for his northern estate. Still recovering from those years of neglect, the locals were rattled by recent events and expected their lord and lady to solve the problem sooner rather than later.

That did rather put the pressure on. Graeme and his bride had moved heaven and earth to bring Lochnagar and Dunlaggan back to life, and under no circumstances would Grant allow a gang of scaly bastards to damage or even destroy all their hard work.

Mr. Harrison, the local butcher, emerged from his shop and began sweeping the stoop. Grant nodded in greeting.

"Guid day to ye, Sir Graeme," the butcher called.

"It's Grant this time, Mr. Harrison," he replied with an apologetic smile.

More than once since his arrival, someone had mistaken him for his twin. Hannah, Sabrina's maid, had repeatedly done so, much to Graeme's amusement. A few times, Graeme had even pretended to be Grant. Once Hannah had twigged to the deception, it had earned them both another scold. When Grant tried to defend himself, Hannah had replied that he was no better than his *nigmenog* of a twin, and that it was a lucky thing Sir Graeme was the magistrate. Otherwise, she would have reported them to the law for their tomfoolery.

"Och, my pardon," Harrison said. "But there's not a farthin' between ye. How milady tells ye apart is a wonder."

"Easy. I'm the one with the brains."

With a snort, the butcher waved him on.

Actually, Sabrina had always been able to tell the twins apart, even from a distance. Kathleen had the same knack for it, never once confusing him for his brother.

Grant found that . . . interesting.

He trotted along the neatly maintained row of stone houses with their scrubbed stoops, flower-filled window boxes, and brightly painted doors in red or blue. Dunlaggan might be just a quaint wee spot of civilization in the midst of a craggy, rather inhospitable landscape, but it was a comfortable sort of place, nonetheless.

Not for him, though. Unlike his twin, Grant would probably go out of his mind with boredom.

There's one thing here that wouldn't bore you, though.

Firmly repressing any more thoughts of Kathleen, he reined in the gelding when he reached the pub.

As usual, the rustic bench out front was occupied. Graeme joked that the village elders took assigned shifts, since a worthy ancient invariably occupied the bench, observing whatever there was to observe. Today, it was Mr. Chattan, a canny fellow who served as unofficial mayor of Dunlaggan. He sat quietly, puffing out acrid plumes of smoke from a pipe that looked as old as he was.

Grant dismounted. "Good afternoon, Mr. Chattan. I hope the day finds you well."

"Och, somethin's always achin' at my age, Mr. Grant," he said with a dramatic sigh.

Grant knew that Chattan was in fact both spry and sharp

as a tack. In many ways, the old boy reminded him of Angus.

"I am sorry to hear that," he politely replied.

"The old bones are nae what they used to be, what with the rheumatics. Still, there's nae use to complain, I suppose. All I ask for is a wee dram now and again, just to keep out the cold."

"That's easy enough to fix. I'll have one sent out to you."

"Och, yer a good man, just like yer twin. Ye'll be wantin' me to watch yer nag, I ken?"

"If you wouldn't mind."

"Nae trouble for ye, sir."

With nary a hint of rheumatics, the old fellow stowed his pipe in a nearby flowerpot and bustled over to take charge of the bay.

"Much of a crowd this afternoon?" Grant asked.

"The usual lot. Yon parson is in there, along with that brother of his."

Grant heard the note of derision. "Not too impressed with Captain Brown, are we?"

"Since the captain be mighty impressed with himself, he has nae need for my admiration. And Reverend Brown." He shook his head. "He's a wee bit starry-eyed when it comes to his big brother. A very trusting sort is our vicar."

"That's rather in the job description." Grant studied the old man, curious. "And why shouldn't Mr. Brown trust and admire his own brother?"

"We'll see how far it gets him," Chattan replied.

"And what do you think it will get him?"

"Trouble." Chattan took the horse's reins and disappeared around to the back of the building.

It was a typically cryptic remark from the village

Methuselah. Chattan knew everything there was to know about Dunlaggan's residents and was usually spot-on with his analysis. He also had an annoying tendency to keep much of that analysis to himself. Unlike the rest of the elderly gents who lounged about the pub, this old duffer was no gossip.

Grant ducked under the low doorway and stepped into the pub. The large, timbered room had a mismatched collection of tables and chairs, a polished bar at one end, and a large stone hearth with a cheerful peat blaze at the other. Mullioned windows let in the late afternoon sunlight and lamps dotted the tabletops, imparting a cheerful glow. Like the rest of Dunlaggan, the pub was simple, neat, and homey, inviting all and sundry to stop in for a wee dram.

The pub was about half full now, but would slowly fill up as the workday drew to a close.

Mr. Monroe, the publican, greeted him with a smile. "A guid day to ye, Mr. Grant. Will ye be having a dram of Lochnagar's finest?"

"Just ale, thanks."

While the publican drew off a mug, Grant leaned an elbow on the bar and cast a look about.

Captain Brown and the vicar occupied a table in front of the hearth, and several of the other patrons had pulled their chairs around, listening to their conversation. From what Grant could tell, the captain was holding court to a spellbound audience, expounding with verve, as well as the occasional jest if the general laughter was any indication.

The vicar sat mostly quiet, cast into a shade by his older brother. Although there was a strong physical resemblance between the brothers, the difference in manner was striking. For all Mr. Brown currently annoyed Grant with his awkward courtship of Kathleen, he was a modest and gentle-mannered fellow, as befit a vicar.

In contrast, Captain Brown struck Grant as a jolly dog, always ready for a drink or a jest. His easy, expansive manner probably appealed to both men and women.

And Grant didn't trust him one damn bit. His instincts told him the man was not a Captain Brown but a Captain Sharp, in Lochnagar for something other than a friendly but unexpected visit with the brother he'd not seen in over four years, according to Sabrina.

Of course, it was entirely possible that Grant mainly disliked the man for interrupting what had been shaping up to be a very pleasurable first kiss with Kathleen.

"The vicar must be pleased to see his brother," he remarked to Monroe.

The publican turned a jaundiced eye toward the captain. "It's a rare bit of mystery, if ye ask me. Never once showed his face around here in all the years the vicar has been seein' to us. Then he pops up all of a sudden like, just for a wee visit with his brother, or so he claims. Except the captain's been in here for the last two days yacking about a land scheme and fillin' some heads with barmy ideas."

Grant frowned. "What sort of land scheme?"

"He claims there's land in South America needin' settlers, ye ken. Hardworkin' Highlanders can make their fortunes farmin' the land." He snorted. "As if anyone ever made a fortune in farmin'."

"Except for the landowners who squeeze every farthing out of their tenants," said an attractive, red-haired young woman who joined Monroe behind the bar. "Our present lord and lady exceptin', of course," she added, flashing a smile at Grant.

He returned the smile. "Ah, Patty. Back at the pub,

are you? I thought Magnus was keeping you busy at the distillery."

Monroe's daughter, Patty Barr, had worked at the Deer and Hound until she'd wed Magnus a few months ago. Since she had excellent organizational skills, she now helped run the office at the distillery.

"Just helpin' until the regular barmaid is over the grippe," she said. "Poor Da was at sixes and sevens without me."

Monroe gave his daughter a quick hug. "It was a sad day when ye left me for that big lug of yers. Dinna think I'll ever get over it."

She scoffed. "Since ye live with me and Magnus, that's not really a problem. Not to mention that my husband keeps ye in the best whisky this side of Inverness—at cost, ye ken."

"Now that is an excellent deal," Grant said.

"Aye," Monroe agreed. "Magnus might be a little short in the brainbox, but he brews a fine whisky."

His daughter elbowed him. "None of that, Da. Ye'll hurt my man's feelins."

Monroe looked incredulous. "Lass, I insult yer man every day. And he *agrees* with me."

"Anyway, we canna all be geniuses like Mr. Grant or Sir Graeme," Patty said.

"Actually, Lady Sabrina is the brains of the outfit," Grant replied. "Graeme and I just do what she tells us."

Patty gave an approving nod. "It's a wise man, ye are. Now, are ye peckish, sir? Would ye like a bit of stew from the kitchen?"

"Thank you, no. I'll join the others. I'm curious to hear more about the captain's land scheme."

Patty's snort was an uncanny echo of her father's. "That one. He's a flash, if ye ask me."

Monroe shrugged. "As long as he pays his bills."

After asking Patty to take old Chattan a dram, Grant strolled over to join the gathering around the brothers.

The vicar gave him a friendly wave. "Mr. Kendrick, how are you? I do believe you've met my brother, John."

The captain stood, casting Grant a broad smile from under his broad mustache. "We had the pleasure of meeting the other day, along with an *excessively* charming young lady."

He winked at Grant.

Bastard.

Grant had to control the impulse to drag the captain across the table by his waxed mustachio and toss him out the window, mostly because of the promise he'd made to himself to stop breaking other people's furniture. He and Graeme had demolished more than a few pubs in their wild youth, not to mention the occasional society drawing room.

The vicar looked startled. "Who are you referring to, John?"

"The lovely young lass who was hanging about your garden with Kendrick, here," his brother replied. "They seemed much engaged . . . in conversation."

Grant mentally frowned. Was the idiot trying to provoke a fight with him?

"It was Miss Calvert," he said to the vicar. "I was helping her repair the damage to your garden."

"Is that what you were doing?" Captain Brown mockingly asked.

Grant crossed his arms and gave the captain the slow smile that had sent more than one bullyboy into rapid retreat. The man blinked, momentarily disconcerted.

"That's *exactly* what I was doing," Grant replied.

The vicar cast a swift look between them before smiling at Grant. "That was exceedingly kind of you and Miss Calvert. Coming home to find my garden so well restored was a great comfort after such wanton destruction."

The captain rolled his eyes. "Good God, David, it was simply a bunch of flowers. Hardly the end of the world."

His brother stiffened. "Perhaps not, but losing the church's silver was a blow, I hope you'll admit."

The captain gestured to Patty before sitting back down. "Yes, bad luck, that. Sorry, old boy."

"Och, it was more than bad luck," said one of the local crofters. "'Twas a sin, is what it was."

The vicar mournfully nodded. "Indeed it was, Mr. Robertson."

"A bleedin' crime," Robertson's wife piped up. "A body canna sleep safe in her bed, what with villains roamin' the countryside. They'll be murderin' us next, mark my words."

Patty marched up and thumped another mug of ale in front of Captain Brown. "Och, stop yer nonsense, Jennie Robertson." Then she whacked one of the other villagers on the shoulder. "Make room for Mr. Kendrick, ye booby. Where are yer manners?"

"It's fine, Patty." Grant quickly hooked an empty chair and pulled it over to sit across from the vicar.

"And I am forgetting my manners," said the vicar with an apologetic smile. "Please do join us, sir."

"Yes, do." John tilted his head, inspecting Grant. "Kendrick, I believe you run the Glasgow offices of your family's trading company, do you not?"

Grant impassively returned his gaze. "I do."

That earned him another broad, mustachioed smile. "I've

been meaning to speak to you and Sir Graeme about an investment opportunity that I'm sure you'll find most interesting."

The vicar shifted uncomfortably. "This is not the place for such a discussion, my dear John. I suspect Mr. Kendrick simply wishes to enjoy his pint."

His brother waved an expansive arm. "We're all friends here. We've already had quite a good discussion with some of the villagers, have we not?"

An approving round of assents greeted the captain's statement. Clearly, some of the locals were receptive to his pitch.

"I don't generally discuss business outside the office," Grant replied. "But please feel free to give me the broad outlines."

"Och, Mr. Fancy and his *broad outlines*," Jennie Robertson muttered.

Her husband shushed her, but Grant ignored her sarcasm. Jennie was a bit of a troublemaker, so he'd give her no fuel to add to the fire.

The captain leaned forward, suddenly eager. "From what my brother tells me, the Kendrick family is well acquainted with doing business in the Americas."

"True, but we only work out of Canada."

"Hardly any difference from north to south, my good fellow. It's all the same, league after league of fertile land, just sitting there empty. It's a crime, all that land going to waste."

"I suspect the native people who inhabit those lands would disagree with you," Grant dryly said. "Not to mention the settlers who've been there for, oh, three hundred years or so."

Brown scoffed. "Natives? They're hardly worth mentioning."

Grant leaned a casual elbow on the table. "My brother Logan is the principal owner of Kendrick Shipping and Trade, and he would not countenance such a view. His son is part Mi'kmaq, from one of the native peoples of Canada."

Like Grant, the vicar now regarded his brother with clear disapproval. "We are all God's children, and are equally loved in His eyes, John. There's no need to be so dismissive."

Captain Brown raised his hands, flashing a rueful smile. "Apologies, Mr. Kendrick. Sometimes my enthusiasm runs away with me."

It was as insincere an apology as Grant had ever heard, but he simply nodded.

"Ahem. Well, with the help of backers in both Edinburgh and London," Brown continued, "I have secured an extensive tract of land in South America, in Belize. It's rich in timber, and there is substantial mineral wealth. Silver, and quite a lot of it, I'm sure."

Grant raised his eyebrows. "Are you sure? Have you seen the land?"

"Indeed I have. My long service in the military brought me to the Americas more than once over the years. I spent quite a bit of time in the Venezuelan Republic."

"My brother joined the army when he was only seventeen," the vicar explained to Grant. "He's had quite a storied career, mostly spent in fighting Napoleon and the French." He smiled at his brother. "We are very proud of John. He's a genuine war hero."

John clapped his brother on the shoulder. "You make too much of it, David. Besides, Mr. Kendrick has two war heroes in his family. My efforts no doubt pale compared to theirs."

Ah. So this was no casual encounter, after all. The man had done some research.

"Nonsense, John," the vicar said. "Your service has been exemplary."

"Simply doing my duty, old boy," his brother replied. "Besides, it gave me the chance to travel the world, didn't it? Provided me with all sorts of opportunities." He met Grant's eye. "Like this particular one."

"When did you acquire this tract of land?" Grant asked.

"I made a scouting trip last winter. When I returned to England to begin rounding up investors, I'm happy to say that I found two excellent ones in London. That allowed me to obtain the capital to make an initial purchase of land three months ago. I'm still seeking additional investors, but we're now ready to also offer shares to settlers."

"Now all that's needed is to *find* those settlers," David said, getting caught up in his brother's enthusiasm. "John hopes to have the first group depart for Belize this spring. Isn't that right?"

"Indeed it is. For a very small price, anyone looking for a better life can stake a claim and sign up to board that first ship. The land is ready to be cleared and farmed." The captain slapped the table in his enthusiasm. "It's so bloody lush down there that the land practically farms itself. Why, you can grow just about anything. And there are great profits to be made in timber from cleared land, too."

Grant crossed his arms and leaned back in his chair. "So, you're here to look for potential settlers?"

The captain waved a casual hand. "Why, I'm here to visit

with David, of course. It's been much too long. Dreadful neglect on my part."

David smiled at him. "And I am grateful, dear brother, but I think we know that Mr. Kendrick is at least partly correct."

"Nothing wrong with killing two birds with one stone, eh?" John said. "Besides, I've heard such grand things about the folks in these parts. Who better than Highlanders to take on the challenge? None are stronger, braver, or more adventurous." He suddenly adopted an outraged expression. "And with all these blasted Clearances, who is more deserving of a chance at a better life? Kicking them off their ancestral lands was the true crime, I say."

"Ye be right about that, Captain," Jennie Robertson piped in. "Robbed of our birthright, we've been."

Her declaration was followed by nods and murmured agreement all around.

The vicar shot Grant a concerned look. "That's certainly not the case at Lochnagar. Sir Graeme and Lady Sabrina have restored lands to any who were dispossessed."

"And there's the distillery," Grant said. "I don't think anyone in Dunlaggan or in this whole district is lacking for good work or land."

"No, we'll just be robbed blind or murdered in our beds," Jennie retorted. "What good will those jobs do us then, I ask ye?"

Grant shifted slightly so he could see the rest of the gathering. Although some were clearly annoyed with Jennie's last outburst, others looked worried—or fashed. And when Highlanders got fashed, trouble usually followed.

"Sir Graeme and I will run this gang to ground soon enough," he said. "These troubles will not be allowed to continue."

"And do ye know who they are?" asked one of the other crofters. "Because my wife wilna even go out to milk our cow in the shed first thing in the mornin'. She's that scared."

"Mayhap you could go do the milkin' for her, Bob Perley," Monroe tartly said from behind the bar.

Only a few chuckled.

"I understand your fears," Grant replied. "But I give you the word of a Kendrick that we'll bring an end to these criminal acts."

Jennie snorted. "Och, that means ye dinna have a clue. Why, it's just like when them Barrs were runnin' amok, makin' life a misery. And what happened to them, I ask ye? Nothin'. They're still runnin' things."

Patty left the bar and stormed over. "It's nae the same thing, Jennie Robertson. There was only one Barr causin' all the problems, and he's in the clink now in Edinburgh."

"Says the woman married to a Barr," sneered Jennie.

"Why, ye—"

Grant swiftly rose and got between the two women. "Patty, she's talking nonsense. Everyone knows Magnus is a fine man."

Monroe, who had hurried over to join them, gave his daughter a quick hug. "It's nae worth the trouble, love. Go back to the bar, like a good lass."

"I'll nae have her defamin' my husband, nor the Kendricks," Patty replied with a scowl.

Grant flashed her a wry smile. "Not to worry. We're used to it."

The vicar, who'd also risen to his feet, cast a worried look around the room. His brother, on the other hand, looked pleased.

"Such angry words are uncalled for, Mrs. Robertson,"

David said in a gentle reproof. "The Barrs are a very decent family. They're our neighbors and our friends."

The woman snorted. "Save yer lecturin' for Sunday, vicar."

"And ye can save yer drinkin' for somewhere else, Jennie Robertson," Monroe snapped, "if ye canna keep a civil tongue in yer head. That goes for yer husband, too."

Mr. Robertson almost fell off his stool. "Nae need to be hasty, Monroe. The missus didna mean nothin' by it."

While Robertson and the missus launched into an argument, with the vicar manfully trying to referee, Grant headed to the bar for another pint. When he was halfway there, the pub door opened and in came Kathleen and Jeannie.

"There you are," Kathleen said. "We've been looking all over for you."

He bit back a smile, taking a moment to relish the picture she made. Only his Kathleen would think a riding habit in an improbable shade of primrose was suitable for a jaunt in the country—or anywhere, for that matter. But improbable suited her perfectly, and she looked as pretty as a field of daisies on a bright summer's morn.

"Not by yourselves, I hope," he said.

Kathleen looked at Jeannie. "Told you he'd say that."

Her sister giggled.

"Yes, how foolish of me to worry about your safety," Grant sardonically replied.

"You'll be happy to know that Jeannie and I were accompanied by a groom."

"I am happy. And surprised."

Her mouth twitched with a small smile. "However, the groom has a few errands to see to, so I'm afraid you'll have to escort us back."

"I'm happy to do so."

"Look, it's Mr. Brown," Jeannie exclaimed.

When she darted off to the vicar's table, Kathleen sighed.

"I'll fetch her," Grant said. "You wait here."

"I cannot ignore poor Mr. Brown forever."

"Yes, you can."

She huffed out a laugh, then followed her sister over to the Browns' table.

Monroe clucked his tongue. "That wee little sister be a handful, I reckon."

"Aye, that," Grant replied before heading over himself.

"I *clearly* remember Miss Calvert," Captain Brown was saying as Grant joined them. "It's a distinct pleasure to see you, ma'am."

Grant curled his fist behind his back to prevent himself from hammering it into Brown's ridiculous mustache.

"And this is Miss Jeanette Calvert," the vicar said, smiling at Jeannie.

"How do you do, sir?" she absently replied, never taking her eyes off David.

Captain Brown slid a swift, calculating gaze between the sisters.

Don't even think about it, ye bastard.

"Won't you ladies join us?" Brown said with a sweeping gesture.

Kathleen gave him an apologetic smile. "I'm afraid—"

Jeannie plopped down on a stool. "Certainly. Thank you."

"Please, Miss Calvert," David said to Kathleen with a pleading smile.

"Well, just for a moment," she replied with obvious reluctance.

"Don't let us keep you, old man," Captain Brown said, giving Grant an easy smile. "I can toddle on up to the big house tomorrow, if you like. Show you and your brother my plans."

Grant grabbed another stool and settled in right next to Kathleen.

She threw him a startled glance and then bit her lip, trying not to laugh. He'd bet she knew exactly what he was doing.

Staking a claim to her.

The vicar frowned, while his brother merely looked amused.

"We were actually looking for Mr. Kendrick," Jeannie said. "We have something to tell him." She leaned over the table, closer to David. "Something *quite* dreadful, in fact."

"Not all that dreadful," Kathleen said in a warning tone. "And we can talk once we've—"

"Ah, a secret, is it? What fun." The captain turned a charming smile on the girl. "You can surely trust the vicar and his brother with a secret, can you not?"

"Now, John, we shouldn't pry," David admonished.

The captain winked at Jeannie. "Of course we should."

The lass responded with a giggle.

"It's nothing, really," Kathleen firmly said. "Just a little kerfuffle up at—"

"Lochnagar Manor," Jeannie interrupted. "Someone broke into one of the outbuilding storerooms and made a *complete* mess of things. The servants are in an absolute uproar over it. Bags of flour and grain were ripped open and strewn everywhere. And some tools were stolen, too."

David blanched. "That's dreadful. And so soon after—"

Grant cut in. "Ladies, I think we'd best get back to the manor."

He stood, offering a hand to Kathleen.

"But we just got here," Jeannie protested. "And I wish to speak to Mr. Brown."

"And I'm sure Mr. Brown wishes to speak to you," the captain said. "After all, to have more robbery and vandalism so soon after the theft at the church? A shocking turn of events."

"Another robbery?" yelped Jennie Robertson from the other table. "Where?"

"At Lochnagar Manor," the captain unhelpfully supplied.

"I'm sure my brother has the situation under control," Grant said.

"And I'm *sure* we'll all be murdered in our bleedin' beds," Jennie angrily retorted. "If Sir Graeme canna protect his own house, what does that mean for the rest of us? We're like sittin' ducks."

Just like that, the room erupted into the thing Highlanders did better than anyone—arguing. It quickly became a *loud* argument that involved much leaping up and waving of arms, as people tried to speak over one another.

The vicar also jumped to his feet, flapping his hands and looking a bit like a deranged raven. "Everyone, please stop yelling," he yelled.

Naturally, no one complied.

Grant quickly helped Kathleen to her feet. "Time to go."

She grimaced and urged Jeannie up.

"Sorry about this," Kathleen said.

Grant steered them to the door through the growing commotion. "No worries, lass. Just another day in the Highlands."

Chapter Seventeen

On the expansive front lawn of Lochnagar Manor, the men's archery competition had entered the final round. Kathleen couldn't help noting that betting on the outcome was brisk, albeit conducted somewhat surreptitiously.

Vicar Brown had obviously noticed, too, and was delivering a bit of a scold to Mr. Monroe for placing a bet.

Sabrina, standing next to Kathleen at the edge of the lawn, rolled her eyes. "I do wish our vicar could take the day off. What man doesn't place a harmless bet now and again?"

"Or woman, as the case may be," Kathleen said.

Sabrina threw her a laughing glance. "Did you really place one?"

"I had Angus do it for me before the tournament began." Kathleen grinned. "Don't want to shock the locals, you know."

"I think your outfit shocked a few of the locals, though, especially poor David. He seemed quite disconcerted."

Kathleen glanced down at herself. "What, this old thing?"

For the fete, Kathleen had chosen a hunter-green riding

skirt trimmed in red braid. She'd paired it with a white cambric blouse and a leather jerkin specially made for her by a London tailor. It was perfect for casually knocking about in the outdoors and for a village fete like this.

"It's a very dashing outfit," Sabrina replied. "Obviously *too* dashing for David. If he found out you'd also laid a bet, he'd have a fit."

"He'll have an even bigger fit if he finds out who'd organized the betting in the first place."

"Who?"

"His brother."

Sabrina's eyebrows shot up. "But Mr. Robertson is the one holding the book and taking the money."

"According to Angus, the captain put him up to it."

"That hardly seems fair, given that he's a finalist."

"I agree, but Captain Brown seems to have gathered influence over some of the villagers. Jennie Robertson hangs off his every word."

"That woman is a menace, I swear. And I must say that I cannot approve of Captain Brown, even if he is David's brother. He strikes me as rather . . ."

"Scaly?" Kathleen ventured.

"You've been hanging about with Angus, I see."

"That's your fault, pet. Whenever Gus has a bout of wind, the nursemaids come running for me or Angus, begging for our help."

Sabrina laughed. "You're both so good with my little darling that I cannot really blame them. And I *am* very grateful for your help."

"I don't mind. And I like your grandfather. He's as outrageous as I am." Surprisingly, Kathleen found she also liked taking care of Gus, at least in moderate doses.

"No one's as outrageous as Angus, not even you. And

speaking of outrageous behavior, care to tell me on whom you're betting? Not the captain, I'll wager."

Kathleen glanced around at the lively crowd milling on the lawns. In addition to the archery tournament, there were children's games and footraces overseen by Graeme. The lord of the manor had played the pied piper all afternoon, with a gaggle of little ones trailing behind him.

"No one can hear us over all this commotion," Sabrina assured her.

"It's supposed to be a secret. I'm a reformed character, remember?"

"I wonder what Grant thinks of your reformation?" Sabrina asked with a sly smile. "And speaking of Grant, doesn't he look splendid in Kendrick plaid?"

Kathleen refused to respond to her cousin's bait as she watched the man in question. Carrying a large yew bow as he strolled onto the archery field, Grant *did* look splendid in kilt, leather vest, and tall boots. And from the moment she'd laid eyes on him this morning, she'd been seized with a compelling desire to answer that age-old question: What *does* a Scotsman wear under his kilt?

Nothing, if you're lucky.

"Kathleen, I think you might be getting a sunburn," Sabrina said. "You look quite flushed."

"Hush, you. We don't want to distract the archers."

Sabrina cupped a hand to her ear. "What's that? I couldn't hear above all the cheering for Grant."

"You are *so* annoying."

Her cousin snickered.

Grant assumed a bowman's stance, one that showcased his brawny form. He nocked the arrow and then easily drew the massive bow. Once loosed, the arrow flew downfield and thudded into the canvas, just to the right of the bull's-eye.

"Blast," muttered Kathleen.

Sabrina tsked. "He'll have to do better if you're to win your bet."

"Who said I bet on Grant?"

"Your freckles are glowing. They only do that when you're looking at him."

Well, that was embarrassing.

"You're right. I'm likely getting sunburnt," Kathleen replied. "It's so sunny today. But it's perfect weather for the fete, thank goodness."

"Dearest, we've already determined that it's a certain *someone* who sets you all aglow."

"I don't know what you're talking about."

"You most certainly do," Sabrina firmly said. "It's silly to keep denying it."

"And I intend to keep denying it, or even acknowledge the need to discuss him. I mean, discuss it."

"We need to talk about it because you've developed feelings for him."

"I'm in denial about that, too."

"Grant's not," Sabrina replied. "He's mad for you, as evidenced by his behavior whenever poor David comes within hailing distance of you."

Kathleen couldn't hold back a chuckle. "He does become rather growly over the vicar, I must say."

"Growly? He turns into a complete bear. I thought he was going to toss David out the window when the poor man stopped by this morning to drop off that lovely corsage for you."

Kathleen had to admit she liked the sound of that. "Goodness, how terribly awkward."

"Especially for me, once Graeme removed his twin

from the scene," Sabrina replied. "I had to explain to David why Grant was acting so rudely."

"What did you tell him?"

"That the fumes from the distillery were giving our poor Grant the headache."

Kathleen burst into laughter. "And David believed you?"

"He was highly sympathetic, and took the opportunity to lecture me once more on the evils of strong drink."

Kathleen scrunched her nose. "Poor you."

"At least we prevented Grant from pitching my vicar out the window." Sabrina held up a finger. "Which brings me back to my point. You've grown very fond of Grant, no matter how much you might deny it."

Kathleen returned her gaze to the field. Captain Brown was now up, the only remaining contestant besides Grant. So far, they'd been fairly evenly matched, although the captain seemed to possess a slight edge. Another reason to dislike the man.

Sabrina nudged her. "You are, aren't you?"

Kathleen blew out an exasperated sigh. "Yes, probably more than I should."

That almost-kiss in the vicar's garden, which she couldn't help wishing had been a *real* kiss, was proof of that.

Sabrina frowned. "But you and he would make a splendid pair, and there are certainly no impediments to marriage. Grant could easily support you. The man practically prints money."

"I have plenty of money, Sabrina."

"Of course. I just meant that your parents couldn't raise any objections on that score. Grant comes from one of the best families in Scotland, too."

Kathleen waved her arms. "We have absolutely *nothing*

in common. He's a boring old businessman who wants to spend the rest of his life in Glasgow—"

"He's not boring—"

"And I want to be in Ireland, where I can live as I choose, without lectures from him on how to behave."

"Grant would never do that."

Kathleen cast her an incredulous look. "He tells me what to do all the time."

"That's only because he's worried about your safety right now. Graeme does the same to me."

"And how do you respond to all that ordering about?"

"When he makes sense, I follow it. When he doesn't, I ignore it."

"As I have every intention of ignoring Grant . . . Mr. Kendrick from now on."

Sabrina looked skeptical. "Then you'll be wearing David's corsage to the ball tonight?"

"Good God, no. Jeannie would pitch a fit." She glanced around. "Where is that scamp, by the way?"

"She's helping Graeme with the cricket game for the older children."

Kathleen exhaled a relieved breath. "Thank goodness she's not trailing after David."

"So, what *are* you going to do with David's corsage?"

"I gave it to Hannah." Kathleen pointed to the large tent, where Hannah was helping to set out the al fresco supper. "She's already wearing it."

Sabrina chuckled. "Poor David."

"Poor me. I have to keep fending him off."

"I could think of one way to solve that problem. Or one *person*."

"Relentless, that's what you are," Kathleen wryly said.

"Very well, dearest. Discussion concluded."

"Thank you."

Kathleen took in the lively crowd of villagers, strolling the grounds or participating in the games. Even the ancients from the village had their own special tent, where they could play whist and smoke their pipes undisturbed.

"You've done a wonderful job, old girl," she said. "No one knows how to throw a party like Sabrina Kendrick."

"It was your idea, Kathleen. It was an excellent one, and so necessary after recent events. We practically had revolt on our hands after the vandalism in our storerooms. I'm afraid that having an incident on the grounds of Lochnagar itself was very upsetting for the villagers. Some think it suggests that we cannot protect them."

Kathleen grimaced. "I tried to stop Jeannie from blurting it out in the middle of the pub, but I underestimated her lack of discretion."

"From what Grant told me, Captain Brown was more than happy to encourage her."

"It practically started a melee. I do believe the captain is something of a troublemaker."

"Graeme thinks he's playing on people's anxieties in the hope of persuading them to sign up for his land scheme."

Kathleen shot her a frown. "That's seems rather desperate of him. And silly, if you ask me."

"Still, it's a bother, and it's useless to deny that most of the locals are perturbed about the break-ins and thefts. Thank goodness Nick sent reinforcements from Glasgow."

At Graeme's hastily written request, Lord Arnprior had dispatched two footmen and a groom from Kendrick House to assist in patrolling the estate and the village.

"And fortunately they arrived in time to help with the fete," Kathleen said. "Fingers crossed it does the trick and gives the villagers a welcome respite from their worries."

In order to ensure that all could enjoy the festivities, Graeme had organized a watch over the village for the entire day, overseen by Mr. Chattan. With houses and cottages locked up tight, and guards posted throughout Dunlaggan, the locals were able to take a much-needed break and carouse to their hearts' content, care of Sir Graeme and Lady Kendrick.

The bustling preparations had yielded another benefit, that of keeping Jeannie busy and away from the vicar.

In fact, everyone at Lochnagar had been working from dawn until well after dusk, including Grant. In his case, however, he was busy hunting villains. When he returned home in the evening, he usually disappeared into the study with Graeme and Angus.

Kathleen had barely seen him, and the fact that she found that annoying was . . . well, annoying.

Sabrina linked arms with her. "I see the archery match is winding up. I'm still rooting for our Grant. If he loses to Captain Brown, I'll be most disappointed."

"And I'll be out a bob."

"Ah, so you did bet on Grant."

"Yes, and if you tell anyone, I'll have to murder you."

"But I have to tell Graeme," Sabrina replied in an innocent tone. "I never keep secrets from him."

Kathleen cast her a jaundiced look. "Do you prefer poisoning, or shall I simply push you off a nearby cliff?"

Her cousin laughed.

They crunched across the gravel drive toward the small crowd watching the archers. Kathleen repressed a sigh when she saw that Jeannie had abandoned cricket in favor of sidling up to the vicar. Her sister was talking a mile a minute as she gazed adoringly up at David. As usual, he regarded her with a slightly befuddled but kind smile.

Kathleen found it mind-boggling that he somehow could not see the obvious problem. It was soon coming to the point where she'd flat out have to tell him. And wouldn't that be a jolly conversation, especially if it prompted the vicar into making an amorous declaration of his own.

Grant's last arrow thudded into the bull's-eye, off center by an inch or so. Still, it was an excellent shot and the onlookers cheered with enthusiasm. It wasn't surprising that he was the favorite. Grant carried himself with a quiet confidence that naturally generated respect, and he treated everyone with equal courtesy.

He was more than a brawny, handsome Highlander. More than a successful businessman. Grant Kendrick was a good *man*, down to the depths of his bones. No wonder she found herself falling in love with him.

Kathleen's brain stuttered on that thought and a roaring filled her ears. She had to shake her head to ease the startling clamor and refocus her scattered wits.

"Good shot, old man," Captain Brown said with phony bonhomie. "You've left me in quite the pickle. Don't know how I'm going to improve on *that* performance."

Grant simply gave him a nod, though Kathleen sensed him mentally rolling his eyes.

"Give 'im what-for, Captain," Jennie Robertson shouted from the edge of the crowd. "We're in yer corner."

"Here, here," added David. "Not that I mean any disrespect to you, Mr. Kendrick," he hastily added, casting Grant an apologetic smile.

"No apologies necessary," Grant replied. "After all, blood is thicker than water."

A smattering of applause and a few cheers greeted the captain as he took his place at the mark. He acknowledged them with a flourishing bow, casting an especially wide smile at Jeannie and David. Kathleen frowned to see her sister applauding so enthusiastically. When Captain Brown winked at her, she gave him a dimpled smile in return.

"Well, that's a surprise," Sabrina commented.

"Not a pleasant one," Kathleen grimly replied. "If that man goes near Jeannie, I *will* actually murder him. What sort of idiot flirts with a sixteen-year-old girl?"

"What's amiss, lassies?" Grant said as he joined them. "Yer lookin' a wee bit fashed, ye ken."

Just for a moment, Kathleen allowed herself to be distracted by how very fine he looked at close quarters. His plain linen shirt showcased his broad shoulders and chest, and his kilt emphasized his lean hips and long legs. It was impossible to be physically unmoved by the sight of Grant Kendrick in a kilt. She even found herself rendered speechless, which was not a helpful sensation.

"We're worried that David's brother is flirting with Jeannie," Sabrina quietly said.

Her words and the sudden scowl on Grant's face unstuck Kathleen's tongue.

"We're probably overreacting," she said. "After all, Jeannie has been following the vicar around like a puppy since we arrived. It's hard to believe she would throw him over so easily."

"I hope not," Sabrina said. "David is harmless, but his brother is . . ." She trailed off with a slight grimace.

"Untrustworthy?" Kathleen finished.

"Aye, that," Grant said as he studied the captain through a narrowed gaze.

Brown had already taken his first shot, with the arrow thudding into the edge of the bull's-eye. He acknowledged the few calls of encouragement and Jeannie's enthusiastic clapping before turning back for his second shot.

"Do you want me to speak with him?" Grant asked, glancing at Kathleen.

She waggled a hand. "I don't want to make a mountain out of a molehill. I'll keep a careful eye on her."

"As long as she's with David, she's safe," Sabrina added.

Grant snorted. "Poor fellow's completely oblivious, for one thing."

"Thank goodness, or you and Jeannie would be rivals," Sabrina teasingly said to Kathleen. "I do hope your sister won't challenge you to a duel."

"Please. Trying to keep the vicar at arm's length while not arousing Jeannie's suspicions has been exhausting."

"Especially since David has been underfoot all week, helping with fete preparations." Sabrina shook her head. "I almost wish a villager would take to his deathbed, so he'd be forced to attend to him and stop pestering us."

Kathleen sputtered out a laugh. "That is positively wicked, Sabrina Kendrick. And the sort of thing I'm supposed to say."

"It's the Kendrick influence. It's corrupting."

The smile Grant directed at Kathleen was also positively wicked. "With the emphasis on *very*," he said.

"You are both ninnies," she said to compensate for the heat making her flush. "And there will be no corrupting behavior around my sister."

"Do you want me to give yon vicar and his brother a good thrashing?" Grant suggested. "I'm happy to oblige."

Sabrina patted his arm. "How kind of you, dear. But I feel certain that David, at least, has no idea how to engage in corrupting behavior."

"I wouldn't know about that," Kathleen muttered.

Just yesterday, he'd volunteered to help her cut flowers for table decorations. Not wishing to be rude, she'd agreed.

The gardens were right behind the house, and staff regularly bustled between the kitchen and the outbuildings. Even if gripped by passion, she'd felt sure the vicar would be on his best behavior in such public conditions.

Sadly, she'd underestimated his misplaced sense of romance. He'd begun to recite a Shakespearean love sonnet as Kathleen was struggling with an overgrown bush of thyme. Although she'd been able to deflect him by commenting that she loathed poetry, he'd quickly rallied. When he'd tried to seize her hand, she'd been forced to accidentally catch her clippers in the hem of his coat, making quite a dreadful tear. She'd then knocked over a nearby watering can that soaked his shoes. Thankfully, that had effectively quenched his passion and he'd made an apologetic retreat.

Grant's eyes narrowed even farther to glittering emerald slits. "Something you'd like to share about the vicar, lass?"

"Not at all. Oh, look, Captain Brown is about to make his final shot."

Grant studied her suspiciously for a few moments before turning his attention to the field. "About bloody time he got to it. Pompous ass."

"Let's hope you best him," Sabrina said.

"At this point, I hardly care. After listening to his land scheme twaddle for half the afternoon, I'm in dire need of a drink." He cut Sabrina a wry glance. "Lemonade and cakes are fine for the kiddies, but I think I've had my fill at least for a month."

Sabrina laughed. "Not to worry. I see that supper is almost ready, and Graeme asked Magnus to bring his best whisky from the distillery. We want everyone to be happy."

"The villagers are having a splendid time. You've done a bang-up job, both of you."

"I've always said that a good romp can solve many a problem," Kathleen said.

Grant's gaze went from warm to downright smoky. "I couldn't agree more, lass," he all but purred.

She tried to ignore the sensation of her body going up in flames.

Sabrina jabbed her brother-in-law. "Grant Kendrick! That sounded downright salacious."

"Really? Sounded perfectly normal to me. What say you, Kathleen? Me, salacious?" He waggled his eyebrows.

Kathleen was thankfully spared the need to reply by the sound of cheers from the crowd. The captain's last shot had hit the center of the bull's-eye dead-on.

"Dratted man." Sabrina shook her head in disgust.

"A pompous ass but a first-rate archer," Grant said.

"You're a very gracious loser, dear. Good for you."

Kathleen grimaced. "I'm not. I just lost a bob."

Grant's eyebrows shot up. "You bet on me?"

"Oh, ah, did I? Honestly, I can't remember. It's been *such* a commotion all day."

He flashed her a charming grin. "I suppose I'll have to figure out a way to recompense you."

"Make it easy on yourself and just give me the bob."

"While you two are flirting, I'd best go and award the annoying captain his prize," Sabrina said.

"I'm not flirting," Kathleen protested.

"Of course you are." Her cousin turned and marched off.

After a few moments of silence, Grant shrugged. "That's a spot of awkward, isn't it?"

"You don't look bothered in the least. Of course, neither am I," she hastily added.

He gently tapped her cheek. "Your freckles are glowing, though."

Kathleen sighed.

"I like your freckles," he said.

"You do?"

"Yes. I've been wondering how many you have. I wouldn't mind counting them, ye ken."

It took her a moment to muster an answer. "Now *that* was a salacious remark."

"All in the name of science. The counting, I mean."

The deep purr in his voice was back. Kathleen had to resist the sudden urge to look for a fainting couch. What in heaven's name had happened to her sober-sided businessman?

She tried to regroup. "Mr. Kendrick, you simply must—"

Grant took her arm and aimed her toward the refreshment tent. "You can give me a proper scold after we've had something to drink. I'm parched."

"You really are a dreadful man."

"You must be thinking of Graeme. I'm the nice one, remember?"

He was more than nice. He was absolutely wonderful. And wasn't that just an irritating state of affairs? She had no room in her life for a man. No man, not even Grant Kendrick.

Then make room, you booby.

"Huh, that's odd," he said.

She glanced up at him. "What's odd?"

"It's Angus. Something's up at the supper tent."

He increased his stride, and she had to scurry to keep up with him.

As they hurried toward the tent, Graeme suddenly fell in stride with his brother.

"Trouble," Graeme said.

"Aye."

Kathleen was amazed, as always, at how attuned they were to each other.

The supper tent was the largest on the lawn, and was set up behind the side terrace of the house. The dining room table, which had been moved inside it, was covered in starched linen and decorated with Kathleen's floral center-pieces. A smaller table next to it held a large punch bowl and various other beverages. Hannah and Angus stood behind that smaller table, engaged in a quiet but fraught discussion.

"What's amiss, Grandda?" Graeme asked.

"Trouble, ye ken," Angus grimly replied.

"Obviously," Grant said. "What sort of trouble?"

Hannah, a slender girl in her mid-twenties, dressed in a neat gray dress with a starched apron, pulled an unhappy face.

"It's the children's punch, sir." She pointed to the large crystal bowl. "It ain't right."

"Ye were to be keepin' an eye on the beverages, lass," Angus said with disapproval.

"I did keep an eye after *ye* mixed the punch and left it out in the kitchen," Hannah retorted. "Once the kitchen maid told me it was ready, one of the lads and me brought it straight out."

"We can apportion blame later if necessary," Graeme said. "What's wrong with the damn stuff?"

"Ye ken it's my secret punch recipe," Angus explained. "So after it's settled a wee bit, I test it to see if it needs more sugar."

"And?" Grant impatiently put in.

"Somebody's spiked it," Hannah said.

The twins exchanged a startled glance.

"With whisky?" Graeme asked with disbelief.

"Well, nae with sugar, ye jinglebrain," Angus tartly replied.

Grant stepped forward and dipped a cup into the strawberry-colored beverage. He took a sip, and then grimaced. "Aye, it's whisky, and sufficient to harm a child if he drank enough. The punch covers most of the taste, so a little one might not catch it."

"My God." Kathleen pressed a hand to her suddenly roiling stomach. "Who would do such a thing?"

Graeme cursed. "I think we know the answer to that."

"And given the circumstances," Grant grimly added, "I'd say we have a spy in our midst, as well."

"Aye," said Angus, "and a right nasty bugger he is."

Chapter Eighteen

It wasn't difficult to spot Grant, since he towered over most everyone in the ballroom. Although he appeared to be lounging against the doorframe, he was on the lookout for trouble.

The entire household had been on the lookout after the afternoon incident with the punch. Fortunately, the rest of the day had gone as planned, and the villagers had enjoyed a generous picnic supper before returning home to prepare for tonight's party.

They'd debated canceling the evening's festivities, of course. Graeme and Sabrina, along with Kathleen, Grant, and Angus, had thrashed it out in a tense session in the kitchen garden during the picnic, before finally concluding that the ball should proceed. Canceling it would have caused upset and even panic amongst the villagers. Graeme was growing increasingly concerned that the locals might take matters into their own hands, with possibly unfortunate results.

But the pressure was certainly on to track down the criminals as soon as possible.

Kathleen murmured an apology as she tried to slip by the butcher's wife.

Mrs. Harrison, a comfortably plump woman with a kind face, moved aside. "Bless me, Miss Calvert, I'm squeezing ye against the wall. I dinna wish to wrinkle yer pretty dress."

"It's rather a crush, isn't it?" Kathleen replied.

"Aye, it's a grand party. Have ye met Mrs. Ferguson? She's Dunlaggan's linen draper."

"Not formally. It's a pleasure, Mrs. Ferguson."

Mrs. Ferguson, a middle-aged woman in a well-tailored gown of gray silk, returned her smile. "The pleasure is mine, especially since I get to see yer wonderful gown up close. That's a lovely shade of satin, Miss Calvert. And Brussels lace, I take it?"

"That is correct."

Mrs. Harrison shyly touched the lace trim on Kathleen's puffed sleeve. "Lady Kendrick has some right pretty gowns, ye ken. But I've never seen the likes of this one. Ye look like a princess."

"To tell you the truth, I feel overdressed," confided Kathleen.

She'd only bought a few evening gowns with her, and this one, white lace over a rose satin slip, seemed better suited to a *ton* ball than a country party.

"Ye look a treat," said Mrs. Ferguson. "We don't often see such lovely things here in Dunlaggan."

"But all the draperies you've done for the manor house are wonderful," Kathleen replied. "I especially love the tartan silk drapes in the dining room."

"Chattan plaid. My lady's clan, ye ken."

"If her ladyship doesn't mind, I'd love a gown made in that fabric. I think it would be very dashing."

The two women exchanged a glance.

"There's more than a wee bit of purple in that plaid," Mrs. Ferguson said in a dubious tone.

"That's why I like it so much. It reminds me of the vibrant heather I see in the glens."

The butcher's wife smiled. "Well, I reckon ye have the dash to carry it off. It's nae wonder the men are sneakin' peeks at ye, especially our vicar. He's fair smitten, I'll wager."

"Who can blame him?" said Mrs. Ferguson. "Such a pretty lass in such a pretty dress."

Kathleen mentally winced, having dodged the vicar all evening.

"Of course, Vicar Brown is nae the only man with a fancy for Miss Calvert," Mrs. Harrison added to her friend.

Clearly, the ladies of Dunlaggan were not shy about exchanging a wee bit of gossip.

"Mrs. Ferguson," Kathleen hastily said, "shall I stop by your shop in a few days to see about that dress?"

"I would be that honored, Miss Calvert."

"Splendid. I'll see you soon."

"And be sure to have a dance with Mr. Brown," Mrs. Harrison said. "He'll be fair chuffed if ye do."

Kathleen beat as quick a retreat as one could make in a room packed to the rafters.

She finally reached the wide, arched doorway that divided the main drawing room from the smaller one behind it. The doors between the two had been thrown up to create a ballroom. By filling the space with dozens of candelabras, vases of mums, and swags of heather draped over windows and doorways, Sabrina and the staff had transformed the old-fashioned pair of rooms into a festive space for country dances and Highland reels.

The cheerful crowd seemed to be properly appreciative. A colorful gathering, everyone easily mingled, regardless of wealth or station. Even the village ancients had deigned to attend, and were now lounging on padded benches against the wall as they chatted with Graeme. Gentlemen farmers and crofters discussed the state of their crops, the women chatted about children, gardens, and prized recipes, and the young people flirted as they eagerly waited for the dancing to commence.

Kathleen found it all incredibly refreshing. She'd almost forgotten the ease of country life, and how distant it was from the pressures of London's competitive social milieu.

Encouragingly, she'd not heard anyone complain about the vandalism or robberies. That suggested the festivities were achieving their intended goal of reminding Dun-laggan that it was a close-knit community, united against any and all threats.

The only irritation for her was Captain Brown, holding court by the drinks table with a smattering of locals—no doubt expounding on his dreary land scheme. Kathleen would happily have seen him ejected from the party for acting like a pest, especially with Jeannie.

According to Sabrina, Brown had presented his archery prize to Jeannie after the tournament, making a show of it. The prizes for the games weren't much, truth be told, wreaths made of bay leaves and heather, along with silk scarves in Chattan colors. Kathleen had fashioned the wreaths, and Hannah had whipped up the scarves from remnants of leftover drapery fabric.

Unfortunately, Jeannie had been rather dazzled by the captain's gesture. If the dratted man kept it up, she might rethink Grant's offer to thrash the man, or even take on the task herself.

She squeezed past a group of farmers who were complaining about the latest tax outrage from Westminster and finally made her way to Grant. With a shoulder still propped against the doorframe and whisky in hand, he quietly studied the room.

He smiled as she joined him. "How are the Mistresses Ferguson and Harrison? You seemed to be having quite the chew."

"Were you spying on me, sir? I thought that was your brother's job."

"He's turned the position over to me on a temporary basis. And speaking of the Dunlaggan ladies, any chatter about our little problem this afternoon?"

"None at all. You deflected any curiosity quite ably."

He snorted. "You mean Angus and Hannah did. They performed their roles to perfection."

"Yes, but it was your idea."

Once they'd made the discovery that the punch had been spiked, it became necessary to dispose of it without raising suspicion. Grant had suggested that Hannah accuse Angus of adding too many lemons, thus making the punch too tart. The pair had thrown themselves into the charade by loudly exchanging insults. Much to the amusement of the villagers, Graeme had dramatically separated the faux combatants, while Grant had calmly picked up the punch bowl and carried it back to the kitchen.

"Your grandfather is a very convincing actor," Kathleen said.

"No one is better at telling whoppers—or acting outraged at a moment's notice—than our grandda. It's quite a talent."

"Yes, he's a true original."

Grant tilted his head, his gaze warm and slightly amused. "And so are you, lass."

She crinkled her nose. "So I've been told."

THE HIGHLANDER'S IRISH BRIDE

"Yes, but I meant it as a compliment. And speaking of compliments, you look very fetching in that gown."

She dropped him a little curtsy. "Thank you, kind sir. According to the Dunlaggan ladies, I look like a princess."

He settled his broad shoulders more comfortably against the doorframe. Kathleen couldn't help thinking he looked like a handsome Highland prince in the dress kit of his clan. In a fine wool kilt in Kendrick plaid, topped by a tailored black coat, he was absolutely delicious.

"A fairy princess, I would say," Grant said. "There's something quite fey about you."

"It's the Irish, and I hope *that* was meant as a compliment, too."

He smiled. "Kathleen, I could spend all night complimenting you."

She had a sudden mental image of what spending *all night* with Grant could possibly turn out to be.

"And I've noticed you're quite fond of pink," he added. "It's a very flattering color, especially with that overskirt of Brussels lace."

She choked on a laugh. "Mr. Kendrick, this will never do. Men are generally not thought to notice such things as the details of a lady's dress."

His gaze went positively smoky. "Lass, I notice *everything* about you."

Kathleen resisted the temptation to snap open her fan and flap away at her suddenly overheated cheeks.

"Clearly not," she managed to reply. "Because this gown isn't pink."

"No?"

"It's rose satin, as anyone with an eye for fashion can see. I'm afraid you do not have an eye for fashion."

He laughed. "Perhaps not, but I know what I like. And

I like that color on you. It matches your freckles when you blush."

She heaved a sigh. "Really, sir, only you would point that out."

"But I like your freckles." He leaned closer. "*Verra* much," he added in a deep brogue.

Goodness.

Kathleen had no choice now but to open her fan and start fanning herself. Grant chuckled and resumed his position against the doorframe.

"So, no disturbing gossip, thus far?" he asked.

Kathleen breathed a sigh of relief. Flirting with Grant Kendrick was a risky proposition, especially to her heart.

"All seems well." She glanced around. "Where's Sabrina? I haven't seen her in some time."

"She slipped upstairs. To check on Gus, I'm thinking."

Kathleen was suddenly horrified at the notion that little Gus might be at risk. "I . . . I never even thought of that."

Grant rested a big hand on her shoulder, his thumb sliding over the exposed skin above her puffed sleeve. Her anxiety began to ease at his gentle touch.

"There's no reason to worry," he said. "The nursery is well guarded, as is the rest of the house."

She'd seen some precautions put in place, but had been too busy with the floral arrangements and getting ready for the party to pay much attention.

"What about the kitchen? Keeping the food safe, I mean."

He snorted. "Hannah suggested that Angus serve as the official taster. She noted that he's such an ornery old bird no one would care if he popped off."

She couldn't help but smile. "Oh dear. Poor Angus."

"No, poor me. I had to separate them."

"I can well imagine the scene. But I do hope there's

truly no concern about the kitchen. Sabrina told me that Cook and the housekeeper would check everything and make sure only the regular kitchen staff were involved in preparations." The very idea of someone tampering with the food made her queasy.

Grant shook his head. "Lass, there's naught to worry about. Trust me, all right?"

She stared up at him, lost for several heartbeats in the depths of his forest-green gaze.

"I do," she finally whispered.

They were the truest words to ever cross her lips.

For long moments, they just stared at each other. Then his head dipped a bit, as if he would actually kiss her, before he straightened up to put space between them again. Kathleen had to resist the temptation to press a hand to her fluttering heart.

"Gracious," she squeaked.

His mouth twisted into a wry smile. "What I wouldn't give for a quiet little corner right now."

"That sounds . . . quite improper, sir."

She'd been about to say, *wonderful*, like a complete ninny.

"Perhaps later, then?"

"You are incorrigible, Mr. Kendrick."

"I believe that's the nicest thing you've ever said to me. And didn't we agree you should call me Grant?"

She adopted a mock frown. "No, I don't think we did."

His answering laugh reminded Kathleen once again how much she loved the sound—warm and welcoming, like a hot toddy but infinitely more stimulating.

She made a concerted effort to rein in her skittering emotions. After all, they were in the middle of a ballroom.

She hardly needed another scandal on her hands, triggered by publicly mooning over Grant Kendrick.

"To return to the original point of our discussion, sir—"

"Would that be sneaking off to find a nice, quiet corner?"

"No, you booby," she tartly replied.

"Och, it's a hard lass, ye are," he said with a dramatic sigh.

"Mr. Kendrick—"

"Grant."

"*Mr.* Kendrick, do not force me to whack you over the head with my fan."

His grin was unrepentant. "No need to fash yourself, Kathleen. I mean, *Miss* Calvert."

"You know, you're as bad as your twin."

"No one's as bad as Graeme. Except possibly our older brother Logan."

"Then I will be sure to avoid that brother at all costs."

"Don't count on that happening, lass."

She frowned, this time with genuine confusion. "But he's in Canada, is he not?"

He skated over her question. "As to the point of our discussion, I assume you're asking if we're safe from having further incidents like this afternoon's unfortunate occurrence."

"Yes."

"For the moment we are, but we need to bring a stop to this as soon as possible. I should be out there looking for the blighters right now, not standing about guarding the punch bowl."

"As competent as you are, Mr. Kendrick, even you can't see in the dark. There's no moon, and it's now overcast."

His smile returned, as did the wicked gleam in his eyes. "I can see some things *verra* well in the dark, ye ken."

She shook her head. "You're hopeless."

"All right, I'll stop teasing. You can be assured that for tonight, at least, everything is fine. We have guards posted everywhere, including in the village. So you should just try to enjoy yourself."

"Speaking of enjoying one's self, I seem to have lost track of Jeannie." She craned up on her toes again. "I had a good eye on her for most of the evening, until now."

Until she'd let herself get distracted by Grant.

"Jeannie left the main drawing room a few minutes ago while we were talking. She seemed to be following some young ladies to the supper room, so I assumed she was going with them."

Kathleen *very* much doubted that. "Can you see David?"

"He was with his irritating brother not ten minutes ago. Now I only see the captain. No David."

"Drat. I need to find her right now."

"I'll go with you."

Forging a path through the cheerful mob, Grant led her to the main corridor that ran the length of the manor house. He stopped a footman hurrying toward the supper room with a tray of glasses.

"Davey, have you seen Miss Jeanette?"

The footman shook his head. "It's a fair crush, sir. But I can help ye look, if ye want me to."

Grant shook his head to dismiss Davey, then glanced down at Kathleen. "She's probably in the dining room. Why don't you check there while I pop upstairs for a look in the family parlor and Graeme's study?"

She nodded and started off, but he suddenly reeled her back in. "Hang on. Here's Sabrina, and she's looking fashed."

Sabrina hurried toward them from the front hall. She did look annoyed, although she managed a smile for some of the village ladies chatting outside the ballroom.

"It's Jeannie, isn't it?" Kathleen asked her with a sinking heart.

"I'm afraid so. She's in Graeme's study with David. Graeme's keeping an eye on them." She winced. "He discovered them, in fact."

"Blast and damnation," Kathleen muttered as she turned on her heel and strode off with the other two following.

When they reached the center hall with its wide, circular staircase that led to the family rooms, Kathleen glanced over her shoulder at Grant.

"You needn't come, sir. Jeannie will be difficult enough to manage even without an audience."

"No, we definitely need Grant," Sabrina said.

Grant shook his head. "I take it my twin is acting like an idiot?"

"He's gone full Highlander, as Nick would say."

"What does that mean?" Kathleen asked as they hurried up the stairs.

"It means that he caught Jeannie trying to kiss our vicar."

Kathleen nearly tripped at the top step. "Please tell me you're joking."

"Sadly, I cannot. She had him backed against the bookshelves, apparently. I was coming from the nursery and heard Graeme leveling dire threats at poor David."

"Och, yon vicar's a hapless idiot," Grant said.

"Since he allowed a sixteen-year-old girl to lure him upstairs, I cannot disagree," Sabrina replied.

"And I'm going to find out exactly how she did it." Kathleen marched off down the hall.

"The offer to thrash the hapless idiot is still open," Grant said as he strode with her.

"I'm reserving that honor for myself."

She certainly felt like giving someone a good whack, including herself for losing control of the situation. Again.

The study was at the back of the house and thankfully well away from the party. Her sister might be only sixteen, but that didn't mean she wasn't old enough to ruin her reputation. Or to force a vicar into marriage to preserve *both* their reputations.

As they approached the end of the hall, they heard raised voices coming from the study.

"Why the hell is Angus in there?" Grant asked.

"He wasn't when I left," Sabrina said.

Kathleen stopped outside the door, drawing in a calming breath as she prepared for the upcoming fireworks. When a brawny arm wrapped around her shoulders and pulled her close, she had an overwhelming urge to shut her eyes and snuggle against Grant's chest.

"No worries, lass. We'll get it sorted." He pressed a quick kiss to the top of her head before letting her go.

"Grant, dear, that was an extremely anemic first kiss," Sabrina said with disapproval.

He winked at his sister-in-law. "How do you know it was our first kiss?"

"I have an infallible instinct for such matters."

"You are both ridiculous," Kathleen said.

He smiled. "Aye, that. Want me to go in first? I can tackle Graeme to the floor and clear the field."

"That sounds very helpful," she retorted.

The silly exchange, however, had done the trick. Kathleen no longer felt like leaping out the nearest window and fleeing into the night.

She squared her shoulders, stalked into the room, and came to a dead halt. Grant almost ran over her, side-stepping at the last moment.

"Jeannie, what in God's name are you doing?" she blurted out.

The vicar was squeezed between Jeannie and the bookshelves to the left of Graeme's desk. One part of Kathleen's mind registered that he looked utterly horrified. A larger part, however, noted that Jeannie was standing with her back to him, facing Graeme with her arms spread wide.

"What do you think?" Jeannie snapped. "I'm saving David from being murdered."

"Och, nae worries," said Angus as he held Graeme's arm, trying to pull him back. "Our lad will nae be killin' anyone."

"That remains to be seen," Graeme barked. "No one takes advantage of a girl in my house, not even the bloody vicar."

"But . . . but I didn't take advantage of anyone," David stuttered, turning whiter than his clerical collar.

"Don't worry, David," Jeannie passionately exclaimed. "I'll protect you."

Kathleen threw off her paralysis and rushed to her sister. "Dearest, I'm sure this is all a misunderstanding. And there's no need to squish poor Mr. Brown against the bookshelf. It's a wonder he can even breathe."

"I'll not move one inch until I know he's going to be safe. We're going to be married, so it's my duty to protect him."

David let out a whimper.

Graeme overrode the whimper with a growl. "So ye *have* been taking advantage of yon lass. Now I will have to kill ye."

"Sabrina, could you *please* get your husband under control?" Kathleen gritted out.

Her cousin marched up and took Graeme's other arm,

giving it a shake. "Graeme, you are acting like a jinglebrains. I am sure there's a perfectly reasonable explanation for this."

"I've yet to hear it," Graeme snapped.

"I already explained it, if people would just listen," Jeannie said. "David and I are getting married, so he's not taking advantage of me."

"You are most certainly *not* getting married," Kathleen said. "For heaven's sake, Jeannie, look at the poor man. He's utterly terrified."

"I say," protested Brown, "it's only because Sir Graeme keeps threatening to murder me."

Kathleen all but goggled at him. "So you do want to marry my sister?"

"No, of course not! I want to marry—"

"Please don't say another word about marriage," Kathleen hurriedly cut in.

Stricken, Jeannie twisted around to face him. "David, of course you want to marry me. After all, you kissed me."

He emphatically shook his head. "No, you kissed *me*."

"But you didn't push me away," Jeannie said with a frown.

"I didn't want to hurt you," he exclaimed.

"A likely story," Graeme retorted. "Why else would you come up here with her?"

"I came up here to fetch a book her ladyship said I could borrow," David protested. "Miss Jeannie followed me."

Graeme snorted his disdain for that explanation.

Angus elbowed him. "Leave off. Yer actin' like a complete booby."

"I'm sure you find this vastly amusing, Grant," Sabrina said in a stern voice. "But will you please do something with your idiot twin?"

Grant *did* look like he was stifling laughter, but he went

over and dropped a hand on his brother's shoulder. "Come on, old son. Let's leave the ladies to it."

"Absolutely not."

Grant began to look irritated. "Can you at least stop growling like a tiger with a thorn in his paw? You sound ridiculous."

His twin cast him an incredulous glance. "This situation doesn't bother you?"

"What bothers me most is that you're distressing the ladies."

Since Graeme winced, that was obviously a home hit.

"As Kathleen said, I'm sure it must be a misunderstanding," Grant added.

"It's not," Jeannie stubbornly put in.

"I know you want to protect him, lass," Grant replied in a kind tone. "And that's a generous instinct. But Vicar Brown is a grown man, many years older than you. He's well able to speak for himself."

"I won't let anyone hurt him," Jeannie said.

"No one will. You have my word."

"We'll see about that," Graeme retorted.

His twin gave him a sharp elbow in the side.

"That actually hurt," Graeme muttered with a scowl.

Grant ignored him. "I do believe we need to hear from Mr. Brown, and without any more declarations or threats."

Since Jeannie was clearly beginning to waver, Kathleen took her hand. "I think David is embarrassed by what's happening here, love. I'm sure you don't want that."

Jeannie glanced over her shoulder at the vicar, who now appeared to be praying for a miraculous escape from the humiliating scene.

"All right," she reluctantly agreed. "But nobody's to start yelling at David again."

"No yelling allowed," Kathleen replied in a soothing tone as she gently pulled her sister away from the object of her devotion.

David breathed out an audible sigh of relief and made an attempt to straighten his mangled collar.

"Go on, lad," Angus said in an encouraging voice. "We're listening."

"Ahem, thank you. As I was trying to explain, her ladyship had recommended a book she thought I would like, one by Sir Walter Scott—"

"Of course, it *would* be one of those inane novels," Graeme interrupted.

"She had generously offered to lend it to me," the vicar finished with wounded dignity.

"That's right," Sabrina said. "I told David he could borrow my copy whenever he wished."

"I meant to pick it up the other day, but I, er, experienced a small accident with a watering can in the garden, which forced me to return home."

When David then darted a glance at Kathleen and blushed, she had to swallow a curse.

Grant looked at her. His mouth twitched, but then he simply nodded at the vicar. "Carry on, Mr. Brown."

"Anyway, I didn't wish to miss another opportunity. So before supper, I came upstairs to retrieve the book. I was looking through the shelves when Miss Jeanette came into the room."

"I followed him up," Jeannie said with fatal candor. "I thought it would finally be our chance to be alone." She gazed defiantly around the room. "I wanted to tell David that I loved him."

Kathleen sighed. "Dearest, that was neither wise nor

appropriate. You put both Mr. Brown and yourself in a very awkward position. If anyone else had found out—"

Jeannie flung away from her. "You have no right to speak to me like that, Kath. You're not my mother or my guardian. And if I want—"

"Vicar, I believe Captain Brown will be wondering where you are," Grant smoothly put in. "And the ladies will no doubt wish to talk without us hanging about like useless ninnies."

"Oh . . . oh, indeed," David said with a grateful smile. "Certainly, poor John will be wondering where I am. I've been gone for much too long."

Graeme stepped forward and took him by the arm. "Splendid. I'll escort you downstairs."

Before anyone could say another word, he frog-marched David from the room.

"Best go and make sure he doesna throw yon vicar over the banister," Angus said to Grant.

"Indeed," Grant dryly replied.

When Kathleen cast him a grateful smile, he gave her a thoroughly roguish wink in reply. That brought a heated blush to her cheeks, but he was already striding from the room.

Angus waggled his bushy eyebrows at Kathleen. "Looks like there's hope for our Grant after all, eh, lass?"

Jeannie scowled. "I wish people would stop saying things I don't understand."

"Grandda, you can go any time," Sabrina pointedly said.

"Happens yer right. The lads will probably get into it once Graeme gives yon vicar and his scaly brother the boot."

Sabrina pointed at the door. "Out. Now."

"Nae need to get fashed, missy. I'm off."

After he'd stomped out and slammed the door shut, Kathleen sagged against the bookshelves. "Thank God. What an utterly dreadful scene."

"Only because you were all so mean," Jeannie said in a surly tone.

Still, she didn't miss the tearful shimmer in the girl's eyes. Jeannie was obviously mortified and hurt. And now Kathleen had to hurt her even more.

She lovingly placed her hands on her sister's shoulders. Jeannie's gaze was filled with both a wounded defiance and a vulnerability that made Kathleen's heart ache.

"Darling, I know you think you love Mr. Brown—"

"I do," Jeannie exclaimed.

"All right, let's accept that is so. Can you honestly say Mr. Brown returns your feelings?"

Jeannie's lips pressed tight, as if refusing to allow the words to escape.

"Sweetheart, Mr. Brown is almost twice your age," Sabrina said in a kind voice. "And you have quite a lot of growing up to do before you're ready for marriage."

"Other girls get married at my age," Jeannie protested. "And I'm sure he'd wait for me, anyway."

Kathleen steeled herself for the necessary cut. "I'm sorry, darling. Mr. Brown is a very kind man, and I'm sure he thinks you're a terribly sweet girl. But I can say without a shadow of a doubt that he does not love you."

"You don't know that!"

She held Jeannie's gaze. "I assure you, I do."

The girl stared at her for a moment. Then she gasped. "You want him for yourself, don't you?"

"I absolutely do not," Kathleen emphatically replied.

Jeannie pulled from her loose grasp. "I don't believe you. You always have to have everything, don't you? You always have to have *all* the attention." She dashed a hand across her eyes. "It's not fair."

"Dearest, I swear to you—"

The girl pushed past her and stormed for the door. When Kathleen started after her, Jeannie spun around and flung up her hands.

"Leave me alone, Kath. I hate you. I *hate* you." Then she ran from the room.

Stunned, Kathleen sank into the club chair in front of Graeme's desk. "I made a mess out of that, didn't I?"

Sabrina grimaced. "It couldn't be avoided, I'm afraid. Now, can I get you a whisky, old girl? You look like you could use it."

"Please. And make it a large one."

Chapter Nineteen

Despite the darkness, Grant easily spotted Kathleen in the new gazebo at the far end of the kitchen garden. She'd designed the elegant little folly, incongruously set amidst vegetable beds. She had a knack for bringing beauty to the odd corners of life that everyone else forgot, filling them with laughter, joy, and even love.

When she'd burst into his quiet life like quicksilver and moonlight, she'd yanked him awake. Grant now knew that Kathleen Calvert was exactly what he'd been looking for all along.

He walked past the neatly tended beds, some already mulched and ready for the colder months ahead. Would Kathleen spend those months up here, separated from the wider world and from him? That was a question that needed answering.

She sat on a wrought-iron bench in the corner, her legs tucked under her skirts. Deep in thought, she didn't glance up until he stepped into the gazebo.

"Getting a bit of fresh air, are we?" Grant asked.

"I'm hiding," she tersely replied. "This place seemed safe from discovery."

"Ah. Would you rather I go away?"

"Oh . . . no. I'm sorry to snap your nose off. You startled me, that's all."

He leaned against a support post. "I should have called out before sneaking up on you."

"You Kendricks do seem to excel at popping up out of nowhere."

"Then perhaps you could bell me, like a cat."

She chuckled. "I'd say you're much too big, and more like a tiger than a harmless tabby cat."

Grant rather liked the sound of that. "Seen any tigers lately? Besides me, of course."

"Only in illustrations, but I think they have green eyes, also like you."

"And like me, they have excellent night vision." He shook out the wool cloak he'd slung over his arm. "I can see you shivering, lass. That pretty dress is not nearly warm enough for lurking in gardens at night."

"I did bring a shawl, as you can see."

"Och, that little scrap of fabric?" He draped the cloak around her slender form and carefully pulled the hood over her coiffure.

"Thank you. I *was* getting a bit chilly and was just contemplating a return to the house. But I'm terrified of running into the vicar—or my sister." She sighed. "Coward that I am."

Grant settled next to her on the bench. "You're safe from David. He fled posthaste after my deranged twin put a scare into him. I doubt yon vicar will be showing his face around Lochnagar anytime soon."

"That's one small blessing." She suddenly started to

scramble up. "I don't suppose you know where Jeannie is? I hope she didn't go after David."

Grant gently pulled her back down. "No worries. According to Sabrina, she went to her room."

She peered up at him. "I suppose Sabrina told you what happened after you escorted David from the room?"

He snorted. "Escorted him is putting it nicely. Graeme probably would have tossed him out a window if I hadn't been there. I was tempted to let him do it, too. The good vicar is a nincompoop."

"I cannot entirely blame him, since Jeannie is a very determined girl. She gets that from my example, I'm afraid."

"I'm guessing you were never as naïve as our Jeannie."

"I think losing my mother at such an early age forced me to leave my childhood behind."

"Aye, that," he quietly replied.

She glanced up at him, her expression hidden in the shadows cast by the hood. "Of course you would understand, having lost both your parents so early."

What could he possibly say? That his innocence had buckled under the weight of grief? That he'd believed for too long that any chance for true happiness had died that day he'd been unable to save his father?

She slipped a hand out from the cloak and rested it on top of his. "I'm so sorry."

"Kathleen, your wee hand is as cold as snow," he gruffly said, tucking it back under the thick wool. "We should go back inside before you catch a chill."

When Kade was a little boy, he'd caught a terrible chill that had almost killed him. It had taken years for him to regain his strength. The idea of anything like that happening to Kathleen . . .

He stood. "Back ye get."

She grabbed his sleeve and yanked him down to the bench with a surprising strength. "Don't be such a fussbudget. I'm perfectly warm."

"Fussbudget, am I?"

"Sometimes. When you're worried about someone."

Grant settled back down. "Very well, we'll stay but not for much longer. It's the Highlands, and our nights get cold this time of year."

"I'm getting used to it, which is an alarming notion."

"Wait until January. This weather will seem like the middle of the summer."

She chuckled. "Are you trying to scare me?"

"Nothing scares you, lass."

"That is certainly not true."

"Name one thing that frightens you—and I'm not talking about spiders, or a mouse running across your foot."

"I must say that I cannot stand spiders."

"Do you run screaming for the nearest footman to kill it whenever you see one?"

"Spiders do serve a purpose, you know, especially in the garden. They eat other bugs that damage the plants, for one thing."

"So you leave them be?"

"We have reached a mutually acceptable solution. I try to avoid them, and they try to avoid me."

Her laugh echoed his own. The warmth of her laughter wrapped itself quietly around his heart.

After they sat for a minute in companionable silence, she spoke again.

"There is one thing that does scare me. Right now, at least."

"And that is?"

"That something bad will happen to Jeannie. That I'll fail her somehow." She exhaled a sigh. "I'm already failing her."

"As someone with six brothers, most of them hellions, I can tell you conclusively that you are not failing your sister."

"She told me that she hates me."

Grant wrapped his arm about her shoulders, drawing her close. Kathleen's entire body startled, and she hesitated for a moment before settling against him. He had the oddest sensation he'd held her a thousand times before.

"She didn't mean it," he quietly replied.

"She sounded like she did."

He thought for a moment. "Kathleen, I know what true hate looks like in families, many times over. What Jeannie is going through with you is not hate."

When she tilted her head to look up at him, the hood slipped back. Starlight seemed to glimmer in her eyes. Never had she looked more fey or more beautiful.

"I'm sorry," she said. "Do you wish to tell me about your family?"

Tell her about his brothers Nick and Logan and their years-long estrangement? Or how badly his father had treated Graeme when he was just a sad, wee boy? Such pain and ugliness couldn't be conveyed in a few bare sentences, if ever. Nor would it help Kathleen with her present dilemma.

He pressed a kiss to the top of her head and then tucked her back under his arm.

"Some other time. Let me just say I suspect Jeannie is acting this way because she feels safe with you. She knows you will never betray her."

"Of course I won't."

"So there you are. She is simply acting like a . . ."

"Brat," she ruefully finished.

"That's one way of describing it. However, I also think she's trying to emulate you. She wants to be as dashing as you are."

She sighed. "I am a terrible role model."

"Not true. You're teaching her how to perceive right from wrong, and how to stand up for herself. Those are valuable lessons, especially for a girl who's led such a sheltered life."

"That's incredibly kind of you to say, Mr. Kendrick."

He wanted her to think of him as more than simply *kind*. Yon booby-headed vicar was kind, and look how far it had gotten him with her.

"Enough with calling me Mr. Kendrick, lass. You're making me feel old before my time."

She chuckled. "God forbid anyone should think you were old."

"Och, I'm practically on the shelf, ye ken. My family despairs of me."

"Mine, too."

"Your family is lucky to have you, and I'll be happy to defend that point with anyone who says otherwise."

"I might say the same for you." She twisted a bit under his arm so she could see him. "You're very good at taking care of people, you know. It's . . . nice."

"Nice sounds rather boring."

"You're not boring at all." Her tone suggested she was a bit perplexed by such a notion.

"You used to think I was, though."

"Only because I was a ninny."

"You were never a ninny."

"Well, I still say you're very good at taking care of people."

You'll never know if you don't ask.

"I'd like to take care of you, Kathleen, if you let me."

She snuggled back under his arm, as if dodging the question. "I never thought of myself as someone who needed to be taken care of."

"We all need help now and again, sweetheart."

"Even you?"

"Definitely me."

While she pondered his admission, Grant did his best to be patient. Yet all he wanted to do was kiss her breathless.

"I believe I would like you taking care of me, now and again," she finally whispered.

Relief all but staggered him.

"Aye, that," he managed.

When he bent down to kiss her, she pressed a finger against his mouth. "But only when truly necessary."

Grant smothered a grin as he took her hand and pressed a kiss to her palm. He felt her tremble. It was slight, but telling, so he cupped her chin, finally giving in to the craving he'd been fighting for days—or weeks, if he were honest.

Taking that first, precious kiss.

As soon as their lips touched, as gentle as a snowflake drifting down from the heavens, she breathed out a funny little sigh. At that moment, Grant knew he would never forget this kiss. Kathleen's lips were as soft as rose petals, and as sweet as the ripest of berries.

For long moments, he simply enjoyed the feel of her smooth skin under his fingertips as he brushed feather-light kisses against her mouth. He wouldn't rush her. As confident as she was, Kathleen was a novice to lovemaking. Her response was shy, almost tentative, as if she were exploring a world without a map, not quite sure which way to go.

Holding his instincts in check took a mighty effort. He longed to take her mouth in the same way he wanted to take her body, with complete and total abandon. But he'd be damned if he rushed her. He'd give her all the time she needed to—

When Kathleen's tongue surged between his lips, Grant almost fell off the bench. She grabbed his shoulders, huffing out a laugh before slipping inside once more. Her innocent eagerness caught him completely off guard.

And set him aflame like a torch.

Brushing aside her cloak, he circled Kathleen's waist and pulled her close. She quivered as her breasts pressed against him. Grant let his fingers drift over her rib cage, brushing her plump curves before settling on the gentle swell of her hip. He imagined stripping off her silky gown to explore every inch of her even silkier skin, licking his way down her body to the intimate secrets hidden between her thighs.

Hold back, ye randy bastard.

They were on a damn garden bench on a cold autumn night, and all he could think of was having his way with her? He'd never been so close to losing control. But her delicate kisses, followed by the luscious sweep of her tongue, turned him rock-hard with desire.

Unable to hold back, he finally stroked into her mouth with greedy, demanding desire. Shuddering, Kathleen dug her fingers into his coat before responding with a passion that almost knocked him off the bench a second time.

After heated minutes that brought him to the brink of

losing every vestige of control, Kathleen gasped and pulled back.

Grant stilled. "Do you want me to stop?" he gritted out.

She peered up at him, puzzled. "Why would I want you to stop?"

"Because *you* just stopped. I don't want to push you, sweetheart."

She made an exasperated noise. "Silly. I just had to catch my breath."

When he chuckled, she started to pull him back down. He evaded her mouth, pressing kisses along her jawline before flicking her dangling earbob with his tongue and then licking the edge of her ear.

"Goodness," she breathily said.

He nipped her earlobe. She dug her fingers into his coat, as if needing to keep her balance. Smiling to himself, Grant moved down the lovely line of her neck, kissing his way to the dainty curve of her breasts. Kathleen pressed a hand to the back of his skull, melting in his arms.

When he flicked his tongue over the top of her plump breast, she squirmed. Grant came to the belated realization that she was now fully bent over his arm. He'd soon be dipping under the edge of her stays and searching for her tender nipple. Under the circumstances—sitting on a cold bench with a house party roaring away behind them—it counted as supremely idiotic behavior.

Regretfully, he moved away from the temptation posed by her breasts. But when he paused to drag his tongue over the fluttering pulse in her throat, Kathleen breathed out a delicious moan that sent a bolt of heat to his groin.

He lifted his head and took her mouth in a deep, devouring kiss. As she trembled in his arms, Grant thanked every saint in the heavens for the fact that she wanted him as much as he wanted her.

But then something penetrated the haze of passion in his brain, something that had been trying to punch through.

He froze.

Kathleen's eyelids fluttered open. "What's wrong?" she asked in a soft, husky voice.

That voice tempted him to forget what his brain was trying to tell him.

He couldn't, though.

"Do you smell smoke?" he asked.

She looked befuddled for a moment, then her brows snapped together. "Yes."

Grant kept a loose hold on her as he scanned the back of the house, looking for the source.

"It's quite strong," she added in a concerned tone.

"Yes." And it smelled wrong. Not like a normal fire from the kitchens or one of the chimneys.

"You can let me go," she said. "I won't topple over."

He glanced at her and grimaced. Both her dress and her hair were more than a wee bit disheveled. "Sorry, lass."

"It doesn't matter."

He gave her a hand up. She drew the cloak around herself and followed him out of the gazebo. Grant again scanned the house, then cast a quick glance toward the stables and outbuildings. He saw nothing, even though the acrid smell was growing stronger.

"Can you go to the kitchen and alert the housekeeper?" he asked. "Mrs. Wilson needs to check the house."

She nodded. "Where are you going?"

"The stables and outbuildings. They look all right, but—"

He broke off at the sound of hooves pounding along the

path from the distillery. A rider was hell-bent for leather from the sounds of it. He strode to the gate with Kathleen scurrying behind him, just as a familiar figure pulled up and flung himself off the horse.

"Mr. Kendrick," gasped Dickie Barr. "The distillery is on fire."

Grant's heart slammed into his ribs. Fire and explosion were a distiller's greatest fears. He and Graeme had almost set themselves on fire more than once back in the day. But Graeme had learned from those near mishaps and made the new building as fireproof as possible.

"How did it start, Dickie?"

"Arson. Some bastard climbed in through the back window and—"

Grant didn't need to hear those details. "Is there anyone in the building?"

"Adams, the night watchman, was upstairs when it happened. It started at the base of the stairs, cutting them . . . uh . . ."

Grant almost shook him. "What do you mean, them?"

"Miss Jeannie's with Adams, ye ken," Dickie blurted out. "She came to see the cat."

When Kathleen gasped, Grant snaked an arm around her waist.

"You're saying Jeannie is trapped?" she choked out.

Dickie grimaced. "I was about to try to get up the stairs, but Adams shouted I had to run for help, instead."

Grant knew what he had to do. "I'll take your horse, Dickie. You run to the kitchens and raise the alarm. Get all the help you can. Kathleen, go with him."

"I'm going with you," she snapped.

"Lass, I don't have—"

She pulled away and hurried through the gate, taking the reins from Dickie. Cursing, Grant followed her.

"Run!" he ordered Dickie.

As the young man took off toward the house, Grant hauled himself up into the saddle. The horse shied a bit, but Kathleen firmly held him. Once she'd transferred the reins, Grant reached down a hand for her.

"This is a bad idea," he grimly said.

"It's not up for debate."

He reached down for her. It was a bit of a scramble, but he got her quickly settled in front of him. Then he turned the jittery animal on the narrow path.

"Hold tight," Grant said.

Kathleen wove her fingers in the horse's mane. "I'm not an idiot, sir."

She'd gotten her fear under control, but it went against all his protective instincts to bring her toward danger. Still, he understood, and knew he would do the same if in her position.

He prodded the horse into a canter, resisting the urge to gallop. It was dark, and he didn't know the path as well as Dickie.

"This is my fault." Her voice was tight with anguish. "If I'd gone up to check on her—"

"The only ones at fault are the bastards who set the damn fire. And I'm bloody well going to kill them when I find them."

When they rounded the long curve in the path, Kathleen let out a strangled cry. Grant hissed a curse under his breath.

Flames were visible through the windows on the ground floor, and smoke seeped out from doors and windows. He couldn't see any flames on the upper floors, so Jeannie and Adams should still be relatively safe. Unless—

"What if the fire reaches the casks?" Kathleen asked, seeming to read his thoughts.

"I'll get them out before it does."

If even one cask caught fire, the building could go up like a torch. And if fumes were left in the stills . . .

Grant reined in before the gate to the distillery. Kathleen pushed herself off the horse, all but tumbling down into the dirt.

"Dammit, lass," he barked as he pulled the panicking horse away from her.

Ignoring him, she scrambled up and pelted down the path toward the distillery. Grant swung his leg over the saddle, slid to the ground, and took off after her. Her dark cloak streamed behind her as she raced for the front door, and Grant had to lengthen his stride to catch her.

When he did, he pulled her to a halt just as her hand reached out for the door handle.

Kathleen struggled in his arms. "Let me go!"

He pulled her tight against his body, where he could feel the frantic beat of her heart.

"You can't touch the handle. You'll burn your hand."

She wriggled like a worm on a hook. "I don't care! I have to get to her."

Grant put steel into his voice. "Not by running straight into the fire, you won't. We'll all end up dead."

She froze in his arms, her breathing erratic. "We have to do something," she managed.

"I know. I'm going to—"

"Kath!" cried Jeannie's voice from above.

Her sister leaned out the window, the cat clutched to her chest.

Kathleen sagged in Grant's arms. "Are you all right, love?" she called out.

A grizzled head poked out of the window beside Jeannie.

"Aye, we're fine," Adams said. "But it's getting' smoky up here."

"And very hot," Jeannie added in a tearful voice.

"Darling, we're going to get you down right now," Kathleen replied. "Just stay calm."

"Adams, take Jeannie and go to the north end of the building, the part closest to the stream," Grant ordered.

Every distillery had a source of water close by. At Lochnagar, it was a deep, swift-moving stream that drained into a nearby loch. At the far end of the building, the stream ran right beneath the windows, kept in its course by bulkheads. Jeannie and Adams could always jump for it, if everything else failed, though it was not a good option.

Adams nodded, clearly taking Grant's meaning. "Come along, lass," he said to Jeannie.

"I don't want to leave Kath," she tearfully replied.

As Kathleen persuaded her sister to go with Adams, Grant took a quick look into the closest window. There was a hell of a lot of smoke, and flames were visible at the back of the building, around the stairs, and close to the still chimneys. Fortunately, Graeme never left the peat fires burning at night unless a full crew was working. And most of the casks were stored by damn good luck against the wall closest to the office, thus away from the fire.

But the stairs *were* bloody well blocked, as fire licked its way up the staircase and the wall behind.

Kathleen joined him at the window. "What can you see?"

"The stairs are on fire."

She pressed a hand to her mouth.

"But Jeannie and Adams are safe for now," he quickly added. "This building is new, so the wood is fresh and shouldn't burn too fast."

She made a visible effort to control her fear. "What can we do?"

He stepped back, looking for footholds on the building. Unfortunately, it was built too damn well for him to scale the wall to an upper window.

"We need a ladder, or something I can climb on and get purchase on that window sill."

She whipped around. "The horse—"

But it had bolted, because Grant had been chasing after her instead of lashing him to the gate.

"There's a work shed around the back," he said. "I'll look there for a ladder or something else first. You go round the other side of the building and see if you can find anything."

She raced off while he ran around the building to the shed. Smoke and blazing heat poured out from a broken window where the arsonist had gained entry.

The shed door was locked. Ignoring his watering eyes, he drove a kick just above the lock that knocked the door half off its hinges. A quick survey of the room—mostly by feel—told him there was no damn ladder. He found an axe, though, and snatched it up just in case.

Outside again, he searched the back of the distillery for a way in. The back door was too near the stairs, which were now almost engulfed in flames. He'd have to try to scale up the building somehow and hope he didn't slip on the whitewashed walls and tumble down, splitting open his skull.

He was looking for handholds, when Kathleen came pelting toward him.

"I found one," she gasped. "At the north end of the building. It was just lying there in the grass."

Thank God.

"Grant, where are you?" roared a familiar voice.

A moment later, his twin stalked around the corner. They rushed to meet him.

"Jeannie's inside, upstairs," gasped Kathleen. "With the watchman. But there's a—"

"Ladder, I know," Graeme said. "Captain Brown is already on it. He and the others will get Jeannie and Adams out."

Kathleen took off, racing around the corner of the building.

"We've got to get this bloody fire out before the casks go up," Graeme said.

"Do we have enough equipment for a bucket brigade?" Grant asked.

"Aye, but not enough to get around from the stream to the front of the building. We've got to get that back door open."

"Agreed. But it's damn close to the fire. It'll be hot as Hades, and I doubt the key will even work in the lock."

Graeme shoved a frustrated hand through his hair, making it stand straight up. "It's a bloody sturdy door. We'll have to take that axe to it, and then kick it open."

They could now hear shouts from the front of the building. Sabrina came pelting around the corner to join them, the greatcoat over her gown flapping out behind her. When she reached them, she bent over, gasping to catch her breath.

Graeme crouched down beside her. "Love, are you all right?"

"I . . . I just ran the whole way, that's all." She straightened up with a grimace. "Angus says the fire is getting close to the casks."

Graeme nodded. "We're going to get this door open. Tell Angus to bring the men back here with the buckets."

"What about Jeannie and Adams?" Grant asked Sabrina.

"The captain was bringing Jeannie down when I arrived," she said.

"Good. Now hurry and get Angus and the others, all right?" Graeme said.

Sabrina threw her arms around Graeme's neck. "You be careful, husband."

"I'll take care of him," Grant promised.

"You'd best, or I'll murder you both." Then Sabrina raced back the way she came.

"Bloodthirsty lass," Grant commented.

"She learned it from me," his twin replied as he studied the back door. He carefully touched it and yanked his hand back. "Hot as hell, as predicted."

"Remember how we got into the kirk at Kinglas? We'll need to do it like that, I reckon."

When they were sixteen, they'd broken into the local kirk to raid the collection plate. It was a prank, and they'd always intended to return the money. The vicar had caught them dead-to-rights as they kicked in the lock on the back door.

Graeme snorted. "Aye. I'll use that axe you've got on the lock."

Grant handed it over. "Might be a backwash once we get the blasted thing open, so be prepared."

His twin nodded and then swung the axe in a mighty heave at the door handle. The blow knocked the door handle off, and hopefully broke the lock.

"Ready?" Graeme asked, glancing at Grant.

Grant nodded, and they positioned themselves, side by side, a few feet from the door.

"Count of three," Graeme said.

He counted off. Then, as one, they took flying kicks at the wide wooden door.

It gave, crashing inward. A blast of heat and smoke rushed over them as they both fell flat on their backs in the dirt.

For a moment, Grant lay stunned, trying to collect both his breath and his wits.

"Lads, are ye all right?"

Grant took his grandfather's hand and scrambled up, while Dickie assisted Graeme to his feet. They turned, gazing into the flames.

Graeme started to talk, but broke off with a cough.

"The buckets, Grandda," Grant hoarsely ordered.

"Aye."

Within moments, the men formed a line from the stream to the back door, mostly staff from the manor. They began passing buckets along to Graeme, who stood by the door ready to heave in the water.

"Grandda, we need more men and buckets," Grant said as he handed a full pail to his brother.

"We've got plenty of men. Not sure about the buckets."

"Go see. We can get a second brigade through the back window."

Sabrina came hurrying back. "Jeannie and Adams are both safe. Kathleen and Captain Brown are taking them to the manor."

"Have one of the footmen go with them," Graeme said. "Davey, if he's free."

Sabrina frowned but went off to do as he asked.

Grant exchanged a glance with his twin as he handed him a bucket. Clearly, neither of them trusted the captain, but that was a discussion for later. Now that everyone was out of danger, they had to focus on keeping Graeme and Sabrina's investment—and the hope of future prosperity for Dunlaggan—from being completely lost to the flames.

Angus returned with men who quickly formed a second water line. Magnus came with him, carrying what looked to be a pile of blankets.

"I'm goin' to soak yon blankets and throw them over the bigger casks," he yelled to Graeme. "Them casks are too big to move without puttin' the men in danger."

"Aye, that," Graeme called back.

In grim silence they worked, staff from the manor and men from the village working hard and efficiently. It was brutal and desperate, and Grant lost track of time. Smoke billowed as water doused flames, all but choking them. But still they kept on.

After what seemed a lifetime, the fire appeared finally beaten. Graeme wrapped a kerchief around his face and went farther inside for a look.

"All right, lads," he called. "It's all out."

The men dropped their buckets, and most sank to the ground. A few staggered to the stream to splash water over their heads.

"As bad as it looks?" Grant asked as his brother came out.

"A bloody mess, but we'll have to go around front to get a better look before we know how bad."

As they walked around the front of the building, Grant felt someone had pummeled him.

"God, I could use a drink," he rasped out. "Got any whisky about the place?"

His twin's derisive snort turned into a cough.

As they came around the corner, Sabrina rushed over and threw herself into her husband's arms.

"Lass," he protested, "I smell like the depths of hell."

"I don't care," she said in a muffled voice. "As long as you're all right."

"Och, I'm fine."

She raised her head to look at Grant. "And you?"

"We're both fine."

"And ye saved the building," Angus said, clapping Graeme on the shoulder.

Magnus emerged from the front door, his face as grimy as his clothing.

"How bad is it?" Graeme asked.

"The stills are ruined, sir, and God knows what the heat did to the brew in the casks."

"What about the building?"

"From what I can tell at first look, the staircase is fair wrecked, but the structure seems solid. Nae that canna be fixed, thank the guid Lord."

Graeme heaved a sigh. "And no one was hurt, which is most important."

Magnus looked down at the ground. "I'm right sorry, Sir Graeme. I shoulda been more careful, what with all that's been goin' on."

"None of this is your fault, Magnus," Graeme said.

Sabrina patted the big man's arm. "Indeed, no. Who could ever imagine someone could do something so dreadful?"

Graeme muttered a curse.

His twin's bleak expression made Grant want to put a fist through a wall. Graeme and Sabrina had worked so hard, and now this, on top of everything else?

"It's time we run that someone to ground," he said, grasping Graeme's shoulder. "Once and bloody for all."

Chapter Twenty

Sabrina looked up from the stack of mail by her plate as Kathleen entered the breakfast parlor. "There you are. Did you get any sleep last night?"

Kathleen headed straight for the coffeepot that beckoned from the mahogany sideboard. "A bit. Jeannie wanted to sleep with me but insisted that Mrs. Wiggles join us. I can tell you with absolute certainly that your cat came honestly by her name."

"Oh, dear." Sabrina crinkled her nose. "She must have been covered in soot."

"We tried to wipe her down, but Mrs. Wiggles preferred to clean herself—for half the night. I know because she was sitting on my legs for most of it."

Sabrina looked torn between exasperation and amusement. "Kath, you should have put the dratted thing out in the hall."

"Hannah conveyed that message quite emphatically when she saw the state of my bed linens this morning."

"The whole house is in an uproar, I'm afraid. But that's no reason for you to put up with one of Hannah's scolds or our ridiculous cat."

Kathleen took a seat across from her. "I rather enjoy Hannah's scolds. They're colorful. And I truly don't think I would have slept much, anyway, after all that commotion."

Commotion that included a stimulating encounter with Grant in the gazebo.

Sabrina grimaced. "What a dreadful visit this is turning out to be for you. I do apologize, dearest. I cannot imagine what you must think of us."

Kathleen pointed a finger at her. "Sabrina Kendrick, don't you dare apologize. You're in the middle of a crisis, and our presence has caused one complication after another."

"At least I don't think we'll have to worry about our vicar. After that scene in the study, I shouldn't be surprised if the poor man went home, packed his bags, and left Dunlaggan with all speed."

"Another bad outcome you can lay at my door."

Sabrina scoffed. "It's just stuff and nonsense, especially compared to our other problems."

Kathleen glanced at the clock when it chimed out the hour. "I take it the men are already back at the distillery?"

"Yes. Graeme and Grant left at first light, and Angus shortly thereafter. The twins wanted to have a good look around the place in the daytime, to see if they could find any clues."

"Any real chance of that?"

"Graeme thinks it doubtful, given how carefully these bounders covered their tracks. But he needed to get a work crew organized for repairs, as well."

Kathleen squeezed her cousin's hand. "I'm so sorry, old girl."

"Truly, I feel the worst for poor Magnus. He was dev-

astated. Most of the last distillation was ruined, I'm afraid."
Sabrina shook her head. "And I've never seen my husband
as furious as he was over the danger to Jeannie and Adams."

"I cannot say that I blame Graeme, which brings me to
my next point."

"You wish to return to Glasgow with Jeannie." Sabrina
nodded. "I'll miss you, of course, but it's perfectly under-
standable."

Kathleen shook her head. "I have no intention of abandoning you. I'm only surprised your husband hasn't loaded
you and Gus into the carriage already."

"He did try that on last night until I made the case that
we would be perfectly safe as long as we didn't stray beyond
the gardens. Besides, I have no intention of deserting my
people in the middle of this uproar."

"Graeme actually accepted that?" Kathleen skeptically
asked.

Sabrina wrinkled her nose. "Not immediately. But Grant
backed me up, thank goodness. He's very good at calming
my Highland warrior's agitation down to a dull roar."

"He's very good at a lot of things."

When Sabrina's eyebrows ticked up, Kathleen hastily
went on.

"But it's Jeannie I want to talk to you about. If she
would truly listen to me, it might not be a problem to let
her stay. But as it is . . ."

"But surely she'll listen to you now, after last night."

"Maybe, but it won't last." Kathleen felt sure of that. "I
do think she must go home to London."

"Have you discussed it with her?"

"I thought I would do it over breakfast."

Sabrina chuckled. "With me providing cover?"

"Sorry," Kathleen sheepishly replied.

"Don't be. It makes perfect sense. And here she is now," Sabrina brightly added as the door opened and Jeannie shuffled in. "Good morning, my dear. I hope you slept well."

The girl sat in the chair next to Kathleen, looking pale and wan.

"Not really." Jeannie took a scone from the generous plate of pastries. "I couldn't help worrying about David. He must be *terribly* upset about last night. Captain Brown said he would make sure to tell him that I wasn't injured."

Argh.

Kathleen forced a calm reply. "That was very kind of the captain, but I hardly think the vicar's feelings is the worst of our problems at the moment."

Jeannie paused while ladling marmalade onto her scone. "What are you talking about, Kath?"

"The fire, pet. You could have been killed."

"It wasn't my fault, though," her sister protested. "I had no idea that was going to happen."

"Of course not, but you left the house without telling me. There are very dangerous men about, Jeannie. And they are doing dreadful things. You cannot be wandering about on your own."

Her sister's chin went up in a familiar mutinous tilt. "It's just a short walk to the distillery, and nothing happened on the way there."

"True, but you could have been seriously hurt, dearest," Kathleen said. "Can you imagine how our parents would feel if anything happened to you?"

"But nothing did. And I'm fine."

"Yes, but—"

"I'm *fine*."

Kathleen was beginning to hate that phrase.

"I think what we're trying to say, dear," Sabrina said, "is that it might be time for you to return to London. The situation here is quite volatile."

Jeannie put down her knife. "Are you going back to London, Kath?"

Kathleen fixed her with a firm gaze. "No. Sabrina needs my help."

"Then I'm staying, too," Jeannie said.

"Dearest, that's not a very sensible—"

"Well, if it's not sensible for me to stay, then it's not sensible for you to stay," her sister retorted.

"It's different, Jeannie. As I said, Sabrina needs me. Besides, I'm older."

Her sister bolted up. "I can help too, Kath. I'm not stupid, you know. Stop treating me like I'm just a little girl."

Kathleen also rose. "Of course you're not a little girl. But at the moment you're rather acting like one."

When Jeannie began to argue, Kathleen held up a hand. "This is not up for discussion. In the absence of our parents, I am your guardian. And it's best you return to London."

Her sister's glare was hot enough to singe Kathleen's eyebrows. "I'm not leaving and you can't make me."

"Dearest, please be re—"

Jeannie stamped her foot. "No! I'm not leaving David, and nothing you can say will change my mind."

And with that, she stormed out of the room.

"Oh, Lord." Kathleen sank back into her chair. "Do you think it's too early to have a drink?"

Sabrina grimaced in sympathy. "At this rate, I might very well join you."

* * *

Rather than take refuge in a morning tipple, Kathleen had turned to the garden. She'd mulched vegetable beds, sorted herbs for drying, and carted dirt back and forth in a wheelbarrow. Though one of the stable boys had offered to help, she'd needed the hard work to keep her mind off what to do with her stubborn little sister and what to do with Grant Kendrick.

The first problem was immediate and evoked anxious frustration. That Jeannie was as out of control as a wobbly top had been amply demonstrated by last night's events. The only realistic way to keep her sister from harm was to get her back to London and under Helen's watchful eye. But short of tying Jeannie up and sitting on her for the entire trip, Kathleen very much doubted she would prevail.

She knelt down on the grass verge to yank out an especially recalcitrant beetroot and then tossed it into the wheelbarrow.

"Face it, old girl," she muttered to herself, "you've royally cocked it up."

"Did you say something, Kathleen?"

She let out an exasperated sigh at the sound of the voice before looking up at the giant looming over her. The blasted man was so handsome in his riding gear, with a smile lifting the corners of his oh-so-delectable mouth, that she almost forgot to be annoyed with him.

"Sneaking up on me again, Mr. Kendrick? Such a bad habit."

He crouched down beside her. "As I suggested last night, you should put a bell on me."

"That wouldn't be very practical for someone skulking about after various and sundry villains, now would it?"

"You have me there, lass."

She eyed him. Despite the warmth of his expression, she could see the fatigue in his eyes and the lines of worry around his mouth.

"I take it you've been doing just that this morning," she said.

"Yes, without much success. Graeme and I went over the scene very thoroughly but found little that could point us in the right direction." He grimaced. "Or any direction."

"I'm sorry. It must be so frustrating."

"Especially for my brother. He's ready to go on a rampage. Stealing, vandalism, and even a highway robbery are significantly different from arson."

"I'm sure Graeme is very grateful to have your help and support."

"He is. Not that I've been able to do much thus far."

She glanced down at his feet. "It seems you've been out scouring meadow and glen, though. Getting rather muddy, if your boots are any indication."

"I was following a set of fresh footprints along the stream and then through a barley field behind one of the tenant farms. Turns out they belonged to the farmer's son."

She gave him a gentle poke on his brawny bicep. "Surely you're not giving up? That's not the Kendrick way, from what I understand."

"No, it's not. I only returned to the manor because bad weather is heading our way."

She hadn't noticed until now the dark storm clouds gathering over the craggy peaks in the distance. "That does look quite ugly."

"Quite. We've got a few hours before it hits, but I figured there was no point getting caught in the middle of it. I'll go back out again once it's passed."

"Well," she said, "I suppose I should start cleaning all this up then."

Grant rose and helped her to stand. "We could take shelter in the gazebo."

She stripped off her work gloves. "Since the gazebo has no walls, I will treat that comment with the consideration it deserves."

He tilted his head, his forest-green gaze studying her with an intensity that made her pulse flutter. "I found it quite cozy last night. Didn't you?"

"That is entirely beside the point."

"What point are you referring to?"

"That there will be no repeats of last night's incident."

"I hope you're talking about the fire." He crouched a bit, resting his hands on his knees so they were at eye level. "And not about our kiss, because I was truly hoping for another one of those."

With his mouth only inches away from hers—and knowing what pleasures his mouth could provide—Kathleen had to muster an unfortunate degree of willpower to stand her ground.

"In case you've failed to notice, sir, it's broad daylight and we're in the middle of the kitchen garden. In full view of the house."

"Ah. We simply have to wait for nightfall." He straightened up and took out his pocket watch. "Which is in approximately—"

"Don't be ridiculous."

He raised his russet eyebrows. "We don't have to wait for darkness? Even better."

When he leaned down as if to kiss her, she whacked him on the arm with her dirty garden glove.

"Och, lass. The laundry maid will nae be happy about that, ye ken. Ye've left muck on my sleeve."

"And I'll be thankin' you not to be such a booby, Grant Kendrick," she sarcastically echoed him with her own brogue.

He grinned, unrepentant. "I simply wish to be clear about the rules of conduct when it comes to kissing. And, might I note, that for someone with a reputation for scandalous behavior, you're being quite missish."

"I've given over scandalous behavior, remember?"

"That is a terrible shame, Miss Calvert."

Since the seductive gleam in his gaze was temptation itself, and since she very much wished to engage in a spot of scandalous behavior, Kathleen forced herself to act stern.

"You wouldn't be the first man to experience an unfortunate accident with my watering can, sir."

Grant snorted. "So that's what yon vicar was referring to the other day. You gave him a soaking."

"Not just that. His frock coat had a distressing encounter with my garden clippers, as well. Therefore, since you seem to value your clothing so much—"

"I could take them off," he suggested. "But you'd have to promise to put your clippers down first."

Kathleen felt her eyes all but roll from their sockets. "Grant Kendrick, if you do not behave yourself—"

He laughed. "All right, I'll stop teasing. Still, at some point we need to talk about what happened between us last night."

He was right. But at the moment, she didn't feel equipped for that particular conversation.

When she bent to retrieve her garden tools, he wrapped a hand around her wrist and brought her back up.

"Sweetheart, what's amiss?"

His voice was so gentle, and his expression so kind, that she longed to throw herself into the shelter of his embrace.

"Jeannie and I had another fight."

"About her running off to the distillery and getting trapped by the fire?"

She flapped a hand. "She skimmed right over that, believe it or not. No, it was over my insistence that she return to London."

He winced in sympathy. "That must have gone down a treat. Is it David she's not wishing to leave?"

"In a nutshell. How she can think there's any hope with a man almost twice her age—and a vicar, no less—is beyond me. If it were Kade, I could understand. But this infatuation with David is absolutely dotty."

"Infatuations usually are. Jeannie is young and impressionable, and Brown has become something of a hero to her. She'll get over it soon enough."

Kathleen sighed. "I used to be her hero."

"And you will be again, sweet girl."

After casting a quick glance around the garden, he tipped up her chin and pressed a kiss to her lips. He lingered for a few moments, and it was all Kathleen could do not to press her body against his.

When he pulled back, she had to struggle to find her voice. "That . . . that was very naughty of you."

"My fair colleen," he murmured in a deep brogue, "I am just getting started."

Suddenly, she felt a great deal better than she had even a few minutes ago. Kathleen had the sensation that with Grant by her side, any problem could be solved.

"Grant Kendrick, stop flirting and bring Kathleen inside," called a crisp feminine voice from the back door.

"Good Lord," Kathleen muttered as she glanced over her shoulder at Sabrina.

Grant rolled his eyes. "Och, Sabrina's as bad as my twin."

"I just need to put my gardening tools away," Kathleen called back.

Sabrina waved an impatient hand. "The gardener will take care of it."

"She's fashed about something," Grant said, taking Kathleen's arm.

"Not more trouble, I hope."

"What's wrong?" Grant asked Sabrina when they reached her.

"I cannot find Jeannie."

Kathleen's heart banged against her ribs. "She went up to her bedroom after breakfast. When I tried to speak with her before coming out to the garden, she told me to go away. That she wasn't coming out of her room."

"When Mrs. Wilson brought the tea tray to the drawing room, I asked one of the maids to fetch Jeannie," said Sabrina. "I thought she'd be hungry, since she'd not had any breakfast. But her room was empty."

"Did you try the study? She likes to read there in the afternoon."

Sabrina grimly shook her head. "Hannah and I have looked everywhere on the main floors. I sent Davey to poke around the rest of the house—"

She broke off when the Kendrick footman hurried toward them down the hallway. Kathleen rushed to meet him.

"Any luck?" she asked.

Davey grimaced. "Nae, miss. She's not in the house. Me and the housemaids looked everywhere, and we couldna find her. She's nae in the stables, either."

Kathleen shook her head in disbelief.

"Blast," said Sabrina. "I'm sorry, dearest. I should have kept a better eye on her."

"No, it's my fault. I am an absolute idiot."

"We can debate fault later," said Grant. "There's a storm coming, and it's a bad one. If she's caught in it—"

Kathleen didn't let him finish. "I'm going to change into my riding habit. Sabrina, please have someone saddle my horse."

She lifted her skirts and pelted down the hall, ignoring Grant's calls to wait.

Chapter Twenty-One

Grant reined in his bay at the top of the gentle rise that overlooked the small loch and scanned the area below. Kathleen, atop her mare, came up beside him.

"We should have found Jeannie by now," she said in a worried tone.

"Not if she's hiding. And given the row you had this morning, that's a distinct possibility. She probably needs a few hours to calm down and come back to her senses."

"But she's been gone for longer than a few hours, and dusk will be on us soon." Kathleen grimaced. "I'm worried that she's stumbled across that gang."

When she tightened her grip on the reins, her horse shook its head in protest.

Grant shot out a restraining hand. "Careful, lass. We don't want you getting tossed out here in the middle of nowhere."

He'd already lived that nightmare, and he'd be damned if he went through it again.

"Sorry, I'm being an idiot. But those awful men—"

"Graeme and I have been all over these grounds, and

we can't find the blasted thieves. Jeannie is not going to stumble upon them while walking across a field."

"I suppose you're right. Still, we should have come across her by now."

"She might never have come this way in the first place. That crofter only saw her from a distance, remember—if it even was her."

After their first hour of fruitless searching, they'd come across one of Graeme's tenants, who claimed to have seen a girl on the path to the loch. At the time, the man had not thought anything of it.

Kathleen stripped off one of her gloves, stuck two fingers in her mouth, and blew out an ear-splitting whistle. In the distance, a dog responded with a mournful howl, while the horses waggled their heads.

Grant tugged on his ear. "Bloody hell, lass. A bit of warning might have been helpful."

"Sorry, but I know Jeannie would recognize my whistle if she heard it."

"I imagine they heard it all the way back in Dunlaggan. It's quite impressive."

"One of my few genuine talents," she ruefully said.

"Och, sweetheart, you have many talents."

"Finding my sister isn't one of them."

Grant again scanned the surrounding area. "I'm rapidly coming to the conclusion that Jeannie didn't come this way."

Kathleen sighed. "I was so certain she had. Dickie told Jeannie about the smugglers' hut a few days ago, and how they used it as their hideout. She thought it all sounded terribly exciting."

Grant studied the simple hut, tucked up below on the

shoreline. "Aye, it's exactly the sort of place that would appeal to her."

"Perhaps she's hiding in it?"

Although it was obviously no longer used for smuggling purposes, Graeme had maintained the upkeep on both the hut and its long, sturdily built pier in the event that he expanded operations to this location. The lake eventually emptied out into Loch Laggan, which made it a prime route for shipping to Inverness and points beyond.

Graeme also kept the hut stocked with fuel, blankets, and other basics in case of emergencies. The weather changed quickly in the Highlands, and dangerously so in winter. The hut could serve as shelter for any crofter or shepherd caught out in the open.

His instincts told him, however, that Jeannie was not in there. "I think—"

A rumble of ominously loud thunder cut him off. Kathleen's horse skittered a bit, but she quickly brought the mare under control.

"That's getting too close for comfort," she said as she peered at the storm clouds piling up over the loch.

"Aye, there's no avoiding that mess now. That's why I wanted you to remain at the house."

They'd had a short but heated argument before beginning the search. After threatening to bash him over the head with a vase, Kathleen had marched off to the stables, leaving Grant with no choice but to lock her in her bedroom or go searching with her. Since he prided himself on both his logic and his sense of self-preservation, he'd chosen the second alternative.

Kathleen flashed him a scowl. "We've had this discussion."

"Without effect."

"Grant Kendrick, I will clobber you over the head if you don't cease pestering me," she threatened again, looking adorably fierce.

"Lass, I know you're worried, but I'm fairly convinced at this point that one of the others has found Jeannie or she returned home on her own."

They weren't the only ones searching, of course. Davey and one of the grooms had headed out in the opposite direction, and Sabrina had sent one of the stable boys running for Graeme and Angus.

"For us, though," he added, "that storm's about to hit. So *we* will now be taking shelter in the blasted hut."

The first drops of rain began to splatter in the dust and on their clothing. The rising wind kicked up dirt devils, and as if to hurry them along, a bolt of lightning shot across the sky, followed by growl of thunder.

Kathleen grimly nodded. "Lead on, sir."

By the time they reached the hut, the loch frothed with whitecaps and a heavy curtain of rain swiftly approached across the water. Graeme dismounted then went to help Kathleen down from her horse. As she came gracefully into his arms, her glossy curls brushed against his cheeks. For a moment, when their bodies pressed together, he had to fight the overwhelming urge to capture her lush lips with his mouth.

As if in rebuke for his wandering thoughts, a gust of wind snatched off his hat.

Grant nudged Kathleen toward the cabin. "Inside with you, while I take care of the horses."

She shielded her eyes from the wind. "Let me help."

"No need. There's a horse shed out back. It'll only take me a few minutes."

She seemed inclined to argue, but suddenly the wall of rain finally hit them with driving force.

"Go," he barked.

Kathleen dashed up onto the small porch, wrenched the door open, and disappeared into the hut.

Grant led the increasingly skittish animals around to the back. The sturdy shed behind the hut was big enough for two horses or a pair of cattle. Thankfully, Graeme had recently restocked it with hay and blankets for just such an emergency.

Grant unsaddled the horses, gave each a quick rub-down, and got them settled as best he could.

As the rain poured down in sheets, he ran around the hut and took the steps in one leap. Kathleen, who'd obviously been watching for him, opened the door.

Grant swiped his dripping hair aside as he glanced around the hut. "No Jeannie."

Kathleen unpinned her once-jaunty riding hat. "No."

Clearly frustrated, she tossed the bedraggled hat onto the table in the center of the one-room hut. "I can only hope she's home by now. Jeannie hates thunder and lightning."

Grant took off his greatcoat and slung it on a hook by the door. "She probably saw the storm coming in and scurried back home to safety."

Kathleen stared at him, her pewter-gray eyes as turbulent as the skies outside. "Do you truly think that, or are you just trying to make me feel better?"

"I would never insult your intelligence like that. For one thing, you would likely smash me on the noggin—a threat you made only a few hours ago, as I recall."

"I did, but only because you were acting like a thickhead. And *you* said that I was as reckless as Jeannie, which was very annoying of you."

"I simply said that you tended to be a bit cavalier with your own safety."

"I have been the opposite of cavalier since we arrived in Scotland. I'm so bloody careful about *everything* that I'm ready to murder myself out of boredom."

"Being careful does not make one boring, Kathleen. It makes one *careful*."

She jabbed a finger at him. "Name one time when I've acted irrationally, or without care for my safety."

"Well, there was—"

"And do *not* mention that stupid cricket game, because none of that was my fault."

He repressed a smile. "All right, I won't mention that particular incident."

She scowled and crossed her arms under her breasts, which nicely squeezed into plump mounds. In fact, Grant could see—

"Oh, is there another incident you'd like to mention?" she asked.

"Not one in particular. You do, however, have a marked inclination to risk both your reputation and safety to protect your sister."

"Wouldn't you do the same for your siblings?"

"That's different."

"Why?" Her voice was sugary-sweet. "Because you're a man?"

Grant shook his head. "I'm not walking into that trap, lass, so don't even try."

"Fah," she said, perfectly imitating Angus. "And by the way, you're staring at my chest. How very rude of you."

To be precise, he was staring at the pert outline of her nipples, which he could see through what had to be several layers of fabric. Very damp fabric.

"I'm only staring because it has finally occurred to me—thickhead that I am—that you're obviously wet and cold."

She looked perplexed for a moment but then shrugged. "I am feeling a bit soggy, but you're soaked, Grant. Your hair is positively dripping."

"Fortunately I was wearing a greatcoat. It held up better than your riding jacket."

"I'm fine." She then promptly shivered.

"Och, you should bash me over the head for letting you stand about in that damp outfit for even a moment. We need to get a fire going right now."

"I already tried while you were stabling the horses. I don't seem to have the knack for it."

Grant crouched down in front of the stove and began rearranging the haphazard stack of peat. "There is a bit of a trick to it." He glanced back at her. "Please take off that riding jacket. You've got to dry out, love."

"Ah . . ."

"Kathleen, your lips are turning blue."

She gave him a weak smile. "My shift was muddy from the garden, so I took it off. And I forgot to put on a blouse. I dressed in rather a hurry, as you know."

No wonder he'd been able to see the outline of her nipples. "Are you saying . . ."

She flapped a hand. "I'm wearing stays, so it's all perfectly respectable. Well, mostly, anyway."

Since Grant had already seen a pair of her stays, he knew they were the opposite of respectable.

He nodded toward a trunk on the other side of the room. "There are clean blankets in there. Off with the jacket, and wrap yourself in one of them while I get this fire going."

"All right, but keep your back turned."

"Lass, I'm the boring one, remember? So boring it wouldn't even occur to me to take a peek."

"It's my opinion that your so-called boring behavior is nothing but a ruse to lull the rest of us into complacency." She waved a hand. "Now, turn around."

He snorted but complied with her direction and turned back to the stove. "Why, exactly, am I so intent on lulling everyone into a state of complacency?"

"It's how you get people to do what you want."

He glanced over his shoulder in disbelief, just as she slipped off her jacket to reveal her stays. They weren't the ones from the day of the robbery but they were still very pretty, trimmed in blue ribbons instead of pink. Fortunately, since she was facing the trunk, she didn't see him gaping at her like an untried schoolboy.

Hastily, he turned back to the stove. "Lass, you're confusing me with someone else. My family rarely does what I want. It's the opposite, in fact, as is evidenced by our trip to Lochnagar."

"They ask you to do that sort of thing because they can depend on you."

"That sounds rather boring," he dryly replied.

There was silence for several moments before she answered. "I used to think that always being the reliable one is such a bore. But now I think there's nothing more tiresome—more *boring*, in fact—than constantly dashing about and raising a ruckus. Because if you're doing that all the time, it probably means you're . . ."

"Bored?"

"Yes. Or something isn't right, and you're not quite sure what it is. It's exhausting trying to figure it out."

Her voice was quiet, as if she were speaking to herself. She sounded rather lost and alone, and not the confident lass who always faced the world with courage and more than a bit of dash.

Resisting the urge to get up and pull her into his arms, Grant retrieved the flint from the basket next to the stove and started the fire.

"And there's certainly nothing interesting about an unreliable person," Kathleen added in a firmer tone. "In fact, it's immensely irritating."

"I assume we're now speaking about a certain little sister who shall remain nameless."

"Ha ha, how terribly amusing."

Smiling to himself, Grant added another square to the smoldering peat. It properly caught, and soon a welcome heat poured out into the room.

He stood. "Is it safe to turn around?"

"I am now perfectly respectable."

Grant turned to find her sitting in one of the cane chairs at the rough-hewn table. Wrapped in a plaid blanket that covered her to the knees, with her thick hair haphazardly contained by a messy topknot, she looked quite raffish and anything but boring.

In fact, she looked like she'd just rolled out of bed after a cracking good tumble. And that mental image now set his mind in an entirely inappropriate direction, especially given their circumstances. At the moment, he could think of nothing he'd rather do more than carry his fey colleen over to the narrow bed in the corner and give her a right, good tumble on the spot.

Kathleen's smile was a half wince. "I must look a wreck."

"You look entirely charming. How are your boots? Did they get wet?"

She stuck a foot out, showing him an impressively sturdy

boot. "I bought these in Glasgow. Vicky said I would need them in the Highlands."

"What about the rest of you? You're starting to get warm enough?"

She rolled her eyes. "I might be skinny, but I'm no Dresden miss, sir."

Skinny was not how he would describe her. "If I return you to Lochnagar with even a sniffle, Sabrina will murder me."

"You're the one who got soaked, not me."

When she snaked an arm from under the blanket and pointed at him, he caught an enticing glimpse of creamy freckled skin and blue bows.

He again raked back his wet hair. "Just my head."

"There are towels in the trunk."

Grant retrieved a sturdy cloth and went to work on his hair. Once done with that, he pulled off his riding jacket. Hooking one of the cane chairs, he placed it close to the stove and hung his jacket over the back.

"Where's your jacket, lass?"

When she didn't answer, he glanced over to find her staring at him, rather wide-eyed. A flush stained her cheeks, making her freckles glow.

"Kathleen?"

She gave a start. "Sorry, it's on that bench by the trunk."

Grant retrieved the crumpled jacket and shook it out before carefully hanging it next to his. "Should be dry in no time."

When another crack of thunder shook the cottage, she grimaced. "I wonder how long this will go on?"

"Another hour or so, I imagine."

She muttered something unhappy about her sister.

Grant crossed to a set of shelves that contained crockery,

tumblers, and, thankfully, a full decanter of Lochnagar's finest. He uncorked the bottle and poured out two glasses.

"I will bet you a bob that she's back at the house by now," Grant said.

"What if she's not?"

"Then she'll get a good soaking."

She bristled. "Is that supposed to make me feel better?"

He handed her a glass. "No, but this will. And try to stop worrying about Jeannie. Don't forget this is the girl who survived two days in a carriage boot."

"Yes, but—"

"You never finished telling me how I'm able to get my family to do what I want. I still have my doubts about that."

Her smile was rueful. "Because of our trip to Lochnagar, you mean."

"That's one example."

"Very well, then. Once someone has convinced you that something is necessary, you then arrange for how it gets done, in the way *you* want it done. People only think they're getting their way, but it's really you."

"That's sounds rather manipulative of me."

She waggled her sleek eyebrows. "Oh, it's very manipulative. But also very helpful. And you're so good at it that most people never even notice."

He pointed to himself. "Old sobersides, bending everyone to my evil will?"

"Exactly. You have them all fooled."

It was so ridiculous that he had to laugh. "Kathleen, my family runs me from pillar to post."

She cocked her head and studied him. "It seems to me that you're also quite good at holding your family at arm's length. You can be very reserved, in your own quiet way."

Home hit, old boy.

"And how do I do that?" he asked in a neutral tone.

"For one thing, you don't yell." She rolled her eyes. "Other Kendricks yell *quite* a lot."

He snorted. "Noticed, did you?"

"One would have to be dead not to notice. You sit there and let them storm and bluster. Then, when they've blown themselves out, you make a suggestion." She shrugged, revealing more bare shoulder. "From what I can tell, at that point they usually do what you suggest."

That was precisely how he'd learned to manage his family.

She gave him a rueful smile. "I wish I had the knack for it, at least with Jeannie."

They drank their whisky, listening to the hard drum of rain on the roof. Kathleen shifted to rearrange her blanket more closely around her shoulders.

"Can I ask you a question?" she said softly.

"Of course."

"Why have you never married?"

Grant blinked. "Sorry?"

"I know it's very forward of me, but most men of your age and social standing are married by now."

"Perhaps I'm simply a confirmed bachelor, too fussy for my own good."

She scoffed. "Balderdash. I'd wager you've had legions of girls trailing after you. As a longtime denizen of the Marriage Mart, I'm quite expert on these matters."

He thought it best to deflect the uncomfortable discussion about his life. "Well, you're an exceedingly eligible young lady. Why aren't *you* married?"

"Simple. No one has asked me."

"Are all the men in London complete boobs?"

She chuckled. "Apparently so. Now, stop dodging the question."

"Frankly, I've just never given the matter much thought."

That wasn't entirely true. He'd met several interesting girls over the years who likely would have made splendid wives if he'd taken the trouble to court them. Except for that one ridiculous episode in his youth, he'd never been willing to put forth the effort.

Until now.

Kathleen wisely nodded. "That makes sense, given the sort of person you are."

That did *not* sound promising.

"And what sort of person am I?"

"A solitary one."

He snorted. "Surrounded by so many noisy Kendricks? Impossible."

"On the contrary. One can live surrounded by people and still feel alone."

And wasn't that a twist of the knife in the heart? It seemed impossible that someone as bright and vivacious as Kathleen, so full of light and warmth she practically shimmered, could feel alone. Could *be* alone.

If there was ever a woman who deserved loving, who deserved to be the heart and soul of a man's life, it was Kathleen Calvert.

"Sweetheart, I—"

Lightning exploded outside, followed by a deafening roll of thunder that seemed to vibrate through the whole hut. Kathleen startled, then made a grab for her blanket as it began to slide from her shoulders.

"Good Lord, that was awful," she exclaimed.

Grant rose and crossed to the small window. He tried

to see through the driving rain, but couldn't because it was practically a bloody gale out there.

They wouldn't be leaving anytime soon.

And that could be a problem. Dusk would come fast on the heels of the storm. As it was, they were skating on the very edges of propriety. If they were stuck here alone much longer—

"I hope the horses don't take fright," Kathleen said.

Grant returned to the table. "They should be fine. The shed is new and sturdily built."

Her lips rolled inward, tight with anxiety.

"You're worried about Jeannie."

She gave a morose little nod.

To hell with it.

The time for caution had passed, blown to tatters by the storm.

He pulled his chair close to hers and sat. Then he wrapped an arm around her shoulders, tucking her against him. She sank into his embrace with a funny little sigh.

"I did almost marry," he confessed. "When I was young and exceptionally stupid."

She wriggled sideways to look at his face. The motion pushed her breasts against him, a sensation he thoroughly enjoyed.

"Really? What happened?"

"Graeme and I eloped."

She choked out a laugh. "I know you and Graeme are exceedingly close, but that seems a bit much."

He pressed a kiss to the top of her messy curls. "Cheeky lass. I mean we jointly eloped with two young ladies of our acquaintance."

"Not very successfully, obviously."

"It was an epic disaster from beginning to end."

"They why did you do it?"

"It was my grandfather's idea, so that should tell you something."

When she tilted her head, her face was so close that he could practically count the freckles that danced across her cheekbones.

"I've noticed he's something of a matchmaker, but that idea seems rather deranged, even for him."

"When it comes to matchmaking, Angus lets no obstacle stand in his way, including the feelings of the various parties."

She wrinkled her nose. "How did this all come about?"

"Mostly as a result of our own bad behavior. The family consensus was that at the advanced age of twenty-two, it was time for the terrible twins to grow up. Angus believed that the most expedient path to such a laudable goal was marriage."

"Did he also pick out the girls for you?"

"I'm happy to say we managed that bit on our own."

She chuckled. "So much initiative."

"Angus planned the rest, though. He even came with us to direct the proceedings."

She jerked upright. "Your grandfather went with you on your elopement? Now you must be joking."

Grant resettled her under his arm. "Alas, no. Royal also participated in this mad scheme, although his efforts were markedly more successful. He and Ainsley eventually did get married."

"It sounds a rather crowded affair."

"It required two overloaded carriages to transport the lot of us from Glasgow to Kinglas."

"Really, it all sounds insanely complicated. Why didn't you simply sneak off and get married in Glasgow?"

"Not dramatic enough for a Highlander, ye ken. Besides, Graeme and I feared a concerted resistance from the fathers of our intended brides—not to mention from Nick. So we thought it best to put some distance between us and all of them." He shook his head. "It was an absurdity from beginning to end."

She made an impatient noise. "More details, please."

"Hmm. Well, Royal and Ainsley spent most of the journey yelling at each other, which unnerved the other girls and prompted them to begin having second thoughts. Naturally, this irritated Angus, which led to fairly predictable results."

"More yelling?"

"Exactly, and an unfortunate degree of name-calling. By the time we reached Kinglas, both girls swore they would rather be boiled in oil than marry a Kendrick. And that was even before the avalanche, and Graeme falling off the carriage and breaking his leg. We capped off this catalogue of disasters by coming down with wretched colds after we reached Kinglas. Suffice it to say that our intended brides were greatly relieved at the failure of our demented plan."

Kathleen twisted around again to stare up at him. "An avalanche? Really?"

"Really."

"That's . . . that's . . ." She dissolved into laughter.

"Go ahead and laugh," he said with a dramatic sigh. "Don't spare my feelings."

She shook even harder in his arms.

It was hilarious, of course, but also embarrassing. Even thinking about it made him feel like a bottle-headed moron. Yet if it served to distract his sweet lass from her troubles, it was worth it.

"Fortunately, Vicky and Nick caught up with us and quashed any gossip or scandal," he added. "It was a miracle poor Nick didn't shoot us for the crime of capital stupidity."

She giggled before subsiding against him.

Despite the raging storm outside, a quiet contentment settled over them. The peat fire gently hissed, pouring out a comforting heat, and the whisky drove out any lingering chill in his muscles. With Kathleen snuggled in his arms, Grant felt more at peace, more *himself*, than he had in a very long time.

She stirred, half turning her face into his shoulder.

"Were you sorry you didn't marry?" Her voice was muffled.

"I was sorry I caused so much trouble."

"But the young lady . . . did you love her?"

Now she was no longer resting softly in his embrace. Rather, her slender form felt rigid, as if tension had just invaded her limbs.

"I certainly liked her," he said, "but I'm not ashamed to admit that I mostly felt relief. I was far too stupid to know what I wanted at that point in my life."

"Do you know what you want now?"

He propped his chin on her head, smiling to himself. "I think so."

"And do you think you could love me . . . I mean, like me?"

There was a momentary silence before she tried to slide out of his embrace.

"Never mind," she hastily added. "Silly question. Just forget I asked it."

Grant gently pulled her back, turning her to face him. Her eyes were huge, her cheeks flushed, and her expression a heart-twisting mix of defiance and self-doubt. Never had he met someone who seemed so confident and yet so unsure—or unaware—of how bloody wonderful she truly was.

He cupped her chin. "Sweet lass, I *more* than like you."

Then he bent and captured her lips, determined to show her just how much.

Kathleen fell into the midst of a storm as Grant's desire swept over her. She rose up to meet it, all the emotion she'd denied for so long bursting forth. It seemed to invade every muscle and nerve in her body, causing her to tremble within his strong embrace.

And yet, at the center of it all was a sensation of peace unlike anything she'd ever felt. It was like coming home, only deeper and more certain.

She snaked a hand out from under the blanket to clutch the edge of his waistcoat. Grant murmured, pulling her closer as he deepened the kiss.

With a happy sigh, she opened to him. Grant tasted like whisky and heat as he explored her mouth, stealing the breath from her lungs. It wasn't just peace that she felt in his arms. It was a growing sense of excitement, one that made her want to squirm in her seat.

Better yet, squirm on top of him.

Kathleen clutched at his shoulders, trying to find mental purchase. Was this truly Grant, the man who valued control over everything else? Because what he was doing to her was the opposite of control. He'd hardly begun kissing her, and yet she was ready to climb onto his lap and do things that no proper young lady—or barely proper, in her case—should contemplate. They weren't even betrothed, for heaven's sake. She should stop him. He'd *want* her to stop him before events overtook them.

And in another minute or two . . .

Grant nipped her lower lip. Any notion of stopping him dissolved into the ether. Along with her maidenly qualms, which weren't very strong to begin with.

When her nipped her again, then softly nuzzled her mouth, Kathleen couldn't hold back a moan.

"Did ye like that, sweet lass?" His brogue was deep and oh-so-seductive.

Her eyelids fluttered up—she hadn't realized she'd closed them—and found herself staring into a gaze so fiery it was a miracle she didn't instantly go up in flames.

"I think so," she managed. "But perhaps you'd best do it again to make sure."

His chuckle was wicked as he leaned down to nuzzle her lips. Slowly, expertly, he ravished her mouth until she *was* squirming like a mad thing. His kisses were lovely, but they weren't *nearly* enough.

"Grant," she gasped, "you're driving me insane."

He studied her with a teasing smile. Unlike her, Grant seemed to be in control, although his gaze glittered with sensual intent.

"Am I now?" he purred. "And what would you like me to do about that, Kathleen?"

She huffed. "Has anyone told you that you're a dreadful tease?"

His smile turned rueful. "No, actually. You're the first."

"You're quite good at it, you know. And you're working me up into *quite* a state."

He leaned down and pressed so tender a kiss to her mouth that unexpected tears gathered behind her eyelids.

Kathleen blinked them back. She would not spoil this splendid moment with silly sentimentality.

Silly? You love him, you ninny.

"We cannot have that," he murmured. "So what would you like me to do, sweet lass?"

She suddenly realized it wasn't an idle question on his part. Grant was asking her something vitally important. Was she ready to step across that threshold of trust? Was she ready to fully and finally be with him?

Yes.

She reached up to stroke his bristled cheek. "Do everything, please."

His gaze sparked even hotter. "Ye shall have everything ye want, and more."

Then Grant reached over and swept her up from the chair. She quickly found herself nestled on his lap. The plaid blanket slid off her shoulders, exposing her stays.

With an appreciative murmur, he adjusted her across his brawny thighs. Kathleen blinked in surprise because his muscled legs weren't the only things that felt brawny. Even through the sturdy wool of her skirt, she could feel his erection. It felt huge and hard, a little intimidating, and incredibly exciting.

"Goodness," she said.

"Are you comfortable, love?"

"Um, quite. Thank you." Then she winced, realizing she sounded like a henwit.

Grant didn't seem to notice. He was too busy running his calloused fingertips along her collarbone.

"So pretty," he rumbled. "And your sweet freckles." He trailed one finger down to the top of her stays. "I've been wanting to see exactly where they go for weeks."

"Everywhere, I'm afraid."

The corners of his eyes crinkled with amusement. "Then I'll have a path to follow."

"I'm glad they're good for something."

He didn't reply, his gaze now focused on her body. His hand drifted down to cup her breast. When he swiped a thumb over the outline of her nipple, Kathleen bit back a gasp. He did it again, and sensation shot from the tip of her breast to deep between her thighs. When she squirmed to relieve the growing ache, Grant hissed out a breath.

"Och, lass," he muttered. "You're going to drive *me* mad."

She pressed a steadying hand to his chest. "Sorry."

"Don't apologize, sweetheart. I will happily lose my mind to you."

It was so silly that she couldn't help but giggle.

He briefly smiled. "Kathleen, are you warm enough?"

"I'm roasting, actually."

Between the heat pouring from the stove and Grant's ministrations—not to mention her heavy skirt, stockings, and boots—any chilliness had long since dissolved.

He flicked the blanket away from her arms. "Then let's get rid of this. By the way," he added as he tugged on one of the blue bows trimming her stays, "you have very pretty underclothes. Have I told you that?"

"That would have been most improper, sir," she replied with mock severity.

He laughed before pressing a lingering kiss to her lips, dipping briefly inside. When Kathleen sucked on his tongue, his hips jerked, pressing his erection into her bottom. Once again, a sultry heat cascaded through her body to settle between her thighs. She had a sudden mental flash of how that heat would feel with him buried deep inside her, and she couldn't hold back a whimper.

"Och, lass," he murmured.

He stroked his fingers over the swell of her breast, and then dipped down under her stays, brushing the edge of her nipple. The sensation was electrifying.

"Oh, Grant," she gasped.

"More?" This time, he brushed right across the hard tip.

"Yes," she managed in a strangled tone.

"Good. Because I want to see your pretty freckles," he growled. "I want to see everything."

He gave two hard tugs on the top of her stays. Her breasts popped free. Her nipples were dark and already stiff with arousal, and seemed to grow even tighter under his avid gaze.

"Yer so damn lovely, my Kathleen," he growled.

His voice alone made her go weak. And damp.

Grant lowered his head to her breast. His tongue flicked out, laving the tight point. Kathleen wriggled, silently urging him to increase the pressure, but he kept a firm grip as he gently tortured her into a state of near frenzy.

He went from one breast to the other, teasing and tweaking until her nipples were flushed and hard. Sensation pulsed through her body, and she had to bite on her lip to keep from groaning.

"Make as much noise as you want," he rasped out. "It's just me."

She clamped a hand on the back of his skull, jerking him down for a frantic kiss. As their tongues tangled, his arm locked around her shoulders.

A moment later, he broke free of her greedy kiss.

"Grant," she moaned. "Don't stop—"

She bit off her words as he squeezed a nipple between his fingertips. Then he bent down, and his mouth was on her. She jerked and probably would have tumbled out of his arms, but he held her tightly. He lavished attention on her breasts, kissing her nipples before sucking them into his mouth.

Kathleen's world went up in flames. Outside, rain beat against the windowpanes, and a cold wind howled overhead. But inside everything was hot and wet, her body craving him, making itself ready. She arched her back, pressing her breast against his lips, giving him everything.

A moment later, he pulled back.

"Why . . . why are you stopping?" she stuttered.

"I'm not."

He fisted a hand in her skirt, sweeping it up to her belly. Kathleen trembled, shocked and excited to be so suddenly exposed.

"Goodness," she squeaked.

Grant settled a hand on her thigh, above her garter and stocking. "You are so bloody gorgeous, Kathleen."

Her thoughts were so scattered, she could hardly muster a coherent response. "I have freckles down there, too."

He flashed her a grin. "One of these days, I'd like to count them. And kiss them, each one."

That sounded . . . wonderful.

"That will take quite a while," she replied.

"Then we'll leave it for next time."

"Oh, very well," she said, trying not to sound disappointed.

As odd—and as nerve-wracking—as it was to be so vulnerable, Kathleen did not want him to stop. Not when she felt ready to crawl out of her skin with restless desire.

He flashed her a quick look, his gaze like emerald fire. "Oh, love, I'm not done yet."

"Really, it's fine . . ."

The air caught in her lungs as he spread her thighs wide.

His hand settled on the soft tangle of curls at the top of her thighs.

"So soft," he murmured. "So damn pretty."

Kathleen trembled as she watched him play with the curls hiding her sex. It was thoroughly wanton, and she found his touch almost unbearably exciting. But Grant also cradled her so protectively, and his gaze held such tenderness— even awe—that she had to blink back tears.

"All right, lass?" he murmured.

She smiled at him. "Aye, that."

He gently cupped her sex and kissed her with a passion that set her on fire. When he parted her folds, Kathleen moaned against his lips.

And then he played with her, murmuring husky, erotic encouragement. Grant slicked his fingers over her until she was trembling, aching for release. Stifling a cry, she arched her back, pushing against his hand to increase the torment-ing, delicious pressure.

"Och, that's my beauty," he purred.

He teased her, circling the hard bud, making her strain for his touch.

"Grant," she finally gasped out. "Please!"

He leaned down and briefly nuzzled her mouth. "Ye are so ready, so hot. I want ye to come, now."

The blunt demand, uttered in a low, sensual growl, pushed her right to the edge. Once more, she arched her back, pushing hard.

He pushed back, right on the aching knot of her sex. Then he slowly pressed two fingers inside her tight, slick channel. She cried out as waves of luxurious contractions rippled out from her core. His hand moved over her, inside her, urging her to release.

Kathleen squeezed her eyes shut as Grant flung her

body up to the heavens. Starlight burst under her eyelids as she surrendered to the most intense pleasure she'd ever felt. She was weightless, and almost terrifyingly free.

Then he caught her as she fell back to earth, gently kissing her forehead and cuddling her in a protective embrace.

The storm had passed, both inside and out. As Kathleen drifted back to sanity, she became aware of the silence. Over the pounding of her heart, she heard only a gentle rustle of fabric as Grant smoothed down her riding skirt and tucked the blanket around her.

She rested against him, her face turned into the soft wool of his vest, savoring the moment and absorbing it into every fiber of her being. She breathed in his scent of rain and whisky, smoky peat and crisp Highland air. It was utterly and completely Grant.

Part of her wished this moment would never end. Part of her wished she didn't have to sit up, straighten her clothes, and reenter the world with all its problems. Because she was exactly where she wanted to be.

As the seconds slid by, Kathleen let herself drift in a lovely haze. Eventually, though, Grant shifted her a bit and brushed a tangled lock of hair from her brow.

"All right, Kath?"

She mentally blinked at the gruff, decidedly unromantic tone of his voice. It was a marked change from only a few minutes ago.

"Yes, thank you."

She tilted her head back so she could see his face. His features were in shadow, which made it difficult to read the expression in his eyes. But his mouth was quirked up in a wry smile that was also difficult to read.

"Are *you* all right?" she asked.

He leaned down to nuzzle her mouth. When she pressed

a hand to the back of his neck, trying to hold him there, he huffed out a chuckle before pulling back—reluctantly, she thought.

You hope.

"Never better," he finally said. "And I would like nothing better than to tuck you up into that bed and pamper you for the rest of the night. Unfortunately, we don't have time. The storm's passed and we've got to go before we completely lose the light. The path is bound to be a mess after all that rain. It'll be rough enough on the horses without having to navigate in the dark."

While Kathleen couldn't argue with his logic, she'd been hoping for something a little less prosaic and a little more romantic than a discussion about horses and mud. Still, best not to make a fuss over it, she supposed.

"Of course." She struggled to right herself. "Quite correct."

His burnished brows ticked together in a frown. "Are you sure you're all right?"

"Perfectly. Now, if you can help me get upright . . ."

"Oh, yes. Sorry."

He tipped her up and then helped her stand. Since her legs still felt like jelly, she struggled a bit to find her balance.

"Easy." Grant kept his hands on her waist. "We don't want you—"

"Going arse over teakettle. Indeed not. Now, would you be so kind as to fetch my jacket while I try to, er, arrange myself?"

She tugged on the top of her stays, trying to restore them to some measure of respectability. Grant had been *quite* enthusiastic when he'd yanked them down.

"Sorry about that," he said with a wince.

He sounded embarrassed, which was . . . embarrassing.

Kathleen tugged once more before giving up with a sigh. "It's fine. The jacket will cover any defects—if it's dry by now."

"Right. The jacket," he said, coming to his feet.

He plucked it off the chair, carefully feeling it for damp spots.

"Seems completely fine." He handed it to her.

She dumped it on the table before commencing a struggle with her skirt, which was a wrinkled mess and twisted backward. The wrinkles she could blame on spending several hours on a horse and then getting caught in the rain.

"I'm glad something's fine," she muttered.

Grant, pulling on his riding jacket, paused to shoot her a quick frown. "What's wrong, Kathleen?"

She finally got her skirt more or less sorted, then realized that one of her stockings had sagged down to the top of her boot. "Oh, blast."

He came over to the table. "Can I help?"

"No, thank you." She half turned away from him as she retied her garter.

"Lass, what is amiss?" Grant enunciated every word, as if she were a dimwit.

She fussed with her skirt a bit more, working up her courage before turning to face him.

He loomed over her, arms crossed over his brawny chest, a concerned frown marking his brow.

She hoped it was concern for her welfare, and not something else.

So, find out.

"Are you having second thoughts?" she bluntly said.

He looked blank for a few seconds. Then he shook his

head before tipping up her chin and giving her a brief, hard kiss.

"Don't be daft. I'm simply anxious to get you safely back home. I don't want you taking a tumble off your horse in the dark."

"I have never taken a tumble off a horse in my life."

"Splendid, but there's no point in taking chances." He pulled out a small silver watch from an inside pocket and then grimaced. "Bloody hell. It's even later than I thought. The entire damn household will be in a stew. First Jeannie disappears and now us."

Ah. So that's why he was acting so oddly. He was worrying about how their extended absence would appear. It would certainly raise questions that might be difficult to answer. Ones Grant might not want to answer, given the potential consequences.

Consequences like propriety, a woman's honor, and possibly even marriage.

Kathleen felt an awful twinge in her heart, as if something had just sprung loose and dropped to the floor.

Don't think about it right now. Think about Jeannie.

She would sort out her feelings about Grant Kendrick later.

"Let's hope Jeannie is home by now," she said as she stuck her arms into her jacket. "If not, we'll have to get fresh horses and go back out."

Grant shrugged into his greatcoat. "When we get back to Lochnagar, you won't be going anywhere but straight into a hot bath. We still have a long ride back on muddy roads. I will not have you catching a chill, Kathleen."

She fisted her hands on her hips. "As I told you, I am perfectly fine. And Jeannie is what matters most right now. I think we can both agree on that."

He shot her a veiled look as he headed for the door. "Please try not to worry. Jeannie's a smart girl. I have little doubt she's home by now."

"Well, I *do* have doubts," she retorted.

"Then the best way to resolve those doubts is to return home as quickly as possible." His gaze tracked over her, head to toe. "There's a comb and small mirror in the trunk if you need it. I'll saddle the horses and then we'll be off."

"What about the—" She broke off with a sigh, since he was already out the door. "Drat and double drat."

Kathleen stalked over to the trunk, cursing Grant Kendrick and her silly lovestruck self.

Chapter Twenty-Two

The lights of Dunlaggan finally winked into view through the murky night. Grant threw a glance over his shoulder at Kathleen, slightly behind him.

"Not much longer now, sweetheart," he said.

"Thank God. I just pray that someone has found Jeannie, since our efforts were an utter waste of time."

Grant sighed as he returned his attention to the road. Whatever fire had remained from their romantic interlude had been snuffed out on the muddy trail back from the loch. The difficult footing had forced the horses to pick their way interminably back to the main road.

Increasingly fashed about her sister, Kathleen had wanted to cut over the fields and head straight back to Lochnagar. Grant had vetoed that as too dangerous, since the rough country was cut through with ravines and boggy ground. After yet another sharp debate, he'd pointed out that he knew the countryside better than she did, and that he'd be damned if he let her be injured by taking a risky shortcut.

Since that discussion, Kathleen had barely uttered a word. No doubt she thought him too cautious and too annoying to merit any further consideration. As for their sensual interlude, Grant was at a loss how to think about that. From what he could tell, Kathleen wasn't thinking about it at all, which was more than a trifle discouraging.

He couldn't really blame her. After all but ravishing the poor girl, he'd then acted like an unromantic prat. Of course, he'd wanted nothing more than to rip her clothes off, and give in to the desire he'd been fighting for weeks. Not doing so had required an epic feat of self-control. But he'd had no choice, because making love to his sweet lass would have led to an inexorable series of decisions, practically forcing her to marry him regardless of her personal wishes.

As it was, they were already skating on very thin ice, with a full-blown scandal lurking in dark waters below.

His deep concern had led to his odd behavior. When she'd most needed cuddling and reassurance, he'd all but dumped her off his lap and rushed out to saddle the horses, so they could get back to Lochnagar with all speed.

Unfortunately, they'd been alone together for hours now, and it would take a deal of luck to escape their increasingly dodgy situation with Kathleen's reputation intact.

They approached the first house at the edge of the village, which happened to be the vicarage. Light blazed forth from every window. Grant thought it might be worth making a quick stop, since the vicar would probably know if Jeannie had been found. If so, Kathleen could finally relax.

"Do you want me to see if Brown's heard anything about Jeannie?" he asked.

Kathleen brought her mare up beside his. "I'd rather ride straight through. I truly don't think I can face Mr. Brown, especially looking like this."

"Och, you look fine. No worries there."

She shot him a disbelieving look. "You are a—"

"Hallo, Mr. Kendrick. Hold up, will you?" called the vicar from his front door.

"That's just perfect," said Kathleen in a disgusted voice.

"Sorry, lass. We'll just have to brazen it out."

They reined in as the vicar rushed out to the road to meet them. Captain Brown followed him to the gate at a more leisurely pace.

The vicar gaped as he took in Kathleen's appearance. "Miss Calvert! Are you perfectly all right? Did you take a tumble from your horse?"

"Looks like someone took a tumble," Captain Brown drawled.

"She's fine," Grant sharply said. "We got caught in the storm while we were out searching for Jeannie."

"Reverend Brown, do you know if my sister has been found?" Kathleen anxiously asked.

The vicar nodded. "Yes, she's fine but for a twist of the ankle. John happened to come upon her while out riding. He was able to return her to Lochnagar before the weather turned too frightful."

Kathleen slumped in her saddle. "Thank God."

"Thank me," the captain said in jovial tone. "The poor girl would have had a right good soaking if I hadn't found her when I did."

"Is her ankle very injured?" Kathleen asked.

"Not badly, I should think," John answered. "She was limping, but mostly she was annoyed with herself that she'd stumbled over a rock."

Grant pressed Kathleen's shoulder. "See, lass? All's well."

She dredged up a smile for the captain. "Thank you, sir. I'm very grateful."

He gave her a small bow. "Delighted to help, dear lady."

"Miss Calvert, will you come in for a cup of tea?" David asked, obviously worried about her. "You must be chilled to the bone after being stranded out in that terrible storm."

The captain tilted his head. "From the look of things, I'd say they were stranded somewhere inside, not out."

The vicar frowned at his brother. "Sorry, what?"

"David, their clothes are perfectly dry."

"Thank you for the offer of tea, Mr. Brown," Kathleen hastily cut in. "But we must go. My sister will be worried about me."

"As are all the folk up at the manor house," the captain said. "You've been gone so long, after all."

The vicar nodded. "Yes, as soon as the storm passed, Sir Graeme sent men out looking for you. We were all quite worried, you know."

"I would have happily joined the search myself, even though I'd already rescued one damsel in distress today. I'd wager, however, that Mr. Kendrick did his level best to keep Miss Calvert from feeling *too* distressed." The captain's grin matched his smarmy tone.

"John, there is no need to make jest of it," his brother said. "We would have been happy to help, but Sir Graeme felt it unnecessary."

Grant was quite sure that Graeme was trying to control a potentially scandalous situation by keeping others away.

"And he was right," he said. "We were fine."

Captain Brown shot him a broad wink. "Better than fine, I'd wager."

The vicar frowned. "John, why are you talking such non-sense? Clearly Miss Calvert has suffered a difficult day."

"She has indeed," Grant said. "Which is why I'm getting her back to Lochnagar."

He'd deal with bloody Captain Brown and his salacious—if accurate—innuendoes later.

"Yes, it's been a wearying day," Kathleen said.

The vicar nodded. "Then of course you must go, dear Miss Calvert."

Grant gave the brothers a nod and nudged his horse forward with Kathleen following suit right away.

"I'll stop by Lochnagar tomorrow to see how you get on, Miss Calvert," the vicar called after them.

"Splendid idea," said the captain. "We'll visit to see how both you and Miss Jeannie get on."

"Not if I can help it," Kathleen muttered.

"We'll have Sabrina put them off," Grant said. "She can say you're too worn out to see visitors."

"It wouldn't be far off. I cannot wait to get off this blasted horse."

"I imagine our poor horses feel the same."

"Yes, I'm aware today has been a strain on the horses," she snapped.

Grant wrestled his temper under control. "Kathleen, I know it's been a trying day—"

"And I'm acting like a complete henwit," she interrupted. "I apologize, Mr. Kendrick."

"Mr. Kendrick? It's a bit late for that, is it not?"

Her sigh was exasperated. "Please don't remind me."

And wasn't that just jolly?

"Kathleen, I—"

"It's just that Captain Brown was so awful," she burst out. "I was mortified, especially to have it happen in front of his brother."

"I assure you that I'll be having a word with yon captain about his conduct. It's well past due. As for David, I think those inane innuendoes sailed right over his head."

"Those inane innuendoes were unfortunately accurate."

His temper spiked again. "Unfortunately? Is that how you would characterize what happened between us?"

"Yes. No." She flapped a hand. "I don't know, really. I was just so embarrassed, that's all. I don't mean to be rude."

"Och, and I'm being a complete brute," Grant ruefully said. "You're tired and in dire need of a cup of tea and something to eat."

"I'm in dire need of a brandy and a warm bath."

At the moment, Grant could wish for nothing more than to be in that bath with her. Clearly, though, things between them were decidedly unresolved.

"Kathleen, I don't want you to worry about anything. And if the captain knows what's good for him, he'll be keeping his bloody mouth shut."

"Best to leave it alone, I think," she replied in a gloomy tone. "A confrontation would probably just encourage him to foster more gossip."

"There's bound to be a little gossip, sweetheart. We've been gone for most of the day."

"Fine, but can we please not talk about it right now?" she said. "I'm exhausted."

He repressed a sigh. "Of course."

They finished the remainder of the short ride in grim silence. Grant too felt weariness drag at his bones. After the fire last night, he'd not slept much and had risen with the dawn. That plus the tumultuous events of today made him feel like he'd been awake for a week.

Now, on top of everything else, Kathleen clearly was none too enamored of him, despite her earlier enthusiastic indications to the contrary.

When they rode under the stone arch and into the manor's central courtyard, Kathleen breathed out a sigh of relief.

"Thank God," she said.

"Aye, that. You'll be in a hot bath in no time."

She cast him a wary look as they brought their horses to a halt.

"Grant, I—"

The front door flew open and Sabrina appeared in a flood of light from the entrance hall. Graeme loomed behind her.

"At last!" she exclaimed.

Sabrina and Graeme hurried down the stone staircase to greet them, while a groom came around from the stable yard to take the horses.

While Grant dismounted, Graeme helped Kathleen down from her horse. Sabrina threw her arms around her cousin.

"Kathleen, we were so worried about you. Are you all right?" she asked.

"I'm tired, but so relieved to hear Jeannie is unharmed."

"The captain brought her home about an hour after you left on your search," Graeme said. "I was about to send out riders to look for you, but then the storm hit."

"We found shelter in that old smugglers' hut," Grant said as Sabrina whisked Kathleen up the steps. "We just waited there until the storm passed."

Graeme studied him. "Is that all?" he finally asked in a much too innocent voice.

"Yes, that's all," Grant acidly replied.

Then he turned and stalked into the house, ignoring his twin's chuckle.

"Took you long enough to get back, though," Graeme said when he caught up with him at the top of the staircase.

"Do you have any idea how bloody awful those paths

are when it rains?" Grant said. "The horses had to slog through knee-deep mud until we reached the road."

"It was *not* an enjoyable ride back," Kathleen added as she pulled off her bedraggled hat.

Sabrina studied her with a concerned frown. "You do look . . ."

"A wreck. I know."

Light from the overhead chandelier and several branches of candles illuminated how disheveled they both were.

"You look like you've been through the mill, old son," Graeme said, trying not to laugh.

Unsurprisingly, his twin had deduced what had happened in that blasted hut. Grant glared daggers at him in warning.

Graeme held up his hands. "I'm not saying a word."

Sabrina regarded Grant with clear disapproval. "Honestly, Grant, you are as great a menace as your brother."

"That is literally impossible," he replied.

"You're making a good run at it, though," Graeme countered.

"Can someone please tell me how my sister is?" Kathleen asked in a frustrated tone.

Sabrina grimaced. "Forgive me, dearest. Jeannie had supper in bed and is now fast asleep. I think she'll be right as rain after a good night's sleep."

"And her ankle?"

"It's nothing more than a minor strain."

"Where did Brown find her?" Grant asked.

"She'd headed out past the distillery," Graeme replied. "Over the small bridge and out past the Robertsons' croft. I was heading that way myself when I ran into them."

"Nowhere close to where we were searching," Kathleen

said with disgust. "But that farmer was so certain he saw Jeannie."

"That was obviously another girl," Grant said.

"Really? Thank you for that enlightening observation, Mr. Kendrick."

There was a momentary, fraught silence.

"So, I hope you found that old hut a cozy place to hole up together," Graeme said in a hearty voice. "Plenty of whisky there, as well as blankets to keep you wrapped up nice and tight, eh?"

Grant repressed the urge to smack his brother in the back of the head.

Sabrina scowled at her husband. "You are an idiot, Graeme Kendrick."

"What did I say?" Graeme protested.

Hannah came trotting down the stairs. "Miss Calvert's bath is almost ready, my lady, and Cook is sending a tea tray to her room."

"Any chance I could get a brandy, too?" Kathleen asked.

Sabrina led her over to the staircase. "You can have the entire decanter, if you wish."

As she followed Kathleen up the stairs, she glanced over her shoulder at Grant. "Menace," she mouthed.

Hannah, who was eyeing both Grant and his twin with disdain, shook her head. "Feckless, the both of you," she said before following the ladies.

"Not sure why I'm getting it between the teeth," Graeme commented. "Now, old boy. How about a nice glass of whisky? You seem like you could use it."

"You have no idea."

Graeme slung an arm around Grant's shoulders and led him to his study.

"Can't be as bad as all that, lad."

"It's worse," Grant said.

Graeme pointed to one of the wing chairs in front of the blazing hearth.

With a grateful sigh, Grant settled in. "Where's Angus?"

"Upstairs with Gus. No doubt he'll pop down soon enough."

"I'll look forward to it," Grant dryly replied.

Graeme handed him a crystal glass with a hefty portion of whisky. "You know he'll want to find out exactly what happened this afternoon."

"Grandda will no doubt deduce the answer as quickly as you have."

Graeme propped a shoulder against the fireplace mantel. "All jesting aside, I'm afraid your lengthy absence with the fair Kathleen is likely to cause a wee spot of gossip."

"Did you really need to send out a blasted search party?" Grant asked. "I was perfectly capable of getting Kathleen home in one piece."

"More or less."

"I thought we were being serious."

"We are. Of course I knew she was perfectly safe with you. My wife, however, grew more perturbed as the day wore on."

"It was just a storm, Graeme."

"Aye, but let's not forget the villains afoot in these lands. Sabrina was in a complete stew that you'd fallen afoul of them."

"And when Sabrina is in a stew . . ."

"Everyone's in a stew. By dinnertime, Jeannie was convinced her sister had been murdered."

Grant rubbed a hand over his messy hair. "God, what a disaster."

"We'll keep the gossip to a minimum. It's Dunlaggan, not Glasgow." His brother raised an eyebrow. "That's if there *is* a need to contain it."

"There's definitely a need, since the lady isn't best pleased with me. Don't expect wedding bells anytime soon."

"How in Hades did you put Kathleen into such a snit?"

"I'm still trying to sort that out. As for keeping the tittle-tattle under control . . ." Grant shook his head. "When we rode past the vicarage, David came beetling out with his annoying brother, who arrived at the same conclusion you did. He not only read the situation correctly, he made it obvious that he'd done so."

Graeme's eyebrows shot up. "With the vicar standing there?"

"The captain did it deliberately. Although David was mostly confused, I'm sure the captain has cleared that up by now."

"Scaly bastard," Graeme said.

"Kathleen is worried about the captain, too. She's afraid he's flirting with Jeannie, which would be massively inappropriate."

"I saw no evidence of such this afternoon. He was his usual bombastic self with the girl, but more in the way of an avuncular relative."

"How was Jeannie with him?"

"I don't think the vicar has a rival for her affections, if that's what you're worried about," Graeme replied.

"Good. David is harmless. Still—"

The door flew open and Angus barreled into the room.

"Aboot time ye got home," he barked. "What the devil were ye doin' with that poor lassie for hours and hours?"

Graeme winked at the old fellow. "What do you think, Grandda?"

Angus thumped down into the other wing chair. "Oh? Then we'll be hearin' wedding bells verra soon, I'm expectin'."

Grant sighed. "I wouldn't bet on it."

His grandfather started stuffing his ratty clay pipe from his equally ratty tobacco pouch. "Och, ye should have come to me for courtin' advice. Yer out of practice, lad."

"That is definitely not the problem, Grandda."

"If it nae be your wooin' skills, then why aren't we celebratin' yer betrothal to Kathleen?"

"Because she likely would have turned me down flat?"

"She'd best not," Graeme said, "or Sabrina will have something to say about it."

"Then perhaps your wife can try her persuasive skills on her, because I'm certainly not having any luck," Grant tartly replied.

Angus sympathetically patted Grant's knee. "Yer tongue just gets twisted when yer nervous. Ye always had that problem."

"That is a load of bollocks," Grant said. "And I wasn't nervous."

Although he had been less than articulate in the aftermath of their intimate encounter, he was sorry to say.

"Then what *is* the problem?" Graeme asked. "It's obvious Kathleen has strong feelings for you, and you have strong feelings for her. Good God, you practically committed vicarcide over her."

"Look, I won't deny that we have feelings for each other—"

"Verra *strong* feelings," Angus said, before blowing out an enveloping cloud of smoke.

Exasperated, Grant waved it away. "Would you stop doing that?"

"Interruptin' or smokin'?"

"Both."

"I canna think without a pipe, and this tangle needs some thinkin'."

"I haven't noticed that smoking brings clarity to your mental processes," Grant said.

His grandfather and Graeme exchanged long-suffering glances.

"He's fashed, ye ken," Angus said.

"Clearly fashed," Graeme replied.

Grant made a concerted effort to keep an even temper. "The reality is, Kathleen and I are miles apart about everything. Even when we try to talk things through, we end up at cross-purposes."

Angus pointed his pipe stem at him. "It's like I said. Yer nerves are twistin' up yer tongue."

"I can think of one way to use your tongue that doesn't involve talking," Graeme said with a smirk. "It's remarkably effective in resolving even the most vexing of differences with one's beloved."

Angus snickered. "Aye, that."

"You're both revolting," Grant said. "And *massively* unhelpful."

His brother laughed. "All right, lad, we'll stop teasing. But we do want to help, you know."

"I don't think you can, though," Grant confessed. "It appears that Kathleen has developed cold feet."

Angus shook his head. "She's nae a die-away-miss. Kathleen's that brave, ye ken."

"It's not a question of bravery, Grandda. It's a question of what she wants."

"And she doesn't want you?" Graeme asked.

Grant tried for a wry smile. "I can't compete with Ireland, you see. Besides, she thinks I'm a bore, and I think . . ."

She's bloody wonderful. Too wonderful for me.

"I'll wager she wasn't bored this afternoon."

Grant thought about how Kathleen had shivered with passion in his arms. "That's not enough, though."

"It's a start. And by the way, have you actually asked her to marry you?"

"Well, no."

Graeme snorted. "Never took ye for a coward, lad."

"I will knock your block off, twin. Don't think I won't," Grant said with a growl.

"It's nae that," Angus said to Graeme. "It's that our lad doesna think he's good enough for Kathleen."

Graeme rolled his eyes. "Of course he's good enough. He's miles better than the rest of us, especially me."

"Och, yer all good lads. But I agree that yer twin is as fine a man as ye could ever hope to meet."

Grant's throat went suddenly tight. "I appreciate your support. But the fact remains that Kathleen wants a different sort of life than marriage with the likes of me."

Angus kept his focus on Graeme. "It's because of what happened with yer dad. Our Grant has never gotten over the guilt, ye ken."

For an awful moment, Grant's brain seemed to freeze. "That's . . . that's ridiculous," he finally said. "It has nothing to do with our father."

"No, Grandda's right," said Graeme. "You've carried this guilt much too long, old boy."

When Grant responded with a grimace, his brother fetched the whisky decanter and refilled their glasses.

"Ye never told us exactly what happened that day, son," Angus quietly said.

The old bitterness leached up, like a deadly poison. "What for? You all know."

"What happened to our father, but not to you," Graeme pointed out.

The instinct to retreat behind an indifferent façade resurfaced. Grant had never been able to talk about that night, not even to Nick or to Graeme. Both had tried more than once to pry it out of him. But every time, a door in his head had slammed shut, keeping the memories safely locked up.

He realized now he'd been lying to himself, because those memories were always lurking below the surface, whispering awful things that were impossible to forget.

His grandfather's hand came to rest on his arm. "Time to let it out, son."

"Aye, that," Graeme quietly said.

"Och," Grant gruffly replied, "you'll never stop pestering me if I don't, will you?"

"We'll never stop loving ye, lad," Angus said. "Ye can be certain of that."

"Bloody pests." Then he took a deep breath. "All right, then. We were coming up on Kade's second birthday, you remember?"

Angus sighed. "Aye, that was a bad time. Yer da was strugglin'."

"He was drinking himself to death," Graeme said in a

grim tone. "He never even noticed the rest of us were grieving, too."

When their mother died a few days after Kade was born, felled by childbed fever, the effect was catastrophic. The children were left devastated and bewildered, and their father had never recovered from the blow. If not for Nick and Angus, the family would have fallen entirely to pieces.

Angus grimaced. "The laird should have been there for ye. Instead he let his grief and anger poison everything for everybody."

"Not me," Grant softly said. "I was his favorite."

Graeme nodded. "You were the one bright spot in his life. Thank God for you."

"It was rather a mixed blessing," Grant replied.

"Aye, but a blessing nonetheless," Angus said. "Ye were always a guid boy, with yer kind, sunny ways. And ye brought that sunshine into your da's life."

Grant had always possessed a knack for handling his father. Even when Da was in his blackest moods, Grant could usually get a smile out of him or convince him to put aside his whisky glass. They'd go riding, his father on Big Red, an enormous roan, and Grant on Geordie, his Highland pony. Out where water and sky met Kinglas lands, his father's mood would lift.

"It was a hell of a burden to put on a little boy's shoulders, though," Graeme sharply said. "We were only nine when our father died."

"I know, son," Angus said. "But your da was lost. He couldna see a way out."

"He had his children," Graeme argued. "We would have helped him. Instead, he piled it all on poor Grant."

"For all the good it did," Grant said. "I still wasn't able to save him."

And that failure would stay with him for the rest of his days.

After a few moments of silence, Angus gently prodded Grant's knee. "Go on. Tell us what happened."

"I remember that everyone had scattered after dinner."

"Da was in a particularly foul mood that night," Graeme said. "We all wanted to get away from him."

"Yes, but I followed him to the library."

Unfortunately, none of Grant's usual tactics had worked. His father had sat at his desk, pouring whisky down his throat while his state of mind grew bleaker and bleaker.

"I thought if I got him away from the whisky, he would calm down," he added. "So I suggested we go out to the stables. One of the mares had just foaled, and I said I wanted to see the newborn."

Graeme nodded. "Da was usually better around the horses."

But once they'd checked on the mare and her foal, Da had made the impulsive decision to go riding. Grant had tried to talk him out of it, since night was falling and his father was drunk. More drunk than usual.

"The head coachman and the grooms were in the servants' hall, having supper," Grant said. "There was just one stable boy left on duty, and he'd only been working at Kinglas for a few months. Da told him to saddle Big Red."

Graeme winced. "And that poor lad was not been about to argue with the Laird of Arnprior."

"No."

When his father then ordered Grant to go back to the house, for once, he'd disobeyed him.

"After Da rode out, I asked the boy to help me saddle one of the mares. I knew my pony could never catch up.

Then I sent the lad to find our coachman and tell him what happened."

"Ye were a brave lad, even back then," Angus said with pride.

"Grandda, I was scared to death," Grant ruefully replied.

"Aye, but ye didna let it stop ye."

Grant had spotted his father cantering toward a stand of woods east of Kinglas. "It was daft to be riding into the woods, especially with night coming on so fast. So I called out to him, and he stopped and waited for me."

"What happened when you got there?" Graeme asked. "How did he react?"

"He gave me a good tongue-lashing."

"Of course his did." His twin sighed.

"You suffered worse."

"Yes, but that was not the last conversation anyone would wish to have with his father." Graeme's gaze was full of understanding.

"It was what I said next that truly upset him."

"What was it, son?" Angus gently asked when Grant paused for a few moments on the horrible memory.

"I called him a mean old man and said he was scaring everyone. I told him that if he didn't stop it, I would never talk to him again."

Graeme covered his eyes. "Poor, poor lad."

Angus sighed and again patted Grant's arm. "The laird did not take that well, I reckon."

"He cursed at me and told me to go home. Then he lashed out at Big Red. The poor horse was already jittery from all the yelling, so when Da hit him with his crop, he reared and almost went right over on his back. It was a miracle he didn't."

What happened next wasn't a miracle, though. As his father pitched off the horse, one foot caught in the stirrup. Big Red bolted and dragged him for several dozen yards over the rocky ground before he came free. Grant threw himself from the mare and ran to his father, who was motionless, his face covered with blood.

Grant had shrieked at him to open his eyes, to get up, even move a hand. Over and over again, he'd begged his father not to leave him. The only answer had come from the wind, a hollow cry that echoed his boyish sobbing.

By the time he finished describing the scene, Grant had to clear his tight throat. "You know the rest, Grandda. You and Nick found me. I don't know how long it took, but it seemed forever."

"We found ye almost right away," Angus said. "But I have nae doubt it felt like forever. I wish I could have spared ye that sight, lad. I wish I could have spared all of ye so much."

Grant shook his head. "If I'd listened to Da when he told me to stay behind, or even if I hadn't said those terrible things to him, he might still be alive today."

It had been an accident, of course, but there was no denying his actions had played a role. It was something he'd never get past.

Graeme crouched down in front of him, his gaze now almost stern. "Grant, it wasn't your fault. You were only a little boy."

"A little boy who disobeyed his father. If only I'd listened—"

"We all disobeyed Da at one time or another," Graeme said. "It was practically my mission in life to drive the old man crazy. And Logan was a bloody master at it."

"But it was different with me. Da *listened* to me. And I

could get him to do things, at least sometimes. He let me take care of him."

"The way yer always tryin' to take care of the rest of us now?" Angus put in. "Like it's yer job?"

Grant frowned at the sharp note in his grandfather's voice. "I'm not sure what point you're making, Grandda."

"Mayhap the point that ye feel so responsible for the old laird's death that ye have to make up for it. By tryin' to keep *us* all safe."

Graeme straightened up. "That does sound right, Grandda. He's always trying to take care of everyone. Especially me—we all know that."

"You're my twin," Grant protested. "I'm supposed to take care of you."

"Do I look like I need taking care of?"

"At one point you did," Grant said, feeling defensive.

"Well, those days are long gone," Angus barked. "And I have news for ye, son, there was nothin' ye could have done to save the old laird, anyway."

"But—"

Angus jabbed his pipe at him, scattering tobacco on the floor. "Yer dad was on the path to ruin long before that sad night. He was set on killin' himself, if not on a horse then with all his drinkin'. The drink would have taken longer, draggin' us all down with him." He let out a disgusted snort. "There be days where I wish yer da *was* alive, so I could wring his neck for puttin' ye all through hell, the nasty old bastard."

Grant exchanged an astonished look with his twin. They'd never heard Angus talk of their father with anything but the respect due to a laird and one of the great clan chiefs of Scotland.

"And another thing. Who said ye were the old laird's favorite?" Angus barked at Grant.

Graeme frowned. "I did. It was obvious."

"Well, ye were wrong, ye booby. Nick was always his favorite. He couldna put a foot wrong with his father. And after yer mother's death, yer da relied on Nick to keep everythin' goin'. If ye want to feel sorry for anyone, save it for yer puir brother, not yer da." Their grandfather shook his head in disgust. "Jinglebrains, the pair of ye."

Grant threw a perplexed glance at his brother. Graeme shrugged, clearly as mystified as he was.

"I didn't mean to upset you, Grandda," Grant said.

Angus made a visible effort to control himself. "Ye had a terrible time of it, and I'm right sorry for that. All ye lads had a hard time. But what about how I felt, I ask? Did ye ever think about that?"

"Felt about our father's death?" Graeme cautiously asked.

"No, about yer blessed mother. How do ye think *I* felt after she died? She was my dear daughter, and my only child. And I'd already lost my Fiona, yer grandmother. To then lose my daughter . . ."

He broke off, muttering and making a show of knocking his pipe tobacco into the grate.

Widening his eyes, Graeme looked at Grant. "We are a pair of jinglebrains, aren't we?"

"The worst, apparently."

Grant stood and reached out to his grandfather, carefully pulling him up from his chair.

"Och, ye big oaf," Angus exclaimed. "What are ye doin' now?"

When Grant wrapped his arms around him, his heart wrenched at the feel of his grandfather's skinny limbs.

They'd always thought the old fellow was invincible. Right now, though, he seemed so frail in Grant's arms.

"I'm hugging you, you old goat," he said. "And telling you how much I love you. We never would have made it without you, Grandda. We owe you everything."

"Aye, that," Graeme softly said.

For a moment, his grandfather returned his embrace before shoving his way free.

"Apologies are all well and good, laddie boy," he said with a scowl designed to cover his show of emotion. "But that nae fixes the problem."

"What problem is that, again?" Graeme asked.

Angus pointed a gnarled finger at him. "That yer twin needs to stop bein' a bloody ninny and ask Kathleen to marry him." Then he rounded on Grant. "And I'll nae have more excuses from ye. Get the job done."

Then the old man turned on his boot heel and stomped out, slamming the door behind him.

"What the hell just happened?" Grant asked.

"Angus happened, as usual."

Grant couldn't hold back a laugh. "I just bared my soul to the man, and he called me a bloody ninny."

"That's our grandda."

"Our entire family is completely deranged."

Graeme's smile was wry. "And we wouldn't have it any other way."

Chapter Twenty-Three

"I thought I'd find you here," Grant said.

Kathleen put down her trowel. Of course he would find her grubbing about in the dirt, even though she'd picked a secluded corner behind the gazebo. "I suppose I have become entirely predictable."

"Just a lucky guess."

She scoffed. "Sabrina told you, didn't she?"

"Och, yer too smart for me, lass," he teased.

"I thought I would be safe out here." When his eyebrows shot up, she flapped a hand. "From David, not you."

Never you.

She eyed him, feeling a little annoyed. Grant looked perfectly wonderful in his tailored coat, form-fitting breeches, and polished boots. Even his cravat was starched to a nicety and crisply folded.

"I do wish that just once we could have a conversation where I wasn't covered in dirt," she groused.

"You look beautiful. I wouldn't change a single thing about you, love."

Kathleen felt a flush rising to her cheeks. "That's hard

to believe, given how dreadfully I behaved yesterday. May I have a hand up, please?"

Grant cupped her elbows, lifted, and set her on her feet.

"Which part of yesterday are we talking about?" he asked. "Because I distinctly remember some very delightful behavior, too."

Since she was not ready to have *that* conversation, she made a show of batting dirt and bits of grass from her skirts.

"You should use a pillow or a blanket to kneel on while you're working," he suggested.

"So I wouldn't get so dirty?"

"Because it would be easier on your knees, daft girl."

She sighed. "We're doing it again, aren't we?"

"Talking at cross-purposes?" Grant casually shrugged. "Seems to be the way we go about things."

"And that doesn't bother you?"

"It's bound to get better if we keep working at it. Practice makes perfect, after all."

She huffed out a laugh. "In our case, I think it would take a great deal of practice."

"Probably even a lifetime."

Kathleen decided she was still not ready for that conversation. "Is it safe to assume that David has departed the premises?"

Fortunately, Grant went along with the change in topic. "Sweetheart, you cannot permanently hide in the garden like a deranged hermit. One of these days you'll have to tell yon vicar the truth."

"I know. I just couldn't face him after that dreadfully awkward encounter outside his house last night. And Jeannie was so eager to see him, too. It's a gruesome tangle, I'm afraid."

"Aye, it's a ridiculous situation."

"And Captain Brown—I'm still tempted to stab him with my clippers."

Grant laughed. "I love a fierce, bloodthirsty lass."

"You absolutely do not. You and your twin act like Sabrina and I are frail princesses who must be locked away in a tower for our own good."

"Och, no tower could hold you lassies. You'd just break out."

She started to clean up her tools, dumping them into her workbasket. "Well, this princess is going to clean up—if the coast is clear, that is."

"After exactly one cup of tea, Sabrina promptly sent the brothers Brown on their way. She made the required apologies on your behalf and kept Jeannie well in hand."

"How do you know?"

"I was there, and what fun it was. David glared daggers at me while the captain smirked like a simpering dandy."

"How awful. Why did you go in the first place?"

"I wanted to make sure Captain Brown kept his blasted innuendoes to himself. He quickly figured out that I would knock his block off if he didn't."

She exhaled a sigh of relief. "That was *so* kind of you, Grant. Thank you. I do worry about the captain's behavior with Jeannie, though."

"His conduct was more akin to that of an older brother. He brought her a collection of Celtic fairy tales to entertain her while she recovers from her injury. Sabrina deemed it appropriate for a girl her age."

Kathleen couldn't help feeling dubious. "Jeannie didn't seem inclined to flirt with him?"

"She very prettily thanked the captain, but it's clear she still fancies herself in love with David."

"I can't imagine the vicar found it very comfortable spending time with Jeannie—or with you, apparently."

Grant shrugged. "When he wasn't sending me death threats with his eyes, he was exceedingly kind to Jeannie. The fellow does have good manners, I'll give him that."

Kathleen crinkled her nose. "Except toward you. And I'm such a bounder for dumping that unpleasant scene on you and Sabrina."

His mouth tilted up in a dangerously seductive smile. "I suppose you'll have to make it up to me, then."

She adopted a puzzled frown. "Hmm. There is one way I can think of."

"Yes, lass?" he purred in his lovely brogue.

"You can let me give you a proper apology about yesterday. You were simply trying to help me, and I was a complete hag to you. You didn't deserve it, and I most sincerely apologize."

He eyed her with polite skepticism.

Kathleen had to resist the urge to shuffle her feet. "What?"

"Is that it?"

"Is what it?"

"Is that how you're going to make it up to me?"

"It was just tea with David and his brother," she said. "It wasn't as if you flung yourself in front of a bullet for me."

"I might have preferred a bullet than tea with Vicar Brown and his idiot brother."

"Now you're just being ridiculous."

Instead of replying, he took her by the elbow and started to march her along the path.

"And where are we going now?"

"To the gazebo. We need to talk."

He was right, of course. But just thinking about yesterday's illicit encounter put her in a stew. She'd been doing her best not to think about it, because she hadn't a bloody clue what to *do* about it.

"All right, but no canoodling," she blurted out.

When Grant laughed, Kathleen couldn't help sighing.

"God, I'm a complete ninny," she said.

"There's no reason to be nervous, sweetheart. We'll just talk, I promise."

He handed her up the stairs into the gazebo. Kathleen settled on the bench, smoothing down her skirts and trying to calm her jangled nerves. Grant leaned against a railing, arms crossed, as he watched her with a slight smile.

Kathleen had the impression he was trying not to crowd her, both physically and emotionally. She was grateful for that, since she felt out of her depth. Grant was obviously about to make a proposal of marriage, and while that was exciting, it was also terrifying. She needed to keep her wits about her—thus, the prohibition on canoodling—in order to make the most important decision of her life.

The fact that she needed to make a decision at all was mind-boggling. Until very recently, she'd been firmly set on a course back to Ireland, come hell, high water, or Grant Kendrick.

That will teach you to kiss a Highlander.

"Properly sorted now, are we?" Grant asked after a few moments.

"Yes, I'm as ready as I'll ever be."

"Lass, you may look like a fairy princess, but you've the heart of a lion. You're ready for anything."

His words sparked a lovely, warm glow in her chest. "I do believe that's the nicest thing you've ever said to me."

"I'm just getting started."

"Then since I am not immune to flattery, I shall have to be on my guard."

His expression turned serious. "It's not flattery, Kathleen. You're brave and kind, and you're a hell of a lot smarter than I am."

She held up a finger. "But you're much better with numbers. You practically print money, remember?"

"And you joke when you're nervous."

She crinkled her nose. "My father and Helen remind me of that on numerous occasions. I've tried to break the habit, but I can't seem to manage it."

He looked comically dismayed. "Och, please don't compare me to your parents when I'm about to launch into a marriage proposal. It's deflating, ye ken."

"We certainly cannot have you deflating." She flapped a hand. "Oh, dear. That sounded rather improper, didn't it? I'm sorry. I'm terrible at this sort of thing."

Grant pushed off from the rail and joined her on the bench. When he took her hand, her insides skittered. But then he wove their fingers together, and it suddenly felt like the most natural thing in the world.

For several long moments, they sat in comfortable silence. When she tilted her head to study his profile, she found him staring at their hands, a frown marking his brow.

"Is something wrong?" she softly asked.

"It would seem I've been getting everything wrong from the beginning."

Now it was her turn to frown. "What do you mean?"

"Kathleen, I know that I have seemed disapproving at

times, and I truly apologize for giving you the impression that you are anything less than wonderful and perfect."

She felt another flush rise into her cheeks. "No one is perfect, sir."

"You're perfect for me."

"But I'm dreadful with rules and propriety. As much as I might try, I truly don't think I can change that."

"And you think I would object to that?" He shook his head. "Sweetheart, I wouldn't change a damn thing about you."

"Actually, you already *have* objected, and more than once."

"Touché," he wryly replied. "But only when I thought you were putting yourself in a dodgy situation or in harm's way."

"I wasn't in harm's way yesterday when we were in that smugglers' hut and we . . ." She twirled her free hand. "You know. And you were an absolute bear, afterward. I was *quite* annoyed."

He grimaced. "You're right, and I've been kicking myself about that ever since. I should have been more attentive to your feelings. And to my feelings, to tell you the truth."

"Instead, you immediately began managing the situation."

"I tend to do that. But I know it was not helpful or appropriate given yesterday's circumstances."

"Then why *did* you get so fashed?"

"Because we'd already been gone a hell of a long time, by ourselves."

She sighed. "You were worried about the gossip."

"I was worried about *you*, and how the gossip might affect you. But there was another compelling reason, too."

"Which was?"

When Grant played with her fingers, clearly delaying, Kathleen nudged him.

"Well?" she prompted.

He snorted. "Bossy lass."

"Best get used to it, laddie boy. Now, please answer the question."

He shifted to look her straight in the eye. "It's because I wanted to rip your clothes off and make love to you until I thoroughly wore you out. And then let you rest a bit before I did it again." He leaned close, almost nose-to-nose. "All night long."

All she could do was gape at him.

Grant's smile was wry. "You're staring, sweetheart."

She managed to collect herself. "This is an incredibly shocking state of affairs. Such behavior will never do, and certainly not for a sobersides such as yourself."

"It's not my fault, lass. You're so sweet and lovely that I can't help wanting to make love to you all the time."

Over the years, Kathleen had been called charming, great fun, and even a jolly good sport by her erstwhile suitors, but never sweet and lovely.

"Truly?" She felt almost shy.

"Truly. I've even been tempted to murder the vicar over you. Almost tossed the poor fellow out the nearest window on several occasions, in fact."

"That's terribly sweet. But if I married David, my sister would toss *me* out a window."

"Sounds like we're both in a pickle. What do you propose?"

"I believe proposals are your department, Mr. Kendrick."

He pressed his lips to her forehead. Kathleen had to resist

the temptation to melt into his arms—or say yes before he even asked.

Buck up, old girl. Be sure of yourself.

"Shall I go down on one knee?" he asked in a husky voice.

"I'd suggest not. The gazebo floor is in need of a sweeping."

"That's a shockingly prosaic consideration for someone of your romantic temperament."

"Indeed. I hardly know myself anymore."

She was jesting, but it was the truth. Grant Kendrick had turned her world completely on its head.

As he gathered up her hands, his gaze turned intent. "I know you, dearest girl. I feel like I've known you my entire life. I *see* you, too. And what I see is more than I could ever be worthy of. But I hope you'll let me try, because you're the most wonderful woman I've ever met."

Kathleen blinked back the sting of tears. "Thank you."

His mouth curved into a loving smile. "Miss Calvert, I hope you will do me the great honor of agreeing to be my wife."

"I . . ."

She wanted to say *yes* more than anything she'd ever said yes to in her life. But the words stuck in her throat.

Grant's smile faded. "Kathleen?"

"I . . . I'd like to, but I'm just not sure," she finally stammered.

His eyes opened wide with disbelief. "You're joking."

"I'm afraid not."

He let go of her hands and crossed his arms over his chest. "You did just ask me to propose, did you not? What in Hades have we been talking about for the last fifteen minutes?"

"Well, I'm not entirely sure."

When he started to protest, she flapped a hand. "All right, yes. I suppose I did suggest—"

"Suggest? Och, lass." His brogue was heavy, a sure sign of irritation.

Kathleen couldn't blame him, since she sounded like a henwit.

"What I meant is that I'm not entirely sure . . . I mean, I *want* to say yes, but it's just that—"

She broke off, annoyed by how frazzled she felt. She sucked in a calming breath and tried again. "Grant, forgive me. But lately I feel like a kite battered in a high wind. So I want to be sure that I'm making the right decision for both of us."

When his eyebrows shot up practically to his hairline, she grimaced.

"I know," she said. "It's absurd. Me being the cautious one."

"It's a wee bit disconcerting, I'll admit."

"Imagine how I feel."

He took her hands again, holding them in his lap.

"Then let's start at the beginning," he said in his calm, Grant-like way. "What exactly are you worried about? That we're too different from each other?"

She nodded.

"Then I suggest you look no further than Graeme and Sabrina for confirmation that opposites can get along perfectly well."

"That's an excellent point," she admitted.

"Good. What else, then? Are you worried I'm a fortune hunter? I am well able to support you, Kathleen."

She scowled at him. "You are a booby, Grant Kendrick. Besides, I have it on good authority that you make a great deal of money."

"Yes, it's my one true talent," he sardonically replied.

"You have many talents, dear sir. Which brings me to my next point. I would make a terrible wife for a businessman."

He looked genuinely surprised. "It's not a job that one applies for, Kathleen. Nor is there a list of duties that one is required to follow."

"Aren't you afraid I'll accidentally offend the right sort of people? I do that, you know."

He simply shrugged.

"What about scandals?" she persisted. "I'm quite good at those, you'll recall."

"You must remind me to introduce you to my family sometime, especially my grandfather."

"I know, but—"

Grant withdrew one hand from their loose clasp and pointed to himself. "Scandalous elopement, remember? And when we have a few hours to spare, I'll relate some of those stories I wouldn't let Graeme tell you because they were too outrageous."

"I would like to hear them," she confessed.

"Then you shall. Now, do you want to keep listing objections, or shall we get to what is truly worrying you?"

"And you think you know what that is?" she warily asked.

"It's Ireland."

"Well . . . yes."

"Ireland is not the back of beyond, sweetheart."

"True, but it's not Glasgow. I'm not fond of living in the city. And Glasgow is where you need to be. I don't see how we can get around that."

"Kathleen, you stood on your head trying to avoid leaving Glasgow for Lochnagar. And Lochnagar, I might point out, is both the country *and* an actual back of beyond."

She sighed. "I know. I'm terribly inconsistent. It's just

that my brain is in such a muddle these days with Jeannie and everything else."

"Everything else including our interlude yesterday?"

When she gave him a sheepish smile by way of reply, Grant chuckled, not looking the least bit put out. The man had the patience of a saint, in addition to all his other fine qualities. Any woman in her right mind would crawl over hot coals to marry him.

And she *did* want to marry him. It was just that—

"Please tell me what else is bothering you," he quietly asked.

Apparently, he could read minds, too.

"I can't tell what you're thinking most of the time," she said. "You're very reserved, while I'm the opposite. I feel like we're not on equal footing."

He pondered that for several seconds before responding. "Would it surprise you to know there are many times when I cannot tell what you're thinking?"

"This conversation would suggest otherwise," she ruefully replied. "I know it's a dreadful cliché, but I'm an open book compared to you."

"To expand on that cliché, you only let people read what you want them to read. In fact, I'd say you're as reserved as I am, only in a different way."

She frowned. "I don't think that can be true."

"And *I* think it's a way of protecting yourself. You keep others from getting too close, or from talking about the painful events of the past. It's a form of armor." He grimaced. "Believe me, I understand."

Expressed like that, his observation made sense. She did go out of her way to avoid speaking or even thinking of painful things. It was one of the reasons she liked to keep busy, she supposed. Better to be busy than sad.

"You understand, because you needed to protect yourself, too," she softly replied.

After they sat in silence for a bit, she nudged him. "So, where does that leave us?"

Grant gathered up her hands again and held them to his chest.

"Right where we need to be, I hope. My darling, behind this boring exterior is a man who loves you very much. And he would be very happy if you could manage to love him in return."

The emotion in the forest-green depths of his gaze perfectly matched his words. Kathleen had no doubt that he loved her with all his heart.

She couldn't hold back a few sniffles. "Blast. I told myself I wouldn't cry."

"Is that a yes?"

"Very likely. But would you mind if I thought about it a bit more? It's my first proposal. A lady is required to quibble and prevaricate, is she not?"

That was nonsense, of course. But she wished to recover her equilibrium and not burst into emotional and messy tears in front of him.

"Daft girl." Then he turned serious. "I know this isn't the life you envisioned, Kathleen. Or what you necessarily wanted. But please also know that I will spend the rest of my life trying to make you happy. Make *us* happy."

She smiled mistily at him. "You are the nicest man I've ever met."

"Thank you," he wryly replied.

And because he was so nice, a horrible thought darted into her brain. It had been there earlier but had slipped away in the mental commotion of their discussion. "And you're sure you're not simply proposing to me because of yesterday? Because there would be gossip about us?"

"Lass, I just told you that I loved you," he said, exasperated. "Have you already forgotten?"

She narrowed her eyes. "So, you are worried about gossip."

He closed his eyes and muttered something under his breath.

Kathleen tugged on his hands. "Well?"

He opened his eyes. "What I'm worried about is you, and what *you* want. I would never pressure you to marry me, Kathleen. My rush back from that smugglers' hut was precisely so you would *not* be backed into in a corner by gossip and left without a choice. Frankly, I shouldn't wish to marry you if that were the case."

By now, he looked so annoyed that she couldn't help beaming at him.

"You know, I think you must be the nicest man in the entire world," she said.

"Splendid. And since I am the nicest man in the world, I'm now going to leave you alone. Because if I don't leave, something drastic is bound to happen."

"What's that?"

"I will toss you over my shoulder and carry you straight to my bedroom, where I will then take you to bed. I can safely say you would be left in no doubt as to the sincerity of my proposal."

He stood, but then leaned down, his arms caging her. He brought his face so close that Kathleen almost saw double.

"I'd have ye screaming with pleasure in no time, lass," he added in a murmur. "Count on it."

Her heart skipped at least three beats. "That . . . that sounds like fun."

"Now, you have a decision to make, so I'll leave you to it," he gruffly replied.

And then he was gone.

Chapter Twenty-Four

"I thought I'd find you here," Sabrina said as she walked into Lochnagar's stables.

Kathleen blew out a dramatic sigh. "I truly am becoming a predictable person. How dreadful."

Her cousin joined her at one of the stalls, where Kathleen had been silently communing with a placid mare. "It was either here or the garden. They're your favorite spots, especially when you wish to hide."

"Oh, Lord. So I'm a coward, too."

Sabrina laughed. "Not at all. You were exceedingly wise to avoid that gruesome little tea with David and his brother."

Kathleen made a show of wiping her brow. "Whew. Not a coward, thank goodness, but still predictable."

"What's wrong with being predictable? It simply means one behaves in a consistent fashion."

"I just never thought of myself that way."

"How we think of ourselves is often the result of labels that others apply to us, especially when we're young."

Kathleen went back to rubbing the mare's soft nose. "I suppose we sometimes grow into those labels, too."

"Or try to fit ourselves into someone else's expectations of those labels?" Sabrina shrewdly asked.

"Tell that to Helen. She would say I do the exact opposite."

"Your stepmother is completely dreary. What she thinks about you isn't important."

Kathleen propped her elbow on the half door and studied her cousin. "Then what is important, Sabrina? Please tell me, because I can't seem to figure it out."

Sabrina gently poked her on the chest. "What's important is how *you* think of yourself. Everything else flows from that. So, tell me what's truly bothering you?"

Kathleen grimaced. "I'm in a muddle."

"And that's why you're here. The horses have always calmed you down."

"True enough."

The scents and sounds of a stable, the beauty of the horses, and even the gruff comments of grooms hard at work had always been a comfort to her. Life was so much simpler with horses. It was the same with gardening. In a garden or a stable, she could be as solitary and eccentric as she wished, and no one seemed to mind.

They were also the only places where she felt in control of her life.

She glanced at Sabrina, the picture of domestic elegance in a blue kerseymere dress and matching plaid shawl, with not a hair out of place. Her cousin was a woman in control of her life—a miracle, that, considering the complications of running a large estate and a distillery.

"How do you do it?" Kathleen exclaimed. "How do you manage it all without going batty?"

The mare snorted and moved away, clearly disapproving of her little outburst.

"I ask for help when I need it," Sabrina calmly replied. "That's something you might think about."

"I did ask for help with Jeannie," Kathleen pointed out.

"I meant when *you* need help, not when someone else does. You tend to go it alone, dearest. I think that's because you don't wish to appear vulnerable or not in control."

"I always said you were the smartest person I know," Kathleen ruefully replied.

Sabrina tilted her head. "Shall I hazard a guess as to your trouble right now?"

"That shouldn't be difficult. After all, you told Grant where I was hiding."

"Only because Angus was preparing to make you a proxy marriage proposal, since he was convinced that his grandson would make a hash of it. Grant had to threaten to lock him in his room to keep him from pestering you."

Kathleen had to laugh. "That's ridiculous, if rather sweet."

"Angus wants you and Grant to be happy. We *all* want that."

"I want that too, of course, but . . ." She sighed. "I worry that I'll make a bungle of married life."

"Grant clearly does not agree, dearest. He loves you just as you are."

Kathleen thought of the expression in Grant's eyes when he proposed to her. "I know," she softly replied.

"But you still have doubts? That wouldn't be unusual, even when you love a person."

It was a surprising admission from her always-decisive cousin. "Did you have doubts about Graeme?"

"Not at all. He needed convincing, though."

Kathleen covered her mouth, trying not to laugh.

Sabrina shook her head. "My poor lamb was so skittish that I had to storm his bedroom and attempt, rather clumsily, to seduce him."

"Good God. How did that end up?"

Her cousin pointed back to the house. "Baby in nursery."

"Huzzah for you, old girl. But as for me . . . well, I've done quite a good job of convincing myself that I'd never get married. It would just be me, my gardens, my horses . . ."

"And Ireland. Kathleen, you do not have to give up all your dreams. Just shift them a bit. I'm sure you could visit Ireland whenever you wished."

"I suppose," she doubtfully replied.

Sabrina snapped her fingers. "Perhaps Grant could establish an office in Dublin. Kendrick Shipping and Trade will be setting up one in London next year, so why not Dublin, too? Then there'd be lots of excuses to go to Ireland."

Kathleen rolled her eyes. "Why would Grant listen to me about something like that?"

"Because he loves and respects you. Kendrick men make a habit of listening to their wives, which is an excellent quality of theirs. Now, what else is bothering you?"

Kathleen stewed for a few seconds before voicing her fears. "He's so reserved. I chatter away like a magpie, while he imitates a bloody sphinx. How the devil will we ever learn to properly communicate?"

Frowning, Sabrina stared at her feet for several long seconds. "You know that the twins lost their parents at an early age?" she finally said.

Kathleen nodded.

"But what you probably don't know," Sabrina continued,

"is that Grant was present when his father died. It was a dreadful riding accident, and there was no one else there to help. It was incredibly traumatic for the poor boy."

Kathleen's stomach spun into a hard knot. "That's . . . that's awful."

"It certainly was. The Kendricks have weathered many tragedies over the years, but that one was particularly Grant's. According to Graeme, after his father's death Grant went from cheerful and happy to quiet and reserved. Much of that has carried over into adulthood."

"I can understand that." Kathleen had grieved terribly after her mother died, even without such a shattering experience.

"The point is that Grant's reserve is not due to a lack of emotion. It's because he feels emotion very deeply. So he does his best to control it." Sabrina briefly smiled. "Frankly, we were beginning to worry that he'd never fall in love. But now he has, and he's tumbled hard. Graeme and I believe he's holding back precisely because he loves you so much. He doesn't want to scare you off."

When put like that, his behavior made perfect sense. "I'm generally not the scaring-off type."

"Agreed. So the question then becomes, do you love Grant?"

"I do."

"Then give yourself a chance, dearest—a chance to love *and* to be vulnerable. Grant will be there to catch you."

Kathleen thought about it. "And I can be there to catch him, too."

Sabrina nodded. "After all, that's what love is truly about."

* * *

Kathleen stealthily made her way down the stairs. The center hall was deserted at this late hour but, thankfully, a lamp burned on one of the side tables. She'd forgotten her candle and had already bumped into a bloody footstool while sneaking through the darkened house.

Aside from that little mishap, an undisturbed peace reigned in the halls of Lochnagar Manor, with most of the other residents now safely abed.

Grant, however, was *not* abed. That was why she was creeping about like a footpad.

He'd not been at dinner, either. A neighboring estate owner had found evidence of trespassers on his lands, and Grant had volunteered to ride over and investigate. It made perfect sense that he should do so. But Kathleen had a sneaking suspicion that he was now avoiding her, so as to give her time to think about his offer without pressuring her.

Of course, Grant was now *all* she could think about, and she wouldn't get a moment's sleep until she spoke with him.

Because her bedroom overlooked the back gardens, she had a view of the adjacent stable yard—which meant she'd been able to see Grant's return to Lochnagar over an hour ago. He'd not gone up to his room, however. She was certain of that, because she'd sneaked two doors down in her stocking feet to knock quietly on his door.

When there'd been no answer, she'd mustered up the courage to peek in. His room was dark and the bed untouched. Thoroughly annoyed, she'd promptly gone off looking for him—in her stocking feet, her hair down, and without a candle to light her way.

You're a ninny.

After a quick glance around the hall, she hurried across

the flagstones to the corridor that led to the library. She'd already checked Graeme's study and the family drawing room, finding both empty. That meant Grant was likely holed up down here, once again going over survey maps to deduce where the gang of thieves might be hiding.

When the light of a candle flickered toward her—and she made out who was carrying that candle—she let out a sigh as she waited for Graeme to reach her.

"Out for a midnight stroll, I see." His amused gaze tracked her from head to toe. "Looks like you forgot your shoes. And your candle."

"You know, you can be almost as annoying as your twin."

He laughed. "Actually, I am much more annoying than my twin. He's the nice one, remember?"

"And the smart one, I hear."

"Smart enough to fall in love with you."

She wrinkled her nose. "Some might think that's a poor show of judgment on Grant's part."

"Then some are complete morons."

She flashed him a wry smile, though what she mostly felt was relief. While the most easygoing of men, Graeme was fiercely protective of his twin. Grant would always be his own man, but Graeme's approval *would* be important to him. Kathleen would never wish to disrupt the incredibly strong bond between the brothers.

"Thank you, Graeme."

"By the way, thank *you* for working your magic on wee Gus tonight. Sabrina tells me that he was yelling his head off until you got your hands on him."

"Until *he* got his hands on my hair ribbons," she joked, pointing to the tumble of hair over her shoulders.

"My boy knows a pretty lass when he sees one. You're

a miracle worker with him, Kathleen. We're going to miss you."

"But I'm not going anywhere."

"Not even back to Glasgow?"

She narrowed her gaze. "Who told you? I haven't even spoken with Grant, yet."

"Nobody told me." Then he waggled a hand. "Well, Angus did."

"Of course he did." She couldn't help asking, just to be sure. "And you're all right with it? I mean, with us?"

"Kathleen, you make my brother happy. For that, I will always be grateful. *All* of us are grateful, and we count ourselves exceedingly lucky you have chosen to be part of our family."

Her throat grew suddenly tight. "I'm the lucky one."

Graeme wrapped an arm around her shoulders and dropped a quick kiss on the top of her messy hair. "Och, you're a grand lass, ye ken. Now, go see your man. He's in the library."

"Working as usual?"

"Yes, and he's due for a break."

She smiled and pressed his arm before moving past him.

"Oh, Kathleen?"

She turned. "Yes?"

"Be sure to lock the door."

She huffed out a chuckle. "And I thought I was the incorrigible one."

He walked backward from her. "We're Kendricks. Incorrigible is our middle name."

Kathleen was still smiling when she raised her hand to knock on the library door. She stilled, then turned the knob and walked into the room.

The sudden blaze of light made her blink. Branches of

candles dotted the tabletops, and a pair of candelabras, one on each corner, sat on the large mahogany writing desk in the middle of the room. A cheerful fire blazed in the hearth, sending warmth and light streaming into the room.

Unlike the study, which served as Graeme's office for his estate and magistrate duties, the library was given over to reading or writing letters. The room was old-fashioned, with its cozily faded carpets on polished oak floors, and a comfortable sofa on the other side of the desk, facing the fireplace. A soft woolen blanket was draped over the sofa, and plump pillows nestled in the armchairs. Jeannie in particular loved this room and spent a great deal of time here, nose deep in a book.

Right now, though, the room was all about Grant and his search for the elusive bandits. He stood in front of the desk, coat discarded, his hands flat on the littered tabletop as he frowned down at a survey map. In the flickering glow of the candles, his hair gleamed almost as brightly as flame.

Absorbed in his work, he continued to stare at the map. Kathleen indulged herself in covert appreciation of his brawny form and handsome profile. How she'd ever found him a bore was a mystery. She knew now that he was a superbly controlled man who never wasted a word or an action. That quiet intensity was immensely appealing.

"Knock, knock," she said. "May I come in?"

Grant slowly straightened up and turned to face her, his distracted frown easing into a smile. The smile turned into a grin as he took in her messy hair and stocking toes peeking out from under her skirts.

"Just larking about at this hour, are we?" he said. "But I think you forgot your shoes."

"I didn't forget them. I was sneaking. Successfully, I might add, since you didn't hear me come in."

"I'll wager you didn't sneak past Graeme."

"You would win that wager. I'd successfully navigated the house only to be tripped up by your annoying brother."

"He was a spy, ye ken."

"There wasn't much spying involved, since I practically barreled straight into him."

"Bad luck, that. But why the need for sneaking?" He looked at her feet again. "And your poor toes. They must be freezing by now, daft lass."

"All in a good cause," she said.

His eyebrows notched up. "Which is?"

She turned the key in the lock before calmly facing him. At least she hoped she appeared calm, because her heart was racing like a horse at full gallop.

"Because I'm going to seduce you, sir. One generally sneaks about when embarking on such a course of action."

He choked out a laugh. "You are?"

Kathleen waved an airy hand. "Of course, I do not wish to disturb if you're working. Shall I leave you to it?"

"Only if you want me to chase you down the hall and drag you back."

"That might be fun, although we'd probably wake up half the house."

He strolled over—though prowled would be a better description—and joined her at the door. Propping one hand against the wood panels, he leaned down to feather a kiss across her lips.

"It would be worth it," he murmured.

She rested a hand against the silk of his waistcoat. "You were working, though. I'm sure it's important."

"I'd consign every bit of work to the flames if you would be so very kind as to seduce me."

The heated glitter in his gaze practically set *her* on fire.

"Not necessary," she managed to reply. "I shall be happy to seduce you, forthwith."

He braced his other hand against the door, caging her in.

"And does that mean you've decided to marry me, Kathleen?"

She huffed out a breath. "Of course it does, you booby. I hardly seduce men I'm *not* going to marry."

"Excellent. Now I won't be required to hunt down your previous suitors and throttle them."

She patted his chest. "You can be well assured that none of my suitors inspired in me the least desire to engage in seduction."

"Excellent judgment on your part, lass."

"Naturally, you would think so."

He chuckled, and then started to bend down to kiss her again.

Kathleen pressed two fingers to his mouth. "Before I commence the seduction, I wish to tell you something. I promise it won't take long, but it's important."

He kissed her fingers before curling his hand around hers and bringing it down to his chest. "Sweetheart, you can take as much time as you need. As eager as I am to be seduced, there is no need to rush or feel any pressure. Whatever you wish to do or not do is fine."

It was a wonder she didn't melt right at his feet. "You truly are the nicest man in the world."

"As we have previously ascertained. Now, come along before you freeze your toes. Nothing is more fatal to love-making than chilblains."

Before she could respond to that bit of silliness, he swept her up and carried her to the sofa.

"Feel free to sweep me off my feet, Mr. Kendrick," she said rather breathlessly as he lowered her to the cushions.

He took up the fireplace poker and rearranged the logs before adding another one to the flames. "Can't have you wandering about barefoot, lass."

She stuck out one foot. "I'm not. These are woolen stockings, very sturdy and warm."

Still, she was grateful for the heat now pouring out from the fireplace. She'd probably be even more grateful once they divested themselves of their clothing, which would likely happen sooner rather than later.

He joined her on the sofa, settling her under the crook of her arm. Kathleen snuggled against him with a happy sigh.

"Now, what did you wish to talk about?" he said. "The marriage settlements? I must warn you that I'm a skilled negotiator."

She poked him. "You're ridiculous. And since we both have quite a bit of money, that will hardly be necessary."

"But I could be a nefarious fortune hunter. You have only my word that I'm not."

"Your grandfather is right. You are a jinglebrains."

"Yes, but I'm your jinglebrains, and that makes all the difference."

"And here I was all these weeks, thinking you lacked a sense of humor."

Keeping his arm draped over her shoulder, he turned a bit so he could look down at her. "You weren't wrong. I'd completely forgotten how to have fun until you reminded me. I bless the day you came into my life, Kathleen Calvert."

Since both his words and the tenderness in his gaze made

her want to cry, she took herself in hand. "If what we've been going through the last several weeks is your idea of fun, you're not just a jinglebrains. You're a lunatic."

Grant simply smiled and settled her back under his arm. "All right, lass, what is it you wish to tell me?"

"Well, I know I've been rather a pain lately—"

He cuddled her. "Never."

"That's very kind, but you know I've been a bear to you, and you didn't deserve it."

"To say we've all been under a great deal of pressure would be an understatement. I believe I've been growly once or twice, too."

She craned her head back, looking at him with mock astonishment. "No, really?"

"Cheeky lass," he said with a smile. "But I agree that we've had many challenges these last weeks. On top of everything going on around us, you also needed to make difficult decisions about your future. Believe me, love, I'm incredibly grateful for the sacrifice you're willing to make."

"But it's *not* a sacrifice, and I don't want you thinking it is."

His eyebrows ticked up. "I recall a conversation this afternoon that suggested otherwise."

"I know, and I've been thinking about it ever since. And I believe that I've been approaching the question from the wrong angle."

"Interesting. What's the correct angle?"

"I was looking at life as . . . as a binary choice. It was either having one thing or the other."

He nodded. "Me, or Ireland."

"Yes. And Ireland seemed so simple. But when I started

to fall in love with you, I realized that such wasn't the case. Ireland presented just as many problems as you did."

"Thus, the binary choice."

"Yes, but what a silly way to look at things. Because whatever choice one makes, there will always be challenges. Difficulties don't disappear when you fall in love, nor does falling in love solve all your problems." She gave him a wry look. "Despite what any romantic book or poem might claim to the contrary. I was thrown off a bit until I realized that."

"I always thought the opposite," he confessed. "Love . . . marriage seems insanely complicated to me, even a happy marriage. That's one reason I avoided thinking about it."

"You're right. Love and marriage *are* very complicated."

He tilted his head. "Are we talking ourselves out of it? Because if we are, perhaps we should skip this discussion and proceed directly to seduction."

Kathleen scoffed. "Now you're being silly again."

By way of reply, he leaned down and kissed her, sliding his tongue along the seam of her lips. She felt herself melting against him, and had to muster a strong effort to draw back from his oh-so-tempting mouth.

"That is not playing fair," she sternly said. "You made me lose my train of thought."

Grant chuckled.

She cleared her throat and started again. "Where was I? What these last several weeks have taught me is that complicated and difficult situations are simply one part of life. Complications will continue to exist even if you happen to fall in love with the most wonderful man in the world."

His gaze grew tender again. "Och, Kathleen."

"And it's perfectly fine when it's difficult sometimes,

because you no longer have to manage it alone. Even when it's particularly complicated, it's worth it. Because the people you love are worth it." She placed a hand to his cheek, feeling a day's worth of bristle scratch her palm. "Because *you* are worth it, Grant. Because of you, I can shoulder my burdens and know I don't have to carry them alone."

When he kissed her palm, Kathleen couldn't hold back a shiver.

"And you'll never be alone again," he replied in a husky voice. "I promise I will always be there for you."

She smiled up at him. "I am counting on it."

Unceremoniously, he lifted her up and plopped her onto his lap. "Then, sweetest girl, in lieu of our discussion about marriage settlements, may I formally ask you— again—to marry me?"

After she regained her equilibrium, Kathleen brought a finger to her lips. "Hmm . . ."

"Lass," he growled.

She couldn't help grinning. "I accept, sir. Gladly."

"Thank the good Lord. Now, can we get on with the seduction or is there anything else we need to thrash out?"

"I believe we have concluded our discussion."

"Excellent. Have at it."

She blinked. "Er, what?"

"You're supposed to be seducing me."

"Oh, yes." She rubbed her nose. "Well, this is rather embarrassing, but I'm not really sure how to go about it. I was hoping for some assistance from you."

"Assistance like this?"

He lifted his hips and nudged, pushing something quite large and quite hard against her bottom.

Kathleen felt her eyes pop wide. "Ah . . ."

He chuckled and stretched his arms along the length of the sofa. "Let's try this for a start. Why don't you straddle me and see where that leads."

"That sounds *quite* naughty."

"I believe that's the point."

She took in his sly grin and the heat in his gaze. Clearly, he was challenging her.

Kathleen could never refuse a challenge. "Very well, sir."

When she started to slide off his lap, Grant clamped his hands around her waist. "Kathleen, one generally doesn't commence a seduction by abandoning the object of one's seducing."

"I'm getting up so I can take off my gown, silly. I thought you would enjoy watching me do that."

He smiled. "Despite your protestations to the contrary, you do seem to have a good sense of how to go about seducing a fellow."

"I'm a quick learner."

"I noticed that the other day."

She teased him with a quick kiss. When Grant tried to deepen the caress, she wriggled off his lap—and she *did* wriggle, making sure to press her bottom against his erection.

"Hell and damnation, lass," he groaned. "You'll probably kill me before the night is out."

"That would be most unfortunate," she replied as she reached over her shoulder to start unbuttoning her gown.

Grant once more stretched his arms along the back of the sofa. "I'm willing to make the sacrifice, and I would certainly die happy."

"You truly *are* a jinglebrains. Now, instead of foolish commentary, I suggest you divest yourself of some of your clothing, starting with neckcloth and vest."

"I was hoping you would do that for me."

"I'm having enough trouble reaching these blasted buttons," she muttered as she strained to reach the middle of her back.

He snorted. "Come here and let me get those for you."

She turned her back to him. "So much for my seducing expertise."

"Rule number one—wear a dress that fastens in the front." Grant made swift work of her buttons. "You're all set, and can recommence the seduction."

"Thank you, sir—" She squawked when he goosed her bottom.

Turning around, Kathleen sternly eyed him. Her betrothed looked entirely unrepentant.

"What was that about?" she demanded.

"Sorry, lass, but I've been wanting to do that for weeks. You have such a sweet little bottom."

"So, you've been staring at my backside all this time?"

He lifted an eyebrow as if to say, *Of course I have.*

She pointed a finger at him. "You've been tricking me all along, Grant Kendrick. You are a complete rogue."

"At the moment, this rogue would like you to take off your gown."

Taking a mental breath—because she really *was* rather nervous—Kathleen grabbed her skirts and yanked her dress up over her head. Unfortunately, she also got her shift tangled in there, too, which meant *she* got tangled up. By the time she got the bloody dress off, she was flushed and thoroughly annoyed with herself.

Grant, however, had a hand pressed to his mouth, clearly trying not to laugh.

"If you utter so much as a chuckle, I will walk out of this room," she threatened.

He plucked the gown from her loose hold and tossed it behind the sofa. "Not without your dress, you won't."

"That was a new gown, I'll have you know. At this rate, I won't have anything left to wear, what with riding about in thunderstorms and you tossing my clothing on the floor."

It took her a moment to notice that Grant was staring at her with an expression she could only describe as . . . greedy.

"Yer bloody gorgeous, lass." When Grant stroked his erection through his breeches, Kathleen almost fainted.

She had to swallow twice before she could answer. "Thank you. Now, please take off some of *your* clothing. Fair play, and all that."

He flashed a wicked smile. "I'll be playing, all right. And while I'm undressing, why don't you start on your stays—which, I might add, are very pretty."

She'd worn one of her nicest pairs, front lacing and cream colored, and trimmed with tiny embroidered flowers and pink ribbons.

From the size of Grant's erection—which was now tenting his breeches *quite* impressively—he also liked her stays.

She began to slowly unlace the garment. Grant quickly unwound his cravat and tossed it aside, then went to work on the buttons of his waistcoat. When one snagged, he simply jerked on the vest, sending the button whizzing past her.

"You lost one," she politely said.

He snorted. "I think I'm also losing my mind. Now, would you please come back here while I still have a few wits left?"

She strolled over to stand right in front of him, continuing to leisurely unlace her stays. Grant brushed her hands aside and finished the job.

"I thought I was supposed to be seducing you?" she said, resting her hands on his shoulders.

"Trust me, I am thoroughly seduced."

Grant eased her stays off and dropped them to the floor, leaving her clad only in her shift and her stockings.

"Och, yer like a fairy princess in yer dainty things," he rasped.

She'd worn one of her nicest shifts, too. It was sheer cambric, tied with pale pink ribbons.

With a teasing smile, she played with one of the ribbons. "So, you like my shift, too?"

Grant reached out and pulled her between his legs. "I certainly like this."

He dragged a thumb over the outline of her already stiff nipple. Kathleen couldn't hold back a moan.

"That's my lovely girl," he murmured.

Both of his hands now came up to her breasts. He took his time playing with them, teasing the taut nipples through the fabric. Kathleen's knees actually went wobbly, and she had to keep a grip on his shoulders.

She arched her back when he tugged one of the throbbing peaks. "Oh, Grant!"

His only response was to lean forward and suck her nipple into his mouth, and then begin licking her through the cambric. She squirmed as he lavished caresses, and she had to clamp her legs tight against the luxurious sensation already building between her thighs.

Grant finally pulled back. "Now that's a pretty sight."

The wet and now completely transparent fabric clung to her nipples. They were flushed, stiff and hard, and still aching for his tongue. She dug her fingertips into his shoulders, silently begging for more.

Instead, his focus slid lower. Grant slowly trailed a hand down her belly, making her quiver, before cupping her sex. Kathleen whimpered when he rubbed her through the thin material.

"Spread your legs for me, love," Grant rumbled.

"I feel like I'm going to fall over."

He braced a hand on her hip. "Just keep holding on to my shoulders. I won't let you fall."

Kathleen parted her legs. Grant rubbed and teased her bud to hard prominence through the damp fabric. She closed her eyes and let her head fall back, giving herself over to pleasure, drowning in waves of sensation. Her heart pounded, and tiny contractions began to ripple from deep inside, taking her almost to the edge.

When he suddenly withdrew his hand, she almost toppled over. He clamped a hand on her bottom, holding her upright.

Kathleen glared at him. "Really? Now you stop?"

His chuckle was deep and rasping. "Love, you're not coming until I'm deep inside of you."

She rather lost her breath, because that particular mental image was both intimidating and incredibly exciting.

"And when is that going to happen?"

"Soon."

Then, without warning, Grant swept the shift over her head. Stunned to be suddenly naked before him but for her stockings, she bit back a gasp.

His eyes flared like a torch. "Can you stand on your own?" he rasped out.

"I . . . I think so." She braced her feet and let go of his shoulders.

As Grant unlaced his shirt, his gaze roamed over her body. It was so intent that she could almost feel it trailing over her skin. It took all her willpower to remain standing when all she wanted to do was crawl into his lap and collapse.

"Spread your legs a bit more," he ordered.

Swallowing, she complied with the sensual demand. Grant delved a hand into her curls, then slowly, carefully, pushed two fingers inside of her. Kathleen grabbed his shoulders and cried out as her channel clenched around him.

"Aye, yer ready," he growled.

He pumped his fingers once, wrenching a moan from her throat, and then slowly withdrew them. With his help, she climbed onto his lap and straddled him. Loving the feel of his erection pressed against her exposed sex, she rubbed against him.

Grant hissed. "Hell, yes. That's my beauty."

He steadied her, and then dragged his shirt over his head and tossed it aside. Kathleen's mouth went entirely dry, because Grant Kendrick without a shirt was a sight to behold. His shoulders were broad and his arms bulged with muscle. Dark red hair dusted his brawny chest, and narrowed down in a tempting line over his taut stomach.

"Like what you see?" he murmured.

Kathleen smiled. "I do. I like what I feel, too."

Liked it so much that she wriggled against him.

"Bloody hell," Grant muttered. "That's it, love. Move however you like."

She flexed her hips, rubbing against him, building the

lovely ache between her thighs. It was delicious, and even more delicious when he began massaging her breasts. Kathleen shivered at the sensations storming her body.

When she felt ready to tip over the edge, Grant suddenly bent her back over his arm, thrusting her breasts up. He devoured one, and then the other, drawing on her nipples until they ached with delicious torment. Kathleen squirmed, trying to relieve the ache between her thighs, but Grant's powerful arms held her in position while he lavished kisses and little nips on her breasts.

Desperate, she clamped a hand to the back of his head. "Grant, please!"

He finally drew back. His eyes glittered with a passion that set her entire being on fire.

"Ready for me, sweetheart?" he asked in a husky voice.

She frantically nodded.

"Lift up," he said.

When she shakily complied, he snaked a hand between them and began to unbutton his breeches. When he fumbled a bit, cursing, she couldn't hold back a smile.

He finally freed himself. Kathleen gasped as his erection—so thick and so hard—slid between her slick folds. For a few minutes, he teased her with it, rubbing until the hard little bud ached once more for release.

"Lift up again, my darling," he murmured.

When she did, he fitted himself at her entrance. He felt huge, and she felt a wee bit scared.

Mostly, though, she couldn't wait to be finally and truly his.

Gently, oh-so-gently, he forged into her. Kathleen grabbed his shoulders, feeling her eyes pop wide.

"Ah, love," he gritted out, his eyes narrowing to emerald slits.

There was a sharp sting—her turn to hiss—and then he was fully seated within her. Grant rested his damp forehead against hers, breathing heavily as he held them both still.

After a minute or so, the sting faded, and Kathleen became aware of a beautiful sense of fullness. Grant was inside her—so deep—and it was incredible.

When he opened his eyes, she saw a gaze full of passion, but also a tenderness that brought a quick rush of tears. He brushed a thumb across her cheek before kissing her.

"All right, my bonny lass?" he whispered.

She gave him a misty smile. "Aye, that."

When he chuckled, she felt it in the very depths of her being.

"I am very happy to hear that," he said.

"I would, however, like to . . ." She twirled a hand.

His smile was slow and wicked. "You'd like to come?"

Well, there was no point in being squeamish about it. After all, she was naked and the man was buried inside her.

"Yes, please. As soon as possible."

Grant chuckled. "Put your hand down there, love."

She blinked in shock when he guided her hand to her own sex. "Um, what do you want me to do?"

"Touch yourself, like I just did. I'll do all the rest."

Tentatively, she fingered the hard bud as he began to flex his hips, rocking inside her. That felt rather wonderful, so she rubbed harder. And that felt . . .

Amazing.

While Kathleen pleasured herself, Grant slipped a hand under her bottom, holding her steady against his thrusts. His other hand went to her breast. She moaned as he dragged a calloused thumb over the rigid tip. She rubbed herself harder, teasing the slick, hard knot. Intense pleasure radiated throughout her entire body, rapidly taking her to the edge.

Suddenly, Grant tilted her back and fastened his mouth to her breast, sucking hard. With his mouth on her breasts and his erection stroking her, Kathleen gave herself up to the tiny contractions now starting to ripple out from her core.

Her body was on fire—consuming, delicious fire. She rubbed herself one more time just as Grant nipped her. She cried out, climaxing instantly.

She grabbed his shoulders, shuddering as her channel clenched around him. It was like nothing she'd ever felt before, drowning her in sensation. Grant thrust into her once more, and then groaned as he came with a hard shudder. Kathleen curled herself around him, clinging tight, finding her anchor as she rode out the storm.

And then the waves turned into ripples, and the storm drifted away. In the aftermath, there was only Grant, brushing her tangled hair away from her face, and murmuring sweet endearments in her ear.

As she lay in his arms, recovering her breath, Kathleen's world subtly shifted on its axis. For so long, she'd assumed she'd spend the rest of her life as a spinster, and quite happily so.

For once, she was grateful to have been proven wrong.

Chapter Twenty-Five

Kathleen took a sip from her teacup, and then grimaced at the stone-cold brew. A glance at the clock on one of the library's bookshelves confirmed that the entire morning had slipped by. Stifling a yawn, she considered taking a brisk walk before joining her sister for luncheon. Several hours of researching and sketching designs for new flowerbeds had left her with a fuzzy brain.

Part of that condition could be placed at Grant's door. Or her door, actually, since she'd been silly enough to open it to him each of these last three nights. He always left before the servants were up, giving her a lingering kiss and a stern admonition to sleep in. Kathleen was an early riser, though, even if her future husband had kept her up half the night. But if it came to getting a good night's sleep or making love with Grant, she'd choose the latter every time.

Of course, they needed to be careful, or Kathleen might find herself with child before her betrothed had even put a ring on her finger.

Grant had initially suggested a grand wedding in London with all her friends and their extended families in attendance. Although touched by his generosity, she'd told him

a smaller affair in Glasgow was infinitely preferable to the
circus of a *ton* wedding. Helen would no doubt kick up a
fuss at having to travel to Scotland, but that was no longer
Kathleen's problem.

Besides, she now firmly believed that Jeannie should
spend the rest of the winter in Glasgow with the Kendricks.
Jeannie had seemed genuinely happy to hear of her betrothal to Grant, but also oddly unsettled. The girl had
grown increasingly quiet these last few days, avoiding
company as much as possible. When Kathleen had gently
probed, Jeannie had burst into tears and begged her not to
abandon her *just yet*.

It seemed an overreaction, but it was clear that Jeannie
still relied on her, and equally clear that she dreaded returning home to Papa and Helen. So for now, Kathleen
would do her best to keep Jeannie with her despite the
challenges of managing a moody, complicated girl.

Overarching all these other considerations was the ever-
lurking problem of the bandits. Though matters on that
front had been quiet since the distillery fire, none of them
were under the illusion the troubles were over. Grant and
Graeme were continuing their investigations, but until that
issue was successfully resolved, Kathleen and Grant's future
would have to wait.

Still, despite the delay, a quiet joy to her life persisted,
because now she *did* have a future. And it was better than
anything she'd ever imagined.

Kathleen was rolling up her sketches when Hannah hurried into the library, a troubled frown marking her brow.

"Is something wrong, Hannah?"

"Very wrong. You best look at these, Miss Kathleen."
The maid thrust some crumpled papers at her.

Kathleen placed them on the desk and started to smooth out what appeared to be scrawled notes.

"They're notes to Miss Jeannie," Hannah said. "Secret ones, from the look of it."

"What? Who would send her secret notes?"

Hannah pointed to the bottom of one. Kathleen felt her jaw sag.

"Captain Brown?" she gasped.

"Looks like," Hannah grimly replied. "I just glanced at one of 'em, but that told me enough."

"Where did you find them?"

"In Miss Jeannie's room. I'd gone there to fetch a gown that needed repairing. Since one of the housemaids is out with a nasty cold, I thought I'd straighten up, too. When I picked up the books by her bed, these fell out of one of 'em. I couldn't help seeing Captain Brown's name, and I knew that wasn't right." She pointed at one of the notes. "Read this one."

Hannah's dismayed expression reflected Kathleen's growing horror as she started to peruse the page.

"Captain Brown asked my sister to steal Sabrina's pearls, the ones she received from the king," she blurted out.

"And it looks like she already did."

The floor seemed to tilt under Kathleen's feet, causing her to grab the edge of the desk. "You checked?"

"Just now. Them pearls are gone, all right."

"You're absolutely sure."

"I take care of my lady's jewels, so I know where everything is. Because she hardly wears that set, they're always in the bottom of her jewel case. I also searched all her drawers, just in case."

Kathleen scanned the rest of the notes. There were three in all, and the first obviously inserted into the book the day the captain had presented it to Jeannie. Fury now replaced horror as she realized how thoroughly the brute had hood-winked her sister.

"Yer both lookin' as queer as Dick's hatband, lassies. What's amiss?"

Kathleen wrenched her gaze up to see Angus in the doorway.

"Do you know where Grant is?" she hoarsely asked. "Or Graeme and Sabrina?"

"Grant's out searchin' again with a few of the grooms. Graeme's at the distillery, and Sabrina went down to the village to see some of the shopkeepers."

"I have to find Jeannie," Kathleen said, starting for the door.

"She's not upstairs," Hannah said. "I think she's gone, too."

"What's amiss?" Angus repeated in a louder voice.

Kathleen thrust the notes at him. "Captain Brown has been using my sister to steal for him. It appears she's taken Sabrina's pearls." She turned to Hannah. "Can you make sure she's not here? Get help from Davey and come find me when you know. I'll check the kitchen garden and stables."

Hannah rushed from the room.

As Angus read the notes, his scowl transformed from angry to ferocious. "Scaly, nasty-faced bastard. Do ye think yon vicar is involved?"

"No, but the captain told Jeannie that David is nursing a secret affection for her, and has been held back by his scruples over their difference in station and wealth."

As she headed out to the hall, Angus kept pace with her. "So, if the vicar only had enough money, he'd offer for our Jeannie. Is that the story?"

"Yes, and Captain Brown would sell the pearls and give

the money to David, so David could then ask Jeannie to marry him."

"Without tellin' the vicar it was money from stolen goods? How would that work?" Angus skeptically asked. "Yer sister's no cakedoodle, Kathleen. She'd nae fall for such nonsense."

"I'm sure the captain had some ready explanation, and Jeannie is naïve enough to believe a cunning cheat like him. She *wants* to believe it, because she still thinks she's in love with David."

"Aye, but *stealin'* Sabrina's pearls, lass."

"I know. It's beyond dreadful."

She felt sick over her sister's actions. In retrospect, Jeannie's troubling behavior these past days now made sense. Kathleen hadn't wanted to push her, but it had been yet another capital error on her part.

Panic threatened to overwhelm her. One of the notes alluded to Jeannie meeting up with the captain at some point today. The thought of her little sister in that man's clutches . . .

"I swear, if Brown hurts Jeannie, I will throttle him with my bare hands," she gritted out.

Angus opened the door to the kitchen garden. "Aye, that. But how did the bastard get to our Jeannie in the first place?"

"It probably happened that day he found her in the rain. God only knows what stories he put into her head during their ride back to Lochnagar. What I cannot understand is how he delivered all those notes. The first one, yes. That was in the book he gave her. But the others?"

"All questions that need answerin'."

"Including one about his ultimate game," she said as

they strode between the vegetable beds. "Is the captain simply a common thief and Jeannie a convenient mark?"

"Probably got something to do with his land scheme. Grant got a letter from Nick just this mornin' with none too good a report on the captain's investors. There's no proof they even exist."

Clarity struck Kathleen with the force of a slap to the cheek, bringing her to a halt.

Angus stopped mid-stride. "Lass?"

"The gang of thieves," she whispered.

He looked blank for a moment before shaking his head. "But they were thievin' a good three weeks afore Brown showed up."

"That would provide him the perfect cover. He wasn't even in Dunlaggan when the thieving and vandalism began. Plus, no one would suspect him because the blasted vicar is his brother."

Angus shoved a hand through his bristly white hair, making it stick straight up. "The thievin' makes sense. But the vandalism and fire—that doesna connect."

"It's a terrible muddle." She took his arm and headed for the stables. "But whether he was involved in those crimes or not, Brown is endangering my sister. We have to find her."

"And we need to warn the lads and get them lookin' for Brown."

"Of course, this *would* be the day when everyone has gone off in different directions," she groused as they hurried through the open doors of the stables.

The stable boy came out of the tack room. "Can I help ye, Miss Calvert?"

"Have you seen my sister, Brian?"

"She went out on one of the ponies an hour ago. I saddled Betsy myself."

Kathleen grimaced. "But none of us are supposed to go without an escort."

Brian nodded. "I offered to go with her, but Miss Jeannie said she was only goin' to the distillery to see the cat, and that she had yer permission. It's but a mile, and the workmen repairing the damage are using that path all day. She'd nae be out of anyone's sight."

Kathleen pressed a hand to her suddenly perspiring forehead. "Oh, my God."

"Och, that girl is too smart for her own good." Angus patted Kathleen's shoulder. "Steady on, lass. We'll find her."

She nodded and forced herself to think. "Brian, please saddle the mare for me. A regular saddle, not a lady's."

The boy eyed her morning dress. "But miss—"

"Hop to it, lad," Angus barked. Then he cocked an eyebrow at Kathleen. "We're goin' to the vicarage, I take it?"

"Yes. The captain has been staying there, so it's the best place to start looking."

"I'll saddle up."

Angus followed Brian into the tack room. A moment later, Hannah and Davey rushed into the stables.

"She's nowhere in the house, miss," Hannah wheezed. "I'm sure of it."

"I know. She left an hour ago."

"We found out how she was gettin' the notes," Davey said. "The kitchen boy told us the captain's man was passin' them to him, to give to Miss Jeannie."

Kathleen frowned. "The captain has a servant?"

"His batman," Hannah said. "And a pert fella he is, too. He made a show of courting one of the housemaids. That was why he'd drop by, all casual-like. The kitchen boy's a bit slow, Miss Kathleen, so he wouldn't know it was a wrong thing to pass them notes."

"The captain certainly thought of everything." When Kathleen found him, she *would* wring his blasted neck.

"Davey," she continued, "go to the distillery and tell Sir Graeme what's happening. Since Captain Brown is staying at the vicarage, Mr. MacDonald and I will ride straight there and start looking about."

"I'll run, miss. Be faster than waitin' for a horse." The footman took off at a dead run toward the distillery path.

"Hannah, does Lady Sabrina have an escort?"

"She took the coach, so there's a footman and the coachman."

"Good. If we see her in the village, we'll tell her what's happened. You keep an eye out for Jeannie. If she comes back, send word to the vicarage."

"Aye, miss."

Brian led the mare out of the stall.

Hannah grimaced. "You can't go riding in that outfit, miss."

"I'm wearing my gardening boots, so they'll do. I just need a—"

"Coat." Hannah disappeared into the tack room.

"Brian, do you have gloves?" Kathleen asked.

The boy pulled out a pair of plain leather gloves from his jerkin. Then Hannah returned with a wool jacket, the sort grooms wore in colder weather.

Kathleen pulled on the gloves and shrugged into the coat. It swamped her, but would keep her warm. "Hannah, hold the bridle while Brian gives me a leg up."

The maid looked scandalized but did as she was told.

Brian boosted Kathleen onto the mare just as Angus led a saddled bay out of its stall.

"Ridin' hell-bent for leather, are we?" he said to Kathleen as she settled, draping her skirts over her legs.

"That we are."

"That fella's skittish, Mr. MacDonald," Brian said, eyeing the bay's twitchy behavior. "Mayhap ye should take one of the mares?"

Angus scoffed. "Och, there's nae horse I canna handle, lad."

The old man nimbly mounted, and quickly brought the fidgety horse under control.

Kathleen led the way to the stable yard and around the house. Once they passed through the courtyard and onto the main drive, she prodded the mare into a gallop. Angus kept pace, easily controlling the big bay.

As they raced toward the main road, Kathleen's heart pounded, seemingly in time with the mare's hooves. When they reached the estate's gates a few minutes later, they slowed to make the turn to Dunlaggan.

Kathleen's breath caught when she saw a rider coming toward them from the village, still several hundred yards out. "Can you tell who that is?"

"Looks like a man."

Drat. Not Jeannie.

She shielded her eyes from the afternoon glare. "Maybe it's Grant."

Angus peered forward and then spat out a curse. "Nae. It's the scaly bastard."

Brown was riding straight toward them at an easy canter. It seemed almost impossible to believe.

Kathleen gathered her dumbfounded wits. "At least Jeannie isn't with him, so I hope that's a good sign. He doesn't seem the least bit disturbed, does he?"

"Happen yer right about that."

A moment later, the captain waved his hat in greeting.

"He obviously thinks we don't know what he's up to," she said.

Angus glanced at her. "What's the plan, lass? Shall we take him?"

She grimaced. "I didn't think to bring a pistol."

The old fellow patted his pocket. "I got a nice popper from the tack room. No worries about that."

"Thank goodness one of us is thinking ahead. Let's slow down. We can't rush in unprepared."

This might be their only chance to capture Brown. More importantly, they didn't yet know where Jeannie was. If Brown had done anything to her, they couldn't afford to let him get away.

"We'll take him," Angus said.

"Agreed, but wait till he's close before drawing your pistol. You can't afford to miss."

"Och, I never miss."

Grant had once commented that his grandfather was a terrible shot. She had to trust that, for once, he'd been exaggerating.

"We'll simply act like friends who happened to run into each other," she said.

Angus nodded. "Then I'll pull out my popper and make the bastard get off his horse. He'll be easier to control that way."

"That . . . that sounds fine."

It actually sounded horrible, but she didn't have a better idea.

"Good day to you, Miss Calvert," the captain cheerfully called out as he approached.

Kathleen reined in her horse. Angus did likewise, staying

close. His bay sidled a bit, but the old fellow kept him under control.

Captain Brown came to a halt about a dozen yards away. Was he suspicious already? Still, he seemed his usual jovial self, so she managed to pin on a smile.

"Good afternoon, sir," she said. "Are you off to Lochnagar?"

"Yes, to call on Lady Kendrick and the rest of you ladies. I must make my departure tomorrow, so I've come to say goodbye. Business calls, I'm afraid."

"How unfortunate. I'm sure your brother will miss you."

"Yes, I'm afraid he will. Especially since he's nursing a broken heart, eh, Miss Calvert?" He gave her a knowing wink.

Kathleen returned a polite smile. Blast the man, though. Why wouldn't he come closer?

Angus glanced at her before pulling out a horse pistol and leveling it straight at Brown. Obviously, he'd decided the captain was close enough.

Brown's eyebrows shot up in exaggerated surprise. "Is this a jest? Miss Calvert, has the old codger lost his wits?"

"Ye'll hold yer bleedin' tongue and get doon off that horse," Angus snarled.

Brown adopted an outraged expression. "I'll do no such thing. What the devil is going on, here?"

"You've been using my sister to steal for you," Kathleen snapped. "Where is she, you bounder?"

"Hell's bells, that's a jolly rude thing to say to a friend."

"We found your notes. Jeannie was to meet you this afternoon, bringing Sabrina's necklace. My sister had best be unharmed if you don't wish to get shot."

"I'll shoot ye anyway, ye blasted varlet," Angus said. "Now, get off yer damn horse."

Brown's gaze darted between them. Then, oddly, he smiled and held up a hand. "I think not."

Boom.

A thundering shot echoed nearby. It startled Kathleen's mare, though she didn't lose control. But Angus's nervous bay shied badly, nearly dismounting him. Struggling with the reins, he dropped the pistol.

When it hit the ground, it discharged. The bay reared again and sent the old man tumbling backward onto the grassy verge. The horse then jumped a low wall and took off across the field.

"Angus," Kathleen gasped, starting to dismount.

"Hold right there, Miss Calvert."

Brown had leveled a pistol at her and regarded her with a cold smile.

Angus let out a groan as he struggled to sit up. He looked dazed, and there was blood on his forehead.

"Please let me go to him," she said.

"Don't move," Brown ordered.

Just seconds later, she heard pounding hooves from behind.

A stranger pulled up in a flurry of dust. "All right, Cap'n?"

"Fine, although it took you long enough."

"I had to cut through the woods. Didn't expect you to have company."

"No, that was a surprise," replied Brown. "But your shot was the distraction I needed."

Kathleen stared at the big man in the greatcoat and slouchy cap. She didn't recognize his face, but she definitely recognized the voice. "You're one of the robbers, the one who went through my trunk."

"Happens you're right, miss. And a nice haul it was."

He flashed an ugly leer. "Liked them dainties of yours, too. Pretty, like you."

She ignored his salacious remark and turned back to Brown. "You apparently are the leader of that blasted gang. How appalling."

"I must say, Miss Calvert, we've had a grand time here in Dunlaggan. Yet now we must depart for richer pastures. Once we take care of you and your ridiculous escort, that is."

Bile rose into her throat. "Please just tell me if Jeannie is unharmed," she hoarsely said.

Brown's gaze suddenly filled with a cold, unnerving anger. "I have no idea where your sister is. She did not keep to our rendezvous, unfortunately. Now, I must do my best to track her down."

Kathleen could only hope that Jeannie had come to her senses, and was now safely back at the manor. "My sister is obviously smarter than you are. And don't even think to go to Lochnagar. The game is up, sir. If you have any brains, you'll make your escape now."

Brown studied her for several long seconds before flicking a glance at his henchman. "Get that old fool up onto the horse behind the woman. And make sure you tie his hands."

"We're taking 'em with us?"

"For now, yes." Brown gave Kathleen a toothy, avaricious grin. "One never knows when one needs a hostage, my dear. You might prove to be useful, after all."

Chapter Twenty-Six

Kathleen studied the rock wall, searching for any kind of possible handhold. If she couldn't get them out of this cave, they would be abandoned to their fate or to the tender mercies of Captain Brown.

She held the lantern over her head. "Do you see that bit of rock near the top? I might be able to toss the end of the rope ladder around it. If so, maybe I could scramble out from there."

After making Kathleen and Angus descend the ladder, Brown had tossed it down after them, into the cave.

Angus, who was sitting on a blanket and calmly stuffing his pipe, shook his head. "Lass, I'm not the sort to give up, but there's nae gettin' out of this cave without help. The scaly bastard has seen to that."

She sighed. "I suppose you're right. These walls are too bloody steep."

"It's a grand hiding place for that band of rank riders. It's nae to be wondered that the lads couldna find them."

"I cannot believe the thieves were able to find this place. It's almost invisible from the outside."

Tucked beneath a large rocky overhang, the cave was a

deep hole that was impossible to see until one was virtually upon it. About twenty feet down with steep walls, the space remarkably resembled a large room. The floor was dry and relatively flat, several dozen feet across in diameter. There was no way out but up.

Brown using them as hostages was probably the best they could hope for. If he decided to leave them here, Kathleen feared they had no hope of escape unless they were found. Those desperate thoughts tied her stomach up in knots.

Angus patted the blanket. "Lass, sit yerself down. Yer burnin' up yer energy wanderin' aboot like that."

"I can't help it. I'm so worried about Jeannie, and I'm furious that I allowed Brown to trick us."

"I'm the ninny that dropped the pistol, ye ken."

"That wasn't your fault. I'm just relieved that you weren't hurt any worse."

"It was just a wee knock on the head. After the twins, I've got the hardest noggin in the family."

When Angus had tumbled off his horse, she'd been terrified he'd been shot either by Brown's henchman or by the discharge of his own pistol. Thankfully, both shots had gone wide. He had a nasty bump and a small cut on his forehead but otherwise seemed unharmed.

Roger, the captain's revolting accomplice, had made short work of tying up the old fellow and boosting him onto the back of Kathleen's horse. She'd been tempted to see if she could give him a good kick as he was securing Angus behind her, but Brown had read her thoughts. He'd noted in a regretful tone that though he didn't wish to shoot her, he would if she forced his hand.

They'd ridden across several fields into a stand of trees. Once through, they'd come upon a rocky terrain dotted with ravines and caves. Astoundingly, the cave the gang used for their bolthole was less than an hour's ride from Lochnagar.

"I was quite proud of myself when I found it," Brown had boasted with an irritating smirk. "It's impossible to see, and yet so close to Dunlaggan. You all wondered how we escaped so easily after our escapades. This is the reason."

Kathleen had glared at him. "Do you even own land in the Americas or was that all a lie, too?"

"I have the land, but it's all swamp and jungle. Can't clear it long enough to grow a bloody thing. I lost every shilling on the blasted venture, so I have to recoup my losses one way or the other, and this is it."

His plan had been to find gullible investors, and also to dupe the villagers into buying worthless shares of land.

"But why the vandalism and the fire?" Kathleen had asked. "And why in God's name did you tamper with the children's punch at the fete? What purpose could be served by such vile acts?"

The captain had casually shrugged. "The more frightened the villagers were, the more likely they would be to buy shares. Many Scots are leaving for the Americas to start a new life, especially after the Clearances. If I made Dunlaggan unattractive to them, it might convince some to leave."

"So you would rob them, and then leave them with nothing." Kathleen had been tempted to spit at his feet. "You are a vile man, Captain Brown."

"And ye'll be gettin' yer just desserts for tryin' to hurt the bairns," Angus had growled. "The Kendricks will see to that, ye slimy bastard."

After that jolly exchange, Roger had forced them to

climb down into the cave. After Brown had thrown the ladder after them, Kathleen had tried a final stab of talking sense into him—and keeping her sister safe from him.

"You've already stolen many valuable things, including my jewels," she'd argued. "You should let us go and leave Dunlaggan while you can, since the Kendricks are now onto you. This is your final chance to escape."

Brown had scowled down at her. "I have four other men to pay off, and I must also recoup my losses. Lady Kendrick's pearls will do that and more. Your sister had best have them."

At that point, Kathleen had lost her temper and started issuing dire threats, but the captain and Roger had simply disappeared from view.

Angus held up the whisky bottle he'd found in a crate of provisions. "Have a dram to take off the chill."

Kathleen trudged over to join him on the blanket. "I suppose we should be grateful for the lanterns and the supplies."

Angus handed over the bottle. "And the drink."

After their captors had departed, they'd searched the cave. The hideout was well stocked. There were blankets and cords of wood, as well as lamps, candles, and crockery. Along with the whisky, they'd found hard biscuits and a round of cheese. They certainly wouldn't expire from the cold or die from hunger or thirst. At least not for some time.

"How long have we been down here?" she asked.

Angus checked his pocket watch. "Maybe half an hour. I wasna keeping track, ye ken."

"Blast. It feels like much longer."

"It's cause yer fretting about yer sister, and whether we'll die down here."

"Is that insight supposed to cheer me up?"

"Yer man would tear every hill down to the ground to find ye if he has to, lass. Dinna ye worry."

She couldn't help smiling at the notion of Grant as *her man*. She'd been clinging to his image since this nightmare began, using it as a bulwark against debilitating fear.

"It's Jeannie I'm mostly worried about. I wonder why she didn't make the rendezvous?"

"Thought better of it, I reckon. She's a smart lass, and she kens right from wrong, thanks to you."

"I hope so. But I feel like I've failed her—"

Angus grabbed her arm. "Hush, lass. I heard something."

Kathleen, straining her ears, heard Jeannie faintly calling her name. She scrambled to her feet and then helped Angus to stand.

"Jeannie, we're down here," she shouted.

Long seconds passed before she heard the reply, closer now. "I can't tell where you are."

"Sound echoes off the rock," Angus said. "Hard to tell where it's comin' from."

When Kathleen stripped off a glove, he covered his ears. She stuck two fingers in her mouth and blew a piercing whistle.

"Again," called Jeannie a moment later.

She blew with all her might, almost blasting out her own ears. They heard a scramble of boots and soon Jeannie's head appeared at the top of the cave.

Kathleen's head swam with relief. "Darling, are you all right? You're unharmed?"

"Yes, but I'm scared, Kath. The captain promised that nothing bad would happen, even if I took Sabrina's pearls. Why did he do this to you?"

"The captain tricked all of us, Jeannie. He wants the

pearls for himself. Are you sure you're alone? No one saw you come here?"

"I was very careful. I didn't get too close, and I waited for a long time to make sure they were gone."

"How did you find us, lass?" asked Angus.

"I was riding back from the village across the fields after I . . . I chickened out. Kath, I couldn't do what Captain Brown wanted me to do. I'm sure he's furious with me." She rubbed her cheek, clearly brushing back tears.

"It's all right, sweetheart. Just tell me what happened next."

"I was cutting across the fields because I didn't want anyone to see me. I thought if I could get back to the house and put the pearls in the jewelry box, I could just tell you what happened and you would fix it."

"But you didn't make it back to the house."

"I saw you and Mr. MacDonald on the road. I was just about to call to you when I saw Captain Brown. I got scared, so I hid my pony behind a hedge."

"I always knew ye were a smart lass," Angus said.

"I thought that man with the pistol killed you," Jeannie said, sounding teary.

"Nae, I was just a silly jinglebrains for falling off my horse. Now, dinna ye be tellin' my grandsons, lassie, or they'll roast me forever. Then I'd have to paddle them."

His little jest worked, because Jeannie let out a watery giggle. "I won't."

"So then you followed us here?" Kathleen asked.

"I thought about riding to Lochnagar for help, but I was afraid I would lose you. So I waited until you were almost to the woods, and then I followed."

"That was so brave of you, Jeannie." And horrifying,

given how much danger she could have put herself in. Kathleen felt sick even thinking about it.

"Aye, yer a brave lass," Angus said. "And wise enough not to get too close, I ken."

"I was afraid they would hear me, so I hid with my pony behind some rocks until I saw them come out of the ravine. But I didn't know exactly where to look until you whistled. It's a corker of a whistle, Kath."

"It is at that," Angus dryly replied.

"Sweetheart, that was incredibly smart," Kathleen said. "I am so proud of you."

Jeannie rubbed her nose. "But I was so stupid for believing the captain. Even though he said it was all to help David, I knew it was wrong to steal and keep secrets from you. David was never going to marry me, anyway. I don't think he loves me, after all."

"David would *not* want you stealing for him, no matter what," Kathleen said.

"He'll hate me now," Jeannie said in a despairing voice. "*You* must hate me for getting you into this mess."

"Lass, we need to be gettin' out of here," Angus murmured to Kathleen.

Kathleen gazed up at her sister. "Listen to me, Jeanette. I love you. I will *always* love you, no matter what. We can sort everything out later. Right now, we need to get out of here. Can you look around and see if there's a rope stashed somewhere?"

Her sister disappeared.

"If she canna find anything, she'll have to go for help," Angus said.

"I would hate sending her back by herself. Brown and his men are still out there. What if . . ." Her throat tightened at the idea of what those evil men could do to Jeannie.

Angus pressed a hand to her shoulder. "I ken, but we dinna have a choice. And the longer we wait, the more likely she'll run into them. There's a farm between here and Lochnagar, one of Graeme's tenants. She could stop there first."

Kathleen managed a smile. "That's an excellent idea."

"There's no rope up here," Jeannie called as she reappeared above them.

"All right, this is what I want you to do. Did you see a farm when you followed us?"

"Yes."

"Good. Now, go there and find someone to escort you to Lochnagar. If by some small chance the captain finds you first, just give him the pearls, all right?"

"But they're Sabrina's gift from the king! I can't do that."

"Sabrina won't give a hang about the pearls. She'll only want you to be safe. You *need* to be safe, understand? If Brown should find you, you have to give him the pearls and let him be on his way."

"But what if the captain comes back here, first? He could kill you." Jeannie's face suddenly contorted. "I'd like to kill *him* for doing this to you, and for tricking both me and David. He's a monster."

"He is," said Angus. "But ye need to do just what yer sister says. After that, I'll kill the varlets for ye."

That seemed to perk Jeannie up. "You promise?"

"Aye, that."

"Jeannie, you have to go," Kathleen said firmly. "Now."

"All right."

"If you see anything that makes you nervous—and I mean anything—you hide."

"I will. I love you, Kath."

"And I love you too. So much. Now, off you go."

They heard Jeannie scramble away, and then only silence.

Kathleen shot Angus a disbelieving look. "You'll kill the varlets for her? Really?"

"It worked, didn't it? Cheered our lassie right up."

"Apparently she's as bloodthirsty as you are."

"Och, she's a brave girl, just like ye."

Kathleen grimaced. "Well, she's certainly reckless like me."

Angus reached for the whisky bottle. "Have a wee pick-me-up."

"Why not?" she said with a sigh.

There was nothing else to do but wait. And pray.

Grant climbed over the rocks at the end of the ravine. "Kathleen? Angus?" he called.

A moment later, a piercing whistle sounded from the direction of a large overhang on his left. Frowning, he hurried to it and went under it. There he saw the hole that gaped open near the back.

Hell and damnation.

He and Graeme had scoured this area twice. They'd come within yards of this overhang and never once spotted the cave. No wonder Brown and his crew of blighters had been able to hide out for so long.

Kathleen and his grandfather stood about twenty feet below him in the surprisingly well-lit and obviously well-supplied cave.

Thank God.

Grant had to brace his hands on his knees to catch his breath from his rapid scramble up the ravine, and even more so from the fear that had throttled his breathing since the moment he and Graeme found their grandfather's pistol lying in the grass. They'd split up after that. Graeme had gone off to get as many men as possible from Dunlaggan. Grant had headed out to the fields in the opposite direction. It had taken every ounce of willpower not to panic, with Kathleen and his grandfather in the clutches of a ruthless bastard.

"Took ye long enough," Angus said with a wry smile. "We almost died from boredom waitin' for ye."

Grant choked out a laugh. "Sorry. I've been a wee bit busy, ye ken."

"You're here," Kathleen said, flashing him the most beautiful smile he'd ever seen. "And that's all that matters."

While Angus had a nasty bruise on his face, Kathleen looked fine—better than fine.

"Can you get us out?" she called up.

"I got a rope from the farm. Grandda, you look like hell. Are you all right?"

"Och, just a wee knock. And yer lassie is fine."

"Did you see Jeannie?" Kathleen asked.

"Yes, she's fine. I was coming out of the woods when I saw her pelting out of the ravine. She was a bit incoherent at first, but I got the gist."

Grant had almost fallen off his horse when he'd seen the girl trundling toward him as fast as the pony's stubby little legs could go. She'd thrown herself into his arms, bursting into overwrought tears. He was practically dying from worry by that point, but he'd simply patted her back until she'd calmed down.

"Where is she now?" Kathleen asked.

"I took her to that nearby farm. The farmer and his son are right now escorting her back to Lochnagar," Grant said as he started to unwind the coil of rope he'd carried in. "I also grabbed this rope while I was there."

Kathleen pressed a hand to her head. "Thank God. I've been so scared for her."

"Is Graeme lookin' for Brown and the rest of them rum coves?" Angus asked.

"Yes, he's leading a search."

"Brown knows his story is blown," Kathleen said, " and that'll make him even more dangerous."

"If he has any brains, he'll be riding as fast as he can away from Dunlaggan."

"But Grant, he seemed absolutely determined to get Sabrina's pearls."

"We can deal with that later," he said, anxious to get them out of there. "Grandda, can you tie the rope around Kathleen's waist so I can pull her up?"

"Kathleen is well able to tie a rope, sir," she tartly replied.

Grant snorted. "That's my girl."

He'd waited half a lifetime for her, only to fear he'd lost her forever. By God's grace and Jeannie's bravery he'd found her and his beloved old goat of a grandda. He vowed never again to take for granted the people he loved.

He wound the sturdy rope around his waist and tied it off with a double loop knot.

"Rope coming down," he called, dropping the rest of the coil down to the floor.

Kathleen and Angus had a short argument about who would go up first, until she finally just told him to cease fashing himself. She then quickly and competently tied the rope around his waist.

Angus tested the knot. "Ye can whistle, play cricket, and tie knots. Are ye sure yer not a boy in disguise?"

"I can say with full assurance that she is not," Grant said.

Angus looked up with a grin. "Good for ye, lad."

"Grandda, if you get dizzy on the way up, just tell me. I can do all the work if need be, and pull you straight up."

"I'm nae such a ninny as needin' that, laddie boy. I can do my part."

Grant braced his feet against a small ledge at the side of the cave. "All right, Grandda. When you're ready."

"Ready, son."

Grant held the rope firm as Angus began to pull himself up, using his feet to gain purchase on the cave walls. As the old duffer's head started to come close to the lip of the cave, Grant could see his grandfather was tiring from the strain.

"Ease off, Grandda," he said. "I've got you now."

When Angus nodded, Grant began to quickly pull. Only a few moments later, his grandfather was safely beside him.

Grant wrapped an arm around his waist. "All right, Grandda?"

"Aye." Angus wheezed. Then he started to sink down onto the rock. "Just let me catch my breath."

Grant untied the rope from around his grandfather's waist and dropped the coil back down. Kathleen wasted no time securing it around her waist and then gave a yank to test the knot.

"Ready?" Grant said.

Her beautiful smile glimmered up at him. "More than ready."

"Then come to me, sweet lass."

Kathleen began to pull herself up hand over hand as he kept the rope taut against her weight. She was strong and nimble and utterly determined. Grant watched proudly as she scaled the wall in practically no time. When she reached the top, he gave a little pull and she tumbled into his arms.

"Oh, thank God." She burrowed against him. "When Brown captured us, I was so afraid I would never see you again."

He folded his arms tightly around her. "I will always find you, love. No matter what."

She lifted her head. "Promise?"

Grant took her lips in a soul-searing kiss, pouring out all the love he felt for her. Kathleen quivered in his arms, kissing him back with a desperation that set him on fire.

A bony finger jabbed him in the back.

"There's nae time for canoodling," Angus barked. "We've got varlets to catch."

Kathleen reluctantly pulled out of Grant's arms. "You're right. Sorry."

"Ye'll have plenty of time for kissin' after we run Brown and his gang to ground."

"The only place you two are going is back to Lochnagar," Grant said as he untied the rope and quickly coiled it up.

Kathleen nodded. "Yes, I need to be with Jeannie."

"And Angus needs to have his head looked at," Grant added.

"What about horses?" Angus asked. "They obviously took yon lassie's."

"I borrowed one from the farmer. Kathleen can ride with me on mine."

They made their way to the end of the ravine, where Grant's bay and a sturdy draft horse were tied to a bush. After all were mounted, with Kathleen nestled securely in front of Grant, they picked their way off the rocky ground to the edge of the field.

"Your head all right, Grandda?" Grant asked.

"I'm fine, son. I'll nae be topplin' off another horse today."

They set off at a smart pace. The farmer's horse wasn't built for speed, but they still made good progress. In well under an hour, they rode past the gates of Lochnagar Manor.

Kathleen, who'd been dozing for the last twenty minutes, roused herself as they rode up the drive.

Grant kissed the top of her head. "All right, love?"

"I can't believe I fell asleep."

"Getting kidnapped does tend to wear one out."

"As does a man sneaking into your bedroom at night."

Grant chuckled. "Not tonight. You need your rest."

"I have a feeling we won't be getting much rest until Captain Brown and his men are safely locked away."

"He's probably halfway to Inverness by now."

As they rode into the main courtyard and pulled up, the front door flew open and Sabrina came rushing down the steps.

"Thank God!" she exclaimed. "We've been so worried."

"We're fine, lass," Angus said as he slowly dismounted. "Just a bump on the head and a few aches and pains for me."

"We'll get someone to look at your head," she replied in a distracted manner. "But we have a problem. A *big* problem."

"Did Jeannie get back?" Kathleen anxiously asked. "Is she all right?"

"Yes, she's safe. For now."

"What the hell does that mean?" Grant asked.

"It means she's cornered Captain Brown in the library and is holding him at gunpoint."

"What?" Kathleen yelped.

Grant stared at Sabrina in disbelief. "Anyone else in there?"

"Graeme and the vicar are. I'm afraid Jeannie is going to shoot the captain. She's incredibly upset."

"Grant, hand me down," Kathleen said in an impatient tone.

"Of course, but no running off half-cocked."

"I have to get to her before something terrible happens."

She wriggled, trying to slide off the horse. Grant kept a firm hold.

"Kathleen, if we go charging in there, we might startle her. She could fire the gun, or Brown might take the opportunity to go for her or one of the men. He's probably armed."

"I know, but—"

He gave her a squeeze. "We'll get her safely out, I promise. But we have to be careful."

She obviously didn't like it but gave a terse nod. Grant helped her off the horse and then dismounted.

"Grandda, can you take the horses?"

"Aye, then I'll join ye."

"No, you go up to the nursery and stay with Gus. Keep him safe. Who knows who else is lurking about the damn place?"

Angus nodded and led the horses away.

"Excellent thinking, Grant," Sabrina said as they hurried up the steps. "I've already got an armed footman outside the nursery, but it makes sense to send Angus up there."

"We don't need him rushing into the middle of this," he

said as they entered the hall. "And before *we* rush, tell me how this happened."

"Apparently the captain decided to sneak in and try to find my necklace," Sabrina said. "He seems to be alone."

Grant couldn't believe the gall of it. "Is the bloody idiot insane?"

"He's desperate," Kathleen replied as they headed to the back of the house. "Brown said he needed the necklace to cover his losses on the land scheme and pay his men."

Hell and damnation.

"So, desperate *and* dangerous." He turned to Sabrina. "But how did he end up with Jeannie holding him at gun-point?"

"As far as we can deduce, she spotted him upstairs and retrieved a pistol from Graeme's study," Sabrina said. "Then she followed him to the library. She started shouting at him a few minutes ago. Graeme and I were in the front hall, because David had just arrived to talk to us."

They turned the corner to see one of the grooms stationed outside the library door. He was armed with a pistol and held up a warning hand. They could clearly hear Jeannie, who sounded on the verge of hysterics.

"Oh, God," Kathleen whispered.

Grant put his arm around her shoulder and hugged her. "I still cannot believe Brown took such a risk."

Sabrina made a disgusted noise. "It wasn't much of a risk. Most of the staff are scattered about the countryside, searching for people. Brown probably climbed in through the library window, which is why he's in there now. He was going to leave the way he came."

"Does he have the necklace?" Grant asked her.

"No. I locked it in Graeme's safe in the study."

Kathleen jerked out from under his arm. "What does that matter? I *need* to get in there."

"We might be able to use the blasted necklace as leverage if things go sideways," he replied. "Offer it to Brown, then track him down later."

"I'll go fetch it." Sabrina lifted her skirts and ran.

Kathleen grabbed his sleeve. "Grant, I'm the only one Jeannie will listen to."

"I know, but do everything calmly, all right?"

When she gave an impatient nod and started toward the door, Grant reeled her back. He put his hands on her shoulder and made her look at him.

"Calmly, my love."

Kathleen stared up at him, her silver gaze turbulent as the windswept sea. Then she sucked in a deep breath and control seemed to settle over her like the quiet after a storm.

"Yes, I know," she said.

"Jeannie has the gun, so she's in control at the moment."

"So, we have to make her continue to feel like she's in control."

"Aye."

Kathleen squared her shoulders and walked to the half-open door. The groom stepped aside and let her go in. Grant followed right behind.

The scene in the room stopped them dead in their tracks.

The captain stood near the bay window that was swinging open in the breeze. Jeannie was not more than five feet away from him. Her arm was extended as she pointed a pistol at Brown's head. David stood to the left of his brother, in front of a bookshelf. Graeme was standing behind the desk with his arms held out in a calming gesture.

And a great deal of calm was needed, since Jeannie had

cocked the hammer on the pistol. The captain's face was as white as death as he stared at her, although his eyes blazed with fury and disbelief.

Jeannie flickered a brief glance at Kathleen, then her focus returned to her captive.

"Sweetheart, please give me the pistol," Graeme quietly said. "I promise you Captain Brown will not escape. Justice will be served."

"He lied," Jeannie spat out, "and he *used* me. He's ruined David's life, too. They probably won't let him be a vicar anymore. Captain Brown stole that from him."

"Jeanette, listen to me," David said in a voice tinged with desperation. "I'll be fine, no matter what. But if you shoot John, the consequences could be very bad for you."

"I don't care! He made a fool out of b . . . both of us." Her voice was unsteady, but the arm that held the weapon was not. "He robbed your beautiful church. And he made me think you loved me."

"Yes, it was very wrong, but everything he took can be replaced. However, you cannot be, Jeanette. You're the only thing that matters right now."

Jeannie blinked hard. For a few moments, she seemed to be wavering.

Unfortunately, the idiot captain decided to intervene.

"Right as usual, David," he said, dredging up his travesty of a smile. "No need to go to prison over the likes of me, Miss Jeannie. Put the gun down. There's a good little girl."

If there was anything Jeannie hated, it was being treated like a little girl.

"I should kill you right now," she snapped. "You're a *horrible* man."

Kathleen took a step forward. "And he's certainly a stupid one, dearest. After all, you've outsmarted him every step of the way. Because of you, the captain will spend the rest of his life in prison—or be deported."

Jeannie sniffed a few times. "He should hang for what he did."

Grant moved to stand beside Kathleen. "And he may well do just that. Listen, Jeannie, you've done what we couldn't—you've captured the rogue. Now it's time to leave the rest to us."

"He's right," David said in a stout voice. "You've outdone us all, Jeanette. I could not be prouder of you."

She darted a suspicious glance at the vicar. "Really?"

"Absolutely," he earnestly replied. "You've put us all to shame."

"You certainly have," Kathleen said. "I assure you that Graeme will know exactly what to do with the captain. Now, please let him come to you and take the gun, all right?"

Jeannie grimaced. "Are you sure, Kath? You're sure he'll get what's coming to him?"

"He absolutely will. I promise, darling."

"And can you try to make sure that David isn't hurt by this?"

"Lass, David can be vicar here for as long as he wants," Graeme said. "Now, I'm going to walk over to you, and you're going to hand me the pistol. All right?"

"Please do what Graeme says, dearest," Kathleen said. "I promise it'll be all right."

Jeannie let out a trembling sigh and nodded at her sister, which took her focus off her captive.

Instantly, the man leapt, giving Jeannie a hard shove. She flew forward, losing her balance *and* her grip on the weapon, which sailed toward the wall. Grant wrapped his arms around Kathleen and dove for the floor, shielding her from the expected pistol blast.

But nothing happened.

Kathleen wriggled beneath him. "What . . . what happened?"

"Don't move, Kathleen," Grant urgently said.

"No, you must all get up," the captain said. "*Now*."

Clenching his teeth, Grant rose and then helped Kathleen to stand. Thankfully, Graeme had pulled Jeannie away from Brown's reach. David was still frozen in place by the bookshelves, looking stunned.

The captain was now armed with a pistol, presumably pulled from his coat. And he pointed it straight at Kathleen.

"I'll be leaving now," he said, "and I'm taking Miss Calvert with me for insurance. She's much easier to control than her sister."

A red haze flickered at the edges of Grant's vision. "The hell you will," he snarled, stepping in front of Kathleen.

The captain sneered. "Fine. I'll shoot you instead, and then make my escape during the commotion."

"Don't forget there's a pistol on the floor right behind me," Graeme said in a hard voice. "Trust me, I'll get you squarely between the shoulders while you're running."

"But that gun obviously isn't loaded," Brown contemptuously replied. "Unfortunately, I was unaware of that when the little bitch cornered me."

Jeannie glared at him. "You're a demon."

"He is indeed," said David.

Before Brown could turn, the vicar took two quick steps and whacked him in the head with a book. As the captain staggered, David plucked the pistol from his hand and then whacked his brother again—even harder this time.

The captain dropped to his knees, his eyes glazing, before slowly toppling over.

For a few moments, everyone simply gaped at the prone

figure on the carpet. Then the vicar, carefully holding the pistol with two fingers, brought it over to Graeme.

"I believe you should have charge of this, sir."

Graeme stared at him, stunned. "Er, thank you."

Kathleen wrapped her arms around Grant's waist and leaned into him. She squeezed him before letting go and rushing over to her sister. Jeannie stared forlornly down at David, now crouched beside his unconscious brother.

Kathleen pulled her in for a hug. "Jeannie, you are incredibly brave and I love you so, so much. But please don't scare me like that ever again."

"I'm sorry, Kath," Jeannie said in a small voice. "When I saw him trying to sneak away, I couldn't let him go. I just couldn't."

"I know, sweetheart."

"I . . . I had to make up for how stupid I was. About everything."

Grant's heart ached for both Kathleen and her wee sister. "Och," he said, "the man fooled all of us, ye ken. We were total nincompoops."

David rose to his feet, looking grim. "He certainly fooled me. Sir Graeme, I cannot apologize enough for this disaster. I brought the snake into the garden."

Graeme clapped him on the shoulder. "Hell, David, you're as much a hero as Jeannie. You laid the bastard, er, your brother, out flat. I'll see that you're made a bishop after this."

"Dear me," said David, looking a bit scandalized by Graeme's language. "That is very kind but certainly not necessary."

While Graeme waved in two footmen and told them to secure the captain, Grant retrieved the literary bludgeon from where David had dropped it. When he read the title, he started to laugh.

"What is it?" Kathleen asked.

He held it up. "The book is Fordyce's *Sermons to Young Women*. Ironic, under the circumstances."

"It's such a heavy book. I pulled it out while you were all on the floor," David said.

Kathleen gave him a grateful smile. "It was very well done, sir."

"I couldn't let my brother hurt you, Miss Calvert," he quietly replied. "Or any of you."

Grant extended a hand. "Thank you, sir. I will forever be in your debt."

David gave him a rather shy smile and returned the handshake. "You're most welcome, Mr. Kendrick. It's the least I could do."

He looked sadly at his brother as the footmen carted the captain away. "What happens now?" he asked Graeme.

"He'll have to spend the night in the cellar. Then I'll bring him to the authorities in Inverness tomorrow. And we might yet run the rest of the gang down. At the very least, there will be warrants out for them."

David nodded. "I understand. Would you mind if I stayed with John tonight? I know he's a dreadful man, but he's the only brother I have."

"Of course not," Graeme kindly said. "We'll have to keep him tied up, but I'll try to make things as comfortable as possible for the both of you."

Jeannie pulled out of Kathleen's embrace and shyly approached the vicar.

"Sir, I'm sorry for all the trouble I caused," she said. "I'm sure I must have seemed very silly to you. Of course you could never love me."

David's smile was infinitely kind. "That is only because you're still quite young, my dear. I am very fond of you, and of your sister. But sometimes things don't work out just as we would wish. That can be sad and disappointing, but it doesn't mean the end. You have many things to look forward to, Jeanette. I foresee much good in your future."

The girl awkwardly shrugged. "I know, but . . ."

The vicar held up a finger. "You have your dear sister. She loves you very much, and that is splendid."

"And you have us Kendricks, Jeannie," Grant said. "We love you very much, too."

Kathleen flashed him a grateful smile.

"There now," David said to Jeannie. "What could be better than having a family who loves you?"

"I am lucky," she solemnly replied. "But I'm also very sorry about your brother."

David sighed. "Me too."

Graeme tactfully cleared his throat. "Vicar, if you'll come with me, I'll get you set up. And perhaps you'll take a wee dram of whisky, just this once? I'm sure you could use it."

"I think I will, Sir Graeme." Then David gave Kathleen a courtly little bow. "Miss Calvert, please know that you have my best wishes for your happiness. And for your sister's, as well."

"Thank you," she replied, sounding rather choked up.

David nodded to Grant and then left the room.

"Graeme, wait," Grant said, stopping his brother. "Was Jeannie's pistol actually not loaded, or did it misfire?"

His twin gave him a wry smile. "Of course it wasn't loaded. You know I don't leave loaded guns lying about."

Jeannie wrinkled her nose. "I didn't know that when I took it."

"Your gambit worked," Grant assured her. "That's all that matters."

"I suppose." She looked at her sister. "What happens now, Kath?"

Sabrina dodged around Graeme as they passed each other in the doorway and came over to Jeannie. "Now that all the excitement is over, you need a nice cup of tea and something to eat. Then a hot bath and a rest."

"That sounds just the ticket," Kathleen said.

"Will you come up and see me in a bit?" Jeannie plaintively asked her sister.

Kathleen hugged her. "Yes, dearest. I'll join you shortly."

"And I think *you* need a drink, Kathleen. A nice, big dram," Sabrina said over her shoulder as she led Jeannie out.

"She's not wrong," Kathleen wryly said to Grant.

He dropped a kiss on the tip of her nose before steering her to the couch. "I'll fetch one for both of us."

With a weary sigh, Kathleen dropped onto the comfortable cushions and shut her eyes.

When Grant returned with the drinks, he handed one to her before putting his on the table in front of them. Then he sat and pulled her in for a cuddle. She relaxed against him before taking a cautious sip from her glass.

She grimaced. "I'm still not sure I like whisky. That seems rather dreadful, since I'm marrying a Highlander."

"Just don't tell Angus. You'll cut him to the quick."

"Poor Angus. I was so worried about him."

"No doubt Sabrina has already sent for the local sawbones to doctor him. Try not to worry, love. It's all over."

"I know, but I worry about my sister, too. It's been so hard on her. And I feel simply awful about David. First he clobbered his own brother, then he was so kind to Jeannie, and *then* he offered us his congratulations. I almost burst into tears on the spot."

"He cast me into a complete shade. Are you sure you wouldn't rather marry him than me?"

"David certainly displayed heroic qualities today." Then she pulled out from under his arm to scowl at him. "Speaking of heroic, do not *ever* put yourself in danger like that again, Grant Kendrick. Offering to be shot? Really?"

"Kathleen, I wasn't about to let you get kidnapped again. That's not how Kendricks operate, love. We protect our lassies, ye ken." He would die before he'd see her in that kind of mortal danger.

"Well, I'd rather get kidnapped than you get shot."

He pulled her back under his arm. "Let's make an agreement. You agree not to get kidnapped, and I agree not to get shot."

"There do seem to be a ridiculous number of kidnappings in your family, from what Sabrina tells me."

"I'm hoping you were the last."

She huffed out a laugh and settled back under his arm. For a few minutes, they sat quietly, drinking their whisky and listening to the quiet hiss of the fire. Grant could hardly believe it was all over and that his darling girl was safely in his arms.

"I would rather die than have anything happen to you," he finally said. "I thought I'd lost you, Kathleen. It was . . . not something I ever want to experience again."

"I know. I was so afraid I'd never see you again, too."

He cupped her cheek, gently turning her to look at him. "I love you, Kathleen Calvert. And I would be most happy if we never lost each other for the rest of our lives."

She smiled up at him, her gaze now gleaming like a

thousand silvery stars. "I love you, and I promise that I will never lose you again, no matter what."

As Grant pressed his lips to hers, he knew that all the shadows and doubts were a thing of the past. Their promises would hold for life.

Epilogue

Glasgow
January 1824

Kathleen gazed at the neglected mess of a garden. Flowerbeds were full of weeds, hedges were in need of trimming, and an ornamental pond was choked with lily pads. The lawns surrounding the house were in better form, but barely.

In a word, the garden was a mess.

"It's rather grim," said her husband. "Might be a bit too much work, love."

Kathleen shook her head. "No, it's *perfect*."

Plans for the property were already taking shape in her head. Kathleen was certain she could restore the grounds to their former beauty. It was the sort of challenge she most enjoyed—starting from scratch and creating something beautiful and enduring.

"How did you find it on such short notice?" she asked. "We only returned from Ireland a week ago."

Grant led her down a few shallow stone steps to a gravel path that wandered toward the manor's greenhouse. "I started looking before we left for Ireland, but this property became available only a few days ago. The owner hasn't stayed here in years and wants to sell the place."

After they returned to Glasgow from Lochnagar in November, their wedding preparations had begun. Every other Kendrick wedding had been a rushed affair, according to Grant, so Vicky and the rest of the family insisted on a grand celebration for him and Kathleen. Since everyone, especially Angus, was terribly excited, Kathleen hadn't been able to refuse. The preparations had also served as an excellent distraction for Jeannie, who still brooded about her misadventures in Lochnagar. Vicky, wise as always, had drafted the girl as her assistant in planning the festivities.

"I'm determined to impress your family," Vicky had said. "If we're going to make them travel to Scotland, we'd best put on a good show."

While Kathleen and the Kendricks had busied themselves with preparations, Grant spent long days at the office. Kathleen had fretted that he was working too hard, but he'd insisted it was in a good cause.

"I want a month with my bride in Ireland," he'd said, "with no distractions. If that means long days and a few nights at the office until our wedding, I'm happy to make the sacrifice."

Any subsequent worries had been silenced with activities guaranteed to assure Kathleen that her virile betrothed had energy to spare.

The wedding ceremony had been performed in Glasgow Cathedral by the archbishop, and had been magisterial enough to impress even Helen. A lavish wedding breakfast had followed, and a grand ball at Kendrick House had been held the next evening. Helen had subsequently proclaimed the celebrations most impressive, and Papa pronounced everything first rate.

One of the happiest outcomes was the reunion of Jeannie and her mother. Kathleen had been dreading Helen's reaction to their misadventures in Lochnagar, especially for Jeannie's sake. She and Grant had minimized some of the more alarming details, giving Papa and Helen little more than a basic summary. But anything involving the Kendricks was sure to attract notice, and the trial and subsequent deportation of Captain Brown and his gang had been thoroughly covered in the Scottish papers, as well as in a number of London gazettes.

Jeannie had bravely and honestly owned up to her actions, a sign of the girl's growing maturity. While Kathleen had been both proud and worried for her, the expected explosion of temper from Helen never occurred. While *shocked to the very fiber of her being*, as she'd dramatically put it, Helen had also expressed admiration for Jeannie's courage.

"After all, Jeanette takes entirely after me," Helen had explained. "I would expect nothing less from my daughter than to stand up to a dastardly poltroon like Captain Brown."

In truth, Kathleen suspected that Helen had greatly missed Jeannie and was relieved to be reunited with her youngest child. Jeannie also admitted that she'd missed her parents and was happy to return with them to London.

And although she and Jeannie had shed more than a few tears when her family departed for home, Kathleen had been thrilled to see her sister reconciled with her mother, and in much better spirits.

All in all, it had been a splendid two weeks of family visits and wedding festivities. It had been even more splendid when Kathleen and Grant had finally left on their wedding trip. They'd spent several enjoyable days in

Dublin, visiting with Kathleen's former governess and her family and taking in the sights.

Then they'd finally set out for Greystone Manor, Kathleen's beloved home. By themselves at last for three wonderful weeks, Grant had focused all his attentions on her. They'd spent the days wandering and riding about the estate and the countryside as Kathleen showed her new husband all her childhood haunts. Evenings had been given over to quiet dinners and chats by the fireside, and then delicious lovemaking until the early hours of the morning. It had been nothing short of blissful, and Kathleen had found herself falling more deeply in love with Grant every day.

That she'd made the right decision for her life was made abundantly clear by those weeks in Ireland. Even though she loved Greystone and would always wish to visit, Ireland was now her past. Her future lay with Grant, the Kendricks, and Scotland, and she was excited for the adventures that loomed over this new horizon. Like finding their own home, where they could settle and start a family.

"Of course," Grant said as they strolled toward the greenhouse, "we can keep looking at other houses, if you like. We can even build one, if you prefer."

Kathleen smiled up at him. "No, this property seems exactly right. That should not surprise me, since you're the most terrifyingly efficient man in Scotland. Of course you would find the perfect place."

"What I am is a man very motivated to have some privacy with his bride," he dryly replied. "Kendrick House is a bit crowded these days. I'm continually terrified that Angus or one of the children is going to burst in on us at a decidedly inappropriate time."

"It is a trifle much with that many of us under one roof,"

she admitted. "Especially now that Royal and his family are here for a visit. I only worry that this particular property is too far from the city. I don't want you spending so much time going back and forth between a house in the country and your offices in Glasgow."

"Lass, we're only a twenty-minute carriage ride from the edge of Glasgow. And this place is close to the port, which is certainly convenient for my work."

She cast him a dubious look. "Are you sure?"

He tipped up her chin to give her a thorough kiss.

"What I'm sure of," he finally said, "is that I want my wife to be happy. And I'm happy to live outside of the city— and also happy to have a bit of distance from my family. If we're not careful, Angus will be haunting our doorstep on a daily basis."

She patted his chest. "Your grandfather can visit as often as he likes. I think he's great fun."

"And he thinks you're his special project. He's determined to teach you about our family, the clan, and every arcane bit of Scottish history he can think of. He'll bore you to tears, most likely."

"Then I'll bore him right back with lengthy lectures about optimal growing conditions for orchids and the most effective methods for pruning fruit trees. Trust me, darling, I can arcane with the best of them."

Grant laughed. "That ought to do it. Now, would you like to see the greenhouse and the rest of the place before you make a final decision?"

Kathleen took his arm. "Lead on, husband."

They poked around the greenhouse, a long, sweeping wing that culminated in a lovely octagonal pavilion. Kathleen was charmed by the beauty of the design, and the wonderful light that flooded through the large panes of glass.

"It's splendid. Grant, I think we should take it right now."

"But you haven't even seen the rest of the house. Who knows what the water closets are like, or the chimneys? Remember Lochnagar?"

"Oh, bother the water closets. They can be repaired."

She swept out her arms to take in the greenhouse, the pavilion, and the gardens. "This is what counts. This is where the fun truly happens."

Grant's eyes gleamed with amusement. "What about the bedrooms? As I recall, we seem to have a great deal of fun in those."

"That is an excellent point. Perhaps we'd best survey them, too."

"Perhaps we'd best *test* them out. Find just the right one before we make a final decision," he replied, waggling his brows.

She felt her eyes pop wide. "Right now? You cannot be serious."

He fished a large key out of his pocket. "I've got the house key, and I'm entirely serious. If you're up to it, that is."

"Is that a challenge, Mr. Kendrick?"

"I believe it is, Mrs. Kendrick."

She poked him in the cravat. "Then challenge accepted, sir."

Between one breath and the next, he swept her into his arms and began striding toward the front door.

Kathleen grabbed her hat. "Grant, I can walk into the house, you know."

"Not the first time, sweetheart. The first time you enter your new home, I'm carrying you over the threshold."

She let out a happy sigh. "You are truly the most romantic man in the world."

"Not the most boring?"

"I don't think so, but perhaps you'd best prove it to me again."

He grinned. "Challenge accepted, wife."

Kathleen laughed with sheer joy as Grant carried her over the threshold and into their new and decidedly not-boring life.